1/22

BEAUTIFUL WORLD, WHERE ARE YOU

BEAUTIFUL WORLD, WHERE ARE YOU

SALLY ROONEY

WHEELER PUBLISHING
A part of Gale, a Cengage Company

Wheeler Publishing, a part of Gale, a Cengage Company.

ALL RIGHTS RESERVED
Wheeler Publishing Large Print Hardcover.
The text of this Large Print edition is unabridged.
Other aspects of the book may vary from the original edition.
Set in 16 pt. Plantin.

**LIBRARY OF CONGRESS CIP DATA ON FILE.
CATALOGUING IN PUBLICATION FOR THIS BOOK
IS AVAILABLE FROM THE LIBRARY OF CONGRESS.**

ISBN-13: 978-1-4328-9335-4 (hardcover alk. paper)

Published in 2021 by arrangement with Farrar, Straus and Giroux.

Printed in Mexico
Print Number: 01   Print Year: 2022

When I write something I usually think it is very important and that I am a very fine writer. I think this happens to everyone. But there is one corner of my mind in which I know very well what I am, which is a small, a very small writer. I swear I know it. But that doesn't matter much to me.

— NATALIA GINZBURG,
'My Vocation' (translated by Dick Davis)

1.

A woman sat in a hotel bar, watching the door. Her appearance was neat and tidy: white blouse, fair hair tucked behind her ears. She glanced at the screen of her phone, on which was displayed a messaging interface, and then looked back at the door again. It was late March, the bar was quiet, and outside the window to her right the sun was beginning to set over the Atlantic. It was four minutes past seven, and then five, six minutes past. Briefly and with no perceptible interest she examined her fingernails. At eight minutes past seven, a man entered through the door. He was slight and dark-haired, with a narrow face. He looked around, scanning the faces of the other patrons, and then took his phone out and checked the screen. The woman at the window noticed him but, beyond watching him, made no additional effort to catch his attention. They appeared to be about the

7

same age, in their late twenties or early thirties. She let him stand there until he saw her and came over.

Are you Alice? he said.

That's me, she replied.

Yeah, I'm Felix. Sorry I'm late.

In a gentle tone she replied: That's alright. He asked her what she wanted to drink and then went to the bar to order. The waitress asked how he was getting on, and he answered: Good yeah, yourself? He ordered a vodka tonic and a pint of lager. Rather than carrying the bottle of tonic back to the table, he emptied it into the glass with a quick and practised movement of his wrist. The woman at the table tapped her fingers on a beermat, waiting. Her outward attitude had become more alert and lively since the man had entered the room. She looked outside now at the sunset as if it were of interest to her, though she hadn't paid any attention to it before. When the man returned and put the drinks down, a drop of lager spilled over and she watched its rapid progress down the side of his glass.

You were saying you just moved here, he said. Is that right?

She nodded, sipped her drink, licked her top lip.

What did you do that for? he asked.

What do you mean?

I mean, there's not much in the way of people moving here, usually. People moving away from here, that would be more the normal thing. You're hardly here for work, are you?

Oh. No, not really.

A momentary glance between them seemed to confirm that he was expecting more of an explanation. Her expression flickered, as if she were trying to make a decision, and then she gave a little informal, almost conspiratorial smile.

Well, I was looking to move somewhere anyway, she said, and then I heard about a house just outside town here — a friend of mine knows the owners. Apparently they've been trying to sell it forever and eventually they just started looking for someone to live there in the meantime. Anyway, I thought it would be nice to live beside the sea. I suppose it was a bit impulsive, really. So — But that's the entire story, there was no other reason.

He was drinking and listening to her. Toward the end of her remarks she seemed to have become slightly nervous, which expressed itself in a shortness of breath and a kind of self-mocking expression. He watched this performance impassively and

9

then put his glass down.

Right, he said. And you were in Dublin before, was it?

Different places. I was in New York for a while. I'm from Dublin, I think I told you that. But I was living in New York until last year.

And what are you going to do now you're here? Look for work or something?

She paused. He smiled and sat back in his seat, still looking at her.

Sorry for all the questions, he said. I don't think I get the full story yet.

No, I don't mind. But I'm not very good at giving answers, as you can see.

What do you work as, then? That's my last question.

She smiled back at him, tightly now. I'm a writer, she said. Why don't you tell me what you do?

Ah, it's not as unusual as that. I wonder what you write about, but I won't ask. I work in a warehouse, outside town.

Doing what?

Well, doing what, he repeated philosophically. Collecting orders off the shelves and putting them in a trolley and then bringing them up to be packed. Nothing too exciting.

Don't you like it, then?

10

Jesus no, he said. I fucking hate the place. But they wouldn't be paying me to do something I liked, would they? That's the thing about work, if it was any good you'd do it for free.

She smiled and said that was true. Outside the window the sky had grown darker, and the lights down at the caravan park were coming on: the cool salt glow of the outdoor lamps, and the warmer yellow lights in the windows. The waitress from behind the bar had come out to mop down the empty tables with a cloth. The woman named Alice watched her for a few seconds and then looked at the man again.

So what do people do for fun around here? she asked.

It's the same as any place. Few pubs around. Nightclub down in Ballina, that's about twenty minutes in the car. And we have the amusements, obviously, but that's more for the kids. I suppose you don't really have friends around here yet, do you?

I think you're the first person I've had a conversation with since I moved in.

He raised his eyebrows. Are you shy? he said.

You tell me.

They looked at one another. She no longer looked nervous now, but somehow remote,

11

while his eyes moved around her face, as if trying to put something together. He did not seem in the end, after a second or two, to conclude that he had succeeded.

I think you might be, he said.

She asked where he was living and he said he was renting a house with friends, nearby. Looking out the window, he added that the estate was almost visible from where they were sitting, just past the caravan park. He leaned over the table to show her, but then said it was too dark after all. Anyway, just the other side there, he said. As he leaned close to her their eyes met. She dropped her gaze into her lap, and taking his seat again he seemed to suppress a smile. She asked if his parents were still living locally. He said his mother had passed away the year before and that his father was 'God knows where'.

I mean, to be fair, he's probably somewhere like Galway, he added. He's not going to turn up down in Argentina or anything. But I haven't seen him in years.

I'm so sorry about your mother, she said.

Yeah. Thanks.

I actually haven't seen my father in a while either. He's — not very reliable.

Felix looked up from his glass. Oh? he said. Drinker, is he?

12

Mm. And he — You know, he makes up stories.

Felix nodded. I thought that was your job, he said.

She blushed visibly at this remark, which seemed to take him by surprise and even alarm him. Very funny, she said. Anyway. Would you like another drink?

After the second, they had a third. He asked if she had siblings and she said one, a younger brother. He said he had a brother too. By the end of the third drink Alice's face looked pink and her eyes had become glassy and bright. Felix looked exactly the same as he had when he had entered the bar, no change in manner or tone. But while her gaze increasingly roamed around the room, expressing a more diffuse interest in her surroundings, the attention he paid to her had become more watchful and intent. She rattled the ice in her empty glass, amusing herself.

Would you like to see my house? she asked. I've been wanting to show it off but I don't know anyone to invite. I mean, I am going to invite my friends, obviously. But they're all over the place.

In New York.

In Dublin mostly.

Whereabouts is the house? he said. Can

13

we walk there?

Most certainly we can. In fact we'll have to. I can't drive, can you?

Not right now, no. Or I wouldn't chance it, anyway. But I do have my licence, yeah.

Do you, she murmured. How romantic. Do you want another, or shall we go?

He frowned to himself at this question, or at the phrasing of the question, or at the use of the word 'romantic'. She was rooting in her handbag without looking up.

Yeah, let's head on, why not, he said.

She stood up and began to put on her jacket, a beige single-breasted raincoat. He watched her fold back one sleeve cuff to match the other. Standing upright, he was only just taller than she was.

How far is it? he said.

She smiled at him playfully. Are you having second thoughts? she said. If you get tired of walking you can always abandon me and turn back, I'm quite used to it. The walk, that is. Not being abandoned. I might be used to that as well, but it's not the sort of thing I confess to strangers.

To this he offered no reply at all, just nodded, with a vaguely grim expression of forbearance, as if this aspect of her personality, her tendency to be 'witty' and verbose, was, after an hour or two of conversation, a

14

quality he had noted and determined to ignore. He said goodnight to the waitress as they left. Alice looked struck by this, and glanced back over her shoulder as if trying to catch sight of the woman again. When they were outside on the footpath, she asked whether he knew her. The tide broke in a low soothing rush behind them and the air was cold.

The girl working there? said Felix. I know her, yeah. Sinead. Why?

She'll wonder what you were doing in there talking to me.

In a flat tone, Felix replied: I'd say she'd have a fair idea. Where are we heading?

Alice put her hands in the pockets of her raincoat and started walking up the hill. She seemed to have recognised a kind of challenge or even repudiation in his tone, and rather than cowing her, it was as though it had hardened her resolve.

Why, do you often meet women there? she asked.

He had to walk quickly to keep up with her. That's an odd question, he replied.

Is it? I suppose I'm an odd person.

Is it your business if I meet people there? he said.

Nothing about you is my business, naturally. I'm just curious.

He seemed to consider this, and in the meantime repeated in a quieter, less certain voice: Yeah, but I don't see how it's your business. After a few seconds he added: You're the one who suggested the hotel. Just for your information. I never usually go there. So no, I don't meet people there that much. Okay?

That's okay, that's fine. My curiosity was piqued by your remark about the girl behind the bar 'having an idea' what we were doing there.

Well, I'm sure she figured out we were on a date, he said. That's all I meant.

Though she didn't look around at him, Alice's face started to show a little more amusement than before, or a different kind of amusement. You don't mind people you know seeing you out on dates with strangers? she asked.

You mean because it's awkward or whatever? Wouldn't bother me much, no.

For the rest of the walk to Alice's house, up along the coast road, they made conversation about Felix's social life, or rather Alice posed a number of queries on the subject which he mulled over and answered, both parties speaking more loudly than before due to the noise of the sea. He expressed no surprise at her questions, and

16

answered them readily, but without speaking at excessive length or offering any information beyond what was directly solicited. He told her that he socialised primarily with people he had known in school and people he knew from work. The two circles overlapped a little but not much. He didn't ask her anything in return, perhaps warned off by her diffident responses to the questions he'd posed earlier, or perhaps no longer interested.

Just here, she said eventually.

Where?

She unlatched a small white gate and said: Here. He stopped walking and looked at the house, situated up a length of sloped green garden. None of the windows were lit, and the facade of the house was not visible in any great detail, but his expression indicated that he knew where they were.

You live in the rectory? he said.

Oh, I didn't realise you would know it. I would have told you at the bar, I wasn't trying to be mysterious.

She was holding the gate open for him, and, with his eyes still on the figure of the house, which loomed above them facing out onto the sea, he followed her. Around them the dim green garden rustled in the wind. She walked lightly up the path and searched

17

in her handbag for the house keys. The noise of the keys was audible somewhere inside the bag but she didn't seem to be able to find them. He stood there not saying anything. She apologised for the delay and switched on the torch function on her phone, lighting the interior of her bag and casting a cold grey light on the front steps of the house also. He had his hands in his pockets. Got them, she said. Then she unlocked the door.

Inside was a large hallway with red-and-black patterned floor tiles. A marbled glass lampshade hung overhead, and a delicate, spindly table along the wall displayed a wooden carving of an otter. She dumped her keys on the table and glanced quickly in the dim, blotchy mirror on the wall.

You're renting this place on your own? he said.

I know, she said. It's much too big, obviously. And I'm spending millions on keeping it warm. But it is nice, isn't it? And they're not charging me any rent. Shall we go in the kitchen? I'll turn the heat back on.

He followed her down a hallway into a large kitchen, with fixed units along one side and a dining table on the other. Over the sink was a window overlooking the back garden. He stood in the doorway while she went searching in one of the presses. She looked around at him.

You can sit down if you'd like to, she said. But by all means remain standing if it's what you prefer. Will you have a glass of wine? It's the only thing I have in the house, drinks-wise. But I'm going to have a glass of water first.

What kind of things do you write? If you're a writer.

She turned around, bemused. If I am? she said. I don't suppose you think I've been lying. I would have come up with something better if I had been. I'm a novelist. I write books.

And you make money doing that, do you?

As if sensing a new significance in this question, she glanced at him once more and then went back to pouring the water. Yes I do, she said. He continued to watch her and then sat down at the table. The seats were padded with cushions in crinkled russet cloth. Everything looked very clean. He rubbed the smooth tabletop with the tip of his index finger. She put a glass of water down in front of him and sat on one of the chairs.

Have you been here before? she said. You knew the house.

No, I only know it from growing up in

town. I never knew who lived here.

I hardly know them myself. An older couple. The woman is an artist, I think.

He nodded and said nothing.

I'll give you a tour if you like, she added.

He still said nothing and this time didn't even nod. She didn't look perturbed by this; it seemed to confirm some suspicion she had been nursing, and when she continued to speak it was in the same dry, almost sardonic tone.

You must think I'm mad living here on my own, she said.

For free? he answered. Fuck off, you'd be mad not to. He yawned unselfconsciously and looked out the window, or rather at the window, since it was dark out now and the glass only reflected the interior of the room. How many bedrooms are there, out of curiosity? he asked.

Four.

Where's yours?

In response to this abrupt question she did not move her eyes at first, but kept staring intently at her glass for a few seconds before looking directly up at him. Upstairs, she said. They're all upstairs. Would you like me to show you?

Why not, he said.

They rose from the table. On the upstairs

20

landing was a Turkish rug with grey tassels. Alice pushed open the door to her room and switched on a little floor lamp. To the left was a large double bed. The floorboards were bare and along one wall a fireplace was laid out in jade-coloured tiles. On the right, a large sash window looked out over the sea, into the darkness. Felix wandered over to the window and leaned close to the glass, so his own shadow darkened the glare of the reflected light.

Must be a nice view here in the daytime, said Felix.

Alice was still standing by the door. Yes, it's beautiful, she said. Even better in the evening, actually.

He turned away from the window, casting his appraising glance around the room's other features, while Alice watched.

Very nice, he concluded. Very nice room. Are you going to write a book while you're here?

I suppose I'll try.

And what are your books about?

Oh, I don't know, she said. People.

That's a bit vague. What kind of people do you write about, people like you?

She looked at him calmly, as if to tell him something: that she understood his game, perhaps, and that she would even let him

21

win it, as long as he played nicely.

What kind of person do you think I am? she said.

Something in the calm coolness of her look seemed to unsettle him, and he gave a quick, yelping laugh. Well, well, he said. I only met you a few hours ago, I haven't made up my mind on you yet.

You'll let me know when you do, I hope.

I might.

For a few seconds she stood there in the room, very still, while he wandered around a little and pretended to look at things. They knew then, both of them, what was about to happen, though neither could have said exactly how they knew. She waited impartially while he continued glancing around, until finally, perhaps with no more energy to delay the inevitable, he thanked her and left. She walked him down the stairs — part of the way down. She was standing on the steps when he went out the door. It was one of those things. Both of them afterwards felt bad, neither of them certain really why the evening had been such a failure in the end. Pausing there on the stairs, alone, she looked back up at the landing. Follow her eyes now and notice the bedroom door left open, a slice of white wall visible through the banister posts.

2.

Dear Eileen. I've waited so long for you to reply to my last email that I am actually — imagine! — writing you a new one before receiving your reply. In my defence I've gathered up too much material now, and if I wait for you I'll start forgetting things. You should know that our correspondence is my way of holding on to life, taking notes on it, and thereby preserving something of my — otherwise almost worthless, or even entirely worthless — existence on this rapidly degenerating planet . . . I include this paragraph chiefly to make you feel guilty about not replying to me before now, and therefore secure myself a swifter response this time. What are you doing, anyway, if not emailing me? Don't say working.

I am going crazy thinking about the rent you're paying in Dublin. You know it's more expensive there now than Paris? And, forgive me, but what Paris has Dublin lacks. One of the problems is that Dublin is, and I mean literally and topographically, flat — so that everything has to take place on a single plane. Other cities have metro systems, which add depth, and steep hills or skyscrapers for height, but Dublin has only short squat grey buildings and trams that run along the street. And it has no courtyards or roof gardens like continental cities, which at least break up the surface — if not vertically, then conceptually. Have you thought about it this way before? Maybe even if you haven't, you've noticed it at some subconscious level. It's hard to go very far up in Dublin or very low down, hard to lose yourself or other people, or to gain a sense of perspective. You might think it's a democratic way to organise a city — so that everything happens face to face, I mean, on equal footing. True, no one is looking down on you all from a height. But it gives the sky a position of total dominance. Nowhere is the sky meaningfully punctuated or broken up by anything at all. The Spire, you might point out, and I will concede the Spire, which is anyway the narrowest possible of interruptions, and dangles like a measuring tape to demonstrate the diminutive size of every other edifice around. The totalising effect of the sky is bad for people there. Nothing ever intervenes to block the thing from view. It's like a memento mori. I wish someone would cut a hole in it for you.

I've been thinking lately about right-wing politics (haven't we all), and how it is that conservatism (the social force) came to be associated with rapacious market capitalism. The connection is not obvious, at least to me, since markets preserve nothing, but ingest all aspects of an existing social landscape and excrete them, shorn of meaning and memory, as transactions. What could be 'conservative' about such a process? But it also strikes me that the idea of 'conservatism' is in itself false, because nothing can be conserved, as such — time moves in one direction only, I mean. This idea is so basic that when I first thought of it, I felt very brilliant, and then I wondered if I was an idiot. But does it make some sense to you? We can't conserve anything, and especially not social relations, without altering their nature, arresting some part of their interaction with time in an unnatural way. Just look at what conservatives make of the environment: their idea of conservation is to extract, pillage and destroy, 'because that's what we've always done' — but because of that very fact, it's no longer the same earth we do it to. I suppose you think this is all extremely rudimentary and maybe even that I'm un-dialectical. But these are just the abstract thoughts I had, which I needed to write down, and of which you find yourself the (willing or unwilling) recipient.

I was in the local shop today, getting something to eat for lunch, when I suddenly had the strangest sensation — a spontaneous awareness of the unlikeliness of this life. I mean, I thought of all the rest of the human population — most of whom live in what you and I would consider abject poverty — who have never seen or entered such a shop. And this, this, is what all their work sustains! This lifestyle, for people like us! All the various brands of soft drinks in plastic bottles and all the prepackaged lunch deals and confectionery in sealed bags and store-baked pastries — this is it, the culmination of all the labour in the world, all the burning of fossil fuels and all the backbreaking work on coffee farms and sugar plantations. All for this! This convenience shop! I felt dizzy thinking about it. I mean I really felt ill. It was as if I suddenly remembered that my life was all part of a television show — and every day people died making the show, were ground to death in the most horrific ways, children, women, and all so that

I could choose from various lunch options, each packaged in multiple layers of single-use plastic. That was what they died for — that was the great experiment. I thought I would throw up. Of course, a feeling like that can't last. Maybe for the rest of the day I feel bad, even for the rest of the week — so what? I still have to buy lunch. And in case you're worrying about me, let me assure you, buy lunch I did.

An update on my rural life and then I'll sign off. The house is chaotically huge, as if in the habit of producing new, previously unseen rooms on a spontaneous basis. It's also cold and in some places damp. I live a twenty-minute walk from the aforementioned local shop and feel as if I spend most of my time walking there and back in order to buy things I forgot about on the last trip. It's probably very character-building, and by the time we see one another again I'll have a really amazing personality. About ten days ago I went out on a date with someone who worked in a shipping warehouse and he absolutely despised me. To be fair to myself (I always am), I think I have by now forgotten how to conduct social intercourse. I dread to imagine what kind of faces I was making, in my efforts to seem like the kind of person who regularly interacts with others. Even writing this email I'm feeling a little loose and dissociative. Rilke has a poem that ends: 'Who is now alone, will long remain so, / will wake, read, write long letters / and wander restlessly here and there / along the avenues, as the leaves are drifting.' A better description of my present state I couldn't invent, except it's April and the leaves aren't drifting. Forgive the 'long letter', then. I hope you'll come and see me. Love love love always, Alice.

3.

At twenty past twelve on a Wednesday afternoon, a woman sat behind a desk in a shared office in Dublin city centre, scrolling through a text document. She had very dark hair, swept back loosely into a tortoiseshell clasp, and she was wearing a grey sweater tucked into black cigarette trousers. Using the soft greasy roller on her computer mouse she skimmed over the document, eyes flicking back and forth across narrow columns of text, and occasionally she stopped, clicked, and inserted or deleted characters. Most frequently she was inserting two full stops into the name 'WH Auden', in order to standardise its appearance as 'W.H. Auden'. When she reached the end of the document, she opened a search command, selected the Match Case option and searched: 'WH'. No matches appeared. She scrolled back up to the top of the document, words and paragraphs flying past so quickly as to seem almost certainly illegible, and then, apparently satisfied, saved her work and closed the file.

At one o'clock she told her colleagues she was going to lunch, and they smiled and waved at her from behind their monitors. Pulling on a jacket, she walked to a cafe near the office and sat at a table by the window, eating a sandwich with one hand and with the other reading a copy of the novel *The Karamazov Brothers*. Now and then she put the book down, wiped her hands and mouth with a paper napkin, glanced around the room as if to ascertain whether anyone there was looking back at her, and then returned to her book. At twenty to two, she looked up to observe a tall fair-haired man entering the cafe. He was wearing a suit and tie, with a plastic lanyard around his neck, and speaking into his phone. Yeah, he said, I was told Tuesday but I'll call back and check that for you. Seeing the woman seated by the window, his face changed, and he quickly lifted his free hand, mouthing the word: Hey. Into the phone, he continued: I don't think you were copied on that, no. Looking at the woman, he pointed to the phone impatiently and made a talking gesture with his hand. She smiled, toying with the corner of a page in her book. Right, right, the man said. Listen, I'm actually out of the office now but I'll do that when I get back in. Yeah. Good, good, good to talk to you.

The man ended his call and came over to her table. Looking him up and down, she said: Oh Simon, you're so important-looking, I'm afraid you're going to be assassinated. He picked up his lanyard and studied it critically. It's this thing, he said. It makes me feel like I deserve to be. Can I buy you a coffee? She said she was going back to work. Well, he said, can I buy you a takeaway coffee and walk you back to work? I want your opinion on something. She shut her book and said yes. While he went to the counter, she stood up and brushed away the sandwich crumbs that had fallen into her lap. He ordered two coffees, one white and one black, and dropped some coins into the tip jar. The woman joined him, removing the clasp from her hair and then reinserting it. How was Lola's fitting in the end? the man asked. The woman glanced up, met his eyes, and let out a strange, stifled sound. Oh, fine, she said. You know my mother's in town, we're all meeting up tomorrow to look for our wedding outfits.

He smiled benignly, watching the progress of their coffees behind the counter. Funny, he said, I had a bad dream the other night about you getting married.

What was bad about it?

You were marrying someone other than me.

The woman laughed. Do you talk like this to the women at your work? she said.

He turned back to her, amused, and replied: God no, I'd get in awful trouble. And quite rightly. No, I never flirt with anyone at work. If anything they flirt with me.

I suppose they're all middle-aged and want you to marry their daughters.

I can't agree with this negative cultural imaging around middle-aged women. Of every demographic, I actually think I like them best.

What's wrong with young women?

There's just that bit of . . .

He gestured his hand from side to side in the air to indicate friction, uncertainty, sexual chemistry, indecisiveness, or perhaps mediocrity.

Your girlfriends are never middle-aged, the woman pointed out.

And neither am I, quite yet, thank you.

On the way out of the cafe, the man held the door open for the woman to walk through, which she did without thanking him. What did you want to ask me about? she said. Joining her on the walk back up the street toward her office, he told her he wanted her advice on a situation that had arisen between two of his friends, both of whom the woman seemed to know by name. The friends had been living together as roommates, and then had become involved in some kind of ambiguous sexual relationship. After a time, one of them had started seeing someone else, and now the other friend, the one who was still single, wanted to leave the apartment but had no money and nowhere else to go. Really more of an emotional situation than an apartment situation, the woman said. The man agreed, but added: Still, I think it's probably best for her to get out of the apartment. I mean, she can apparently hear them having sex at night, so that's not great. They had reached the steps of the office building by then. You could loan her some money, the woman said. The man replied that he had offered already but she had refused. Which was a relief, actually, he added, because my instinct is not to get too involved. The woman asked what the first friend had to say for himself, and the man replied that the first friend felt he was not doing anything wrong, that the previous relationship had come to a natural end and what was he supposed to do, stay single forever? The woman made a face and said: God, yeah, she really needs to get out of that apartment. I'll keep an eye out. They lingered on the steps a little longer. My wedding invite arrived, by the way, the man remarked.

Oh yes, she said. That was this week.

Did you know they were giving me a plus-one?

She looked at him as if to ascertain whether he was joking, and then raised her eyebrows. That's nice, she said. They didn't give me one, but considering the circumstances I suppose that might have been indelicate.

Would you like me to go alone as a gesture of solidarity?

After a pause, she asked: Why, is there someone you're thinking of bringing?

Well, the girl I'm seeing, I suppose. If it's all the same to you.

She said: Hm. Then she added: You mean woman, I hope.

He smiled. Ah, let's be a little bit friendly, he said.

Do you go around behind my back calling me a girl?

Certainly not. I don't call you anything. Whenever your name comes up, I just get flustered and leave the room.

Disregarding this, the woman asked: When did you meet her?

Oh, I don't know. About six weeks ago.

She's not another one of these twenty-two-year-old Scandinavian women, is she?

No, she's not Scandinavian, he said.

With an exaggeratedly weary expression, the woman tossed her coffee cup in the waste bin outside the office door. Watching her, the man added: I can go alone if you'd rather. We can make eyes at each other across the room.

Oh, you make me sound very desperate, she said.

God, I didn't mean to.

For a few seconds she said nothing, just stood staring into the traffic. Presently she said aloud: She looked beautiful at the fitting. Lola, I mean. You were asking.

Still watching her, he replied: I can imagine.

Thanks for the coffee.

Thank you for the advice.

For the rest of the afternoon in the office, the woman worked on the same text-editing interface, opening new files, moving apostrophes around and deleting commas. After closing one file and before opening another, she routinely checked her social media feeds. Her expression, her posture, did not vary depending on the information she encountered there: a news report about a horrific natural disaster, a photograph of someone's beloved domestic pet, a female journalist complaining about death threats, a recondite joke requiring familiarity with several other internet jokes in order to be even vaguely comprehensible, a passionate condemnation of white supremacy, a promoted tweet advertising a health supplement for expectant mothers. Nothing changed in her outward relationship to the world that would allow an observer to determine what she felt about what she saw. Then, after some length of time, with no apparent trigger, she closed the browser window and reopened the text editor. Occasionally one of her colleagues would interject with a work-related question, and she would answer, or someone would share a funny anecdote with the office and they would all laugh, but mostly the work continued quietly.

At five thirty-four p.m., the woman took her jacket off the hook again and bid her remaining colleagues farewell. She unwound her headphones from around her phone, plugged them in, and walked down Kildare Street toward Nassau Street, then took a left, winding her way westward. After a twenty-eight-minute walk, she stopped at a new-build apartment complex on the north quays and let herself in, climbing two flights of stairs and unlocking a chipped white door. No one else was home, but the layout and interior suggested she was not the sole occupant. A small dim living room, with one curtained window facing the river, led onto a kitchenette with an oven, half-size fridge unit and sink. From the fridge the woman removed a bowl covered in clingfilm. She disposed of the clingfilm and put the bowl in the microwave.

After eating, she entered her bedroom. Through the window, the street below was visible, and the slow swell of the river. She removed her jacket and shoes, took the clasp from her hair and drew her curtains shut. The curtains were thin and yellow with a pattern of green rectangles. She took off her sweater and wriggled out of her trousers, leaving both items crumpled on the floor, the texture of the trousers a little shiny. Then she pulled on a cotton sweatshirt and a pair of grey leggings. Her hair, dark and falling loosely over her shoulders, looked clean and slightly dry. She climbed onto her bed and opened her laptop. For some time she scrolled through various media timelines, occasionally opening and half-reading long articles about elections overseas. Her face was wan and tired. Outside her room, two other people entered the apartment, having a conversation about ordering dinner. They passed her room, shadows visible briefly through the slit under the door, and then went through to the kitchen. Opening a private browser window on her laptop, the woman accessed a social media website, and typed the words 'aidan lavin' into the search box. A list of results appeared, and without glancing at the other options she clicked on the third result. A new profile opened onscreen, displaying the name 'Aidan Lavin' below a photograph of a man's head and shoulders viewed from behind. The man's hair was thick and dark and he was wearing a denim jacket. Beneath the photograph a text caption read: local sad boy. normal brain haver. check out the soundcloud. The user's most recent update, posted three hours earlier, was a photograph of a pigeon in a gutter, its head buried inside a discarded crisp packet. The caption read: same. The post had 127 likes. In her bedroom, leaning against the headboard of the unmade bed, the woman clicked on this post, and replies appeared underneath. One reply, from a user with the handle Actual Death

Girl, read: looks like you and all. The Aidan Lavin account had replied: youre right, insanely handsome. Actual Death Girl had liked this reply. The woman on her laptop clicked through to the profile of the Actual Death Girl account. After spending thirty-six minutes looking at a range of social media profiles associated with the Aidan Lavin account, the woman shut her laptop and lay back down on her bed.

By now it was after eight o'clock in the evening. With her head on the pillow, the woman rested her wrist on her forehead. She was wearing a thin gold bracelet, which glimmered faintly in the bedside light. Her name was Eileen Lydon. She was twenty-nine years old. Her father Pat managed a farm in County Galway and her mother Mary was a Geography teacher. She had one sister, Lola, who was three years older than she was. As a child, Lola had been sturdy, brave, mischievous, while Eileen had been anxious and often ill. They'd spent their school holidays together playing elaborate narrative games in which they took on the roles of human sisters who gained access to magical realms, Lola improvising the major plot events and Eileen following along. When available, young cousins, neighbours and children of family friends were enlisted to take on the roles of secondary characters, including, on occasion, a boy named Simon Costigan, who was five years older than Eileen and lived across the river in what had once been the local manor house. He was an extremely polite child who was always wearing clean clothes and saying thank you to adults. He suffered from epilepsy and sometimes had to go to the hospital, once even in an ambulance. Whenever Lola or Eileen misbehaved, their mother Mary asked them why they could not be more like Simon Costigan, who was not only well behaved but had the added dignity of 'never complaining'. As the sisters grew older, they no longer included Simon or any other children in their games, but migrated indoors, sketching up fictive maps on notepaper, inventing cryptic alphabets and making tape recordings. Their parents looked on these games with a benign lack of curiosity, happy to supply paper, pens and blank tapes, but uninterested in hearing anything about the imaginary inhabitants of fictional countries.

At the age of twelve, Lola moved on from their small local primary school to an all-girls Mercy convent in the nearest large town. Eileen, who had always been quiet in school, became increasingly withdrawn. Her teacher told her parents she was gifted, and she was taken to a special room twice a week and given extra classes in reading and Maths. At the convent, Lola made new friends, who started coming to the farm to visit, sometimes even to sleep over. Once, for a joke, they locked Eileen into the upstairs bathroom for twenty minutes. After that, their father Pat said Lola's friends weren't allowed to visit anymore, and Lola said it was Eileen's fault. When Eileen was twelve she was also sent to Lola's school, which was spread over several buildings and prefab units, with a student population of six hundred. Most of her peers lived in the town and knew one another from primary school, bringing with them prior alliances and loyalties in which she had no part. Lola and her friends were old enough to walk into town for lunch by then, while Eileen sat alone in the cafeteria, unpeeling tinfoil from home-packed sandwiches. In her second year, one of the other girls in her class came up behind her and poured a bottle of water over her head on a dare. The vice principal of the school made the girl write Eileen a letter of apology afterwards. At home, Lola said it would never have happened if Eileen didn't act like such a freak, and Eileen said: I'm not acting.

The summer she was fifteen, their neighbours' son Simon came over to help her father out on the farm. He was twenty years old and studying Philosophy at Oxford. Lola had just finished school and was hardly ever in the house, but when Simon stayed for dinner she would come home early, and even change her sweatshirt if it was dirty. In school, Lola had always avoided Eileen, but in Simon's presence she began to behave like a fond and indulgent older sister, fussing over Eileen's hair and clothes, treating her like a much younger child. Simon did not join in this behaviour. His manner with Eileen was friendly and respectful. He listened to her when she spoke, even when Lola tried to talk over her, and looking calmly at Eileen he would say things like: Ah, that's very interesting. By August she had taken to getting up early and watching out her bedroom window for his bicycle, at the sight of which she would run downstairs, meeting him as he came through the back door. While he boiled the kettle or washed his hands, she asked him questions about books, about his studies at university, about his life in England. She asked him once if he still suffered from seizures, and he smiled and said no, that had been a long time ago, he was surprised she could remember. They would talk for a little while, ten minutes or twenty, and afterwards he would go out to the farm and she would go back upstairs and lie in bed. Some mornings she was happy, flushed, her eyes gleaming, and on other mornings she cried. Lola told their mother Mary it had to stop. It's an obsession, she said. It's embarrassing. By then, Lola had heard from her friends that Simon attended Mass on Sunday mornings even though his parents didn't, and she no longer came home for dinner when he was there. Mary began to sit in the kitchen herself in the mornings, eating breakfast and reading the paper. Eileen would come down anyway, and Simon would greet her in the same friendly manner as always, but her retorts were sullen, and she withdrew quickly to her room. The night before he went back to England, he came over to the house to say goodbye, and Eileen hid in her room and refused to come down. He went upstairs to see her, and she kicked a chair and said he was the only person she could talk to. In my life, the only one, she said. And they won't even let me talk to you, and now you're going. I wish I was dead. He was standing with the door half-open behind him. Quietly he said: Eileen, don't say that. Everything will be alright, I promise. You and I are going to be friends for the rest of our lives.

At eighteen, Eileen went to university in Dublin to study English. In her first year, she struck up a friendship with a girl named Alice Kelleher, and the following year they became roommates. Alice had a very loud speaking voice, dressed in ill-fitting second-hand clothes and seemed to find everything hilarious. Her father was a car mechanic with a drinking problem and she'd had a disorganised childhood. She did not easily find friends among their classmates, and faced minor disciplinary proceedings for calling a lecturer a 'fascist pig'. Eileen went through college patiently reading all the assigned texts, submitting every project by the deadline and preparing thoroughly for exams. She collected almost every academic award for which she was eligible and even won a national essay prize. She developed a social circle, went out to nightclubs, rejected the advances of various male friends, and came home afterwards to eat toast with Alice in the living room. Alice said that Eileen was a genius and a pearl beyond price, and that even the people who really appreciated her still didn't appreciate her enough. Eileen said that Alice was an iconoclast and a true original, and that she was ahead of her time. Lola attended a different college in another part of the city, and never saw Eileen except on the street by coincidence. When Eileen was in her second year, Simon moved to Dublin to study for a legal qualification. Eileen invited him to the apartment one night to introduce him to Alice, and he brought with him a box of expensive chocolates and a bottle of white wine. Alice was extremely rude to him all evening, called his religious beliefs 'evil' and also said his wristwatch was ugly. For some reason Simon seemed to find this behaviour amusing and even endearing. He called around to the apartment quite often after that, standing with his back against the radiator, arguing with Alice about God, and cheerfully criticising their poor housekeeping skills. He said they were 'living in squalor'. Sometimes he even washed the dishes before he left. One night when Alice wasn't there, Eileen asked him if he had a girlfriend, and he laughed and said: What makes you ask that? I'm a wise old man, remember? Eileen was lying on the sofa, and without lifting her head she tossed a cushion at him, which he caught in his hands. Just old, she said. Not wise.

When Eileen was twenty, she had sex for the first time, with a man she had met on the internet. Afterwards she walked back

45

from his house to her apartment alone. It was late, almost two o'clock in the morning, and the streets were deserted. When she got home, Alice was sitting on the couch typing something on her laptop. Eileen leaned on the jamb of the living room door and said aloud: Well, that was weird. Alice stopped typing. What, did you sleep with him? she said. Eileen was rubbing her upper arm with the palm of her hand. He asked me to keep my clothes on, she said. Like, for the whole thing. Alice stared at her. Where do you find these people? she said. Looking at the floor, Eileen shrugged her shoulders. Alice got up from the sofa then. Don't feel bad, she said. It's not a big deal. It's nothing. In two weeks you'll have forgotten about it. Eileen rested her head on Alice's small shoulder. Patting her back, Alice said softly: You're not like me. You're going to have a happy life. Simon was living in Paris that summer, working for a climate emergency group. Eileen went to visit him there, the first time she had ever got on a plane alone. He met her at the airport and they took a train into the city. That night they drank a bottle of wine in his apartment and she told him the story of how she lost her virginity. He laughed and apologised for laughing. They were lying on the bed in his

46

room together. After a pause, Eileen said: I was going to ask how you lost your virginity. But then, for all I know, you still haven't. He smiled at that. No, I have, he said. For a few seconds she lay quietly with her face turned up toward the ceiling, breathing. Even though you're Catholic, she said. They were lying close together, their shoulders almost touching. Right, he answered. What does Saint Augustine say? Lord, give me chastity, but not yet.

After graduating, Eileen started a Master's degree in Irish Literature, and Alice got a job in a coffee shop and started writing a novel. They were still living together, and in the evenings Alice sometimes read aloud the good jokes from her manuscript while Eileen was cooking dinner. Sitting at the kitchen table, pushing her hair back from her forehead, Alice would say: Listen to this. You know the main guy I was telling you about? Well, he gets a text from the sister character. In Paris, Simon had moved in with his girlfriend, a French woman named Natalie. After finishing her Master's, Eileen got a job in a bookshop, wheeling loaded trolleys across the shop floor to be unloaded and placing individual adhesive price stickers onto individual copies of bestselling novels. By then her parents had run into financial trouble with the farm. On Eileen's visits home, her father Pat was sullen and restless, pacing around the house at strange hours, switching things off and on. At dinner he barely spoke, and often left the table before the others had finished eating. In the living room one night when they were alone, her mother Mary told her that something would have to change. It can't go on like this, she said. With a concerned expression, Eileen asked whether she meant the financial situation or her marriage. Mary turned her hands palm up, looking exhausted, looking older than she really was. Everything, she said. I don't know. You come home complaining about your job, complaining about your life. What about my life? Who's taking care of me? Eileen was twenty-three then and her mother was fifty-one. Eileen held her fingertips lightly against one of her eyelids for a moment, and said: Aren't you complaining to me about your life right now? Mary started crying then. Eileen watched her uneasily, and said: I really care that you're unhappy, I just don't know what you want me to do. Her mother was covering her face, sobbing. What did I do wrong? she said. How did I raise such selfish children? Eileen sat back against the sofa as if she was giving the question serious thought.

What outcome do you want here? she asked. I can't give you money. I can't go back in time and make you marry a different man. You want me to listen to you complaining about it? I'll listen. I am listening. But I'm not sure why you think your unhappiness is more important than mine. Mary left the room.

When they were twenty-four, Alice signed an American book deal for two hundred and fifty thousand dollars. She said no one in the publishing industry knew anything about money, and that if they were stupid enough to give it to her, she was avaricious enough to take it. Eileen was dating a PhD student named Kevin, and through him had found a low-paid but interesting job as an editorial assistant at a literary magazine. At first she was just copy-editing, but after a few months they allowed her to start commissioning new pieces, and at the end of the year the editor invited her to contribute some of her own work. Eileen said she would think about it. Lola was working at a management consultancy firm then and had a boyfriend called Matthew. She invited Eileen to have dinner with them in town one night. On a Thursday evening after work, the three of them waited forty-five minutes on an increasingly dark and chilly street to be seated in a new burger restaurant Lola particularly wanted to try. When the burgers arrived, they tasted normal. Lola asked Eileen about her career plans and Eileen said she was happy at the magazine. Right, for now, said Lola. But what's next? Eileen told her she didn't know. Lola made a smiling face and said: One day you're going to have to live in the real world. Eileen walked back to the apartment that night and found Alice on the sofa, working on her book. Alice, she said, am I going to have to live in the real world one day? Without looking up, Alice snorted and said: Jesus no, absolutely not. Who told you that?

The following September, Eileen found out from her mother that Simon and Natalie had broken up. They had been together for four years by then. Eileen told Alice she had thought they would get married. I always thought they were going to get married, she would say. And Alice would answer: Yeah, you've mentioned that. Eileen sent Simon an email asking how he was, and he wrote back: I don't suppose you're going to find yourself in Paris any time soon? I would really like to see you. At Halloween she went to stay with him for a few days. He was thirty by then and she was twenty-five. They went out to museums together in the afternoons and talked about art and politics. Whenever she asked him about Natalie he responded lightly, self-effacingly, and changed the subject. Once, when they were sitting together in the Musée d'Orsay, Eileen said to him: You know everything about me, and I know nothing about you. With a pained-looking smile he answered: Ah, now you sound like Natalie. Then he laughed and said sorry. That was the only time he mentioned her name. In the mornings he made coffee, and at night Eileen slept in his bed. After they made love, he liked to hold her for a long time. The day she arrived back in Dublin, she broke up with her boyfriend. She didn't hear anything from Simon again until he came over to her family home at Christmas to drink a glass of brandy and admire the tree.

Alice's book was published the following spring. A lot of press attention surrounded the publication, mostly positive at first, and then some negative pieces reacting to the fawning positivity of the initial coverage. In the summer, at a party in their friend Ciara's apartment, Eileen met a man named Aidan. He had thick dark hair and wore linen trousers and dirty tennis shoes. They ended up sitting in the kitchen together until late that night, talking about childhood. In my family we just don't discuss things, Aidan said. Everything is below the surface, nothing comes out. Can I refill that for you? Eileen watched him pouring a measure of red wine into her glass. We don't really talk about things in my family either, she said. Sometimes I think we try, but we don't know how. At the end of the night, Eileen and Aidan walked home together in the same direction, and he took a detour to see her to her apartment door. Take care of yourself, he said when they parted. A few days later they met for a drink, just the two of them. He was a musician and a sound engineer. He talked to her about his work, about his flatmates, about his relationship with his mother, about various things he loved and hated. While they spoke, Eileen laughed a lot and looked animated, touching her mouth, leaning forward in her seat. After she got home that night Aidan sent her a message reading: you are such a good listener! wow! and I talk too much, sorry. can we see each other again?

They went for another drink the following week, and then another. Aidan's apartment had a lot of tangled black cables all over the floor and his bed was just a mattress. In the autumn, they went to Florence for a few days and walked through the cool of the cathedral together. One night when she made a witty remark at dinner, he laughed so much that he had to wipe his eyes with a purple serviette. He told her that he loved her. Everything in life is incredibly beautiful, Eileen wrote in a message to Alice. I can't believe it's possible to be so happy. Simon moved back to Dublin around that time, to work as a policy adviser for a left-wing parliamentary group. Eileen saw him sometimes on the bus, or crossing a street, his arm around one good-looking woman or another. Before Christmas, Eileen and Aidan moved in together. He carried her boxes of books from the back of his car and said proudly: The weight of your brain. Alice came to their housewarming party, dropped a bottle of vodka on the kitchen tiles, told a very long anecdote about their college years which only Eileen and she herself seemed to find remotely funny, and then went home again. Most of the other people at the party were Aidan's friends. Afterwards, drunk, Eileen said to Aidan: Why don't I have any friends? I have two, but they're weird. And the others are more like acquaintances. He smoothed his hand over her hair and said: You have me.

For the next three years Eileen and Aidan

lived in a one-bedroom apartment in the south city centre, illegally downloading foreign films, arguing about how to split the rent, taking turns to cook and wash up. Lola and Matthew got engaged. Alice won a lucrative literary award, moved to New York and started sending Eileen emails at strange hours of the day and night. Then she stopped emailing at all, deleted her social media profiles, ignored Eileen's messages. In December, Simon called Eileen one night and told her that Alice was back in Dublin and had been admitted to a psychiatric hospital. Eileen was sitting on the sofa, her phone held to her ear, while Aidan was at the sink, rinsing a plate under the tap. After she and Simon had finished speaking, she sat there on the phone, saying nothing, and he said nothing, they were both silent. Right, he said eventually. I'll let you go. A few weeks later, Eileen and Aidan broke up. He told her there was a lot going on and that they both needed space. He went to live with his parents and she moved into a two-bedroom apartment with a married couple in the north inner city. Lola and Matthew decided to have a small wedding in the summer. Simon went on answering his correspondence promptly, taking Eileen out for lunch now and then, and keeping his personal life to himself. It was April and several of Eileen's friends had recently left or were in the process of leaving Dublin. She attended the leaving parties, wearing her dark-green dress with the buttons, or her yellow dress with the matching belt. In living rooms with low ceilings and paper lampshades, people talked to her about the property market. My sister's getting married in June, she would tell them. That's exciting, they would reply. You must be so happy for her. Yeah, it's funny, Eileen would say. I'm not.

4.

Alice, I think I've also experienced that sensation you had in the convenience shop. For me it feels like looking down and seeing for the first time that I'm standing on a minuscule ledge at a dizzying vertical height, and the only thing supporting my weight is the misery and degradation of almost everyone else on earth. And I always end up thinking: I don't even want to be up here. I don't need all these cheap clothes and imported foods and plastic containers, I don't even think they improve my life. They just create waste and make me unhappy anyway. (Not that I'm comparing my dissatisfaction to the misery of actually oppressed peoples, I just mean that the lifestyle they sustain for us is not even satisfying, in my opinion.) People think that socialism is sustained by force — the forcible expropriation of property — but I wish they would just admit that capitalism is also sustained by exactly the same force in the opposite direction, the forcible protection of existing property arrangements. I know you know this. I hate having the same debates over and over again with the wrong first principles.

I've also been thinking lately about time and political conservatism, although in a different way. At the moment I think it's fair to say we're living in a period of historical crisis, and this idea seems to be generally accepted by most of the population. I mean the outward symptoms of the crisis, e.g. major unpredicted shifts in electoral politics, are widely recognisable as abnormal phenomena. To an extent, I think even some of the more 'suppressed' structural symptoms, like the mass drowning of refugees and the repeated weather disasters triggered by climate change, are beginning to be understood as manifestations of a political crisis. And I believe studies show that in the last couple of years, people have been spending a lot more time reading the news and learning about current affairs. It has become normal in my life, for example, to send text messages like the following: tillerson out at state lmaoooo. It just strikes me that it really shouldn't be normal to send texts like that. Anyway, as a consequence, each day has now become a new and unique informational unit, interrupting and replacing the informational world of the day before. And I wonder (you might say irrelevantly) what all this means for culture and the arts. I mean, we're used to engaging with cultural works set 'in the present'. But this sense of the continuous present is no longer a feature of our lives. The present has become discontinuous. Each day, even each hour of each day, replaces and makes irrelevant the time before, and the events of our lives make sense only in relation to a perpetually updating timeline of news content. So when we watch characters in films sit at dinner tables or drive around in cars, plotting to carry out murders or feeling sad about their love affairs, we naturally want to know at what exact point they are doing these things, relative to the cataclysmic historic events that structure our present sense of reality. There is no longer a neutral setting. There is only the timeline. I don't know really whether this will give rise to new forms in the arts or just mean the end of the arts altogether, at least as we know them.

Your paragraph about time also reminded me of something I read online recently. Apparently in the Late Bronze Age, starting about 1,500 years before the Christian era, the Eastern Mediterranean region was characterised by a system of centralised palace governments, which redistributed money and goods through complex and specialised city economies. I read about this on Wikipedia. Trade routes were highly developed at this time and written languages emerged. Expensive luxury goods were produced and traded over huge distances — in the 1980s a single wrecked ship from the period was discovered off the coast of Turkey, carrying Egyptian jewellery, Greek pottery, blackwood from Sudan, Irish copper, pomegranates, ivory. Then, during a seventy-five-year period from about 1225 to 1150 BCE, civilisation collapsed. The great cities of the Eastern Mediterranean were destroyed or abandoned. Literacy all but died out, and entire writing systems were lost. No one is sure why any of this happened, by the way. Wikipedia suggests a theory called 'general systems collapse', whereby 'centralisation, specialisation, complexity, and top-heavy political structure' made Late Bronze Age civilisation particularly vulnerable to breakdown. Another of the theories is headlined simply: 'Climate change'. I think this puts our present civilisation in a kind of ominous light, don't you? General systems collapse is not something I had ever really thought about as a possibility before. Of course I know in my brain that everything we tell ourselves about human civilisation is a lie. But imagine having to find out in real life.

Unrelatedly, and in fact so unrelatedly that it comes in at a sharp ninety-degree angle to my last paragraph, do you ever think about your biological clock? Not that I'm saying you should, I'm just wondering if you do. We are still pretty young, obviously. But the fact is that the vast majority of women throughout human history had already had several children by the time they reached our age. Right? I guess there's no good way of checking that. I'm not even sure if you want to have children, now that I think of it. Do you? Or maybe you don't know one way or another. As a teenager I thought I would rather die than have babies, and then in my twenties I vaguely assumed it was something that would just happen to me eventually, and now that I'm about to turn thirty, I'm starting to think: well? There isn't anyone queuing up to help me fulfil this biological function, needless to say. And I also have a weird and completely unexplained suspicion that I might not be fertile. There is no medical reason for me to think this. I mentioned it to Simon recently, in the course of complaining to him about my various other unsubstantiated medical anxieties, and he said he didn't think I needed to worry about that one, because in his opinion I have a 'fertile look'. That made me laugh for like a day. I'm actually still laughing about it while I'm writing this email to you. Anyway, I'm just curious to know your thoughts. Considering the approaching civilisational collapse, maybe you think children are out of the question anyway.

I'm probably thinking about all this now because I saw Aidan randomly on the street the other day and immediately had a heart attack and died. Every subsequent hour since I saw him has been worse than the last. Or is it just that the pain I feel right now is so intense that it transcends my ability to reconstruct the pain I felt at the time? Presumably, remembered suffering never feels as bad as present suffering, even if it was really a lot worse — we can't remember how much worse it was, because remembering is weaker than experiencing. Maybe that's why middle-aged people always think their thoughts and feelings are more important than those of young people, because they can only weakly remember the feelings of their youth while allowing their present experiences to dominate their life outlook. Still, my intuition is that I actually feel worse now, two days after seeing Aidan, than I felt in the moment of seeing him. I know that what happened between us was just an event and not a symbol — just something that happened, or something he did, and not an inevitable manifestation of my failure in life generally. But when I saw him, it was like going through it all over again. And Alice, I do feel like a failure, and in a way my life really is nothing, and very few people care what happens in it. It's so hard to see the point sometimes, when the things in life I think are meaningful turn out to mean nothing, and the people who are supposed to love me don't. I have tears in my eyes even typing this stupid email, and I've had nearly six months to get over it. I'm starting to wonder if I just never will. Maybe certain kinds of pain, at certain formative stages in life, just impress themselves into a person's sense of self permanently. Like the way I didn't lose my virginity until I was twenty and it was so painful and awkward and bad, and since then I've always felt like exactly the kind of person that would happen to, even though before then I didn't. And now I just feel like the kind of person whose life partner would fall out of love with them after several years, and I can't find a way not to be that kind of person anymore.

Are you working on anything new out there in the middle of nowhere? Or just taking recalcitrant local boys out on dates? I miss you! All my love. E.

5.

In the chilled section of a convenience shop, Felix was browsing a selection of ready meals with a slightly unfocused look on his face. It was three o'clock in the afternoon on a Thursday and white light fixtures hummed overhead. The doors at the front of the shop parted but he didn't turn around. He replaced a ready meal on a shelf and took out his phone. There were no new notifications. Inexpressively he put the device back in his pocket, lifted a plastic box off the shelf as if at random, walked over to the till, and paid. On his way out of the shop, in front of the fresh fruit display, he paused. Alice was standing there looking at apples, lifting the apples one after another and examining them for defects. Recognising her, he began to stand a little differently, straighter. It was not clear at first whether he would greet her or just exit without saying hello — he himself didn't seem to know. Holding the ready meal in one hand, he tapped it on the side of his leg absent-mindedly. At that, maybe hearing him or just becoming aware of his presence in her peripheral vision, she did turn, and noticed him, and immediately tucked her hair behind her ears.

Hello there, she said.

Hey. How are you getting on?

I'm good, thanks.

Make any friends yet? he asked.

Absolutely not.

He smiled, tapped the ready meal on his leg again, and looked around at the exit. Ah here, he said. What are we going to do with you? You'll go mad up there on your own.

Oh, I already am, she said. But then maybe I already was before I arrived.

Mad, were you? You seemed pretty normal to me.

Not a word I often hear in connection with myself, but thank you.

They stood there looking at one another until she lowered her eyes and touched her hair again. He glanced over his shoulder once more at the exit, and then back at her. It was difficult to tell if he was enjoying her discomfort or simply taking pity on her. For her part, she seemed to feel obliged to continue standing there as long as he wanted to talk.

Have you given up on the old dating app, then? he said.

With a smile, looking directly at him, she replied: Yes, the last attempt didn't exactly inspire confidence, if you don't mind my saying so.

Did I put you off men entirely?

Oh, not just men. People of all genders.

He laughed and said: I didn't think I was that bad.

No, you weren't. But I was.

Ah, you were alright.

He frowned in the direction of the fresh vegetables before speaking again. She looked more relaxed now and watched him neutrally.

You could come around the house tonight if you want to meet people, he said. Some of the gang from work will be there.

Are you having a party?

He made a face. I don't know, he said. I mean, there will be people there, so. A party or whatever you would call it, yeah. Nothing big, though.

She nodded, moving her mouth around without showing her teeth. That sounds nice, she said. You'll have to remind me where you live.

I'll throw it into Google Maps for you if

you have it, he said.

She took her phone from her pocket and opened the app. Handing him the device, she said: Are you off work today?

He typed his address into the search bar without looking up. Yeah, he said. They have me on really random shifts this week. He handed her back the phone to show her the address: 16 Ocean Rise. The screen displayed a network of white streets on a background of grey, beside a blue area representing the sea. Sometimes they hardly need you in there at all, he added. And then some weeks you're in every day. Drives me mad. He looked around again at the till, seemingly in a different mood now. I'll see you this evening, will I? he said.

If you're sure you'd like me to come, she answered.

Up to yourself. I would go off my bean if I was out there on my own all day. But maybe you like it.

No, I don't really. I'd like to come, thank you for asking me.

Yeah, well, no big deal, he said. There'll be a fair few people there anyway. See you later, then, have a good day.

Without making eye contact with her again, he turned around and left the shop. She looked back at the box of fresh apples, and, as if now feeling it would be inappropriate to continue examining them in any detail, as if the whole process of searching for bruises on the exterior surface of fruit had been rendered ridiculous and even shameful, she picked one up and proceeded to the refrigerator aisle.

16 Ocean Rise was a semi-detached house, with the projecting left half of the facade in red brick and the right half painted white. A low wall separated its concrete front yard from that of its neighbour. The curtains were drawn on the window facing the street, but the lights were on inside. Alice stood at the door wearing the same clothes she had been wearing earlier. She had put powder on her face, which made her skin look dry, and she was carrying a bottle of red wine in her left hand. She rang the bell and waited. After a few seconds, a woman about her own age opened the door. Behind her the hallway was bright and noisy.

Hi, said Alice. Does Felix live here?

Yeah, yeah. Come on in.

The woman let her inside and closed the door. In her hand she was holding a chipped mug that seemed to contain some kind of cola. I'm Danielle, she said. The lads are just down here. In the kitchen at the end of the hall, six men and two women were seated in various positions around the table. Felix was sitting on the counter by the toaster, drinking directly from a can. He didn't get up when he saw Alice enter, he just nodded his head at her. She followed Danielle into the room, toward the fridge, near where he was sitting.

Hey, he said.

Hi, said Alice.

Two of the people in the room had turned to look at her, while the others continued the conversation they had been having before. Danielle asked Alice if she wanted a glass for her wine and Alice said sure. While she was rooting in the cupboard, Danielle said: So how do you know each other?

We met on Tinder, said Felix.

Danielle stood up, holding a clean wine glass. And this is your idea of a date? she said. How romantic.

We already tried going on a date, he said. She said it turned her off men for life.

Alice tried to catch Felix's eye, perhaps to smile at him, to show that she found this remark amusing, but he wasn't looking at her.

I wouldn't blame her, said Danielle.

Putting her bottle down on the counter, Alice looked at the CD library stored along the kitchen wall. Lots of albums, she said.

Yeah, they're mine, Felix replied.

She ran her finger along the spines of the plastic jewel cases, withdrawing one slightly from its slot so it hung out like a tongue. Danielle had by then started speaking to a woman who was sitting on the kitchen table, and another man had come over to open the fridge. Gesturing in her direction, he said to Felix: Who's this?

This is Alice, said Felix. She's a novelist.

Who's a novelist? Danielle asked.

This lady here, said Felix. She writes books for a living. Or so she claims.

What's your name? the man asked. I'll put it into Google.

Alice watched this all unfold with a look of forced indifference. Alice Kelleher, she said.

Felix watched her. The man sat down on an empty chair and started typing into his phone. Alice was drinking her wine and gazing off around the room, as if uninterested. Hunched over his phone now, the man said: Here, she's famous. Alice did not respond, did not return Felix's gaze. Danielle bent down over the screen to see. Look at that, she said. She's got a Wikipedia page and everything. Felix slid off the countertop and took the phone out of his friend's hand. He laughed, but his amusement did not seem completely sincere.

Literary work, he read aloud. Adaptations. Personal life.

That section must be short, said Alice.

Why didn't you tell me you were famous? he said.

In a bored, almost contemptuous tone of voice she answered: I told you I was a writer.

He grinned at her. I'll give you a tip for next time you go on a date, he said. Mention in the conversation that you're a celebrity.

Thank you for the unsolicited dating advice. I'll be sure to disregard it.

What, are you annoyed now because we found you on the internet?

Of course not, she said, I told you my name. I didn't have to.

For a few seconds he continued looking at her and then he shook his head and said: You're weird.

She laughed and said: How insightful. Why don't you put that on my Wikipedia page?

Danielle laughed then too. A little colour had come into Felix's face. He turned away from Alice and said: Anyone can have one of those. You probably wrote it yourself.

As if she were beginning to enjoy herself,

71

Alice responded: No, just the books.

You must think you're very special, he said.

What are you being so touchy about? said Danielle.

I'm not, Felix replied. He handed the phone back to his friend and then stood leaning against the fridge, arms crossed. Alice was standing at the countertop just near him. Danielle looked at Alice and raised her eyebrows, but then the doorbell rang and Danielle went out to get it. One of the other women put on some music, and some of the men at the other end of the room started laughing about something. Alice said to Felix: If you'd like me to leave, I'll go.

Who said I want you to leave? he asked.

A new group of people entered the room and it became noisier. No one specifically came over to speak to either Alice or Felix, and they both stood there next to the fridge in silence. Whether this experience was especially painful for either of them their features did not suggest, but after a few seconds Felix stretched his arms and said: I don't like smoking inside. Will you come out for one? You can get to meet our dog. Alice nodded, said nothing, and followed him out the patio door into the back garden, carrying her glass of wine.

Felix slid the door shut behind them and wandered down the grass toward a small garden shed with a makeshift tarpaulin roof. A springer spaniel immediately bounded up to meet him from the bottom of the garden, sneezed with excitement, placed its front paws on Felix's legs and then let out a single yelp. This is Sabrina, he said. She's not really ours, the last people who lived here just left her behind. I'm mostly the one who feeds her now, so she's a big fan of mine. Alice said that was evident. We don't usually keep her outside, he said. Only when we have people around. She'll be back in tonight when everyone goes home. Alice asked if she slept in his bed and Felix laughed. She tries, he said. But she knows she's not allowed. He ruffled the dog's ears and said affectionately: Fool. Turning back to Alice, he added: She's a complete idiot, by the way. Really stupid. Do you smoke? Alice was shivering and goosebumps were raised on the part of her wrist that extended out from her sleeve, but she accepted a cigarette and stood there smoking while Felix lit one himself. He took a drag, exhaled into the clean night air and looked back up at the house. Inside, it was bright and his friends were talking and gesturing. Around the warm yellow oblong of the patio doors was the darkness of the house, the grass, the clear black void of the sky.

Dani's a nice girl, he said.

Yes, said Alice. She seems that way.

Yeah. We used to go out together.

Oh? For a long time, or?

He shrugged and said: About a year. I don't know — more than a year, actually. Anyway, it was ages ago, we're good friends now.

Do you still like her?

He gazed back into the house as if catching a glimpse of Danielle might help him to resolve this question in his own mind. She's with someone else anyway, he said.

A friend of yours?

I know him, yeah. He's not here tonight, you might meet him again.

He turned away from the house and flicked some ash off his cigarette, causing a few lit sparks to descend slowly through the dark air. The dog bounded away past the shed, then ran around in a circle several times.

In fairness, if she could hear me, she'd be telling you I was the one who fucked it up, Felix added.

What did you do?

Ah, I was cold with her, supposedly. According to herself, anyway. You can ask her if you want.

Alice smiled and said: Would you like me to ask her?

Jesus no, not for me. I already heard enough of it at the time. I'm not still crying over it, don't worry.

Did you cry over it then?

Well, not literally, he said. Is that what you mean? I didn't actually cry, but like, I was pissed off, yeah.

Do you ever actually cry?

He gave a short laugh and said: No. Do you?

Oh, constantly.

Yeah? he said. What do you be crying about?

Anything, really. I suppose I'm very unhappy.

He looked at her. Seriously? he said. Why?

Nothing specific. It's just how I feel. I find my life difficult.

After a pause he looked back at his cigarette and said: I don't think I have the whole story on why you moved here.

It's not a very good story, she said. I had a nervous breakdown. I was in hospital for a few weeks, and then I moved here when I got out. But it's not mysterious — I mean, there was no reason I had a breakdown, I just did. And it's not a secret, everyone knows.

Felix appeared to mull over this new information. Is it on your Wikipedia page? he asked.

No, I mean everyone in my life knows. Not everyone in the world.

And what did you have a breakdown about?

Nothing.

Okay, but what do you mean you had a breakdown? Like, what happened?

She exhaled a stream of smoke through the side of her mouth. I felt very out of control, she said. I was just extremely angry and upset all the time. I wasn't in control of myself, I couldn't live normally. I can't explain it any more than that.

Fair enough.

They lapsed into silence. Alice drained the last of her wine from the glass, crushed her cigarette underfoot and folded her arms against her chest. Felix looked distracted and continued smoking slowly, as if he had forgotten she was there. He cleared his throat then and said: I felt a bit like that after my mam died. Last year. I just started thinking, what's the fucking point of life, you know? It's not like there's anything at the end of it. Not that I really wanted to be dead or anything, but I couldn't be fucked being alive most the time either. I don't know if you would call it a breakdown. I just had a few months where I was seriously not bothered about it — getting up and going to work and all that. I actually lost the job I had at the time, that's why I'm at the warehouse now. Yeah. So I kind of get what you're saying about the breakdown. Obviously the experiences would be different in my case, but I see where you're coming from, yeah.

Alice said again that she was sorry for his loss and he accepted her condolences.

I'm going to Rome next week, she said. Because the Italian translation of my book is coming out. I wonder if you'd like to come with me.

He showed no surprise at the invitation. He put out his cigarette by rubbing the lit end on the wall of the shed in several repeated strokes. The dog let out one more yelp, down at the end of the garden.

I don't have any money, Felix said.

Well, I can pay for everything. I'm rich and famous, remember?

This drew a little smile. You are weird, he said. I don't take that back. How long are you going for?

I'm getting there on Wednesday and then

coming home again Monday morning. But we can stay longer if you prefer.

Now he laughed. Fucking hell, he said.

Have you ever been to Rome?

No.

Then I think you should come, she said. I think you'd like it.

How do you know what I would like?

They looked at one another. It was too dark for either of them to glean much information from the other's face, and yet they kept looking, and did not break off, as if the act of looking was more important than what they could see.

I don't, she said. I just think so.

Finally he turned away from her. Alright, he said. I'll come.

6.

Every day I wonder why my life has turned out this way. I can't believe I have to tolerate these things — having articles written about me, and seeing my photograph on the internet, and reading comments about myself. When I put it like that, I think: that's it? And so what? But the fact is, although it's nothing, it makes me miserable, and I don't want to live this kind of life. When I submitted the first book, I just wanted to make enough money to finish the next one. I never advertised myself as a psychologically robust person, capable of withstanding extensive public inquiries into my personality and upbringing. People who intentionally become famous — I mean people who, after a little taste of fame, want more and more of it — are, and I honestly believe this, deeply psychologically ill. The fact that we are exposed to these people everywhere in our culture, as if they are not only normal but attractive and enviable, indicates the extent of our disfiguring social disease. There is something wrong with them, and when we look at them and learn from them, something goes wrong with us.

What is the relationship of the famous author to their famous books anyway? If I had bad manners and was personally unpleasant and spoke with an irritating accent, which in my opinion is probably the case, would it have anything to do with my novels? Of course not. The work would be the same, no different. And what do the books gain by being attached to me, my face, my mannerisms, in all their demoralising specificity? Nothing. So why, why, is it done this way? Whose interests does it serve? It makes me miserable, keeps me away from the one thing in my life that has any meaning, contributes nothing to the public interest, satisfies only the basest and most prurient curiosities on the part of readers, and serves to arrange literary discourse entirely around the domineering figure of 'the author', whose lifestyle and idiosyncrasies must be picked over in lurid detail for no reason. I keep encountering this person, who is myself, and I hate her with all my energy. I hate her ways of expressing herself, I hate her appearance, and I hate her opinions about everything. And yet when other people read about her, they believe that she is me. Confronting this fact makes me feel I am already dead.

Of course I can't complain, because everyone is always telling me to 'enjoy it'. What would they know? They haven't been here, I've done it all alone. Okay, it's been a small experience in its own way, and it will all blow over in a few months or years and no one will even remember me, thank God. But still I've had to do it, I've had to get through it on my own with no one to teach me how, and it has made me loathe myself to an almost unendurable degree. Whatever I can do, whatever insignificant talent I might have, people just expect me to sell it — I mean literally, sell it for money, until I have a lot of money and no talent left. And then that's it, I'm finished, and the next flashy twenty-five-year-old with an impending psychological collapse comes along. If I have met anyone genuine along the way, then they've been so well disguised in the teeming crowd of blood-thirsty egomaniacs that I haven't recognised them. The only genuine people I think I really know are you and Simon, and by now you can only look at me with pity — not with love or friendship but just pity, like I'm something half-dead lying on the roadside and the kindest thing would be to put me out of my misery.

After your email about the Late Bronze Age collapse, I became very intrigued by the idea that writing systems could be 'lost'. In fact I wasn't really sure what that even meant, so I had to look it up, and I ended up reading a lot about something called Linear B. Do you know all about this already? Basically, around the year 1900, a team of British excavators in Crete found a cache of ancient clay tablets in a terracotta bathtub. The tablets were inscribed with a syllabic script of unknown language and appeared to date from around 1400 BCE. Throughout the early part of the twentieth century, classical scholars and linguists tried to decipher the markings, known as Linear B, with no success. Although the script was organised like writing, no one could work out what language it transcribed. Most academics hypothesised it was a lost language of the Minoan culture on Crete, with no remaining descendants in the modern world. In 1936, at the age of eighty-five, the archaeologist Arthur Evans gave a lecture in London about the tablets, and in attendance at the lecture was a fourteen-year-old schoolboy named Michael Ventris. Before the Second World War broke out, a new cache of tablets was found and photographed — this time on the Greek mainland. Still, no attempts to translate the script or identify its language were successful. Michael Ventris had grown up in the meantime and trained as an architect, and during the war he was conscripted to serve in the RAF. He hadn't received any formal qualifications in linguistics or classical languages, but he'd never forgotten Arthur Evans's lecture that day about Linear B. After the war, Ventris returned to England and started to compare the photographs of the newly discovered tablets from the Greek mainland with the inscriptions on the old Cretan tablets. He noticed that certain symbols on the tablets from Crete were not replicated on any of the samples from Pylos. He guessed that those particular symbols might represent place names on the island. Working from there, he figured out how to decipher the script — revealing that Linear B was in fact an early written form of ancient Greek. Ventris's work not only demonstrated that Greek was the language of the Mycenaean culture, but also provided evidence of written Greek which predated the earliest-known examples by hundreds of years. After the discovery, Ventris and the classical scholar and linguist John Chadwick wrote a book together on the translation of the script, entitled 'Documents in Mycenaean Greek'. Weeks before the publication of the book in 1956, Ventris crashed his car into a parked truck and died. He was thirty-four.

I've condensed the story here into a suitably dramatic form. There were plenty of other classicists involved, including an American professor named Alice Kober, who made significant contributions to the interpretation of Linear B and died of cancer at the age of forty-three. The Wikipedia entries on Ventris, Linear B, Arthur Evans, Alice Kober, John Chadwick and Mycenaean Greece are somewhat disorganised, and some even offer variant versions of the same event. Was Evans eighty-four or eighty-five years old when Ventris attended his lecture? And did Ventris really find out about Linear B for the first time that day, or had he heard of it already? His death is described only in the briefest and most mysterious way — Wikipedia says he died 'instantly' following 'a late-night collision with a parked truck' and that the coroner gave a verdict of accidental death. I have been thinking lately about the ancient world coming back to us, emerging through strange ruptures in time, through the colossal speed and waste and godlessness of the twentieth century, through the hands and eyes of Alice Kober, a chainsmoker dead at forty-three, and Michael Ventris, dead in a car crash at the age of thirty-four.

Anyway, all this means that during the Bronze Age, a sophisticated syllabic script was developed to represent the Greek language in writing, and then during the collapse you told me about, all that knowledge was completely destroyed. Later writing systems devised to represent Greek bear no relation to Linear B. The people who developed and used them had no idea that Linear B had ever even existed. The unbearable thing is that when first inscribed, those markings meant something, to the people who wrote and read them, and then for thousands of years they meant nothing, nothing, nothing — because the link was broken, history had stopped. And then the twentieth century shook the watch and made history happen again. But can't we do that too, in another way?

I'm sorry that you felt so terrible after running into Aidan the other day. These feelings are no doubt completely normal. But as your best friend, who loves you very much and wishes the best for you in every part of your life, would it be aggravating of me to point out that you weren't really

85

happy together? I know that he was the one who decided to end things, and I know that must be painful and frustrating. I'm not trying to talk you out of feeling bad. All I'm saying is, I think you know in your heart that it wasn't a very good relationship. You talked to me several times about wanting to break up and not knowing how. I'm only saying this because I don't want you to start retroactively believing that Aidan was your soulmate or that you could never be happy without him. You got into a long relationship in your twenties that didn't work out. That doesn't mean God has marked you out for a life of failure and misery. I was in a long relationship in my twenties and that didn't work out, remember? And Simon and Natalie were together for nearly five years before they broke up. Do you think he's a failure, or I am? Hm. Well, now that I think of it, maybe all three of us are. But if so, I'd rather be a failure than a success.

No, I never really think about my biological clock. I feel like my fertility will probably continue to haunt me for another decade or so anyway — my mother was forty-two when she had Keith. But I don't particularly want to have children. I didn't know you did either. Even in this world? Finding someone to get you pregnant will not be a problem if so. Like Simon says, you have a fertile look about you. Men love that. Finally: are you still planning to come and see me? I'm forewarning you that I'll be in Rome next week but likely home again the week after. I have made a friend here whose name is (genuinely) Felix. And if you can believe that, you will also have to believe that he's coming with me to Rome. No, I cannot explain why, so don't ask me. It just occurred to me, wouldn't it be fun to invite him? And it seems to have occurred to him that it would be fun to say yes. I'm sure he thinks I'm a total eccentric, but he also knows he's on to a good thing because I'm paying for his flights. I want you to meet him! Yet another reason for you to come and visit when I'm home. Will you, please? All my love, always.

The same Thursday evening, Eileen attended a poetry reading hosted by the magazine where she worked. The venue was an arts centre in the north city centre. Before the event, Eileen sat behind a little table selling copies of the most recent issue of the magazine, while people milled around in front of her, holding glasses of wine and avoiding eye contact. Occasionally, someone asked her where the bathrooms were, and she gave the directions in the same tone of voice with the same hand gestures each time. Just before the reading began, an elderly man leaned over the table to tell her she had the 'eyes of a poet'. Eileen smiled self-effacingly and, perhaps pretending she had not heard him, said she thought the event was about to start inside. Once the reading did begin, she locked her cash box, took a glass of wine from the table at the back and entered the main hall. Twenty or twenty-five people were seated inside, leaving the first two rows entirely empty. The magazine editor was standing at the lectern introducing the first reader. A woman about Eileen's age, who worked at the venue and whose name was Paula, moved in from the aisle to allow Eileen to sit beside her. Sell many copies? she whispered. Two, said Eileen. I thought we might snag a third when I saw a little old man approaching, but it turned out he just wanted to compliment my eyes. Paula sniggered. Weekday evening well spent, she said. At least now I know I have nice eyes, said Eileen.

The event featured five poets, loosely grouped together around the theme of 'crisis'. Two of them read from work dealing with personal crises, such as loss and illness, while one addressed themes of political extremism. A young man in glasses recited poetry so abstract and prosodic that no relationship to the theme of crisis became clear, while the final reader, a woman in a long black dress, talked for ten minutes about the difficulties of finding a publisher and only had time to read one poem, which was a rhyming sonnet. Eileen typed a note on her phone reading: the moon in june falls mainly on the spoon. She showed the note to Paula, who smiled vaguely before turning her attention back to the reading. Eileen deleted the note. After the reading, she picked up another glass of wine and went to sit behind the desk again. The elderly man approached her once more and said: You should be up there yourself. Eileen nodded pleasantly. I'm convinced, he said. You have it in you. Mm, said Eileen. He went away without purchasing a magazine.

After the event, Eileen and some of the other organisers and venue staff went for a drink in a nearby bar. Eileen and Paula sat together again, Paula drinking a gin and tonic served in an enormous fishbowl glass with a large piece of grapefruit inside, Eileen drinking whiskey on ice. They were talking about 'worst break-ups'. Paula was describing the protracted end stage of a two-year-long relationship, during which time both she and her ex-girlfriend kept getting drunk and texting each other, inevitably resulting in 'either a huge argument or sex'. Eileen swallowed a mouthful of her drink. That sounds bad, she said. But at the same time, at least you were still having sex. You know? The relationship wasn't completely dead. If Aidan were to text me when he was drunk, okay, maybe we would end up fighting. But I would at least feel like he remembers who I am. Paula said she was sure he did remember, seeing as they had lived together for several years. With a kind of grimacing smile, Eileen answered: That's what kills me. I spent half my twenties with this person, and in the end he just got sick of me. I mean, that's what happened. I bored him. I feel like that says something about me on some level. Right? It has to. Frowning, Paula replied: No, it doesn't. Eileen let out a strained self-conscious laugh then and squeezed Paula's arm. I'm sorry, she said. Let me get you another drink.

By eleven o'clock, Eileen was lying alone in bed, curled up on her side, her make-up smeared slightly under her eyes. Squinting at the screen of her phone, she tapped the icon of a social media app. The interface opened and displayed a loading symbol. Eileen moved her thumb over the screen, waiting for the page to load, and then suddenly, as if impulsively, closed the app. She navigated to her contacts, selected the contact listed as 'Simon', and hit the call button. After three rings, he picked up and said: Hello?

Hello, it's me, she said. Are you alone?

On the other end of the line, Simon was sitting on the bed in a hotel room. To his right was a window covered by thick cream-coloured curtains, and opposite the bed was a large television set affixed to the wall. His back was propped against the headboard, his legs stretched out, crossed at the ankles, and his laptop was open in his lap. I'm alone, he said, yeah. You know I'm in London, right? Is everything okay?

Oh, I forgot. Is it a bad time to talk? I can hang up.

No, it's not a bad time. Did you have your poetry thing on tonight?

Eileen told him about the event. She gave him the 'moon in June' joke and he laughed appreciatively. And we had a Trump poem, she told him. Simon said the idea made him earnestly wish for the embrace of death. She asked him about the conference he was attending in London and he described at length a 'conversation session' entitled 'Beyond the EU: Britain's International Future'. It was just four identical middle-aged guys in glasses, Simon said. I mean, they looked like photoshopped versions of each other. It was surreal. Eileen asked him what he was doing now, and he said he was finishing something for work. She rolled over onto her back, looking up at the faint pinprick pattern of mould on the ceiling.

It's not good for your health, working so late, she said. Where are you, in your hotel room?

Right, he replied. Sitting on the bed.

She pulled her knees up so her feet were flat on the mattress, her legs making a tent shape under the quilt. You know what you need, Simon? she said. You need a little wife for yourself. Don't you? A little wife to come up to you at midnight and put her hand on your shoulder and say, okay, that's enough now, you're working too late. Let's get some sleep.

Simon switched the phone to his other ear and said: You paint a compelling picture.

Can't your girlfriend go on work trips with you?

She's not my girlfriend, he said. She's just someone I've been seeing.

I don't get that distinction. What's the difference between a girlfriend and someone you're seeing?

We're not in an exclusive relationship.

Eileen rubbed her eye with her free hand, smudging some dark make-up onto her hand and onto the side of her face over her cheekbone. So you're having sex with someone else as well, are you? she said.

I'm not, no. But I believe she is.

Eileen dropped her hand then. She is? she said. Jesus. How attractive is the other guy?

Sounding amused, he replied: I have no idea. Why do you ask?

I just mean, if he's less attractive than you, why bother? And if he's as attractive as you are — Well, I think I'd like to meet this woman and shake her hand.

What if he's more attractive than I am?

Please. Impossible.

He settled himself back a little against the headboard. You mean because I'm so handsome? he said.

Yes.

I know, but say it.

Laughing then, she said: Because you're so handsome.

Eileen, thank you. How kind. You're not so bad yourself.

She nestled her head down into the pillow. I got an email from Alice today, she said.

That's nice. How is she?

She says it's not such a big deal that Aidan broke up with me because we weren't really that happy anyway.

Simon paused, as if waiting for her to continue, and then asked: Did she actually say that?

In so many words, yes.

And what do you think?

Eileen let out a sigh and answered: Never mind.

It doesn't sound like a very sensitive thing to say.

With her eyes closed she said: You're always defending her.

I just said she was being insensitive.

But you think she has a point.

He was frowning, toying with a hotel-branded pen on the bedside table. No, he said. I think he wasn't good enough for you, but that's different. Did she really say it wasn't a big deal?

In so many words. And you know she's going to Rome to promote her book next week, right?

He put the pen down again. Is she? he asked. I thought she was taking a break from all that stuff.

She was, until she got bored.

I see. That's funny. I've been trying to go and see her, but she's always saying it's not a good time. Are you worried about her?

Eileen let out a harsh laugh. No, I'm not worried, she said. I'm annoyed. You can be worried.

You could be both, he remarked.

Whose side are you on?

Smiling, he answered in a low soothing tone of voice: I'm on your side, princess.

She smiled then too, wryly, reluctantly, and pushed her hair back from her forehead.

Are you in bed yet? she asked.

No, sitting up. Unless you'd like me to get in bed while we're still on the phone?

Yes, I would like that.

Ah, well. That can be arranged.

He got up and put his laptop down on a small writing desk in front of a wall mirror. Most of the floor space behind him was taken up by the bed, which was made up with white sheets pulled tightly under the mattress. He was still holding the phone while he plugged his laptop into a charging cable at the wall.

You know, if your wife was there now, said Eileen, she would take your tie off for you. Are you wearing a tie?

No.

What are you wearing?

He glanced at himself in the mirror and looked away again, turning back toward the bed. The rest of the suit, he said. And no shoes, obviously. I take those off when I come in, like a civilised person.

So the jacket comes off next? she said.

Taking off his jacket, which involved switching his phone around between his hands, he said: That would be the usual order of business.

Then the wife would take that off for you and hang it up, said Eileen.

96

How nice of her.

And she would unbutton your shirt for you. Not just procedurally, but in a loving and tender way. Does that get hung up as well?

Simon, who was unbuttoning his shirt with one hand, said no, that would just go back in his suitcase to get washed when he went home.

After that I don't know what's next, said Eileen. Are you wearing a belt of some description?

I am, he said.

Closing her eyes, Eileen went on: She takes that off next, and she puts that away wherever it goes. Where do you put your belt when you take it off, as it happens?

On a hanger.

You're so neat, said Eileen. That's one thing the wife loves about you.

Why, is she a neat person herself? Or she loves it because opposites attract?

Hm. She's not really sloppy or anything, but she's not as neat as you are. And she aspires. Are you undressed now?

Not quite yet, he said. I've been holding the phone the whole time. Can I put it down for a second and then pick it back up again?

With a shy self-conscious smile, Eileen

replied: Of course you can, I'm not holding you hostage.

No, but I don't want you to get bored and hang up on me.

Not to worry, I won't.

He put the phone down on the nearest corner of the bed and finished undressing. Eileen lay with her eyes closed, the phone held loosely in her right hand near her face. Wearing just a pair of dark-grey boxer shorts now, Simon picked the phone back up and lay down on the bed with his head on the pillows. I'm back, he said.

What time do you usually finish work? said Eileen. Just out of curiosity.

Around eight. Probably more like half eight, lately, because everyone's busy.

Your wife would have a job that finishes a lot earlier than that.

Would she? said Simon. I'm jealous.

And when you got home she would have dinner waiting.

He smiled. Do you think I'm that old-fashioned? he asked.

Eileen opened her eyes, as if her reverie had been interrupted. I think you're a human being, she said. Who doesn't want to have dinner waiting for them if they're stuck at work until half eight? If you'd rather come home to an empty house and make your own dinner, my apologies.

No, I don't love coming home to an empty house, he said. And as fantasies go, I don't really object to being waited on hand and foot. It's just not something I would expect from a life partner.

Oh, I'm offending your feminist principles. I'll stop.

Please don't. I want to hear what the wife and I are going to do after dinner.

Eileen closed her eyes again. Well, she's a good wife, obviously, so she will let you do a little bit of work if you must, she said. But not until late. Then she wants to go to bed. Which is where you are now, I take it.

Indeed I am.

Smiling luxuriously to herself, Eileen went on: Did you have a good day at work or a bad day?

It was alright.

And you're tired now.

Not too tired to be talking to you, he said. But tired, yes.

The wife is attuned to all these little subtleties, so she wouldn't have to ask. If you've had a long day and you're tired, I think you'd get in bed around eleven and the wife would give you head. Which she's really good at. But not in a vulgar way, it's all very intimate and marital and all that.

Holding the phone in his right hand, Simon used his left hand to touch himself through the thin cotton cloth of his boxer shorts. Not that I don't appreciate it, but why am I only getting head? he said.

Eileen laughed. You said you were tired, she said.

Ah, I'm not too tired to make love to my own wife.

I wasn't disputing your virility, I just thought you'd like it. Anyway, I can get things wrong, that's alright. The wife would never get it wrong.

It's okay if she does, I'll love her anyway.

I honestly thought you liked oral sex.

Grinning now, Simon replied: I like it, I do like it. But if I only had one night with a fictional wife, I think I'd like to cover more ground. You needn't go into detail if you're reluctant.

On the contrary, I live for detail, said Eileen. Where were we? You undress the wife with your characteristic easy competence.

He put his hand inside his underwear then. You're too kind, he said.

You can take it she's very beautiful, but I won't presume to describe her physique. I know men have their own little tastes and preferences.

Thank you for the licence. I can imagine

her vividly.

Can you? said Eileen. Now I'm curious what she looks like. Is she blonde? Don't tell me. I bet she's blonde and like, five foot two.

He was laughing then. No, he said.

Okay. Well, don't tell me. Anyway, she's really wet, because she's been waiting all day for you to touch her.

He shut his eyes. Into the phone he said: And can I touch her?

Yes.

And what then?

With her free hand Eileen was cradling her breast, tracing a circle around her nipple with the tip of her thumb. Well, you can see in her eyes she's excited, she said. But nervous at the same time. She loves you very much, but sometimes she's anxious that she doesn't really know you. Because you can be distant. Or not distant, but you can be closed off. I'm just sketching in the background so you'll understand the sexual dynamic better. She's nervous because she looks up to you and she wants to make you happy, and sometimes she's frightened that you're not happy, and she doesn't know what to do. Anyway, when you get on the bed she's shaking underneath you like a little leaf. And you don't say anything, you just start to fuck her. Or what did you say before? You make love to her. Okay?

Mm, he said. And does she like that?

Oh yes. I think she was pretty innocent before you married her, so she really clings to you when you're in bed together, because it's overwhelming. She probably wants to come the whole time. And you're telling her that she's such a good girl, you're proud of her, and you love her, and she believes you. Remember how much you love her, that makes a difference. I know a lot about you, but that's the side of you I don't know. How you act with a woman you love. I'm digressing now, I'm sorry. The reason I said that thing about your wife giving you head, I think subconsciously I brought that up because it's something I like to think about. Do you remember we did that in Paris? It doesn't matter. I just remember that you liked it. It made me feel very self-confident. Anyway, I'm getting off the topic. I was describing you having sex with your wife. I bet she's insanely pretty and younger than me. And like, maybe a little bit stupid, but in a sexy way. If I was going to be really self-indulgent, I would make it so that when you're in bed with your wife, not every time but just this one time, you start thinking about me. It doesn't have to be on purpose.

A little idea or a memory goes through your mind, that's all. Not me the way I am now, but when I was twenty or whatever. You really were very nice to me then, you know. So you're having sex with your perfect wife, and she's the most beautiful woman on earth, and you love her more than anything, but just for a second or two when you're inside her, and she's trembling and shivering and saying your name, you're thinking about me, about things we did together when we were younger, like in Paris when I let you finish in my mouth, and you're remembering how good it felt then, to have me in that way, and you told me it was special. And maybe it was, you know. If you're still thinking about it all these years later when you're in bed with your wife, maybe it was special. Some things are.

He was coming then, and his breath was hard. He shut his eyes. Eileen had stopped speaking, she was lying still, her face looked hot. He said something like: Hm. For a short time they were both quiet. Then in a low voice she asked: Can we stay on the phone for one more minute? Simon opened his eyes again, took a tissue from the box on the bedside cabinet and started to wipe his hands and body.

As long as you want, he said. That was

very nice, thank you.

Eileen laughed, almost foolishly, as if she was relieved. Her cheeks and forehead were bright. Wow, you're welcome, she said. I forgot you were one of the 'thank you' guys. It's a great energy from you. You're sort of ninety per cent playboy but you mix it up now and then by acting like a total virgin. I respect it, I have to say. Is it going to be awkward now when we see each other in real life?

Dropping the used tissue on the bedside cabinet and taking another one from the box, Simon said: No, we'll both just act like nothing happened. Right? I believe you once told me I only have one facial expression anyway.

Did I really say that? How cold of me. Anyway, you have at least two. Laughing, and concerned.

He was smoothing his hand down over his chest, smiling. You weren't being cold, he said. You were just kidding.

Your wife would never talk to you like that.

Why, does she worship me?

Yes, said Eileen. You're like a father to her.

He made a humorous groaning noise. That's nice, he said. Eileen was grinning. I bet you think it's nice, she said. I knew you would. Resting his hand on the flat of his stomach, Simon said: You know everything. Eileen screwed up her mouth. Not about you, I don't, she said. His eyes were closed, he looked tired. I think the most realistic part of the fantasy was when I started thinking about you in Paris, he said. She seemed to breathe in deeply then. After a moment, she said quietly: You're only saying that to gratify me. He was smiling to himself. Well, it would only be fair, wouldn't it? he said. But no, I'm telling the truth. Can we see each other sometime soon? Eileen said yes. I'll act normal, he added. Don't worry. After they hung up, she plugged a charging cable into her phone and switched off the bedside light. The artificial orange glow of urban light pollution permeated the thin curtains of her bedroom window. With her eyes still open, she touched herself for a minute and a half, came noiselessly, and then turned over on her side to go to sleep.

8.

Dear Alice. When you say you're going to Rome, do you mean for work? I don't want to be intrusive, but I thought you were supposed to be taking a break for a while? I wish you well on your trip, of course, I just wonder whether it's a good idea to start doing public events again so soon. If you find it cathartic to write me histrionic messages about the publishing world where you say everyone you know is bloodthirsty and wants to kill you or fuck you to death, by all means continue to write them. No doubt you have met evil people through your work, though I suspect you've met a lot of boring, ethically average people as well. I'm not denying you're in pain, by the way — I know you are, and that's why I'm surprised you're subjecting yourself to all this again. Are you flying from Dublin? We could try to see each other before your flight if so . . .

I didn't think I was in a bad mood sitting

down to write this reply but maybe I am. I'm not trying to make you feel that your horrible life is in fact a privilege, although by any reasonable definition it very literally is. Okay, I make about 20k a year and pay two-thirds of that in rent for the opportunity to live in a tiny apartment with people who dislike me, and you make about two hundred thousand euro a year (?) and live alone in a gigantic country house, but for all that I don't think I would enjoy your life any more than you do. Anyone capable of enjoying it must have something wrong with them, as you point out. But we all have something wrong with us anyway, don't we? I looked at the internet for too long today and started feeling depressed. The worst thing is that I actually think people on there are generally well meaning and the impulses are right, but our political vocabulary has decayed so deeply and rapidly since the twentieth century that most attempts to make sense of our present historical moment turn out to be essentially gibberish. Everyone is at once hysterically attached to particular identity categories and completely unwilling to articulate what those categories consist of, how they came about, and what purposes they serve. The only apparent schema is that for every victim group (people born into poor families, women, people of colour) there is an oppressor group (people born into rich families, men, white people). But in this framework, relations between victim and oppressor are not historical so much as theological, in that the victims are transcendently good and the oppressors are personally evil. For this reason, an individual's membership of a particular identity group is a question of unsurpassed ethical significance, and a great amount of our discourse is devoted to sorting individuals into their proper groups, which is to say, giving them their proper moral reckoning.

If serious political action is still possible, which I think at this point is an open question, maybe it won't involve people like us — in fact I think it almost certainly won't. And frankly if we have to go to our deaths for the greater good of humankind, I will accept that like a lamb, because I haven't deserved this life or even enjoyed it. But I would like to be helpful in some way to the project, whatever it is, and if I could help only in a very small way, I wouldn't mind, because I would be acting in my own self-interest anyway — because it's also ourselves we're brutalising, though in another way, of course. No one wants to live like this. Or at least, I don't want to live like this. I want to live differently, or if necessary to die so that other people can one day live differently. But looking at the internet, I don't see many ideas worth dying for. The only idea on there seems to be that we should watch the immense human misery unfolding before us and just wait for the most immiserated, most oppressed people to turn around and tell us how to stop it. It seems that there exists a curiously unexplained belief that the conditions of exploitation will by themselves generate a solution to exploitation — and that to suggest otherwise is condescending and superior, like mansplaining. But what if the conditions don't generate the solution? What if we're waiting for nothing, and all these people are suffering without the tools to end their own suffering? And we who have the tools refuse to do anything about it, because people who take action are criticised. Oh, that's all very well, but then, what action do I ever take? In my defence I'm very tired and I don't have any good ideas. Really my problem is that I'm annoyed at everyone else for not having all the answers, when I also have none. And who am I to ask for humility and openness from other people? What have I ever given the world to ask so much in return? I could disintegrate into a heap of dust, for all the world cares, and that's as it should be.

Anyway, I have a new theory. Would you like to hear it? Ignore this paragraph if not. My theory is that human beings lost the instinct for beauty in 1976, when plastics became the most widespread material in existence. You can actually see the change in process if you look at street photography from before and after 1976. I know we have good reason to be sceptical of aesthetic nostalgia, but the fact remains that before the 1970s, people wore durable clothes of wool and cotton, stored drinks in glass bottles, wrapped food produce in paper, and filled their houses with sturdy wooden furniture. Now a majority of objects in our visual environment are made of plastic, the ugliest substance on earth, a material which when dyed does not take on colour but actually exudes colour, in an inimitably ugly way. One thing a government could do with my approval (and there aren't many) would be to prohibit the production of each and every form of plastic not urgently necessary for the maintenance of human life. What do you think?

I don't know why you're being so coy about this person Felix. Who is he? Are you sleeping with him? Not that you have to tell

me if you don't want to. Simon never tells
me anything anymore. Apparently he's been
going out with a twenty-three-year-old for
about two months and I've never even seen
her. Needless to say, the idea that Simon —
who was already a grown man in his twenties when I was fifteen — is having regular
sex with a woman six years my junior makes
me want to crawl directly into my grave.
And it's never some ugly little nerd with
mousy hair and interesting opinions about
Pierre Bourdieu, it's always an Instagram
model who has like 17,000 followers and
gets sent free samples from skincare brands.
Alice, I hate pretending that the personal
vanity of attractive young women is anything
other than boring and embarrassing. Mine
worst of all. Not to be dramatic, but if
Simon gets this girl pregnant I will throw
myself out of a window. Imagine having to
be nice to some random woman for the rest
of my life because she's the mother of his
child. Did I ever tell you he asked me out
on a date back in February? Not that he
actually wanted to go out with me, I think
he was just trying to boost my self-esteem.
Although, we did have a very funny phone
call last night . . . Anyway: what age is Felix?
Is he an old mystic man who writes you
poetry about the cosmos? Or a nineteen-

year-old county swimming champion with white teeth?

I could arrange to come and see you the week after the wedding, if convenient — arriving the first Monday in June. What do you think? If I could drive it would obviously be easier, but it looks like a combination of trains and taxi journeys might work. You can't imagine how bored I am of rattling around Dublin without you. I quite literally long to be in your company again. E.

112

9.

On Wednesday, Alice and Felix were picked up at Fiumicino by a man holding a plastic pocket with a sheet of paper inside, on which were printed the words: MS KELL-HER. Outside, night had fallen, but the air was warm, dry, saturated in artificial light. In the driver's car, a black Mercedes, Felix sat in the front, Alice in the back. Beside them on the motorway, trucks overtook each other at alarming speeds with horns blaring. When they reached the apartment building, Felix carried their luggage up the stairs: Alice's wheelie suitcase and his own black gym bag. The living room was large and yellow, with a couch and television. Through an open archway was a modern and clean-looking kitchen. One of the bedroom doors led off the back of the living room, and another to the right. After they had looked inside them both, he asked which she would prefer.

You choose, she said.

I think the girl should choose.

Well, I disagree with that.

He frowned and said: Okay, the one who pays should choose.

I actually disagree with that even more.

He lifted his bag onto his shoulder and put his hand to the handle of the nearest bedroom. I can see we're going to disagree a lot on this holiday, he said. I'll take this one here, alright?

Thank you, she said. Would you like to get something to eat before we go to bed? I'll look online to find a restaurant if you want.

He said that sounded good. Inside his room, he closed the door behind him, found a light switch and put his bag on top of the chest of drawers. Behind his bed, a third-floor window faced out onto the street. He unzipped the bag and searched around inside, moving items back and forth: some clothing, a razor handle with spare disposable blades, a foil sheet of tablets, a half-full box of condoms. Finding his phone charger, he took it out and started to unwind the cable. In her room, Alice was also unpacking her suitcase, removing some toiletries from the clear plastic airport bag, hanging up a brown dress in the wardrobe. Then she sat on her bed, opened a map on her phone and moved her fingers with practised ease around the screen.

Forty minutes later, they were eating at a local restaurant. At the centre of the table was a lit candle, a wicker basket of bread, a squat bottle of olive oil and a taller fluted bottle of dark vinegar. Felix was eating a sliced steak, very rare, dressed with Parmesan and rocket leaves, the interior of the steak glistening pink like a wound. Alice was eating a dish of pasta with cheese and pepper. At her elbow was a half-empty carafe of red wine. The restaurant was not crowded, but now and then conversation or laughter from the other tables swelled up and became audible. Alice was telling Felix about her best friend, a woman whose name she said was Eileen.

She's very pretty, Alice said. Would you like to see a picture?

Yeah, go on.

Alice took out her phone and started scrolling through a social media app. We met when we were in college, she said. Eileen was like a celebrity then, everyone was in love with her. She was always winning prizes and having her photograph in the university paper and that kind of thing. This is her.

Alice showed him the screen of her phone,

displaying a photograph of a slim white woman with dark hair, leaning against a balcony railing in what appeared to be a European city, with a tall fair-haired man beside her, looking at the camera. Felix took the phone out of Alice's hand and turned the screen slightly, as if adjudicating.

Yeah, he said. Nice-looking alright.

I was like her sidekick, said Alice. Nobody really understood why she would want to be friends with me, because she was very popular, and everyone kind of hated me. But I think perversely she enjoyed having a best friend nobody liked.

Why didn't anyone like you?

Alice gestured vaguely with one of her hands. Oh, you know, she said. I was always complaining about something. Accusing everyone of having the wrong opinions.

I'd say that gets on people's nerves alright, he said. Putting his finger over the face of the man in the photograph, he asked: And who's that with her?

That's our friend Simon, said Alice.

Not bad-looking either, is he?

She smiled. No, he's beautiful, she said. The photograph doesn't even do him justice. He's one of these people who's so attractive I think it's actually warped his sense of self.

Handing the phone back, Felix said: Must be nice having all these good-looking friends.

They're nice for me to look at, you mean, said Alice. But one does feel like a bit of a dog in comparison.

Felix smiled. Ah, you're not a dog, he said. You have your good points.

Like my charming personality.

After a pause, he asked: Would you call it charming?

She gave a genuine laugh then. No, she said. I don't know how you put up with me saying such stupid things all the time.

Well, I've only had to put up with it a small while, he said. And I don't know, you might stop doing it when we get to know each other better. Or I might stop putting up with it either.

Or I might grow on you.

Felix returned his attention to his food. You might, yeah, he said. Sure anything could happen. So this lad Simon, you fancy him, do you?

Oh no, she said. Not at all.

Glancing up at her with apparent interest, Felix asked: Not interested in the handsome ones, no?

I like him a lot, as a person, she said fairly. And I respect him. He works as an adviser to this tiny little left-wing parliamentary group, even though he could make buckets of money doing something. He's religious, you know.

Felix cocked his head as if expecting her to clarify the joke. As in, he believes in Jesus? he said.

Yeah.

Fucking hell, seriously? He's weird in the head or something, is he?

No, he's quite normal, said Alice. He won't try to convert you or anything, he's low-key about it. I'm sure you'd like him.

Felix sat there shaking his head. He laid his fork down, glanced around the restaurant, and then picked the fork up again, but didn't resume eating right away. And would he be against gays and all that? he said.

No, no. I mean, you should ask him about that, if you meet him. But I believe his idea of Jesus is more friend-to-the-poor, champion-of-the-marginalised kind of thing.

Here, I'm sorry, but he sounds like a headcase. In this day and age a person believes all that? Some lad a thousand years ago popped out from the grave and that's the whole point of everything?

Don't we all believe silly things? she said.

I don't. I believe what I see in front of me. I don't believe some big Jesus in the sky is looking down on us deciding are we good or bad.

For a few seconds she surveyed him and said nothing. Finally she replied: No, maybe you don't. But not many people would be happy, thinking about life the way you do — that it's all for nothing, and there isn't any meaning. Most people prefer to believe there is some. So in that sense, everyone is deluded. Simon's delusions are just more organised.

Felix started sawing a slice of steak in two with his knife. If he wants to be happy, couldn't he make up something nicer to believe? he asked. Instead of thinking everything's a sin and he might go to hell.

I don't think he's worried about hell, he just wants to do the right thing on earth. He believes there's a difference between right and wrong. I suppose you can't believe that, if you think it all means nothing in the end.

No, I do believe there's right and wrong, obviously.

She raised an eyebrow. Oh, you are deluded, then, she said. If we're all just going to die in the end, who's to say what's right and what isn't?

He told her he would think about it. They went on eating, but presently he broke off again and started to shake his head once more.

Not to harp on about the gay thing, he said. But would he have any gay friends, this guy? Simon.

Well, he's friends with me. And I'm not exactly heterosexual.

Amused now, even mischievous, Felix answered: Oh, okay. Me neither, by the way.

She looked up at him quickly and he met her eyes.

You look surprised, he said.

Do I?

Returning his attention to his food, he went on: I just never really had a thing about it. Whether someone is a guy or a girl. I know for most people it's like, the one big thing they really do care about. But for me, it just doesn't make any difference. I don't go around telling people all the time because actually, some girls don't like it. If they find out you've been with guys they think you're a bit not right, some of them. But I don't mind telling you since you're the same yourself.

She took a sip from her wine glass and swallowed. Then she said: For me I think it's more that I fall in love very intensely. And I can never know in advance who it's going to be, whether they'll be a man or woman, or anything else about them.

Felix nodded slowly. That's interesting, he said. And it happens a lot, or not that much?

Not that much, she said. And never very happily.

Ah, that's a shame. But it'll go happily for you in the end, I bet.

Thank you, that's kind.

He went on eating, while she watched him from across the table.

I'm sure people must fall in love with you all the time, she said.

He looked at her, his expression open and sincere. Why would they? he said.

She shrugged. When we first met I got the impression you were always going on dates, she said. You seemed very blasé and cool about everything.

Just because I go on dates doesn't mean people go around falling in love with me. I mean, we've been on a date together, you're not in love with me, are you?

Placidly she replied: I wouldn't tell you if I were.

He laughed. Good for you, he said. And don't get the wrong idea, you're welcome to be in love with me if you want. I would have to put you down as a bit of a lunatic, but I kind of think that about you anyway.

She was mopping the remaining sauce off

her plate with a piece of bread. You're wise, she said.

On Thursday morning an assistant from Alice's publishing house picked her up outside the apartment at ten and took her to meet some journalists. Felix spent the morning wandering around the city looking at things, listening to music on his headphones, taking pictures and posting them in a WhatsApp group. One photograph showed a narrow, shaded cobbled street, and at the end a resplendent white church in the sunlight, with bright green doors and shutters. Another showed a red moped parked outside a shopfront with old-fashioned lettering over the door. Finally he posted a photograph of the dome of St Peter's, creamy blue like an iced cake, seen in the distance from the Via della Conciliazione, sky blazing in the backdrop. In the group chat, someone with the username Mick replied: Where the fuck are you lad??? Someone with the username Dave wrote: Hold on are you in ITALY? what the fuck haha. You not at work this week. Felix typed out a reply.

Felix: Roma baby
Felix: Lmao
Felix: Here with some girl I met on

122

tinder, ill tell you when im back

Mick: How are you in rome with someone you met on tinder?

Mick: This needs way more explanation
hahaha

Dave: Wait what!! did a wealthy old lady
pick you up on the internet?

Mick: Ohhhh

Mick: Hate to say it but ive heard about
this

Mick: You are gonna wake up with no
kidneys

After this exchange, Felix closed out of
that group chat and opened another, which
was titled 'number 16'.

Felix: Hey has sabrina been fed today

Felix: And not just biscuits she wants
wet food

Felix: Post a picture when its done I
wanna see her

No one responded or saw the messages
right away. At the same time, in a different
part of the city, Alice was recording a seg-
ment for an Italian television programme
on which her voice would later be dubbed
over by an interpreter. From a feminist
perspective, it's about the gendered division
of labour, she was saying. Felix locked his

123

phone and continued walking, crossing partway over a bridge and pausing to look down the river at the Castel Sant'Angelo. Through his headphones he was listening to 'I'm Waiting for the Man'. The quality of light was very crisp, golden, casting dark diagonal shadows, and the waters of the Tiber below were pale green, milky. Leaning on the wide white stone balustrade, Felix took out his phone and flicked over to the camera app. The phone was several years old and for some reason opening the camera app caused the music to skip and then switch off. He removed his headphones irritably and took a picture of the castle. For a few seconds then he held the phone out at arm's length, headphones dangling loose over the side of the bridge, and it was not clear from this gesture whether he was trying to see the existing image better, getting a new angle in order to take a different photograph, or simply thinking about letting the device slip soundlessly out of his hand and into the river. He stood there with his arm outstretched and a grave-looking expression on his face, but maybe he was just frowning under the glare of sunlight. Without taking another photograph, he wound up the headphones, pocketed the phone and walked on.

Alice was giving a reading at a literary festival that night. She told Felix there was no need for him to attend, but he said he didn't have other plans. Might as well hear what your books are about, he said. Seeing as I'm not going to read them. Alice said if the event was really good maybe he would change his mind and he assured her he would not. The event was outside the city centre, in a large building that housed a concert hall and exhibitions of contemporary art. The corridors of the building were busy, with various readings and talks going on at the same time. Someone from the publishing house came over before the event and took Alice away to meet the man who would interview her onstage. Felix wandered around with his headphones in, checking his messages, his social media timelines. In the news, a British politician had made an offensive statement about Bloody Sunday. Felix returned to the top of his timeline, refreshed it, waited for new posts to load, and then did the same thing again, several times. He didn't even seem to read the new posts before pulling down to refresh again. Alice was at that point sitting in a windowless room with a bowl of fruit in front of her, saying: Thank you, thank you, that's very kind of you, I'm so pleased you enjoyed it.

About a hundred people attended Alice's event. Onstage she read for five minutes, then engaged in conversation with an interviewer, and then took audience questions. An interpreter sat beside her, translating the questions in Alice's ear and then translating Alice's answers for the audience. The interpreter was fast and efficient, moving a pen rapidly across a pad of paper while Alice was speaking, then delivering the translation aloud without pausing, and then striking through everything she had written and beginning again as soon as Alice resumed. Felix sat in the audience listening. When Alice said something funny, he laughed, along with the others in the audience who could understand English. The rest of the audience would laugh later, when the interpreter was speaking, or else they wouldn't, perhaps because the joke didn't translate or because they didn't find it funny. Alice answered questions about feminism, sexuality, the work of James Joyce, the role of the Catholic Church in Irish cultural life. Did Felix find her answers interesting, or was he bored? Was he thinking about her, or about something else, someone else? And onstage, speaking about her books, was Alice thinking about him? Did he exist for her in that moment, and if so, in what way?

After the event, she sat behind a desk signing books for an hour. He was told he could sit with her but he said he would prefer not to. He walked outside, making a loop around the perimeter of the building, smoking a cigarette. When Alice found him afterwards, she was accompanied by Brigida, a woman from her publishing house, who invited them both to dinner. Brigida kept saying the dinner would be 'very simple'. Alice's eyes were glassy and her rate of speech was more rapid than usual. Felix was by contrast rather quieter than he had been, almost sullen. They all got in a car with Ricardo, who also worked at the publishing house, and drove together to a restaurant in the city. In the front of the car, Ricardo and Brigida carried on a conversation in Italian. In the back, Alice said to Felix: Are you bored out of your mind? After a pause he replied: Why would I be? Alice's face was bright and energetic. I would be, she said. I never go to literary readings unless I have to. Felix examined his fingernails and let out a low breath. You were very good at answering the questions, he said. Did they give them to you beforehand, or were you making it up on the spot?

She said she had not seen the questions in advance. Superficial fluency, she added. I wasn't saying anything really substantial. But I'm pleased I impressed you. He looked at her and said in a slightly conspiratorial tone: Have you taken something? With a surprised, innocent expression on her face, Alice replied: No. How do you mean?

You just seem kind of hyperactive, he said.

Oh. I'm sorry. I think after speaking in public sometimes I get like that. It's adrenaline or something. I'll try to be calmer.

No, don't worry about it. I was just going to ask if I could have some.

She laughed. He lolled his head back on the seat, smiling.

I hear they all take cocaine, she said. In the industry. No one ever offers me any, though.

He turned his head, interested. Oh yeah? he said. In Italy, or all over?

All over, so I've heard.

That's interesting. I wouldn't mind a little bump, if it's going.

Would you like me to ask? she said.

He yawned, glanced at Brigida and Ricardo in the front seats, wiped some sleep from his eye with his fingers. I'd say you'd rather drop dead, he said.

But I'll do it if you'd like me to, she replied.

He closed his eyes. Because you're in love with me, he said.

Hm, said Alice.

He continued to sit there unmoving against the headrest, as if asleep. Alice opened her email app and wrote a new message to Eileen: If I ever suggest I'm going to bring a total stranger to Rome again please feel free to tell me it's a terrible idea. She sent the email and put her phone away in her bag. Brigida, she said out loud, last time we saw one another, you were moving apartments. Brigida turned around in the passenger seat. Yes, she said. I live much closer now to the office. She described her new apartment in comparison with her old one, while Alice nodded and said things like: And the last one had two bedrooms? But I remember there was no lift . . . Felix turned his head to look out the window. The streets of Rome revealed themselves one by one and vanished, pulled backward into the darkness.

10.

Further to my email about the total stranger: Felix is our age, 29. If you want to know whether I've slept with him, I haven't, but I don't think that piece of information can shed much light on the situation for you. We did go on one unsuccessful date, which I told you about at the time, but since then nothing. I suppose what you're really asking is not whether particular sexual acts have taken place between us, but whether my relationship with him has a sexual aspect overall. I think it does. But then, I think that about every relationship. I wish there was a good theory of sexuality out there for me to read. All the existing theories seem to be mostly about gender — but what about sex itself? I mean, what even is it? To me it's normal to meet people and think of them in a sexual way without actually having sex with them — or, more to the point, without even imagining having sex with them, without even thinking about imagining it. This suggests that sexuality has some 'other' content, which is not about the act of sex. And maybe even a majority of our sexual experiences are mostly this 'other'. So what is the other? I mean, what do I feel for Felix — who by the way has never even physically touched me — that makes me think of our relationship as a sexual one?

The more I think about sexuality, the more confusing and various it seems to me, and the more paltry our ways of talking about it. The idea of 'coming to terms' with your sexuality: this seems to mean, basically, coming to understand whether you like men or women. For me, realising that I liked both men and women was maybe one per cent of the process, maybe not even that much. I know I am bisexual, but I don't feel attached to it as an identity — I mean I don't think I have anything special in common with other bisexual people. Almost all the other questions I have about my sexual identity seem more complicated, with no obvious way of finding answers, and maybe even no language in which to articulate the answers if I ever did find them. How are we ever supposed to determine what kind of sex we enjoy, and why? Or what sex means to us, and how much of it we want to have, and in what contexts? What can we learn about ourselves through these aspects of our sexual personalities? And where's the terminology for all this? It seems to me we walk around all the time feeling these absurdly strong impulses and desires, strong enough to make us want to ruin our own lives and sabotage our marriages and careers, but nobody is really trying to explain what the desires are, or where they come from. Our ways of thinking and speaking about sexuality seem so limited, compared to the exhausting and debilitating power of sexuality itself as we experience it in our real lives. But having typed all that to you, I wonder if you think I sound crazy, because maybe you don't feel sexual desire anywhere near as strongly as I do — maybe no one does, I don't know. People don't really talk about it.

At times I think of human relationships as something soft like sand or water, and by pouring them into particular vessels we give them shape. So a mother's relationship with her daughter is poured into a vessel marked 'mother and child', and the relationship takes the contours of its container and is held inside there, for better or worse. Maybe some unhappy friends would have been perfectly contented as sisters, or married couples as parents and children, who knows. But what would it be like to form a relationship with no preordained shape of any kind? Just to pour the water out and let it fall. I suppose it would take no shape, and run off in all directions. That's a little like myself and Felix, I think. There is no obvious path forward by which any relation between us can proceed. I don't believe he would describe me as a friend, because he has friends, and the way he relates to them is different from the way he relates to me. He's much more removed from me than I think he is from them, and at the same time we're in certain senses closer, because there are no boundaries or conventions by which our relationship is constrained. What makes it different in other words is neither him nor me, nor any special personal qualities pertaining to either of us, nor even the particular combination of our individual personalities, but the method by which we relate to one another — or the absence of method. Maybe eventually we will just drop out of each other's lives, or become friends after all, or something else. But whatever happens will at least be the result of this experiment, which feels at times like it's going badly wrong, and at other times feels like the only kind of relationship worth having.

Other than my friendship with you, I hasten to add. But I think you're wrong about the instinct for beauty. Human beings lost that when the Berlin Wall came down. I'm not going to get into another argument with you about the Soviet Union, but when it died so did history. I think of the twentieth century as one long question, and in the end we got the answer wrong. Aren't we unfortunate babies to be born when the world ended? After that there was no chance for the planet, and no chance for us. Or maybe it was just the end of one civilisation, ours, and at some time in the future another will take its place. In that case we are standing in the last lighted room before the darkness, bearing witness to something.

I offer one alternative hypothesis: the instinct for beauty lives on, at least in Rome. Of course it's possible to visit the Vatican Museum and see the Laocoon, or go to that little church and put a coin in the slot to see the Caravaggios — and at the Galleria Borghese there's even Bernini's Proserpina, of which Felix, a born sensualist, professes himself a particular fan. But there are also dark fragrant orange trees, little white cups of coffee, blue afternoons, golden evenings . . .

Have I told you I can't read contemporary novels anymore? I think it's because I know too many of the people who write them. I see them all the time at festivals, drinking red wine and talking about who's publishing who in New York. Complaining about the most boring things in the world — not enough publicity, or bad reviews, or someone else making more money. Who cares? And then they go away and write their sensitive little novels about 'real life'. The truth is they know nothing about real life. Most of them haven't so much as glanced up against the real world in decades. These people have been sitting with white linen tablecloths laid out in front of them and complaining about bad reviews since 1983. I just don't care what they think about ordinary life or ordinary people. As far as I'm concerned they're speaking from a false position when they speak about that. Why don't they write about the kind of lives they really lead, and the kind of things that really obsess them? Why do they pretend to be obsessed with death and grief and fascism — when really they're obsessed with whether their latest book will be reviewed in the New York Times? Oh, and many of them come from normal backgrounds like mine, by the way. They're not all children of the bourgeoisie. The point is just that they stepped right out of ordinary life — maybe not when their first book came out, maybe it was the third or fourth, but anyway it was a long time ago — and now when they look behind them, trying to remember what ordinary life used to be like, it's so far away they have to squint. If novelists wrote honestly about their own lives, no one would read novels — and quite rightly! Maybe then we would finally have to confront how wrong, how deeply philosophically wrong, the current system of literary production really is — how it takes writers away from normal life, shuts the door behind them, and tells them again and again how special they are and how important their opinions must be. And they come home from their weekend in Berlin, after four newspaper interviews, three photo-shoots, two sold-out events, three long leisurely dinners where everyone complained about bad reviews, and they open up the old MacBook to write a beautifully observed little novel about 'real life'. I don't say this lightly: it makes me want to be sick.

The problem with the contemporary Euro-American novel is that it relies for its structural integrity on suppressing the lived realities of most human beings on earth. To confront the poverty and misery in which millions of people are forced to live, to put the fact of that poverty, that misery, side by side with the lives of the 'main characters' of a novel, would be deemed either tasteless or simply artistically unsuccessful. Who can care, in short, what happens to the novel's protagonists, when it's happening in the context of the increasingly fast, increasingly brutal exploitation of a majority of the human species? Do the protagonists break up or stay together? In this world, what does it matter? So the novel works by suppressing the truth of the world — packing it tightly down underneath the glittering surface of the text. And we can care once again, as we do in real life, whether people break up or stay together — if, and only if, we have successfully forgotten about all the things more important than that, i.e. everything.

My own work is, it goes without saying, the worst culprit in this regard. For this reason I don't think I'll ever write a novel again.

You were in a bad mood writing that last message and said some very morbid things about wanting to die for the revolution. I hope by the time you receive this reply you will be thinking more about wanting to live for the revolution, and what such a life would look like. You say that few people care what happens to you, and I don't know if that's true, but I do know that some of us care very, very much — e.g. myself, Simon, your mother. I also feel certain it's better to be deeply loved (which you are) than widely liked (which you probably also are! but I won't labour the point). I'm sorry for complaining so much about book publicity, which is something no sane person could ever care to hear about — and I'm sorry for telling you I was going to take an extended break from publicity and then flying to Rome to promote my book because I am cowardly and hate letting people down. (I would apologise that we didn't get to see each other before my flight, but that actually wasn't my fault — the publishers booked me a car to the airport.) You're right that I make too much money and live irresponsibly. I know I must bore you, but only as much as I bore myself — and I also love you, and feel grateful to you, for everything.

Anyway, yes, please do come to see me after the wedding. Shall I invite Simon along as well? Together, the two of us can surely explain to him why it is wrong for him to date incredibly beautiful women who are younger than us. I'm not totally sure yet why it would be wrong, but between now and then I can definitely come up with something. All my love, Alice.

11.

The evening after she received this email, Eileen was walking through Temple Bar toward Dame Street. It was a fine bright Saturday evening in early May and the sunlight slanted golden across the faces of buildings. She was wearing a leather jacket over a printed cotton dress, and when she caught the eyes of men passing by, young men in fleece jackets and boots, middle-aged men in fitted shirts, she smiled vaguely and averted her gaze. By half past eight, she had reached a bus stop opposite the old Central Bank. Removing a stick of mint gum from her handbag, she unwrapped it and put it in her mouth. Traffic passed and the shadows on the street moved slowly eastward while she smoothed the foil wrapper out with her fingernail. When her phone started ringing, she slipped it out from her pocket to look at the screen. It was her mother calling. She answered, and after exchanging hellos, Eileen said: Listen, I'm actually in town waiting for a bus, can I call you later on?

Your father's upset about this business with Deirdre Prendergast, said Mary.

Eileen was squinting at an approaching bus to make out the number, chewing on her gum. Right, she said.

Could you not have a word with Lola?

The bus passed without stopping. Eileen touched her forehead with her fingers. So Dad is upset with Lola, she said, and he talks to you, and you talk to me, and I'm the one who has to talk to Lola. Does that sound reasonable?

If it's too much bother for you, forget about it.

Another bus was drawing up now and Eileen said into the phone: I have to go, I'll ring you tomorrow.

When the bus doors opened, she climbed on, tapped her card and went to sit upstairs near the front. She typed the name of a bar into a map application on her phone, while the bus moved through the city centre and southward. On Eileen's screen, a pulsing blue dot started to make the same journey toward her eventual destination, which was seventeen minutes away. Closing the application, she wrote a message to Lola.

Eileen: hey, did you not invite Deirdre P to the wedding after all?

Within thirty seconds she had received a reply.

Lola: Lol. Hope mammy and daddy are paying you good money to do their dirty work for them.

Reading this message, Eileen drew her brows together and exhaled briskly through her nose. She tapped the reply button and began typing.

Eileen: are you seriously disinviting family members from your wedding now? do you realise how spiteful and immature that is?

She closed the message application then and reopened the map. When instructed by the dot on the screen, she pressed the stopping bell and made her way downstairs. After thanking the driver she got off the bus, and with frequent cautious glances at her phone began to walk back up the street in the direction the bus had come, past a hairdresser's, a women's clothing boutique, over a pedestrian crossing, until a flag appeared on-screen with a line of blue text reading: You have arrived at your destination. She deposited her chewed gum back into its foil wrapper then and threw it into a nearby waste bin.

The entrance was through a cramped porch, leading onto a front bar, and behind that a private room with couches and low tables, lit entirely by red bulbs. The appearance was quaintly domestic, like a large private living room from an earlier era, but drenched in lurid red light. Eileen was greeted at once by several friends and acquaintances, who put their glasses down and rose from sofas to embrace her. At the sight of a man named Darach she said brightly: Happy birthday, you! After that she ordered a drink and then sat down on one of the faintly sticky leather couches beside her friend Paula. Music was playing from speakers affixed to the walls and a bathroom door swung open at the end of the room periodically, releasing a brief flood of white light before swinging shut again. Eileen checked her phone and saw a new message from Lola.

Lola: Hmmm do I really want to hear about how immature I am from someone who's stuck in a shitty job making no money and living in a kip at age 30 . . . . . .

Eileen stared at the screen for a while and then pocketed her phone again. Beside her a woman named Roisin was telling a story about a broken window in her street-level apartment which her landlord had refused to fix for over a month. After that, everyone began sharing horror stories about the rental market. An hour, two hours, elapsed in this way. Paula ordered another round of drinks. Silver platters of hot food were brought out from behind the bar: cocktail sausages, potato wedges, chicken wings glistening in wet sauce. At ten to eleven, Eileen got up, went to the bathroom and took her phone from her pocket again. There were no new notifications. She opened a messaging app and tapped on Simon's name, displaying a thread from the previous evening.

Eileen: home safe?
Simon: Yes, was just about to text you
Simon: I may have brought you a present
Eileen: really??
Simon: You'll be glad to know the shop on the ferry was doing a special offer

144

on duty free Toblerone
Simon: Are you doing anything tomor-
row night?
Eileen: actually yes for once . . .
Eileen: darach is having a birthday thing,
sorry
Simon: Ah ok
Simon: Can I see you during the week
then?
Eileen: yes please

That was the final message in the thread.
She used the toilet, washed her hands, reap-
plied lipstick in the mirror, and then blotted
the lipstick using a square of toilet roll.
Someone knocked on the outside of the
bathroom door and she said aloud: One
second. She was staring wanly into the mirror. With her hands she pulled the features
of her face downward, so the bones of her
skull stood out harsh and strange under the
fluorescent white ceiling light. The person
was knocking on the door again. Eileen put
her bag on her shoulder, unlocked the door
and went back out to the bar. Sitting down
next to Paula, she picked up the half-empty
drink she had left on the table. All the ice
had melted. What are we talking about? she
said. Paula said they were talking about
communism. Everyone's on it now, said

Eileen. It's amazing. When I first started going around talking about Marxism, people laughed at me. Now it's everyone's thing. And to all these new people trying to make communism cool, I would just like to say, welcome aboard, comrades. No hard feelings. The future is bright for the working class. Roisin raised her glass then and so did Darach. Eileen was smiling and seemed slightly drunk. Are the platters gone? she asked. A man named Gary who was seated opposite said: No one here is really working class, though. Eileen rubbed at her nose. Yeah, she said. Well, Marx would disagree with you, but I know what you're saying.

People love to claim that they're working class, Gary said. No one here is actually from a working-class background.

Right, but everyone here works for a living and pays rent to a landlord, said Eileen.

Raising his eyebrows, Gary said: Paying rent doesn't make you working class.

Yeah, working doesn't make you working class. Spending half your pay cheque on rent, not owning any property, getting exploited by your boss, none of it makes you working class, right? So what does, having a certain accent, is it?

With an irritated laugh he answered: Do you think you can go driving around in your dad's BMW, and then turn around and say you're working class because you don't get along with your boss? It's not a fashion, you know. It's an identity.

Eileen swallowed a mouthful of her drink. Everything is an identity now, she said. And you don't know me, by the way. I don't know why you're saying no one here is working class, you don't know anything about me.

I know you work at a literary magazine, he said.

Jesus. I have a job, in other words. Real bourgeoisie behaviour.

Darach said he thought they were just using the same term, 'working class', to describe two distinct population groups: one, the broad constituency of people whose income was derived from labour rather than capital, and the other, an impoverished primarily urban subsection of that group with a particular set of cultural traditions and signifiers. Paula said a middle-class person could still be a socialist and Eileen said the middle class did not exist. Everyone started talking over each other then. Eileen checked her phone once more. There were no new messages, and the time displayed on the screen was 23:21. She drained her glass and started to put her jacket on. Blowing a kiss, she waved goodbye to the others at the table. I'm off home, she said. Happy birthday, Darach! See you again soon. Amid the noise and conversation, only a few people seemed to notice she was leaving, and they waved and called out to her retreating back.

Ten minutes later, Eileen had boarded another bus, this one heading back toward the city centre. She sat alone by a window on the upper deck, slipping her phone out of her pocket and unlocking it. Opening a social media application, she keyed in the name 'aidan lavin', and tapped the first suggested search result. Once the profile was loaded, Eileen scrolled down mechanically, almost inattentively, to view the most recent updates, as if spurred by habit rather than spontaneous interest. With a few taps she navigated from Aidan Lavin's page to the profile of the user Actual Death Girl, and waited for that to load. The bus was stopping at St Mary's College then, the doors releasing and passengers alighting downstairs. The page loaded, and absently Eileen scrolled through the user's recent updates. As the bus pulled off, the stopping bell rang again. Someone sat down next to Eileen and she glanced up and smiled politely before returning her attention to the screen. Two days previously, the user Actual Death Girl had posted a new photograph, with the caption 'this sad case'. The photograph depicted the user with her arms around a man with dark hair. The man was tagged as Aidan Lavin. As she looked at this photograph, Eileen's mouth came open slightly and then closed again. She tapped the photograph to enlarge it. The man was wearing a red corduroy jacket. Around his neck the woman's arms were attractive, plump, shapely. The photograph had received thirty-four likes. The bus was pulling up to another stop now and Eileen turned her attention out the window. They were stopping at Grove Park, just before the canal. A look of recognition passed over her face, she frowned, and then with a jolt she got to her feet, squeezing past the passenger beside her. As the doors opened she jogged her way almost breathlessly down the staircase and, thanking the driver in the rearview mirror, alighted onto the street.

It was approaching midnight now. The windows of apartments showed yellow here and there above a darkened shop-front on the corner. Eileen zipped her jacket up and fixed her handbag over her shoulder, walking, it seemed decisively, in a particular direction. As she went, she took her phone out once more and re-examined the photograph. Then she cleared her throat. The street was quiet. She pocketed the phone and smoothed her hands firmly down the front of her jacket, as if wiping them clean. Crossing the street she began to walk more briskly, with long free strides, until she reached a tall brick townhouse with six plastic wheelie bins lined up behind the gate. Looking up, she gave a strange laugh, and rubbed her forehead with her hand. She crossed the gravel and rang the buzzer on the front door. For five seconds, ten seconds, nothing happened. Fifteen seconds. She was shaking her head, her lips moving silently, as if rehearsing an imaginary conversation. Twenty seconds elapsed. She turned to leave. Then from the plastic speaker Simon's voice said: Hello? Turning back, she stared at the speaker and said nothing. Hello, his voice repeated. She pressed the button.

Hey, she said. It's me. I'm sorry.

Eileen, is that you?

Yes, sorry. Me, as in Eileen.

Are you okay? he asked. Come up, I'll buzz you in.

The door-release tone sounded, and she went inside. The lighting in the hall was very bright and someone had left a bicycle leaning up against the postboxes. While Eileen climbed the stairs, she felt at the back of her head where her hair had come unravelled from its clasp and carefully with her long deft fingers refixed it. Then she checked the time on her phone, which showed 23:58, and unzipped her jacket. Simon's door was open already. He was standing there barefoot, frowning into the light of the hallway, his eyes sleepy and a little swollen. She stopped on the top step, her hand on the banister. Oh God, I'm sorry, she said. Were you in bed?

Is everything alright? he asked.

She hung her head, as if exhausted, or ashamed, and her eyes closed. Several seconds passed before she opened her eyes and answered: Everything's fine. I was just on my way home from Darach's thing, and I wanted to see you. I didn't think — I don't know why I assumed you'd be up. I know it's late.

It's not really. Do you want to come in?

Staring down at the carpet still, she said in a strained voice: No, no, I'll leave you in peace. I feel so stupid, I'm sorry.

He closed one eye and surveyed her where she stood on the top step. Don't say that, he said. Come in, we'll have a drink.

She followed him inside. Only one of the lights in the kitchen was switched on, illuminating the small apartment in a diminishing circle outward. A clothes horse was set up against the back wall with various items hung out to dry: T-shirts, socks, underwear. He closed the door behind her while she was taking off her jacket and shoes. She stood in front of him then, gazing humbly at the floorboards.

Simon, she said, can I ask a favour? You can say no, I won't mind.

Sure.

Can I sleep in your bed with you?

He looked at her for a moment longer before he answered. Yeah, he said. No problem. Are you sure everything's alright?

Without raising her eyes she nodded. He filled her a glass of water from the tap and they went into his room together. It was a neat room with dark floorboards. In the centre was a double bed, the quilt thrown back, the bedside lamp switched on. Opposite the door was a window with the blind pulled down. Simon turned out the lamp and Eileen unbuttoned her dress, slipping it off over her shoulders, hanging it over the back of his desk chair. They got into bed. She drank some of the water from her glass and then lay down on her side. For a few minutes they were still and silent. She looked over at him but he was turned away from her, only the back of his head and his shoulder dimly visible. Will you hold me? she asked. For a moment he hesitated, as if to say something, but then he turned over and put his arm around her, murmuring: Here, of course. She nestled up close against him, her face against his neck, their bodies pressed together. He made a low noise in his throat like: Mm. Then he swallowed. Sorry, he said. Her mouth was at his neck. That's okay, she said. It's nice. He took a breath in then. Is it, he said. You're not drunk, are you? Her eyes were closed. No, she said. She put her hand inside his underwear. He shut his eyes and very quietly groaned. For a while she touched him like that, slowly, and she was looking up at him, at his closed eyelids, damp, his mouth a little open. Can we? she asked. He said yes. They took their underwear off. I'll get a condom, he said. She told him she was on the pill, and he seemed to hesitate. Oh, he said. Like this, then? She nodded her head. They were lying on their sides, face to face. Holding her by the hip he moved inside her. She drew a quick breath inward and he rubbed the hard fin of her hipbone under his hand. For a few seconds they were still. He pressed a little closer to her and with her eyes shut she whimpered. Hm, he said.

153

Can I put you lying on your back, would that be okay? I think I could get a little bit deeper inside you that way, if you want that. Her eyes were closed. Yes, she said. He pulled out of her then and she turned over onto her back. When he entered her again, she cried out, drawing her legs up around him. Bearing his weight on his arms, he closed his eyes. After a minute she said: I love you. He let out his breath. In a low voice he answered: Ah, I haven't — I love you too, very much. She was moving her hand over the back of his neck, taking deep hard breaths through her mouth. Eileen, he said, I'm sorry, but I think I might be kind of close already. I just, I haven't — I don't know, I'm sorry. Her face was hot, she was breathless, shaking her head. It's okay, she said. Don't worry, don't say sorry. After he finished, they lay in each other's arms for a while, breathing, her fingers moving through his hair. Slowly then he moved his hand down warm and heavy over her belly, down between her legs. Is this alright? he asked. Closing her eyes, she murmured: Yes. Moving his middle finger inside her he touched her clitoris with his thumb and she was whispering, yes, yes. After that they parted and she rolled over onto her back, kicking the quilt down off her legs, catching her breath. He was lying on his side, his eyes half-closed, watching her. Alright? he asked. She let out a kind of trembling laugh. Yes, she said. Thank you. Languidly he smiled then, his gaze moving over her long slim body stretched out on the mattress. Any time, he replied.

In the morning his alarm rang at eight and woke them both, Simon sitting up on his elbow to turn it off, Eileen lying on her back, rubbing her eye with her fingers. Around the edges of the blind leaked a rectangle of white daylight. Do you have plans this morning? she asked. He put his phone back on the bedside table. I was going to go to the nine o'clock Mass, he said. But I can go later, it doesn't make any difference. She lay with her eyes closed, looking happy, her hair disarranged on the pillow. Can I come with you? she said. He looked down at her for a moment, and then answered simply: Of course you can. They got out of bed together and he made coffee while she was in the shower. She came out of the bathroom wrapped in a large white towel, and they kissed against the kitchen countertop. What if I think bad thoughts at Mass? she asked. He rubbed the back of her neck where her hair was damp. Like about last night? he said. We didn't do anything bad. She kissed the shoulder seam of his T-shirt. He made breakfast then while she got dressed. At a few minutes to nine they left the house and walked to the church together. Inside, it was cool and mostly empty, smelling of damp and incense. The priest read from Luke and gave a sermon about compassion. During communion, the choir sang 'Here I Am, Lord'. Eileen let Simon out of the pew and watched him queue with the other members of the congregation, most of them elderly. From the gallery behind them the choir was singing: I will make their darkness bright. Eileen shifted in her seat to keep Simon in sight as he reached the altar and received communion. Turning away, he blessed himself. She sat with her hands in her lap. He looked up at the vast domed ceiling above them, and his lips were moving silently. With a searching expression she watched him. He came and took his seat beside her, laying his hand on hers, and his hand was heavy and very still. Then he knelt down beside her on the cushioned hassock attached to the pew. Bowing his head over his hands, he did not look grave or serious, only calm, and his lips were no longer moving. Lacing her fingers together in her lap, she watched him. The choir sang: I have heard you calling in the night. Simon blessed himself once more and sat up beside her again. She moved her hand toward him and calmly he took it in his and held it, smoothing his thumb slowly over the little ridges of her knuckles. They sat like that until the Mass was over. On the street outside they were smiling again, and their smiles were mysterious. It was a cool bright Sunday morning, the white facades of buildings reflected the sunlight, traffic was passing, people were out walking dogs, calling to each other across the street. Simon kissed Eileen's cheek, and they wished one another goodbye.

12.

Alice, do you think the problem of the contemporary novel is simply the problem of contemporary life? I agree it seems vulgar, decadent, even epistemically violent, to invest energy in the trivialities of sex and friendship when human civilisation is facing collapse. But at the same time, that is what I do every day. We can wait, if you like, to ascend to some higher plane of being, at which point we'll start directing all our mental and material resources toward existential questions and thinking nothing of our own families, friends, lovers, and so on. But we'll be waiting, in my opinion, a long time, and in fact we'll die first. After all, when people are lying on their deathbeds, don't they always start talking about their spouses and children? And isn't death just the apocalypse in the first person? So in that sense, there is nothing bigger than what you so derisively call 'breaking up or staying together' (!), because at the end of our lives, when there's nothing left in front of us, it's still the only thing we want to talk about. Maybe we're just born to love and worry about the people we know, and to go on loving and worrying even when there are more important things we should be doing. And if that means the human species is going to die out, isn't it in a way a nice reason to die out, the nicest reason you can imagine? Because when we should have been reorganising the distribution of the world's resources and transitioning collectively to a sustainable economic model, we were worrying about sex and friendship instead. Because we loved each other too much and found each other too interesting. And I love that about humanity, and in fact it's the very reason I root for us to survive — because we are so stupid about each other.

As to this last point, I speak from personal experience. On the way home from a birthday thing last night, I kind of randomly got off the bus at Grove Park and walked over to Simon's house. I suppose I was a little bit drunk and feeling bad about myself, and maybe I thought I could rely on him to rub my shoulders and give me compliments. Or maybe I wanted him not to be there. Or to be there with this girl he's been seeing, so I could feel even worse about myself. I don't know. I don't know what I wanted, or what I thought would happen. Anyway, when I got upstairs it was obvious the buzzer had woken him up, and he'd had to get out of bed to let me in. It wasn't really late, only around midnight. He was standing in the doorway looking tired and old. I don't mean that in a bad way. But when I see him usually, I suppose I'm used to seeing the same beautiful blonde teenager I've always seen, since I was a little girl. And when he was standing in the doorway last night I realised, he's not that boy anymore. What do I really know about his life? When I developed my first teenage crush on Simon, I didn't understand sexual feelings very well, and I came up with the phrase 'the special touch' to describe to myself how I felt when he touched me. Which, by the way, he only ever did either by accident or in the most chaste ways imaginable. Isn't that a really funny phrase, 'the special touch'? Thinking about it now, it makes me want to laugh. But then last night in bed, he put his arms around me and immediately those words rushed back into my mind, like the last fifteen years were nothing, and the feeling was the same.

We ended up going to Mass together this morning. The church on his street has a very glamorous stone portico at the entrance and the extraordinarily Catholic name 'Church of Mary Immaculate, Refuge of Sinners'. He didn't ask me to come with him, by the way, I wanted to go, though I'm not sure now why I wanted to. It's possible I was getting such a nice feeling from his company that I just didn't want to be physically parted from him for an hour. But it's also possible, and I'm not sure how to put this, that I didn't want him to go without me because I felt jealous. Now that I've said it, I don't really know what I mean by that. Do I resent him for liking the concept of God better than he likes me? The idea seems plainly absurd. But then what? Having put myself back on intimate terms with Simon, albeit for a brief interlude, was I afraid that he was going to Mass to cleanse himself of me? Or maybe in a way I didn't really believe he was going to go through with it, and that if I offered to go with him, he would have to come out and admit he had not been totally serious about the religion thing after all. In the end of course we filed into the church together uneventfully. Inside, it was all white and blue, with painted statues, and dark panelled confession boxes with luxurious velvet curtains. Most of the other attendees were little elderly women wearing pastel-coloured jackets. When the service began, Simon didn't suddenly start acting very intense and spiritual, or crying about the majesty of God the Father or anything like that, he was just his usual self. Mostly he sat there listening and doing nothing. At the beginning, when everyone kept repeating 'Christ have mercy' and all of that, I think a part of me wanted him to start laughing and tell me it was all a joke. In a way I felt afraid of the way he was behaving, saying things like 'I have greatly sinned' — actually saying such things out loud in his ordinary voice, the same way I might say 'it's raining', if I had a sincere belief that it was raining and nothing about this belief struck me as ridiculous. I looked over at him a lot, feeling I suppose alarmed by his seriousness, and he just glanced back at me in a friendly way, as if to say: Yes, this is Mass, what did you expect? Then there was a reading about a woman pouring oil on the feet of Jesus and, I think, drying his feet with her hair? Unless I misunderstood. Simon sat there listening to this patently bizarre and freakish story and looking, as ever, completely calm and ordinary. I know I keep saying how ordinary he was, but it was precisely the seeming absence of any change in his personhood, precisely the fact that he went on being fully and recognisably the same man as always, that was so mystifying to me.

After the readings, the priest started blessing the bread and wine, and then he asked the congregation to lift up their hearts. All at the same time, in a soft collective whisper, everyone in the church replied: 'We lift them up to the Lord.' Is it really possible I witnessed such a scene, right in the middle of Dublin, only a few hours ago? Is it possible such things literally go on, in the real world you and I both live in? The priest said 'Lift up your hearts', and everyone, including Simon, replied without any hesitation or irony: 'We lift them up to the Lord.' Did they believe they were telling the truth, and that their hearts in that moment really were lifted up to the Lord, whatever that even means? If I'd asked myself that question yesterday, I would have said, of course not. Mass is just a social ritual, religious people don't actually spend time thinking about God, and they certainly never try to lift their hearts up toward him or to conceptualise what it would mean to do such a thing. But today I feel differently. I feel that at least some of the people in that church sincerely believed that they were lifting their hearts up to the Lord. And I think Simon believed

163

it. I think he knew what he was saying, and had thought about it, and believed it was true. After that, the priest asked us to give each other the sign of peace, and Simon shook hands with all the silvery little elderly women, and then he shook my hand and said 'Peace be with you', and by then I wanted him to mean it. I didn't feel anymore that I wanted him to be joking, and in fact I felt that I wanted him to be as serious as he seemed, and more serious, and to mean every word.

Can it be that during the service I actually came to admire the sincerity of Simon's faith? But how is it possible for me to admire someone for believing something I don't believe, and don't want to believe, and which I think is manifestly incorrect and absurd? If Simon started to worship a turtle as the son of God, for example, would I admire his sincerity? From a strictly rationalist perspective, it makes as much sense to worship a turtle as it does to worship a first-century Judaean preacher. Considering that God doesn't exist, the whole thing is random anyway, and it may as well be Jesus, or a plastic bucket, or William Shakespeare, it doesn't matter. And yet I feel I couldn't admire Simon's sincerity if he went down the road of turtle worship.

Am I just admiring the ritual, then? Admiring his ability to blandly and uncritically accept received wisdom? Or do I secretly believe there is something special about Jesus, and that to worship him as God, while not quite reasonable, is somehow permissible? I don't know. Maybe it was just the calm, gentle way that Simon conducted himself in the church, the way he recited the prayers so quietly and sedately, just the same as the little old ladies did, and not trying to be any different from them, not trying to show that he believed any more or less ardently than they did, or any more critically or intellectually than they did, but just the same. And he didn't even seem embarrassed that I was there watching him — I mean he wasn't embarrassed for me, at how out of place I was, but he also wasn't embarrassed for himself, to be caught in the act of worshipping a supreme being I didn't believe in.

Afterwards on the street, he thanked me for coming with him. For a second then I was afraid he would make a joke of it after all, just out of awkwardness or nerves, and the idea horrified me. But he didn't. I should have known he wouldn't, because it wouldn't have been like him. He just thanked me and we went our separate ways.

If I say the Mass was strangely romantic I hope you'll know what I mean. Maybe it made me feel there was something deep and serious in Simon, which I hadn't seen for a long time, or maybe it was his gentleness when we were shaking hands. Or, as I'm sure an evolutionary psychologist would suggest, maybe I'm just a frail little female, and after sleeping in a man's bed I come over all weak and tender about him. I make no great claims for myself, it could well be true. And writing this email I do feel a little weak and tender about Simon, and even a little protective, who knows why. If I had gone straight home this morning instead of going with him to the church, I'm not sure I would feel the same way now — but at the same time, if we had just gone to Mass this morning and we hadn't slept together last night, I don't think I'd feel like this now either. It was the seemingly ill-suited combination of sleeping together and then going to Mass afterwards that I think has given me this feeling — the feeling of entering into his life, even just briefly, and seeing something about him that I had never seen before, and knowing him differently as a result.

Speaking of friendship and romance: how is Rome? How is Felix? How are you? The parts of your email about sexuality were very funny. Do you think you're the only person who has ever felt sexual desire?? In case the answer is yes, I am attaching a PDF of Audre Lorde's essay 'Uses of the Erotic', which I know for a fact you will greatly enjoy. Finally — yes of course you should invite Simon to stay! I know he wants to see you, and I can't think of anything better in the world than having the two of you to myself for a week by the seaside. Love always, E.

13.

That same Sunday morning in Rome, Alice couldn't get the shower in the bathroom to switch off. Once she had dried herself and put on a dressing gown, she asked Felix to look at it. He came in and turned the shower head into the wall and examined the unit, clicking the power button on and off to no avail, as she stood behind him with her hair dripping onto her shoulders. Removing the exterior plastic casing of the shower, he squinted at a label inside. With his left hand he took his phone from his pocket and held it out behind him for Alice to accept. Once she had taken it, he read aloud the make and model number and asked her to put it into Google, while he pressed the power button again and watched the interior mechanism move. She tapped the browser icon on the screen of his phone, and it opened on a popular porn website. The page displayed a list of search results for the query 'rough anal'. In the top thumbnail a woman was shown kneeling on a chair, with a man behind her holding her by the throat. Underneath that, another thumbnail showed a woman crying, with smeared lipstick, and mascara running in exaggerated trails from her eyes. Without touching the screen or interacting with the page in any way, Alice handed the phone back to Felix and said: You might want to close out of that. He took the phone back, glanced at it, and instantly flushed all over his face and throat. The plastic covering of the shower unit fell forward again and he had to catch and rebalance it with his other hand. Uh, he said. Sorry. Jesus, that's awkward, sorry about that. She nodded, put her hands in her dressing gown pockets, removed them again, and then went to her room.

A few minutes later, Felix found a solution for the issue with the shower unit. He left the apartment then and went for a walk. Several hours passed, Alice in her bedroom working, Felix walking around the city alone. He wandered down the Corso listening to his headphones, glancing in shop windows and occasionally checking his phone. Back in the apartment Alice came out to the kitchen, ate a banana, some bread and half a bar of chocolate, and then returned to her room.

When Felix got back, he knocked on Alice's bedroom door and, without opening it, asked if she'd like to get something to eat.

I've eaten already, she said from inside. Thank you.

He nodded to himself, pinched the bridge of his nose between his fingers, walked away from her door, and then walked back again. He shook his head and knocked on the door again.

Can I come in? he asked.

Sure.

He opened the door and found her sitting up against the headboard with her laptop on her lap. The window was open. He stood in the doorway, not entering, one hand on the doorframe. She tilted her head to one side enquiringly.

I fixed the shower, he said.

I noticed that. Thank you.

She returned her attention to whatever she had been doing on her laptop. He continued standing there, looking unsatisfied.

Are you mad with me? he asked.

No, I'm not mad.

I feel bad about what happened earlier.

Don't worry about it, she said.

He rubbed the doorframe under his hand, still watching her.

Do you really not want me to worry about it, or are you just saying that? he asked.

What do you mean?

You're acting a bit off with me.

She shrugged. He waited for her to say something and she didn't.

See, like that, he said. You're not really talking.

I don't know what you want me to say. It's your business what kind of porn you like to watch. But it is unfortunate you left the page open because I found it disturbing.

He frowned and said: I wouldn't really say it was disturbing.

No, I'm sure you wouldn't.

What does that mean?

Looking up at him now with a rather fierce expression, she said: What do you want to hear, Felix? You like to watch videos of horrible things happening to vulnerable women, and you want me to say what? That's fine? I'm sure it is fine. You're not going to go to prison for it.

And you think I should, do you?

What I think is really none of your business, is it?

He laughed. He had his hands in his pockets, shaking his head. Lightly he tapped his shoe on the doorframe. I suppose there's nothing embarrassing in your search history, he said.

Nothing like that, no.

Well, you're very superior, then.

She was typing something, no longer looking up at him. He watched her.

I don't think you really care about those women, he said eventually. I think you're just annoyed that I like something you don't.

Maybe.

Or maybe you're jealous of them.

They looked at one another for a moment. Calmly, she said: I think it's a shame you would speak to me like that. But no, I'm not jealous of anyone who has to degrade themselves for money. I consider myself lucky I don't have to.

Your money hasn't gotten you very far with me, though, has it?

Without flinching she replied: On the contrary, I've had the pleasure of your company for the last three days. What more could I ask?

He glanced behind him, into the living room, and then rubbed his hands down over his face in a gesture of total mental or physical exhaustion. She watched him neutrally.

Is that what you were after, the pleasure of my company? he said.

Yes.

And you've enjoyed it, have you?

Very much, she said.

He looked around, shaking his head slowly. Finally he walked into the room and sat on the empty side of the bed, with his back turned to her.

Can I lie down for a second? he said.

Sure.

He lay down on his back. Next to him she continued typing. She seemed to be writing an email.

You're making me feel incredibly guilty over something I don't think was that bad, he said.

Still typing, she answered: It's nice to know you care so much about my opinion.

If you think that's bad, whatever, he said. I've honestly done a lot worse. I mean, if looking at something on the internet is enough to put you off me, we were never going to be good friends, because that's nothing to me. I've done horrible things compared to that.

She stopped typing then and looked at him. Like what? she asked.

Loads of things, he said. Where would I

173

even start. Like, for example, you'll hate this one. About a year ago I brought some girl home after a night out, and then I found out later she was still in school. I'm not just saying that to fuck with you, I'm serious. Sixteen or seventeen, I think she was.

Did she look older?

I want to say she must have. But I didn't think about it. We were both drunk, she seemed like she was having fun. I know that's a horrible thing to say. It wasn't a case of me going after her on purpose because she was a kid, I never would have touched her if I'd known that, but obviously it was still wrong what happened. And I'm not saying, oh, it was just a mistake, it could have happened to anyone. Because actually, it was my own stupidity from start to finish. I'm not going to go on and on about how bad I feel about it. But I do feel bad, okay?

Quietly, she said: I believe you.

And honestly, I've done worse than that. Worst thing I've ever done, if you want to hear —

He broke off, and she nodded for him to continue. He looked away into the room as he spoke, grimacing vaguely, as if staring into a light.

Worst thing I've ever done, I got a girl pregnant when I was in school. She was in

Junior Cert and I was in fifth year. Have you ever heard anything worse than that? Her mam had to take her over to England. I think they got the boat over. She was like fourteen or whatever, a little child basically. We weren't even supposed to be having sex, I talked her into it. I mean, I told her it would be fine. There, anyway, that's the worst thing.

Did she want to do it, or did you make her do it?

She said she wanted to, but she was afraid of getting pregnant. And I told her it wouldn't happen. I don't think I really pressured her into it beyond that, I just said not to worry about it. But maybe that was kind of pressurising in a way. You don't think about this stuff when you're fifteen, or anyway I didn't. I would never do that now — I mean, I would never try to talk someone into it if they weren't interested, I just wouldn't even be bothered. You can believe me or not, I don't blame you if you don't. But when I remember myself saying those words to her I feel really out of my body. I start getting these weird heartbeats and everything. And I start thinking about really evil people, serial killers or whatever, and I feel like maybe that's me, maybe I'm one of these psychopaths you hear about. Because

175

I did say it, I did tell her not to worry, and I was older than she was, so she probably thought I knew what I was talking about. I just didn't think it would actually happen. And you know, I didn't even really have a conscience about it at the time. Only later, after I finished school, I started thinking about how evil it was, what I did to her. And feeling kind of scared and everything.

Do you know what she's doing now? said Alice.

Yeah, I still know her. She's not living in town anymore, she works in Swinford. But I would see her around the odd time when she's home.

Would she say hello to you if she saw you?

Oh yeah, he said. We're not like, not speaking to each other or anything. I just feel awful when I see her because it reminds me of what I did.

Did you ever say sorry?

At the time, maybe. But I never got back in touch with her later when I started feeling really bad about it. I didn't want to drag it all back up and get her upset for no reason. I don't know what she thinks. Maybe she just moved on and it's not on her mind that much. I hope so. But you can judge me if you want, I'm not defending myself.

He was turned to her, his head resting on the pillow, his eyes bright, almost glittering in the white light from the window behind her. She sat upright looking down at him, her face drawn.

Well, I can't judge you, she said. When I think about the worst things I've ever done, I feel the same way you're describing. Panicky and sick and that kind of thing. I bullied a girl I was in school with, really cruelly. For no reason, other than I suppose to torture her. Because other people were doing it. But then they would say they were doing it because I was. When I remember it now, I mostly just feel scared. I don't know why I would want to cause another person pain like that. I really want to believe I would never do that kind of thing again, for any reason. But I did do it, once, and I have to live with it for the rest of my life.

He watched her intently and said nothing.

I can't make it better, what you did, she said. And you can't make it better for me either. So maybe we're both bad people.

If I'm only as bad as you I don't mind that much. Or even if we're both terrible, it's still better than being terrible on my own.

She said she understood that feeling. He wiped his nose with his fingers and swallowed, looking away from her, at the ceiling.

I want to take back a horrible comment I made, he said.

Don't worry. I was horrible as well. What I said about those women degrading themselves for money, that was a stupid thing to say. I don't even think that, really. It doesn't matter, we were both annoyed.

Looking down at his fingernails he said: It's amazing how much you do annoy me.

She laughed. It's not amazing, she said. I have that effect on lots of people.

I'll tell you what it is, you do act very stuck-up at times. But I know other people who can be like that as well, and I wouldn't let it get to me the way it does with you. To be really honest, I actually think it's more the fact that I like you. And then when you act badly it drives me up the wall.

She nodded, silent. For a minute, two minutes, three, they sat on the bed without speaking. Finally he touched her knee in a friendly way and said he was going to have a shower. After he had left the room she sat there unmoving. In the bathroom he switched the shower on and stood looking in the mirror while the water warmed. Their conversation seemed to have had some effect on them both, but it was impossible to

178

decipher the nature of the effect, its meaning, how it felt to them at that moment, whether it was something shared between them or something about which they felt differently. Perhaps they didn't know themselves, and these were questions without fixed answers, and the work of making meaning was still going on.

That evening Alice had dinner with a group of booksellers and journalists in the city, while Felix ate on his own in the apartment. Afterwards they met for a drink and walked over to the Colosseum together. In the darkness it looked skeletal and desiccated, like the dried remains of an ancient insect. You really do see some pretty good stuff here, Felix said. Alice smiled, and he glanced over at her. What? he said. You're laughing at me. She shook her head and answered: I'm just happy you came with me, that's all. Back in the apartment, they wished one another goodnight and Alice went to bed. Felix sat in the kitchen looking at his phone while she lay in the next room with her eyes open, staring at nothing. After midnight, he knocked on her bedroom door.

Yes? she said.

He looked inside, holding his phone in his hand. Are you sleeping? he said. She told him no. Can I show you a video? he asked. She sat up and said yes. He came inside, closed the door and sat down on the bed beside her, where she shifted over to make room. He was still dressed, in a T-shirt and sweatpants. The video showed a raccoon sitting up in a humanoid posture, legs splayed, a bib tied around its neck and a bowl of black cherries in its lap. The raccoon reached into the bowl with its tiny clawed hand, grabbed a cherry and began eating it, all in a very anthropomorphic fashion, nodding its head in gourmet appreciation of the cherry. The caption on the video was 'raccoon enjoying to eat fruits'. It was a minute long and all the raccoon did was eat and nod. Alice laughed and said: Incredible. Felix said he thought she'd like it. Then he locked his phone screen and leaned back against her headboard contemplatively. She lay on her side, facing him, the quilt pulled up to her waist.

Were you sleeping? he asked again.

No.

I didn't interrupt anything, I hope.

What do you mean? she asked. Interrupt what?

I don't know. Whatever girls get up to when they're lying in bed at night.

She looked up at him, intrigued. Ah, she

said. Well, I wasn't touching myself, if that's what you're implying.

I suppose you don't do that, do you not?

Of course I do, but I wasn't just now.

He settled himself down with his head on the pillow, lying on his back and looking up at the ceiling. She had her arm tucked under her head, watching him.

And what do you be thinking about when you do it? he said.

Different things.

Your own little fantasies and things like that.

Indeed, she said.

And who would be starring in these fantasies?

Well, me, of course.

He gave what seemed a very genuine laugh at that. Of course, he said. I would hope so. But who else? Famous actors or celebrities or what.

Not really.

People you know, then.

More often, she said.

He turned to face her where she lay next to him.

And what about me? he said.

She bit on her lower lip for a moment, and then said: I think about you sometimes.

He put his hand out and touched her

nightdress, letting his fingers graze her waist. And what do you think about me doing to you? he asked.

She laughed, and it was impossible in the darkness to tell whether she was embarrassed. I think about you being very, very nice to me, she said.

He seemed to find this amusing. Oh yeah? he said. In what way?

She turned and hid her face in the pillow, which had the effect of suggesting she was in fact embarrassed, but when she spoke she was smiling. You're going to make fun of me if I tell you, she said.

I genuinely won't.

Well, I think about different things. I mean, I don't just have the same fantasy every time. But one thing all the fantasies have in common is — You are going to laugh, because it's so vain. I would never usually say this to someone, but you asked. I like to imagine that you really want me — a lot, not just a normal amount.

Lightly he moved his hand over her ribs, down the side of her body. And how do you know I do? he said. In the fantasy. Do I say it to you or is it just obvious?

It's obvious. But we get to a part later on where you say it as well.

And do you give me what I want, or you

182

just like teasing me?

She turned her face even further into the pillow. He moved his hand back up to her waist, up her ribcage, up to the soft line of her breast. In a low murmuring tone she said: You get what you want.

So why does it make a difference how much I want it? he said. Am I begging you?

No, no, you're not pushy. You're just really into it.

And can I ask, am I any good? Or do you imagine me more kind of nervous because I want it so badly?

She turned to face him, lying on her side again. His fingers moved over the surface of her breast, as far as the strap of her nightdress and back down.

I do sometimes imagine you kind of nervous, she said.

He nodded, his face and manner expressing a keen interest in the discussion. Can I ask something else? he said. You don't have to tell me. But what do you think about when you come?

I think about you coming, she said.

Where, inside you?

Usually.

Slowly, as if in deep thought, he ran the back of his hand over her belly, down over her navel. She was looking at him still.

I know what you're going to say now, she said.

Yeah? What?

I'm going to ask if you ever think about me in that way, and you're going to go: No, not really.

He laughed, stroking the cloth of her nightdress with the back of his hand. No, I'm not going to say that, he said. I can tell you about it if you like, but I'd prefer to hear more what you think. I mean, obviously because it revolves around me I like hearing it, but I also just think it's interesting. I've tried asking people about this stuff before and they never usually tell me anything.

Oh, she said. Were you using a line on me? I thought we were being very intimate.

His laughter had a note of awkwardness in it. We are, he replied. I have asked the question in the past but, as I said, I never usually get anywhere with it. And in fairness I've only ever asked people I'm already with. I've never gone down the route of using it as a pick-up line.

It is a little unorthodox. But then I don't think you're really trying to pick me up.

Well, I could have waited until tomorrow to show you the raccoon video, he said.

She laughed then, and he smiled with the

184

pleasure of making her laugh.

You know well why I'm here, he added.

No I don't! she said. We've been in Rome four nights already and the mood hasn't struck you at all?

We were only getting to know each other then.

What a gentleman.

He turned over again. I don't know, he said. I went back and forth on it. Honestly you can be kind of intimidating in certain situations, I don't know if you know that.

I've heard it from other people, but from you it surprises me, she said.

He shrugged and said nothing.

And I don't intimidate you anymore? she said.

You still do, a small bit. But you know, when someone tells you all their favourite sexual fantasies, that takes the edge off the intimidation a bit. I mean, no offence, but you obviously really fancy me.

Coolly she replied: You told me you weren't going to make fun of me if I told you those things. Feel free, but it doesn't hurt me and I think it's cheap.

He got up on his elbow and looked down at her. See? he said. See, that's intimidating when you talk like that. I wasn't actually making fun of you, by the way, and I'm

185

sorry if you thought I was. But when you're pissed off with me you get this attitude, like you're so above me. It makes me feel like a little worm.

For a while she lay there and said nothing. Then, sadly, she said: Okay, I'm defensive, and I act superior, and I make you feel bad. And besides all that it's obvious I have a crush on you anyway. So I suppose I'm very pathetic to you and not even pleasant to be around.

Yeah, exactly, he said. That's exactly what I think about you. That must be why I spent the last four days following you all over the place like a fucking moron.

What did you come in here for? she asked. Just to tease me?

Fuck's sake. I don't know. I like talking to you. When we go to our separate beds, I find I think about you a bit. So I thought I would come in here and see if you were thinking about me as well. Okay?

What kind of things do you think about?

He probed his back teeth with his tongue, contemplating. It's not that different from what you said, he told her. I imagine you really wanting it. Maybe I tease you a small bit at the start, and I can make you come a lot of times, that type of thing. In the fantasy itself there's nothing that strange. The only weird thing is that when we've been staying here, especially the last two nights, when I thought about you, I felt like you were thinking about me as well, in this room. Were you?

Yes, she said.

And it was like I could feel you near me. Actually, this morning I woke up and for a second I couldn't remember if it was real or not — I mean I was confused whether I was alone in bed or you were there. Because it felt so real.

In a low voice she asked: How did you feel when you realised you were alone?

Honestly, in the split second? he said. Disappointed. Or, I don't know, kind of lonely. He paused for a moment and then asked: Can I touch you now, what do you think?

She said yes. He put his hand under her nightdress and stroked his fingers over her underwear. Her mouth opened and she let out a little breath. Gently, he put his index finger inside her, and she made a whimpering noise. His face was flushed. Ah, you're so wet, he said. Her breath came high and quickly, her eyes still closed. He licked his upper lip and said: Let me take this off you. She sat up a little and he undressed her. After that, he pulled his T-shirt off over his head and with her fingertips she touched his erection through his clothes. I want this so badly, she said. The tips of his ears were red. Yeah? he said. Do you want it now? She asked if he had a condom, and he said yes, in his wallet. While she lay there on her back, he finished undressing and retrieved the wallet from his pocket. She watched him, while with her fingers she absently pinched the skin inside her elbow. Felix, she said. I haven't done this in a while, is that okay? They looked at one another uncertainly then — Alice perhaps uncertain of what he was thinking, Felix maybe uncertain of what the question signified. He had taken a little blue square of foil from his wallet. What do you mean? he asked. She shrugged, looking uneasy, and went on pinching at her arm. He knocked her hand away and said: Stop that, you'll hurt yourself. What's the matter? It's not your first time or something, is it? That made her laugh, a little sheepishly, and he laughed too, perhaps relieved. No, she said. My life has just been weird for a while. Like about two years. But it was normal before. Smoothing his palm down over her thigh, he said sympathetically: Ah, that's alright. Are you nervous? She nodded. He tore open the square of foil then and removed the condom from inside.

Don't worry, he said. I'll look after you. He got on top of her then and kissed her neck. Afterwards, when they parted, Alice seemed to fall asleep instantly, without even moving her arms or legs, which were jumbled awkwardly in the bedclothes. Felix lay down on his side, watching her, and then turned over on his back and stared up at the ceiling.

14.

Dearest Eileen — your email about what happened with Simon brought joy to my withered heart. You deserve romance! And so I feel does he. Can I tell you something about him that I promised I would never tell you but now I'm breaking the promise because the moment is opportune? A few years ago, just after you moved in with Aidan, Simon came over to see me one afternoon for coffee. We chatted about this and that, it was all very normal, and then when he was leaving, he stopped at the doorway of your old room to look inside. It was emptied out already, the bed was stripped, and I remember there was a pale rectangle on the wall where you used to have your Margaret Clarke poster. In a sort of fake-cheerful voice Simon said, 'You'll miss her.' And without thinking about it, I answered, 'So will you.' It didn't really make any sense, because you were actually moving closer to Simon's neighbourhood, but he didn't seem surprised that I had said it. He just replied like, 'Yes, obviously.' We stood there at the door of your room for a few more seconds and then he laughed and said: 'Please don't tell her I said that.' Of course you were with Aidan at the time, so I never did tell you. And I can't say I had always known, because I hadn't. I knew you and Simon were very close, and I knew what had happened in Paris. But for some reason it had never occurred to me that he had been in love with you all along. I don't think anyone knew. Anyway, we never talked about it again. Do you think it's terrible of me to tell you all this? I hope not. It wasn't very clear from your message whether you think you're going to keep seeing each other or not . . . What do you feel?

Yesterday afternoon — just after I got your email, in fact — Felix started to tell me about some things he had done in the past and later regretted. I suppose it was one of those 'worst things I've ever done' conversations — and actually, he has done some pretty bad things. I won't go into the details, but I can say some of it involved his relationships with women. I feel it's not my place to judge him, because I can't think why it should be, and because I'm occasionally wracked with guilt over horrible things I've done too. My impulse was actually to forgive him, especially because he has apparently spent a long time feeling remorseful and blaming himself. But I had to recognise it wasn't my place to do that either, since the actions he described may have impacted other people's lives permanently and would never have any effect on me. I can't step in as a disinterested third party and absolve him of his sins, just as he can't absolve me of mine. So I suppose whatever I felt for him when he confessed these actions wasn't really 'forgiveness', but something else. Maybe just that I trusted that his remorse was real and that he wouldn't make the same mistakes over again. It made me think about people who have done bad things — what they are supposed to do with themselves, and what we as a society are supposed to do with them. At the moment, the cycle of insincere public apologies is probably making everyone suspicious of forgiveness. But what should people who have done terrible things in the past actually do? Spontaneously advertise their own sins in order to pre-empt public exposure? Just try never to accomplish anything that might bring them increased scrutiny of any kind? Maybe I'm wrong, but

I believe the number of people who have done seriously bad things is not insignificant. I mean honestly, I think if every man who had ever behaved somewhat poorly in a sexual context dropped dead tomorrow, there would be like eleven men left alive. And it's not only men! It's women too, and children, everyone. I suppose what I mean is, what if it's not only a small number of evil people who are out there, waiting for their bad deeds to be exposed? What if it's all of us?

You mentioned in your email that you heard a reading at Mass about a woman pouring oil on the feet of Jesus. I might be mistaken, because there are a few similar Gospel stories, but I think the one you mean is the passage in Luke where Jesus has his feet anointed by a sinful woman. I've just read over it again in the little Douay-Rheims translation I brought with me to the hospital. You're right, the story is bizarre, and even (as you put it) freakish. But isn't it also a little bit interesting? The woman in the story really only has one distinguishing characteristic: the fact that she's led a sinful life. Who knows what she's supposed to have done? Maybe she was just a social outcast, essentially a marginalised innocent. But on the other hand, maybe she had actually done some bad things, the kind of things you or I would think of as seriously wrong. It's at least possible, isn't it? She may have killed her husband, or abused her children, or something like that. And having heard that Jesus was staying with Simon the Pharisee, she came to the house, and at the sight of Jesus, she started crying so profusely that she wet his feet with her tears. After that, she dried his feet with her hair and anointed them with perfumed oil. As you point out, it all seems quite absurd, even vaguely erotic — and indeed, Simon the Pharisee seems shocked and uncomfortable that Jesus would allow a sinful woman to touch him in such an intimate way. But Jesus, characteristically puzzling, simply says that all her many sins are forgiven, because she loves him so much. Could it be that easy? We just have to weep and prostrate ourselves and God forgives everything? But maybe it's not easy at all — maybe to weep and prostrate ourselves with genuine sincerity is the hardest thing we could ever learn how to do. I feel certain I don't understand how to do it. I have that resistance in me, that hard little kernel of something, which I fear would not let me prostrate myself before God even if I believed in him.

While I'm here, I may as well tell you that

Felix and I slept together last night. I didn't really want to tell you, if I'm honest, but I think it would have been weird not to. Not that I'm embarrassed — or maybe I am, but not by him. It's more the idea of caring what somebody else thinks about me, when that's exactly what I don't do, and what I'm so good at not doing. It's not easy for me, really. I think we've been having a nice time together — which is me saying that I've had a nice time, and that I never know how he feels. Although our lives have been different in basically every respect, I do feel in a strange way that we've taken different routes to reach similar points, and there's a lot we recognise in one another. You wouldn't believe how long it's taken me to write this paragraph. I feel so frightened of being hurt — not of the suffering, which I know I can handle, but the indignity of suffering, the indignity of being open to it. I have a terrible crush on him and get very excited and idiotic when he shows me affection. So of course in the midst of everything, the state of the world being what it is, humanity on the cusp of extinction, here I am writing another email about sex and friendship. What else is there to live for? Love always, Alice.

15.

On Monday evening at a quarter past eight, the main room of Simon's apartment was empty and dim. Through the small window over the sink in the kitchenette, and the larger window in the living room opposite, the remaining daylight touched the various interior surfaces: the silver basin of the sink, with a single dirty plate and knife lying inside; the kitchen table, dotted here and there with crumbs; a fruit bowl containing one browning banana and two apples; a knitted throw sprawled over the sofa untidily; a thin grey layer of dust on the upper rim of the television; the bookcases, the table lamps, a chess set on the coffee table with what appeared to be an unfinished game on the board. This way in silence the room lay as the light faded, as outside in the hallway people climbed and descended the staircase, and in the street traffic swept past in waves of white sound. At twenty to nine came the noise of a key slipped into the lock, and then the apartment door opened. Simon was talking on the phone as he entered, taking a satchel off his shoulder with his free hand, saying aloud: No, I don't think they're worried about it, really. It's just an annoyance. He was dressed in a dark-grey suit, with a green tie secured by a gold pin. Quietly he used his foot to close the door behind him and hung his bag up on a hook. Aha, he said. Is he there with you? I'll talk to him now if you like. He went into the living room and turned on a floor lamp, dropped his keys on the coffee table. Okay, what do you think is best, then? he asked. Alone in the yellowish light of the lamp, he looked tired. He went to the kitchen and picked the kettle up as if to test its weight. Yeah, he said. No, that's fine, I'll just tell him I've talked to you about it. Replacing the kettle in its cradle, he turned it on, and then sat down on a kitchen chair. Right, he said, but if I'm supposed to pretend you haven't told me, what's my pretext for calling him in the first place? He held the phone between his face and shoulder and started to unlace his shoes. Then, prompted by a remark on the other end of the call, he sat up and put the phone back into his hand again. Clearly that's not what

I meant, he said. The conversation continued like this for some time, while Simon took his shoes off, removed his tie and made himself a cup of tea. When the phone buzzed in his hand, he lifted it away quickly and checked the screen, while the voice on the other end went on talking. An email notification had appeared, with the subject heading 'Tuesday call'. Apparently uninterested, he brought the phone back to his ear and carried the cup of tea over to the sofa to sit down. Yeah, yeah, he was saying, I'm home now. I'm just about to put the news on. He closed his eyes while the voice on the phone was speaking. Sure, he said. I'll let you know. Love you too. Bye. He repeated this last word several times before tapping an icon on-screen to end the call. Looking down at the screen, he opened a messaging app and tapped the name 'Eileen Lydon'. The most recent message was displayed at the bottom of the screen, with the time stamp 20:14.

Simon: Hey, I had a really nice time with you at the weekend. Would you like to see each other again this week?

An icon showed that Eileen had seen the message, but no response had arrived. He closed the app and opened the 'Tuesday call' email, which was part of a longer thread. A previous message read: Yes I am told they have phone records also. Simon or Lisa can you get across this please and get in touch with Anthony if needed. One of his colleagues had replied: If we spend any more time dealing with this non issue I am going to lose my mind. The newest message read: Simon I am attaching Anthony's number and details below. Give him a ring tonight if possible or tomorrow morning? No one is happy about this but it's where we are. Locking his phone, he allowed his eyes to close and for a few moments he sat on the sofa not moving, his chest rising and falling with his breath. After a time he lifted a hand and passed it slowly down his face. Finally he reached for the remote control and turned the television on. The nine o'clock news was just beginning. He sat watching the first few items roll past on the screen, his eyes half-closed, almost as if he was asleep, but sipping now and then from the cup of tea he kept on an arm of the couch beside him. During an item about road safety his phone buzzed, and he reached for it immediately. On-screen a new message displayed.

Eileen: oddly formal tone here Simon

He stared down at this message for several seconds, and then typed out a response.

Simon: Was it?

An animated three-dot ellipsis displayed on-screen, to show that Eileen was typing.

Eileen: why do men over 30 text like they're updating a LinkedIn profile
Eileen: Hi [Eileen], it was great seeing you on [Saturday]. Can we connect again? Try selecting a time and date from the drop down menu

Vaguely now he smiled to himself as his thumbs moved over the keyboard.

Simon: You're right
Simon: If only I were a younger man, I would manually turn off the autocaps function on my phone in order to seem more laidback
Eileen: it's in settings
Eileen: I can help you find it if you get stuck

At the top of the screen, a new email appeared in the 'Tuesday call' thread. The

200

opening text displayed as: Hi all. Have just heard from TJ . . . Simon dismissed the notification without opening it, and began typing another message to Eileen.

Simon: No, that's ok
Simon: I'm always copy and pasting that message saying I had a nice time at the weekend, can we see each other again, etc.
Simon: Never had any complaints before
Eileen: ahaha
Eileen: you can use copy and paste?? I'm impressed
Eileen: anyway yes, we can see each other this week
Eileen: when is good?

Another message appeared at the top of the screen, from a contact listed as 'Geraldine Costigan'.

Geraldine: Your dad says you can give him a ring tomorrow evening if that suits you sweetheart. xxx

Simon let out a long slow breath, and then swiped upward to dismiss the message. His eyes moving back and forth over the messages to and from Eileen, he typed the words Would you, and then deleted them.

He scrolled back up to the previous texts and looked at them once more. Finally, he began typing again.

Simon: Are you busy just now?

The double tick showed that Eileen had seen the message, and then the ellipsis appeared.

Eileen: no
Eileen: I was going to have a bath but my flatmates used all the hot water
Eileen: so I'm just lying on my bed looking at internet
Eileen: why?

On the television, the news had finished and the weather had come on. An illustrated yellow sun hovered over the Dublin region on the map. Simon started typing again.

Simon: Do you want to come over here?
Simon: Endless hot water
Simon: Ice cream in freezer
Simon: No flatmates

A few seconds passed. He rubbed at his jaw with his hand, watching the screen, which reflected on its surface the bulb of the ceiling light in its glass shade overhead.

Eileen: !!

Eileen: I was not fishing for an invite!!

Simon: I know that

Eileen: are you sure?

Simon: Yes

Eileen: it's very nice of you

Simon: What can I say, I have a very nice personality

Eileen: it sounds like fun. . . .

Eileen: but I don't want to intrude on you again!!

Simon: Eileen

Simon: Put your shoes on, I'll call you a taxi

Eileen: hahaha

Eileen: yes daddy

Eileen: thank you

Looking gratified, he closed out of the messages, opened a taxi app and ordered a driver to Eileen's address. He rose from the sofa then, muted the television and went to the sink with his empty cup of tea. After washing up and wiping down the kitchen surfaces, he went into his room and made his bed. Several times while he carried out these tasks, he took his phone from his pocket and checked the taxi app, where a small icon representing Eileen's cab moved slowly and hesitatingly along the quays and southward, and then, closing the app, he pocketed his phone again and returned to what he had been doing before.

When he answered the door twenty minutes later, Eileen was standing in the hallway wearing a cropped grey sweatshirt and a pleated cotton skirt, carrying a tote bag printed with the logo of a London literary magazine. She looked as if she had earlier been wearing dark lipstick but it had faded. He stood still in front of her for a moment before putting his hand to her waist and kissing her on the cheek. Good to see you, he said. She wrapped her arms around his neck, and he let her hold on to him in the doorway. Thank you for inviting me, she replied. They went inside. He closed the door behind them and she produced from her bag a bottle of red wine. I brought you this, she said. We don't have to drink it, I just have a horror of coming over to someone's house and not bringing anything. Especially your house. Imagine what my mother would say. Not that I brought anything last time I dropped by, ha ha. She put the bottle on the table and took her bag off her shoulder. Catching sight of the television, she said: Oh, are you watching Claire Byrne? I won't interrupt. I'll just sit quietly on the sofa. He was smiling, his eyes following Eileen as she hung her bag on the back of a kitchen chair and started to refix her hair, loosening the elastic tie that held it up in a bun. No, I'm not watching it, he said. You look nice. Would you like a cup of tea or something? Or a glass of wine if you'd rather. She went to sit on the couch, pulling off the flat leather shoes she had been wearing and tucking up her feet in their white socks on the cushions. I'll have tea, she said. I don't actually feel like wine. Is this a puzzle? He glanced over from the kitchen and saw her pointing at the chessboard. No, he said, it's a game. Peter was here last night, but he had to head off before we finished. Just as well for me. She went on looking at the board while he boiled the kettle and took a cup down from the press. Did you have the black pieces? she asked. With his back turned to her, he answered no, the white. You're up two pawns, then, she said. And you can check him with your bishop. He was taking a spoon out of the cutlery drawer, amused. Think about it again, he said. She frowned at the board a little longer, while he made the tea and brought it over to the coffee table. Well, I won't mess with it, she said. He sat down at the other end of the sofa and turned off the television. Work away, he said. It's white to

205

move. She picked up the white bishop and checked the black king. Leaning forward, he moved a black pawn to block the attack and threaten her bishop, and she used the bishop to take the pawn. He brought the black knight forward to take the bishop then and fork the white queen and rook. She made a face and said: I'm an idiot. He said it was his fault anyway for leaving himself in such a weak position. She picked up her cup of tea and sat back against the armrest of the sofa. Did I tell you my family are at war with each other about Lola's wedding invites? she said. I really don't know why I got involved, she's just such a nightmare. Do you want to see the texts she's been sending me? He said yes, and she took her phone out and showed him the message Lola had sent her on Saturday night.

Lola: Hmmm do I really want to hear about how immature I am from someone who's stuck in a shitty job making no money and living in a kip at age 30 . . . . . .

His eyes moved over the screen and then he took the device from her hand to read it again, frowning. Jesus, the hostility, he murmured.

Eileen took her phone back from his hand and looked down at it. I only brought up the wedding thing because Mary asked me to, she said. But then when I complained to her about these horrible text messages, she was like, well, that's between the two of you, that's nothing to do with me.

But if you had sent a message like that to Lola —

Right? Exactly. Mammy would be on the phone to me saying, how dare you speak to your sister like that?

I suppose there's no point talking to your dad, he said.

She locked the phone and left it down on the floorboards. No, she answered. He's the only one who's not crazy, obviously. But he knows that we're all crazy, so he's too scared to get involved.

He lifted her feet into his lap. You're not crazy, he said. The other two, yes, but not you.

Smiling, she settled back against the armrest. Thank God there is one person in the world who can see that, she said.

Happy to help.

For a moment she watched him while he rubbed the arch of her foot with his thumb. Then in a different voice she asked: How was your day?

He glanced up at her, and then back down again. Fine, he said. And yours?

You look a little bit tired.

Lightly, without looking up, he replied: Do I?

She went on watching him, while he avoided her eyes. Simon, she said, are you sad today?

He gave a kind of embarrassed laugh. Hm, he said. I don't know. I don't think so.

Would you tell me if you were?

Am I that bad?

Playfully she prodded at him with her foot. I'm asking you about your day right now and you won't tell me anything, she said.

Catching her ankle in his hand, he answered: Hm. Let me see. I had a phone call with my mother this evening.

Oh? How is she?

She's okay. She's worried about my dad, but that's nothing unusual. He has — He's fine, but he has high blood pressure, and she thinks he's not taking his medication properly. It's more psychological than anything else, you know the way families are. And he's pissed off with me because — But that's boring, it's all to do with work.

But your dad isn't working anymore, is he? she said.

Absently he went on circling his hand around her ankle. Right, I mean my work, he answered. You know, we don't see eye to eye politically. It's fine, it's the normal generational thing. He thinks my political views are like, an outgrowth of my stunted personality.

Quietly Eileen said: That's not very nice.

No. I know. Although I think it hurts my mother's feelings more than mine. It's actually — If you heard him, it's quite a detailed theory he's developed. Something to do with a Messiah complex. I'm not going to be able to do it justice, because honestly, I kind of tune out when he starts talking about it. But he seems to think I want to go around saving people because it makes me feel powerful and virile or whatever. The funny thing is that my job has absolutely nothing to do with helping people. Maybe if I was a social worker or a doctor or something, but I actually just sit in an office all day. I don't know. Last time I was home we got into this truly bizarre conflict because I woke up with a headache one morning. He didn't talk to me all day, and then in the evening he gave me this big long speech about how much my mother had been looking forward to seeing me and how I had ruined her whole weekend by having this headache. He can never say he's angry with me himself, he always has to project his feelings onto Geraldine, like it was a personal insult to her that I had a migraine. He has a thing about migraines, because she gets them as well, and he's convinced they're psychosomatic. Anyway, she wants me to call him tomorrow about this medication thing, for his blood pressure. Not that it's going to make any difference what I say. I'm sorry. I feel like I've been talking out loud for about a year now, I'm going to stop.

While he spoke, he had been touching the back of Eileen's calf, the back of her knee, with his fingers, and with his last remark he drew his hand away and sat up.

Don't, she said.

He looked over at her. What? he asked. Don't stop talking, or don't stop doing that?

Either.

He put his hand back where it had been before, under her knee. In response she made a low pleasurable noise like: Mm. He let his thumb brush the inside of her thigh, under her skirt. Kind of sounds like your dad is jealous of you, she remarked. Fondly he went on watching her. What makes you say that? he asked. She leaned her head back on the armrest, looking up at the lit glass lampshade overhead. Well, you're young and handsome, she said. And women love you. Not that your dad would mind that, if you looked up to him and tried to be like him, but you don't. Obviously I don't know him that well, but in my experience he's very domineering and rude. It probably drives him crazy that you're so nice to everyone, and nothing seems to bother you. Simon was stroking the underside of her knee, nodding his head. But in his view, I'm only nice to everyone because it makes me feel good about myself, he said. Eileen made a baffled face. So what? she replied. It's better than bullying everyone to feel good about yourself, isn't it? God knows we have enough sadists in the world. And why shouldn't you feel good about yourself? You have integrity, and you're generous, and you're a great friend. Mildly he raised his eyebrows and for a moment said nothing. Then he replied: Eileen, I didn't know you thought so highly of me. Closing her eyes, she smiled. Yes you did, she said. He glanced over at her where she lay with her head tipped back, her eyes shut.

I'm very happy you're here, he said.

She made a funny face and asked: You mean like, platonically?

Moving his hand up under her skirt, he was smiling. No, not platonically, he said.

She wriggled down a little against the armrest. You know when you sent me that text saying — What did it say? she asked. Put your shoes on, I'm calling you a taxi, or something like that. It was nice.

I'm happy you thought so.

Yeah, it was weirdly sexy. It's funny, I think I enjoy being bossed around by you. A part of me is just like, yes, please, tell me what to do with my life.

He was laughing then, touching the inside of her thigh with his fingers. You're right, he said, that is sexy.

It makes me feel very safe and relaxed. Like when I'm complaining to you about something and you call me 'princess', that turns me on a little bit. Do you hate me saying that? It just makes me feel like you're in control of everything, and you won't let anything bad happen to me.

No, I love that kind of thing. The idea of taking care of you, or you need my help, whatever. I probably have a thing about that anyway. Whenever a girl asks me to open a jam jar, I kind of fall in love with her.

She had the tip of her finger in her mouth. And I thought I was special, she said.

With you it's a little bit more than that, though. Actually, I remember Natalie once said to me about you — This is probably a

212

weird thing to tell you, but anyway. You were coming over to see us in Paris and I was like, worried about you getting on your flight, or whatever. And Natalie said something like, oh, Daddy's little girl is all on her own, something like that. It was funny. I mean, I think she was kidding.

Eileen covered her eyes then, laughing. I have one, she said. I got a text from you one night, and Aidan was just near my phone so he checked the message for me. And when I asked him who it was, he showed me the screen and went, it's your dad.

He was pleased, embarrassed, shaking his head. I feel like if I tried to explain this to anyone else they would call the police, he said.

Just because of the Daddy's princess thing? Or like, you also want to tie me up and torture me.

No, no. But that would be a lot more normal, wouldn't it? My idea is more like — I hope you're not horrified with me saying all this. But I think the fantasy is just that you're really helpless and wet, and I'm like, telling you what a good girl you are.

Coyly she looked up at him through her eyelashes. And what if I'm not a good girl? she said. You don't want to put me over your knee and punish me?

He moved his hand over the thin damp cotton of her underwear. Ah, but not to hurt you, he said. Only to make you behave.

For a moment she said nothing. Then she said: Will you tell me what to do?

In his ordinary, relaxed, half-amused voice he answered: Will you do what you're told?

She started laughing again. Yes. It's funny how much it turns me on. It's weird. I'm really excited to think what you're going to do to me. Sorry if I'm breaking character.

No, don't be in character. Just be yourself.

He leaned over then and kissed her. Her head against the armrest, his tongue wet in her mouth. Passively she let him undress her, watching his hands unbutton her skirt and roll down her underwear. Reaching up under her knee, he lifted her left leg over the back of the sofa and moved her other foot down onto the floor, so her legs were spread wide open, and she was shivering. Ah, you're being very good, he said. Shaking her head, she let out a kind of nervous laugh. Lightly with his fingers he touched her, not penetrating her yet, and she pressed her hips down into the couch and closed her eyes. He put a finger inside her then and she exhaled. Good girl, he murmured. Just relax. Gently then he pressed another finger inside her and she cried out, a high ragged cry. Shh, he said. You're being so good. She was shaking her head again, her mouth open. If you keep talking to me like that I'm going to come, she told him. He was smiling, looking down at her. In a minute, he said. Not yet. He took his clothes off, and she lay with her eyes closed, one knee still hooked over the back of the sofa. In her ear he said: And it's okay if I come inside you? With her hand she clutched at the back of his neck. I really want you to, she said. He closed his eyes for a moment, nodding his head, not speaking. When he entered her, she cried out again, clinging to him, and he was quiet. I love you, she said. He breathed in carefully and said nothing. Looking up at him she asked: Simon, do you like it when I say that? Awkwardly, trying to smile, he said yes. I can feel that you do, she answered. He went on breathing, his upper lip was damp, his forehead. Well, I love you too, he said. She was sucking on her lip now, watching him. Because I'm such a good girl, she answered. With the tip of his index finger he touched her. You are, he said. She closed her eyes again, her lips moving but making no noise. After a few minutes she told him she was coming. Her breath was high and wavering, her body tensed and contracted in his hands. When she was finished, he said quietly: Can I keep going or do you need me to stop? In an exhausted voice, she said sorry, and asked if he would take long. No, I'll be quick, he said. But I can stop if you want, it's alright. She told him it was okay to keep going. He put his hands on her hips and held her against the sofa while he moved inside her. She was limp then, very wet, and unresisting, only letting out a feeble cry now and again. Jesus Christ, he said. Afterwards, he lay down against her body. They were both still, breathing slowly, sweat cooling on his skin. She smoothed the palm of her hand down his back. Thank you, he said. She smiled, glancing down at him. You don't have to thank me, she answered. His eyes were closed. Right, he said. But I'm grateful. Not only — I just mean, it's nice to be with you, I'm happy you came over. Sometimes when I'm here on my own in the evenings, you know, it can be kind of depressing, to be honest. Or just lonely, or whatever. He gave a thin breathless laugh. Sorry, I don't know why I'm saying that, he said. I'm glad you're here, that's all. Do you ever feel, when someone does something nice for you, it's like you're so grateful that you actually start feeling bad? I don't know if other people get that or it's just me. Never mind, I'm being an idiot. He sat up then and started to dress himself. She lay there naked, watching him. But it's not like I was doing you a favour, she said. It was mutual. Without turning around he gave another strained laugh and seemed to wipe at his eyes with his hand. No, I know, he said. I think I'm just grateful that you would want to. I'm sorry, I don't know what's wrong with me.

I don't mind, she said. But I don't want you to feel bad.

He stood up, he was putting his shirt back on. I'm fine, don't worry, he said. Would you like a glass of wine? Or we can have ice cream.

Nodding her head slowly, she sat up. Sure, she said. Ice cream would be nice. He went to the kitchen and over the back of the sofa she watched him while she was dressing herself. From behind he looked tall, his shirt a little creased, and his hair was soft and golden under the overhead lights.

I didn't know you had migraines, she said.

Without turning around he replied: I don't often.

She was buttoning the waistband of her skirt. The last time I had one, I texted you from bed to complain about how bad it was, she said. Do you remember?

He was taking two spoons from the cutlery drawer, answering: Yeah, I think yours are worse than mine.

She nodded her head without speaking. Finally she said: Will I switch the TV back on? We can watch *Newsnight* or something. What do you think?

That sounds good.

He brought over their bowls of ice cream while she turned up the volume on the television. On-screen a British presenter was standing in front of a blue background talking to the camera about a UK party leadership election. With her eyes on the screen, Eileen said: And that's a lie, isn't it? Go on, say it's a lie. But no, they never do. Sitting beside her, Simon was breaking up the ice cream in his bowl with a spoon. You know she's married to a hedge fund manager, he remarked. While they watched, they talked intermittently about the possibility of another general election at home before the end of the year, and which members of Simon's party were likely to hold on to their seats if it happened. He was worried that the people he liked most would lose out, and the 'careerists' would more likely hold on. On the television, a party spokesperson was saying: The prime minister — Excuse me, I'm sorry, the prime minister has said time and time again — Eileen left her empty ice cream bowl on the coffee table and sat back with her feet tucked up on the sofa. Remember when you were on TV? she said. Simon was still eating. For like three minutes, he said. With her fingers she was tightening the elastic in her hair again. I got about a hundred texts that night saying, your friend Simon is on TV! she answered. And one person — I won't say who it was. But one certain person texted me a screenshot of you, and the message said something like, is this the Simon you're always talking about? With his eyes on the television he was grinning then, but he said nothing. Observing his expression, Eileen went on: I don't actually talk about you that much. Anyway, I replied like, yeah, that's him, and she texted back — word for word — no offence, but I want to have his children. He started laughing. I don't believe that, he said. Eileen repeated: Word for word. I would have forwarded it to you, except the 'no offence' part annoyed me. Like, why should I be offended? Does she think we have some kind of sad unrequited friendship where I'm actually in love with you and you don't even notice me? I hate when people think that about us. Simon was looking over at her then, her face in quarter-profile, turned toward the screen, the light of the ceiling lamp white on her cheekbone and the corner of her eyelid. All my friends think the opposite, he remarked. Without turning her face from the television she looked amused. What, that you're unrequitedly in love with me? she said. That's funny. Not that I mind, it's good for my ego. Who thinks that? Peter? I doubt Declan does. The programme was ending then, the production credits rolling. Still with her eyes on the screen she went on lightly: Look, I know you don't want to talk about it. But what you said earlier, about feeling lonely. I feel like that all the time. I'm only saying that because I want you to know you're really not alone in that feeling. In case you think you are. And just from my perspective, whenever I get really lonely, you're the person I call. Because you have a soothing effect on me. You know, the things I would normally worry about, they don't really seem that worrying when I talk to you. Anyway, what I'm saying is, if you ever want to call me when you feel that way, you can. You don't even have to say why you're calling, we can just talk about other things. I'll complain to you about my family, probably. Or I can come over here and we can do this.

Okay? Not that you have to call me, obviously, but you can. Any time. That's all. He did not take his eyes from her while she was speaking, and when she had finished he was quiet for a moment. Then in a mild, friendly tone of voice he said: Eileen, you know on the phone the other night, you were saying I should find a wife for myself? Laughing, she turned to face him. Yes, she said. He was smiling, looking happy and tired. You meant like, some new person who was going to come into my life and marry me, he said. Someone I've never met before. Eileen interjected to add: And very beautiful. A younger woman, I think we said. Not too intelligent, but sweet-tempered. He was nodding his head. Right, he said. She sounds fantastic. Now, I have a question. When I get this wife, whom I can presume from the thrust of your remarks is not the same person as you — With mock indignation Eileen interrupted: Certainly she's not me. For one thing, I'm a lot better-read than she is. He went on smiling to himself. Sure, he said. But once I find her, whoever she might be, will you and I still be friends? She sat back against the sofa cushions then, as if to consider the question. After a pause, she replied: No. I think when you find her, you'll have to give me up. It might even be that giving me up is the precondition for finding her in the first place.

As I suspected, he said. I'll never find her, then.

Eileen lifted her hands up in astonishment. Simon, she said. Be serious. This woman is your soulmate. God put her on earth for you.

If God wanted me to give you up, he wouldn't have made me who I am.

For a moment they looked at one another. She put her hand to her cheek then, and her face was flushed. So you're not going to renounce our friendship, she said.

Not for anything.

She reached her hand out and touched it to his. I wouldn't renounce it either, she said. And you can believe me, because none of my boyfriends have ever liked you, and it never made any difference to me.

He was laughing then, they both were. At midnight she went to brush her teeth and he turned the lights off in the kitchen. Emerging from the bathroom she said: See, I obviously had an ulterior motive, because I brought my toothbrush. She followed him into his room and he shut the door behind them, saying something inaudible. She laughed, and through the door her laughter was softened and musical. In the darkness the main room of the apartment lay quiet again and still. Two empty bowls had been left in the sink, two spoons, an empty water glass with a faint print of clear lip balm on the rim. Through the door the sound of conversation murmured on, the words rounded out, indistinct, and by one in the morning silence had fallen. At half past five the sky began to lighten in the east-facing living room window, from black to blue and then to silvery white. Another day. The call of a crow from an overhead power line. The sound of buses in the street.

16.

Alice, do you remember a few weeks or months ago I sent you an email about the Late Bronze Age collapse? I went on reading about it afterwards, and it seems that while little is known about the period, scholarly interpretations are more various than the Wikipedia page led me to believe. We do know that before the collapse, rich and literate palace economies in the Eastern Mediterranean traded in exorbitantly costly goods, apparently sending and receiving them as gifts to and from the rulers of other kingdoms. And we also know that afterwards, palaces were destroyed or abandoned, written languages were lost, and luxury goods were no longer produced in the same quantities or traded across the same distances. But how many people, how many inhabitants of this 'civilisation', actually lived in the palaces? How many wore the jewellery, drank from the bronze cups, ate the pomegranates? For every one member of the elite, thousands more were illiterate and impoverished subsistence farmers. After the 'collapse of civilisation', many of them moved elsewhere, and some may have died, but for the most part their lives probably did not change much. They went on growing crops. Sometimes the harvest was good and sometimes it wasn't. And in another corner of the continent, those people were your ancestors and mine — not the palace-dwellers, but the peasants. Our rich and complex international networks of production and distribution have come to an end before, but here we are, you and I, and here is humanity. What if the meaning of life on earth is not eternal progress toward some unspecified goal — the engineering and production of more and more powerful technologies, the development of more and more complex and abstruse cultural forms? What if these things just rise and recede naturally, like tides, while the meaning of life remains the same always — just to live and be with other people?

As to the revelation about yourself and Felix: may I say, as your friend, for all your earlier talk about relational formlessness and experimental affective bonds, this did not come as a surprise to me at all. If he's nice to you I will approve of him unconditionally, and if he's not then I'll be his enemy forever. Does that sound reasonable? But I'm sure he'll be nice.

I don't know if I've mentioned this to you before, but a few years ago, I started keeping a diary, which I called 'the life book'. I began with the idea of writing one short entry each day, just a line or two, describing something good. I suppose by 'good' I must have meant something that made me happy or brought me pleasure. I went back to look at it the other day, and the early entries are all from that autumn, almost six years ago now. Dry upturned sycamore leaves scuttling like claws along the South Circular Road. The artificial buttered taste of popcorn in the cinema. Pale-yellow sky in the evening, Thomas Street draped in mist. Things like that. I didn't miss a day through all of September, October, November that year. I could always think of something nice, and sometimes I would even do things for the purpose of putting them in the book, like taking a bath or going for a walk. At the time I felt like I was just absorbing life, and at the end of the day I never had to strain to think of anything good I had seen or heard. It just came to me, and even the words came, because my only aim was to

226

get the image down clearly and simply so that I would later remember how it felt. And reading those entries now, I do remember what I felt, or at least what I saw and heard and noticed. Walking around, even on a bad day, I would see things — I mean just the things that were in front of me. People's faces, the weather, traffic. The smell of petrol from the garage, the feeling of being rained on, completely ordinary things. And in that way even the bad days were good, because I felt them and remembered feeling them. There was something delicate about living like that — like I was an instrument and the world touched me and reverberated inside me.

After a couple of months, I started to miss days. Sometimes I would fall asleep without remembering to write anything, but then other nights I'd open the book and not know what to write — I wouldn't be able to think of anything at all. When I did make entries, they were increasingly verbal and abstract: song titles, or quotes from novels, or text messages from friends. By spring I couldn't keep it up anymore. I started to put the diary away for weeks at a time — it was just a cheap black notebook I got at work — and then eventually I'd take it back out to look at the entries from the previous year. At that point, I found it impossible to imagine ever feeling again as I had apparently once felt about rain or flowers. It wasn't just that I failed to be delighted by sensory experiences — it was that I didn't actually seem to have them anymore. I would walk to work or go out for groceries or whatever and by the time I came home again I wouldn't be able to remember seeing or hearing anything distinctive at all. I suppose I was seeing but not looking — the visual world just came to me flat, like a catalogue of information. I never looked at things anymore, in the way I had before.

Reading the book again now gives me such a strange sensation. Was I really like that once? A person capable of dropping down into the most fleeting of impressions, and dilating them somehow, dwelling inside them, and finding riches and beauty there. Apparently I was — 'for a couple of hours, but I am not that person'. I wonder whether the book itself, the process of writing the book, caused me to live that way, or whether I wrote because I wanted to record that kind of experience as it was happening. I've tried to remember what was going on in my life at the time, in case that might help me to understand. I know I was twenty-three, I had just started working at the magazine, you and I were living together in that horrible flat in the Liberties, and Kate was still in Dublin, and Tom, and Aoife. We went out to parties together, we had people over for dinner, we drank too much wine, we got into arguments. Sometimes Simon would call me on the phone from Paris so we could complain to each other about work, and while we were laughing, I would hear Natalie in the background, putting away plates in the kitchen. All my feelings and experiences were in one sense extremely intense, and in another sense completely trivial, because none of my decisions seemed to have any consequences, and nothing about my life — the job, the apartment, the desires, the love affairs — struck me as permanent. I felt anything was possible, that there were no doors shut behind me, and that out there somewhere, as yet unknown, there were people who would love and admire me and want to make me happy. Maybe that explains in some way the openness I felt toward the world — maybe without knowing it, I was anticipating my future, I was watching for signs.

A couple of nights ago, I was getting a taxi home on my own after a book launch. The streets were quiet and dark, and the air was oddly warm and still, and on the quays the office buildings were all lit up inside, and empty, and underneath everything, beneath the surface of everything, I began to feel it all over again — the nearness, the possibility of beauty, like a light radiating softly from behind the visible world, illuminating everything. As soon as I realised what I was feeling, I tried to move toward it in my thoughts, to reach out and handle it, but it only cooled a little or shrank away from me, or slipped off further ahead. The lights in the empty offices had reminded me of something, and I had been thinking about you, trying to imagine your house, I think, and I remembered I'd had an email from you, and at the same time I was thinking of Simon, the mystery of him, and somehow as I looked out the taxi window I started to think about his physical presence in the city, that somewhere inside the city's structure, standing or sitting, holding his arms one way or another, dressed or undressed, he was present, and Dublin was like an advent calendar concealing him behind one of its million windows, and the quality of the air was instilled, the temperature was instilled, with his presence, and with your email, and with this message I was writing back to you in my head even then. The world seemed capable of including these things, and my eyes were capable, my brain was capable, of receiving and understanding them. I was tired, it was late, I was sitting half-asleep in the back of a taxi, remembering strangely that wherever I go, you are with me, and so is he, and that as long as you both live the world will be beautiful to me.

I had no idea you had been reading the Bible in hospital. What made you want to do that? And did you find it helpful? I thought it was very interesting what you said about the forgiveness of sins. I asked Simon the other night whether he prays to God, and he told me yes — 'to say thank you'. And I think if I believed in God, I wouldn't want to prostrate myself before him and ask for forgiveness. I would just want to thank him every day, for everything.

17.

The second Friday evening in May, Felix spent eight minutes in the security queue leaving work. One of the people ahead of him had set the machine off and was taken into a side room to be searched. A sheet of paper on the door read: SUPERVISORS ONLY, ID TO ENTER. The queue stalled outside and the sound of raised voices came from inside the room. Felix exchanged a glance with the person standing in front of him, but neither spoke. By the time he got through the scanner and into his car, it was thirteen minutes past seven. The sky was dense and white overhead, with shafts of sunlight penetrating here and there through the low cloud. He switched the CD player on, reversed out of the parking space and left the industrial estate.

A few minutes down the road, he pulled off into a flat gravel area overlooking the sea. A wooden visitor centre at the entrance was closed up and no other cars were nearby. At one end a large yellow posterboard displayed information of historical and geographical interest. Felix parked at the outermost edge of the lot, the Atlantic stretching grey and rough outside the windshield. He unbuckled his seatbelt and unzipped the black puffer jacket he was wearing, revealing a faded-green sweatshirt underneath, with a small white embroidered logo. He took his phone out of his pocket, switched it on, and then opened the glovebox and started to roll himself a joint. The phone made various buzzing noises, receiving messages which had come in while he was at work, and his eyes flicked back and forth between the screen in his lap and the rolling paper on the steering wheel. When he was finished, he held the unlit joint in his mouth and scrolled through the messages and notifications onscreen: various social media alerts and app notifications, and one direct text message, from his brother Damian.

Damian: What time are you off tonight? You can come over here or I can bring everything over to yours if it suits better, let me know

Felix reclined the driver's seat, looked up at the fuzzy grey interior of the car ceiling, and sparked his lighter. For a moment he closed his eyes, inhaling, and then he lifted his phone and opened the message thread. The previous text was one Felix had sent yesterday, reading: Off work tmr night, will call u. Before that were several missed call notifications from Damian. Ten days previously, a text from Felix read: Hey sorry no im away. He stared at the thread blankly and then closed it. For a while, taking long drags and exhaling slowly, he scrolled through his other notifications, dismissing or checking them as he went along. He had received one new message through a dating app, which he opened up on-screen.

Patrick: you around tonight?

Felix tapped on the name 'Patrick' and flicked through the uploaded photographs. In one image, a group of men posed at a social event with their arms around one another's shoulders. In another, a bearded man knelt by a body of water holding an enormous fish, its body mottled and iridescent under sunlight. Felix went back to the message and typed in the reply field: Might be, whats up? Without hitting send, he

234

returned to the message he had received from his brother. He locked his phone then and went on smoking and listening to music. At times he hummed or sang along absent-mindedly, his voice light and pleasant. Outside, rain started to drum on the windshield.

At five to eight, he flicked his stub out the window and reversed out of the car park. His eyes were a little glassy now. Approaching the village, he hit the indicator, and then picked his phone up off the dashboard and squinted at it again. There were no new messages. For no apparent reason, he switched off his indicator light and continued driving straight. A car behind him beeped its horn and Felix murmured peaceably: Yeah, alright, fuck off. He kept one hand on the steering wheel and used the other to make a phone call.

After two rings, a voice answered: Hello?

You at home? said Felix.

In my house? Yes.

Busy?

No, not at all. Why?

I'm just out of work, he said. Thought I might swing by and see you if you're around. What do you think?

Well, I'm certainly around. I'm right here.

Be there in a minute, then, said Felix.

He hung up and dropped his phone noise-lessly onto the passenger seat. After a few more minutes on the road, a large white house appeared on the left, and he hit the indicator once again.

It was still raining when he rang the bell. Alice came out to the door wearing a woollen jumper over a dark skirt. Her feet were bare. She had her arms crossed over her chest, and then she uncrossed them. Felix stood looking at her, put a hand in his pocket and slightly closed one eye as if he was having trouble focusing.

Hey, he said. Am I disturbing you?

Not remotely. Would you like to come in?

Seeing as I'm here, I suppose.

He followed her inside, closing the door. She went through to the living room, a large space, painted red, with an open fire in the hearth. Facing the fire was a couch, laden with throws and cushions in various colours. On the coffee table a book was splayed open, pages down, next to a hot cup of tea. Felix stopped inside the doorway as Alice walked in.

All looks very cosy, he said.

She leaned against the couch, crossing her arms again.

What are you up to, reading? he asked.

Yes, I was.

I hope I'm not disturbing you.

You said that already, she said. And I told you you're not.

For a moment neither said anything further. Felix looked down at the fawn-coloured carpet, or at his own shoes.

I haven't heard from you in a while, she said then.

Apparently unsurprised, he continued to study the carpet. Yeah, he answered.

She said nothing. After a moment he flicked a quick glance up at her.

Are you annoyed? he asked.

I'm not annoyed, no. I have been feeling confused. Honestly, I assumed you didn't want to see me anymore. I was wondering if I'd done something wrong.

He frowned. Ah no, he said. You didn't do anything. Look, you're right, I was conscious the days had gone by a bit.

She nodded, inexpressive.

Do you want me to go? he said.

She moved her mouth around uncertainly for a moment. I'm not sure what's going on exactly, she said. But then maybe that's my fault.

He appeared to give this some thought, or perhaps made a show of doing so. Well, I wouldn't say it's your fault only, he said. I know what you mean by it. I think the fault

237

is shared. I'm not really looking for any big commitments in my life at the moment, if I'm honest.

I see.

Yeah, he said. And what with the whole trip to Italy, I thought, you know. Maybe best to take it a bit more casually after that.

Right.

He rocked back a little on his heels. Alright so, he said. I'll go, then, will I?

If you like.

For a few moments he didn't move, but stayed looking around the room vaguely. You don't care anyway, do you not? he said.

Excuse me?

He took a deep breath in through his nose and repeated slowly: You don't care anyway, or do you?

Care about what?

I mean, if I go or I don't go. If you hear from me or not. You don't care either way.

I should think it's obvious I do care, she said. You're the one saying you don't.

But you're not acting like you do.

With a kind of amazed smile, she replied: What would you like me to do, fall on my knees and beg you not to leave?

He laughed to himself. Good question, he said. I don't know, maybe I do want that.

Well, you're not going to get it.

I can see I'm not.

They looked at one another. She frowned at him, and he laughed again, shook his head and turned his face away.

Fuck me, he said. I don't know. Why do I always feel like you're the boss and I just have to do what you tell me?

I have no idea why you feel that way. I don't think I ever tell you what to do.

She was still looking at him but he would not return her gaze, looking off in the direction of the skirting board.

Finally she said: Since you're here, would you like a drink?

Gazing around the room, he gave a kind of shrug. Yeah, alright, why not, he said.

I have a bottle of wine out there, shall I get some glasses?

He frowned to himself, and then said: Okay, yeah. He cleared his throat and added: Thanks.

She went out to the kitchen and he took off his jacket, hung it over the back of an armchair and sat down on the sofa. He took his phone from his pocket and looked at the screen, which displayed a missed call from Damian. He opened the notification with a swipe and then typed a message.

Felix: Hey sorry im not at home tonight.

Might give u a buzz tomorrow

Within seconds a reply arrived.

Damian: It's been nearly 3 weeks. Where are you?

Felix screwed his features up in a frown and began to type his response, deleting and retyping several words as he went along.

Felix: I was away the week before last and this week been at work as I said, im off tomorrow so I will give u a ring then

He sent the message, locked his phone and sat staring into the fire. Alice came back into the room carrying two empty glasses and a bottle of red wine. He watched her while she opened the bottle and filled both the glasses.

Are we going to have one of our deep life conversations now? he said.

She handed him a glass and sat down on the other end of the sofa. Hm, she said. I think I'm still getting my bearings. I'm not sure I feel ready for a deep conversation.

He nodded and looked down into his drink. Fair enough, he said. What do you want to do, watch a film or something?

We can if you like.

She suggested he could look through her Netflix account, and after keying in her password she handed him the laptop. He opened a web browser while she sipped her drink and watched the fire. With two fingers he scrolled aimlessly through a series of thumbnails, glancing up at her now and then as if distracted. Finally he said: Here, I don't know what kind of films you like, you pick something. As long as it doesn't have subtitles, I'll watch it. He handed her the laptop and she took it from him without speaking. He closed his eyes and let his head tip back against the upper part of the sofa. Christ I'm tired, he said. If I drink that now I probably shouldn't drive. She went on scrolling and said: You can stay the night here if you like. He said nothing. The screen displayed a list of category titles like 'Critically Acclaimed Emotional Movies', 'Dark Suspenseful Movies', 'Dramas Adapted from Books'. A dead branch cracked in the fireplace and sent out a shower of sparks, hissing. Alice looked around at Felix, who was sitting very still with his eyes closed. She watched him for a few seconds, and then closed her laptop. He didn't stir. For some time she sat cross-legged on the couch, watching the play of flames in the grate, finishing her glass of wine, and then she left the room, turning out the ceiling light.

Two and a half hours later, seated in the same position, Felix woke up. The room was dark except for the remains of the fire. Running water was audible from somewhere inside the house. He sat up straight, wiped his mouth and took his phone out of his pocket. It was almost eleven at night, and he had received a single new message.

Damian: Cop on to yourself Felix. Where are you now that you can't ring me?

Felix began composing a response, typing How is it and then deleting How and typing Is it your, and then he stopped. For a time he sat staring into the low burning embers in the grate, which cast a deep burnished glow over his face and clothes. Eventually he rose from the couch and left the room. The hallway outside was bright and he stood at the staircase with his brow knitted, as if letting his eyes adjust. In the kitchen, Alice was laughing, and saying aloud: Oh, I wouldn't let a little detail like that bother me. He walked down the hall and stopped in the open doorway. Inside, Alice was look-

242

ing in the fridge, her back turned to him. The light of the fridge formed a white rectangular frame around her body. She was holding her phone to her ear with one hand and propping the door of the fridge open with the other. Perhaps unconsciously imitating her gesture, Felix placed his right hand on the jamb of the kitchen doorway, watching her, saying nothing. She continued laughing. Send pictures, will you? she said. She let the fridge door swing shut and walked over to the sink. In front of her, the black kitchen window reflected the lighted interior of the room. Glancing up then, she caught sight of Felix standing behind her. Without surprise, she said into the phone: I'm going to hang up on you now because someone's just come in, but I'll see you next week, won't I? Felix stood there, no longer watching her but staring down at the floor. I like to keep you guessing, Alice said into the phone. Talk to you soon, goodnight. She left her phone down on the countertop and turned to face Felix. Without looking up, he cleared his throat and said: Sorry about that. I've been working weird hours, obviously I was more tired than I thought. She told him not to worry about it. He moved his jaw a little, nodding. She faced him a moment longer and then, when he still did not look at her, she turned away, wrapping up a loaf of bread.

Did you have a long day at work? she asked.

As if straining to sound amused, he replied: They all feel long in that place.

Now that her back was turned, he had started to watch her again. She emptied some crusts of bread from a small white plate into the pedal bin.

Who was that on the phone? he asked.

Oh, just a friend of mine.

Your friend Eileen?

No, she said. It's funny, Eileen and I never talk on the phone. No, it was a friend of mine called Daniel, I don't think I've mentioned him before. He lives in London, he's a writer.

Felix went on nodding to himself. I'd say you have a lot of writer friends, do you? he asked.

A few.

He lingered in the doorway, rubbing his left eyelid roughly with his fingertips. Alice took a cloth from the sink and wiped down the surface of the kitchen table.

Sorry I never texted you back during the week there, he said.

It's alright, don't worry about it.

I had a good time with you in Italy, I feel

244

bad if you thought I didn't.

That's okay, she said. I had a good time too.

He swallowed and put his hand back down into his pocket. Can I stay the night here? he asked. I think I'm actually too out of it to drive home. I can sleep on the couch if you want.

Putting the cloth back in the sink, she said she would make up one of the beds. He looked down at the floor. She came to stand in front of him, and said in a kindly tone of voice: Felix, are you okay? He gave a half-smile. Yeah, I'm sound, he said. Just tired. Finally he met her eyes and said: You don't want to sleep together, do you? It's alright if you've gone off the idea, I know I was a bit of a prick about it. She looked back at him, her eyes moving over his face. I did feel foolish when I didn't hear from you, she said. Can you understand why I felt that way or do you think I'm being crazy? Apparently uncomfortable now, he said he didn't think she was being crazy, and that he had meant to reply to her message, but time had passed and he had started to feel awkward about it. He was kneading his shoulder under his hand. Look, I'll go, he said. I can drive, I'm grand. I never had that glass of wine in the end anyway. Sorry I interrupted your phone call there, you can ring your friend back if you want.

I'd prefer if you stayed, she said. With me, if that's what you'd like. I don't mind.

You don't mind, or you want me to?

I want you to. Although if you ghost me again afterwards, I might start to suspect you actually hate me.

He looked pleased then, and released his shoulder from under the grip of his hand. No, I'll remember my manners, he said. You'll get a nice normal message tomorrow saying I enjoyed myself.

With an arch look, she replied: Oh, is that the normal thing?

Well, the last person I was with, I never did message her. I think she might be annoyed with me about it, I'm not sure.

Maybe you should try showing up at her house out of the blue and then falling asleep on her couch for two hours.

He put his hand on his chest, as if wounded. Alice, he said. Don't savage me. I'm embarrassed about that. Come here.

She went to him and he kissed her. He moved his hands over her body and she sighed softly. His phone started to vibrate in his pocket, the droning noise of an incoming call. Do you want to get that? she said. No, he replied, it's alright, I'll knock it off. Removing his phone from his pocket, he tapped a button to reject a phone call from Damian's number, and went on: Do you know what I really feel like doing? I want to go up and lie on your bed and you tell me all what you did during the week. Alice said that sounded very innocent. Well, I can take your clothes off while you're talking, he said, how about that? She flushed then, touched her lip, and said: If you like. He watched her with a kind of mischievous amusement. Am I making you blush saying that? he asked. I wouldn't mind, but you're the one who writes filthy books for a living. She said her books were not filthy, and he said he had read on the internet that they were. And I know you don't get embarrassed talking about sex in public, because I've seen you, he said. Up there onstage when we were in Rome, you were talking about it. Alice said that was different, because it was not personal, only abstract. He studied her for a moment. Can I ask, he said, are you going over to London this week, or is your friend coming over here? Not to be nosy, but I heard you saying you'd see him next week. Smiling, she said she had to go to London for work. Such a jet-setter, he replied. Although London's a bit of a kip so I won't be jealous. I used to live there. His phone started to vibrate again and he sighed, removing it from his pocket once more. I won't ask who's calling, Alice said. Holding down the button, Felix answered distractedly: Ah, it's just my brother. I'm not going behind your back falling asleep on anyone else's couches, don't worry. She laughed then, which seemed to please him. Pocketing the phone again, he said: Can we head upstairs? If we stay up much later I won't be any good to you, I'm wrecked.

They went up to Alice's bedroom and sat on her bed together. She took his hand and kissed it, making a line of kisses up from his knuckle along his fingers, and then put the tip of his index finger in her mouth. At first he said nothing and then after a few seconds he said: Ah, fuck. He put his middle finger into her mouth and she ran her tongue along its underside. Alice, he said. Can I ask, do you like giving head at all? It's alright if you don't. Taking his fingers out of her mouth, she said yes. Can we do that now, what do you think? he said. With her mouth open and relaxed-looking, she reached under the waistband of his sweatpants. He lay down on his back with his head propped up on the pillows, and she went down on him. He watched her. A lock of her light hair falling forward, covering part of her face. And her lips wet, her eyes half-closed. She asked him if it was okay. Yeah, it's good, he said. Come here for a second. She moved up beside him and he put his hand under her skirt. Closing her eyes, she held on to the headboard behind him. Do you want to get on top of me? he said. She nodded her head. Clothes on or off? she asked. He frowned thoughtfully. Off, he said. But I'll leave mine on if it's the same to you. Taking her jumper off, she grinned and said: Is that a power play? He put a hand behind his head, watching her undoing the buttons of her blouse. No, I'm just lazy, he said. She took the blouse off and unhooked her bra. Do I look nice with my clothes off? she asked. He was touching his cock slowly while watching her. Yeah, you do, he said. Did I not tell you that before? Pulling her skirt and underwear off over her ankles, she said: I think as a teenager I did, but not anymore. Leaving her clothes hanging over the end of the bed, she got on top of him. I liked having you in my mouth, she said. Her eyes were closed, he was looking up her. That's nice of you to say, he said. What did you like about it? She was breathing deeply. I was afraid you were going to be rough with me, she said, but you were very gentle. I don't even mean rough, I just mean, I was afraid you would want me to try and take more of it when I knew I couldn't. He had his left hand on her hip. You mean like the people in porn, he said. She said yes. Yeah, but I think that's a fairly specialised skill they have, he said. I wouldn't expect your average person to be able to do that. With her eyes closed, Alice said that if he wanted her to learn how to do it, she would want to try. Still watching her face attentively he said: Don't worry about that. You give very good head the way it is. Is that what you prefer to call it, by the way? Or something else? She was smiling, she said she wasn't fussy. But there must be some words that turn you off a bit, he said. Would there not be? Like if I said, I want you to suck my cock, you probably wouldn't like it. She laughed and said she wouldn't mind, but she thought it sounded more funny than sexy. He agreed it was funny, and said it sounded like something from a film. Do you hate the word 'fuck'? he said. Some people do, I don't mind it. But if I said, can we fuck now, would that put you off? She said it would not put her off. Alright, he said, let me fuck you, then. He withdrew his hand, his fingers glistening wet and leaving wet prints on her skin where he touched her. When the head of his cock entered her she took a deep breath and gripped his shoulder under her hand. He was still fully dressed, wearing the same green sweatshirt with the little embroidered logo. You're very small with your clothes off, he said. I don't think I noticed you so small before. She made a moaning noise, shook her head, and said nothing. He sat up a little more and surveyed her. Do you need a second? he asked. She was taking long breaths and releasing them slowly, eyes closed. I'm okay, she said. Is that all of it? Perhaps because she wasn't looking, he allowed himself to smile. Well, nearly, he said. Are you alright? Her face and neck were red. It is a lot, she said. He ran his hand down her side affectionately. Mm, he said. But it doesn't hurt, does it? Still with her eyes held shut she replied: I think it did hurt a little bit the first time. He was touching her breast softly. The first time we were together? he said. You didn't tell me. She shook her head, frowning as if with concentration. No, she said, but I didn't want you to stop, it was nice. It makes me feel very full. He licked his upper lip, still watching her. Ah, I love making you feel like that, he said. She opened her eyes and looked at him. He put his hands on her hips and pulled her down a little, gently, until he was all the way inside her. She drew in one long breath and then nodded, still looking at him. For a couple of minutes they fucked and said nothing. She shut her eyes tightly and he asked again if she was okay. Do you find it really intense, she said. He was looking up at her with an open expression on his face. Yeah, he said. I don't think you could have looked better when you were a teenager than you do now, by the way. You look unbelievable now. And I have one more thought about it. A lot of what's so sexy about you is the way you talk, and the little things you do. And I bet you couldn't behave so nicely when you were younger, could you? And even if you could, not to be soft about it, but I'd still rather have you the way you are. Her breath was ragged then and she reached for his hand, which he gave to her. I'm coming, she said. She was holding his hand very tight. Quietly he said: Look at me for a second. She looked at him. Her mouth was open and she was crying out, her chest and neck pink. He looked back at her, and he was breathing hard. Finally she lay down against his chest, her knees drawn up around him. He ran his hand down over her spine. A minute went by, then five minutes. Here, don't fall asleep like that, he said. Let's lie down properly. She rubbed her eye with the back of her hand, and got up off him. He rearranged his clothes while she lay down naked on the mattress beside him. Then he took her hand and kissed it. That was alright, he said, wasn't it? She nestled her head back on the pillow and laughed. I didn't know you used to live in London, she said. He smiled to himself, still holding her hand. There's a lot you don't know about me, he said. She rolled her shoulders luxuriously against the bedsheets.

Tell me everything, she said.

18.

Friend of my heart! Sorry for the delay — I write to you from Paris, having just arrived here from London, where I had to go and pick up an award. They never tire of giving me awards, do they? It's a shame I've tired so quickly of receiving them, or my life would be endless fun. Anyway, I miss you. I was sitting in the Musée d'Orsay this morning looking at sweet little Marcel Proust's portrait, and wishing John Singer Sargent had painted him instead. He's quite ugly in the painting, but despite this unfortunate fact (and I do mean despite!) something in his eyes reminded me of you. Probably just the glow of brilliance. 'Perhaps indeed there exists but a single intelligence, in which everyone in the world participates, towards which each of us from the position of his own separate body turns his eyes, as in a theatre where, if everyone has his own separate seat, there is on the other hand but a single stage.' Reading those words I feel terribly happy — to think that I might share an intelligence with you.

On the top floor of the museum today, I noticed there were several portraits of Berthe Morisot, all painted by Edouard Manet. In every painting Morisot looks a little bit different, so it's hard to imagine how she really looked — how she combined each different shade of her likeness into one full and recognisable human face. I searched for a photograph afterwards and was surprised by the solidity of her features, which in Manet's work often look cloudy or delicate. In one of the paintings she's handsome, dark, statuesque in a white dress; she sits on a balcony alongside two other figures, her forearm relaxed against the parapet, her hand holding a closed fan; she's looking away, almost frowning, her face is complex and expressive, she's deep in thought. In another painting she's soft-featured, pretty, gazing out at the viewer in a tall black hat and black shawl, her gaze at once uncertain and revealing. She was the model Manet painted more often than any other, more often than his own wife. But when I look at the paintings I don't always recognise her as beautiful right away. Her beauty is something I have to search for, requiring some interpretive work, some intellectual or abstract work, and maybe that's what Manet found so fascinating about it — but then again maybe not. For six years Morisot came to his studio, chaperoned by her mother, and he painted her, always clothed. Several of her own paintings hang in the museum too. Two girls sharing a park bench in the Bois de Boulogne, one in a white dress, wearing a broad straw hat, bending her head forward over her lap, maybe she's reading, the other girl in a dark dress, her long fair hair tied back with a black ribbon, showing to the viewer her white neck and ear. Behind them all the lush vague greenery of the public park. But Morisot never painted Manet. Six years after she met him, and apparently at his suggestion, she married his brother. He painted her just once more, wedding ring glittering dark on her delicate hand, and then never again. Don't you think that's a love story? It reminds me of you and Simon. And to give myself away even further, I duly add: thank God he has no brothers!

The problem with museums like the d'Orsay, by the way and just totally incidentally, is that there's far too much art, so that no matter how well you plan your route or how noble your intentions, you will always find yourself walking irritably past priceless works of profound genius looking for the bathrooms. And you feel slightly cheapened afterwards, like you've let yourself down — at least I do. I bet you never look for the bathrooms in museums, Eileen. I bet as soon as you enter the hallowed halls of Europe's great galleries, you simply leave such corporeal practicalities behind you — if indeed they ever plague you in the first place. One doesn't think of you as a corporeal being really, but as a beam of pure intellect. And how I wish I had a little more of your radiance illuminating my life at the moment.

Yesterday afternoon I gave three interviews and did an hour-long photoshoot, and between two of the interviews, my father called me to tell me that he had a fall and he's back in hospital getting an x-ray. His voice sounded thin and his speech was quite garbled. I received the call while standing in the corridor of my publisher's office building in Montparnasse. In front of me was an entrance to the ladies' toilets, and beside that a large poster for a bestselling paperback by a French writer. I asked him what time the x-ray was scheduled but he had no idea — I'm not even sure how he managed to place the call. When we hung up, I went straight back down the corridor and into an office room, where a nice female journalist in her forties proceeded to conduct an hour-long interview with me about my influences and literary style. The photoshoot afterwards took place on the street. Several passers-by stopped to watch, perhaps curious as to who I was and why my photograph was being taken, while the photographer gave instructions such as: 'Relax your face', and 'Try to look more your normal self.' At eight p.m., a car took me to an event space in Montmartre, where I gave a public reading and answered audience questions, sipping intermittently from a tiny plastic bottle of lukewarm water.

This morning, tired and disorientated, I wandered down the street near my hotel and eventually found and entered an empty church. There I sat for about twenty minutes bathed in the slow serious air of sanctity and cried a few picturesque tears about the nobility of Jesus. This is all by way of explaining to you my interest in Christianity — put simply, I am fascinated and touched by the 'personality' of Jesus, in rather a sentimental, arguably even maudlin way. Everything about his life moves me. On the one hand, I feel toward him a kind of personal attraction and closeness that is most reminiscent of my feeling for certain beloved fictional characters — which makes sense, considering that I've encountered him through exactly the same means, i.e. by reading about him in books. On the other hand, I feel humbled and impressed by him in a different way. He seems to me to embody a kind of moral beauty, and my admiration for that beauty even makes me want to say that I 'love' him, though I'm well aware how ridiculous that sounds. But, Eileen, I do love him, and I can't even pretend that it's only the same love I feel for Prince Myshkin, or for Charles Swann, or for Isabel Archer. It is actually something different, a different feeling. And while I don't, as such, really 'believe' that Jesus was resurrected after his death, it's also true to say that some of the most moving scenes in the Gospels, and some of those to which I return most frequently, take place after the resurrection. I find it hard to separate the Jesus who appears after the resurrection from the man who appears before; they seem to me to be all of one being. I suppose what I mean is that in his resurrected form, he goes on saying the kind of things that 'only he' could say, that I can't imagine emanating from any other consciousness. But that's as close as I get to thinking about his divinity. I have a strong liking and affection for him and I feel moved when I contemplate his life and death. That's all.

Rather than filling me with spiritual peace, however, the example set by Jesus only makes my existence seem trivial and shallow in comparison. In public I'm always talking about care ethics and the value of human community, but in my real life I don't take on the work of caring for anyone except myself. Who in the world relies on me for anything? No one. I can blame myself, and I do, but I also think the failure is general. People our age used to get married and have children and conduct love affairs, and now everyone is still single at thirty and lives with housemates they never see. Traditional marriage was obviously not fit for purpose, and almost ubiquitously ended in one kind of failure or another, but at least it was an effort at something, and not just a sad sterile foreclosure on the possibility of life. Of course if we all stay alone and practise celibacy and carefully police our personal boundaries, many problems will be avoided, but it seems we will also have almost nothing left that makes life worthwhile. I guess you could say the old ways of being together were wrong — they were! — and that we didn't want to repeat old mistakes — we didn't. But when we tore down what confined us, what did we have in mind to replace it? I offer no defence of coercive heterosexual monogamy, except that it was at least a way of doing things, a way of seeing life through. What do we have now? Instead? Nothing. And we hate people for making mistakes so much more than we love them for doing good that the easiest way to live is to do nothing, say nothing, and love no one.

However: Jesus teaches us not to judge. I can't approve of unforgiving puritanism or of moral vanity, but I am hardly perfect in either regard. All my mania for culture, for 'really good' things, for knowing about jazz recordings and red wine and Danish furniture, even about Keats and Shakespeare and James Baldwin, what if it's all a form of vanity, or even worse, a little bandage over the initial wound of my origins? I have put between myself and my parents such a gulf of sophistication that it's impossible for them to touch me now or to reach me at all. And I look back across that gulf, not with a sense of guilt or loss, but with relief and satisfaction. Am I better than they are? Certainly not, although maybe luckier. But I am different, and I don't understand them very well, and I can't live with them or draw them into my inner world — or for that matter write about them. All my filial duties are nothing but a series of rituals on my part designed to shield myself from criticism while giving nothing of myself away. It was touching what you said in your last message about our civilisation collapsing and life going on afterwards. And yet I can't imagine my life that way — I mean whatever goes on, it won't be my life anymore, not really. Because in my deepest essence I am just an artefact of our culture, just a little bubble winking at the brim of our civilisation. And when it's gone, I'll be gone. Not that I think I mind.

PS — I hate to ask, but since Simon says he's coming along with you — should I make up two bedrooms or one?

19

On Friday morning it rained and Eileen took the bus to work. She had finished *The Karamazov Brothers* by then and was reading *The Golden Bowl,* standing up on the bus with one hand gripping the yellow upright rail and the other holding a copy of the novel in paperback. After alighting she put her scarf over her head and walked a couple of minutes to the office on Kildare Street in the rain. Inside, her colleagues were laughing at a satirical video about the Brexit negotiations. Eileen stood at the computer where they were gathered to watch it, looking over their shoulders at the screen, as the rain slid softly and noiselessly down the outer panes of the office windows. Oh, I've seen this one, she said. It's funny. After that she made a pot of coffee and sat down at her desk. She checked her phone and saw a message from Lola about a 'cake tasting' later that week. I'm busy tomorrow evening but otherwise free, Eileen wrote back. Let me know what works. Lola replied within a couple of minutes.

> Lola: What are you doing tomorrow
> Eileen: I have plans
> Lola: Heh heh
> Lola: Are you seeing someone??

Eileen glanced around the office, as if to check that no one was watching, and then, returning her attention to her phone, she began typing again.

> Eileen: no comment
> Lola: Is he tall
> Eileen: none of your business
> Eileen: but yes he's 6'3"
> Lola: !!
> Lola: Did you meet him on the internet?
> Lola: Is he a serial killer?
> Lola: Still if he's 6'3 I suppose it's swings and roundabouts
> Eileen: this interview is terminated
> Eileen: let me know about the 'cake tasting'
> Lola: Do you want to bring him to the wedding?
> Eileen: that won't be necessary
> Lola: Why not??

Eileen put her phone away and opened a new browser window on her work computer. For a moment she paused, staring at the search engine on the home page, and then quickly and lightly she tapped out the words 'eileen lydon' and hit the return key. A page of results showed on-screen, with a set of images displayed at the top. One was a photograph of Eileen herself, sandwiched between two black-and-white historical images. The other results were chiefly social media profiles belonging to other people, along with some obituaries and professional listings. At the bottom of the page, a link to the magazine's website read: <u>Eileen Lydon | Editorial Assistant</u>. She clicked the link and a new page opened. No photograph was included, and the text simply read: Eileen Lydon is an editorial assistant and contributor at the Harcourt Review. Her essay on the novels of Natalia Ginzburg appeared in <u>Issue 43, Winter 2015</u>. The final part of the sentence was hyperlinked and Eileen clicked it, leading her to a page on which the magazine issue could be purchased online. She closed the tab then and opened up her work email account.

At home that evening, Eileen called her parents' landline number, and her father Pat picked up the phone. They talked for a few minutes about a minor political controversy that had been in the news that day, both with similar or even identical tones of disapproval. Please God it won't be long before the next election, Pat said. Eileen told him she would keep her fingers crossed. He asked her how she was getting on at work and she said: Nothing to report. She was sitting on the bed in her room, one arm holding her phone to her ear, the other resting on her knees. I'll put you on to your mother, he said. A rasping noise then, and what sounded like clicking, before Mary's voice said into the receiver: Hello? Eileen gave a strained smile. Hello, she said. How are you? For a little while they talked about work. Mary told an anecdote involving a new member of staff at the school who had mixed up two female teachers who were both named Ms Walsh. That's funny, Eileen said. After that they talked about the wedding, a dress Eileen had seen in a shop window, two different pairs of shoes Mary was deciding between, and finally they moved on to the subjects of Lola's behaviour, Mary's responses to Lola's behaviour, and the underlying attitudes revealed by Mary's responses to Lola's behaviour. When she loses her temper with you, you expect me to take your side, said Eileen. But when she loses her temper with me, you say it's none of your business. Mary sighed loudly into the receiver. Okay, okay, she said, I'm a failure, I've let you both down, what more do you want me to say? Sternly, Eileen answered: No, I never said any of that. After a pause, Mary asked if she had any plans for the weekend. In a guarded tone of voice she said she was going to see Simon on Saturday night. Is he still with the new girlfriend? Mary asked. Eileen closed her eyes and said she didn't know. You were very fond of him at one time, Mary said. Eileen said nothing for a few seconds. Weren't you? Mary prompted. Eileen opened her eyes then. Yes, Mother, she answered. With a smile in her voice Mary went on: He's a handsome boy alright. Although he must be well into his thirties now, is he? I'm sure Andrew and Geraldine wouldn't mind seeing him settled. Eileen was rubbing her fingertip over a piece of embroidery on the quilt. Maybe he'll marry me, she said. Mary gave a shocked hoot of laughter. Oh, you're wicked, she said. And you know, the way you have him wrapped around your finger, I wouldn't be surprised. Is that your new scheme? Eileen replied that it was not 'a scheme'. Well, you'd be a lucky woman, said Mary. Eileen nodded her head in silence for a moment. And would he not be a lucky man? she asked then. Mary laughed again at that. Now Eileen, she said, you know I think the world of you. But I have to say that, because you're my daughter. Eileen went on tracing over the rough stubbled lines of the embroidery with her index finger. If you have to say it, why have I literally never heard you say it before? she asked. Mary was no longer laughing. Okay, pet, she said. I won't keep you any longer. You have a nice evening now. I love you.

After hanging up the phone, Eileen opened a messaging app and selected Simon's name. Their most recent exchange displayed on-screen, from the day before, and she scrolled back up to reread the messages in sequence.

Eileen: send me a photo of your room

The next message was a photograph of a hotel room interior, with a double bed taking up most of the floor space. On the bed was a purple duvet and a folded quilt in a different shade of purple.

Eileen: and now one with you in it . . . . . .
Simon: Haha

Simon: 'Senior political adviser caught sending explicit images from War of Independence commemoration ceremony'

Eileen: what did the IRA fight for if not our freedoms, Simon?

Simon: 'It's what the boys would have wanted,' insists disgraced former aide

Eileen: oh before I forget

Eileen: did you know Alice is in Paris this week?

Simon: You're not serious

Simon: Where did she fly from?

Eileen: didn't say but it has to be Dublin

Simon: International woman of mystery

Eileen: oh god do NOT say that

Eileen: that's exactly what she wants people to be saying

Simon: No, I just hope she's alright

Simon: If I'm back here early tonight I'll give you a ring, ok?

After that Eileen had posted the thumbs-up emoji. No further messages had been exchanged. She exited the thread now and returned to the home screen of the messaging app. For a moment her finger hovered over the button to close the app, and then, instead, as if on impulse, she tapped Lola's name. Lola's most recent message, from earlier that day, displayed onscreen: Why not?? With her thumbs Eileen began typing out a reply.

Eileen: because he's going to be there anyway

She hit send, and almost instantly an icon showed that Lola had 'seen' the message. The animated ellipsis appeared, and within a few seconds a reply arrived.

Lola: Oh my god
Lola: Speaking of serial killers
Lola: Please tell me it's not Simon Costigan

Eileen settled herself back against the headboard, typing.

Eileen: wow
Eileen: all these years and you're still mad that he likes me better than you
Lola: Eileen
Lola: You're not seriously going out with that freak are you
Eileen: if I am it's none of your business
Lola: You realise he goes to confession right
Lola: Like he literally tells his bad thoughts to a priest

270

Eileen: ok

Eileen: firstly, I don't think that's really what happens at confession

Lola: Money down he turns out to be sexually deviant

Lola: He definitely fancied you when you were 15

Lola: And he was at least 20

Lola: Wonder if he told any priests about that

Eileen: lmao

Eileen: in our entire lives, literally one man has ever liked me better than you

Eileen: and you still can't get over it

Lola: Alright kiddo

Lola: Just don't come crying to me when you're married and pregnant

Lola: And some schoolgirls from your neighbourhood start to mysteriously go missing . . . . . .

For a few seconds Eileen stared down at the screen of her phone, her head swaying absently from side to side, before she began typing again.

Eileen: do you know why you hate him Lola?

Eileen: it's because he's the only person who has ever taken my side against you

Lola saw this message, but no ellipsis appeared, and no reply arrived. Eileen locked her phone and pushed it away from her, down the bed. Stretching her legs out, she opened up her laptop and started to draft an email to Alice. Twenty minutes later her phone buzzed again and she retrieved it.

Lola: Actual lol

Reading this message, Eileen took a deep breath in and then allowed her eyes to close. Slowly the breath left her body and re-entered the room, the breath mingling now with the air of the room, moving through the air of the room and dispersing, droplets and microscopic aerosol particles diffusing through the air of the room and dropping slowly, slowly, toward the floor.

By ten o'clock the following night, Eileen was in the kitchen of a house in Pimlico, drinking whiskey from a plastic cup and talking to a woman named Leanne. The hours can be long, yeah, Leanne was saying. I'd be in there until nine a few times a week, anyway. Eileen was wearing a black silk blouse and had a thin gold chain around her neck, which glinted under the light from the ceiling fixture. Music was playing from the living room and beside them, at the sink, someone was trying to open a bottle of sparkling wine. Eileen said she left work before six o'clock most evenings. Leanne gave a high, almost horrified laugh. Jesus, she said. Six p.m.? Where do you work, sorry? Eileen told her she worked for a literary magazine. Paula, who was hosting the party, came over and offered them some sparkling wine. Eileen held up her cup and said: I'm good, thanks. The doorbell rang and Paula put down the bottle and went away again. Leanne started to tell Eileen about various late nights she had recently spent in the office, on one occasion getting a taxi home at half past six in the morning only to return to work in another taxi two hours later. I can't imagine that's good for your health, Eileen said. The door of the kitchen opened then, and Leanne turned around to see who had come in. It was Simon, wearing a white overshirt and carrying a canvas bag on his shoulder. At the sight of him, Leanne let out a cry of greeting. She threw her arms open and he accepted her embrace, looking past her at Eileen with a smile. Hello, he said. How are we?

God, it's been ages, said Leanne. Here, do you know Paula's friend Eileen?

Eileen stood against the kitchen table stroking her necklace absently with a finger-tip, looking back at him.

Ah, he said, we know each other rather well, actually.

Eileen started to laugh then, touching her lip with her tongue.

Oh, said Leanne. I'm sorry, I didn't re-alise.

Taking a bottle of wine out of his bag, he said in a relaxed tone: No, that's alright. Eileen and I grew up together.

Yes, Simon was very fond of me when I was a baby, Eileen said. He used to carry me around my back garden and give me little kisses. So my mother says.

He was smiling to himself, unscrewing the cap from his bottle of wine. Even as a child of five I had beautiful taste, he said. Only the finest babies made the grade.

Glancing back and forth between them now, Leanne asked Simon if he was still working in Leinster House. For my sins, he said. Do you see a glass handy? Leanne said all the glasses were dirty, but there were plastic cups on the table. Let me find a dirty one, I'll wash it, he said. Eileen informed Leanne that Simon would no longer use plastic cups, out of respect for Mother Earth. Simon, who was rinsing a wine glass under the cold tap, said: She does make me sound insufferable, doesn't she? But Leanne, tell me, how is work? Leanne started to tell him about her job, with specific reference to some colleagues of hers who were friends of his. A man in a denim jacket came inside from the back yard, pulling the door behind him, saying aloud to no one in particular: Getting cold out there. Through the kitchen doorway, Eileen caught the eye of their friend Peter, and waving her hand she went out to greet him. She glanced back once over her shoulder to see Simon and Leanne in conversation, Simon leaning against the kitchen countertop, Leanne standing in front of him, twisting a lock of her hair between her fingers.

The living room was small and cramped, with a staircase against one wall and potted plants on the bookcases, leaves trailing over the spines of books. Peter was at the fireplace taking his jacket off, talking to Paula about the same political controversy Eileen had discussed with her father the evening before. No, no one comes out of it looking good, Peter was saying. Well, except Sinn Féin, obviously. Someone had connected their phone to the speakers and an Angel Olsen song started playing, while from the hallway their friend Hannah came inside.

Peter and Eileen allowed their conversation to taper off while Hannah made her way over to join them, holding a bottle of wine by the neck, bangles clinking on her wrists. Immediately she started to tell a story about a problem with the garage door at her house that afternoon, and how long they'd had to wait for the workman to arrive, and how she had been late to meet her mother for lunch in town. While Eileen listened, her eyes travelled back to the kitchen doorway, through which Simon's figure was still partly visible, still leaning against the countertop, though several other people had joined him now. Following her gaze, Peter said: The big man. I didn't know he was here. Hannah had found a clean plastic cup on the coffee table and was pouring herself a drink. She asked who they were talking about and Peter said Simon. Oh, I hope he's brought Caroline, Hannah replied. At this remark Eileen's attention moved quickly from the kitchen doorway back to Hannah. No, Paula said, not tonight. Hannah was screwing the cap back on her bottle while Eileen watched. That's a shame, Hannah said. Leaving the bottle down on the coffee table, she caught Eileen's eye, and asked: Have you met her yet, Eileen?

Caroline, Eileen repeated. Is that . . . ?

The girl Simon is seeing, Paula said.

Eileen was smiling now, with some perceptible effort. No, she answered. No, we haven't met.

Hannah swallowed a mouthful of wine and went on: Oh, she's great. You'll love her. You've met her, Peter, haven't you?

Turning as if to address Eileen, he said: Yeah, she seemed nice. And she's only about ten years younger than him, so that's an improvement.

You are horrible, Hannah retorted.

Eileen gave a brittle laugh. I never get to meet them, she said. For some reason he doesn't like to introduce me, I don't know why.

How curious, said Peter.

I'm sure that's not true, said Hannah.

To Eileen, Peter went on: Because, you know, I've always had that little question mark about the two of you.

Hannah let out a horrified laugh, and grabbed Eileen by the upper arm. Don't listen to him, she said. He doesn't know what he's talking about.

Their friend Roisin came up to join them then, wanting to ask Peter for his take on the same political controversy they had been discussing before. When Eileen went to the kitchen at midnight for another drink, she stopped to look through the back window, where Simon's figure was visible dimly, talking to the woman whose name was Leanne. A cigarette was hanging loosely between Leanne's index and middle fingers, and with her other hand she was touching Simon's shirt collar. Eileen put the bottle away and left the kitchen. In the living room Roisin was sitting on Peter's lap for the purpose of acting out a funny anecdote. Eileen stood by the sofa sipping her drink, smiling at the punchline while everyone laughed. Afterwards she went out to the hallway and took her jacket from underneath a few others that had been left on the same hook. She went out the front door then and closed it behind her. The air outside was cool. Behind her the living room window of Paula's house was lit up, a deep warm golden colour, and from within came the muted noise of music and voices. Eileen took her phone from her pocket. The time on the screen was 00:08. She went out the front gate onto the pavement and put her hands into the pockets of her jacket.

Before she had reached the corner of the street, the door of Paula's house opened up again and Simon came out onto the front step. Without closing the door behind him, he called out: Hey, are you leaving? Eileen turned around. Between them the street was empty and dark, the curved hoods of parked cars reflecting the streetlights dimly. Yeah, she said. He stood there for a moment just looking at her, maybe frowning. Well, can I walk you home? he asked. She shrugged. Wait there for a second, he said. He went back inside and she stood with her hands in her pockets, elbows out, staring down at the cracked pavement surface. When he re-emerged and closed the door behind him, the sound echoed against the walls of the terrace opposite. Bending down, he un-locked his bicycle from the railing of Paula's front yard, and then put his bike lock and key into the canvas bag he had brought with him. She stood watching him. Straightening up again, he wheeled his bike over to where she was standing. Hey, he said. Is everything okay? She nodded her head. You left kind of abruptly, he said. I was looking for you.

You couldn't have been looking for very long, she said. It's an extremely small house.

He gave a kind of puzzled smile. No, well, you hadn't been gone for very long, he said. You're only about fifty feet from the door.

Eileen started walking again and Simon went along with her, his bike clicking quietly between them.

I thought it was nice of Leanne to try and

introduce us earlier, he said.

Yes, I noticed she got a hug. I didn't even get a handshake.

He laughed. I know, I really behaved myself, didn't I? he said. But I think she got the idea.

Tonelessly, Eileen said: Did she.

Looking down at her now, he was frowning again. Well, I didn't want to embarrass you, he answered. What do you think I should have said? Oh, Eileen and I don't need to be introduced. Actually, we're lovers.

And are we? she asked.

Hm. I suppose that's one of those words nobody uses anymore.

They reached the corner of the street and took a left to leave the estate and walk back toward the main road. Above them, narrow trees planted at intervals along the footpath, in full leaf. Eileen's hands were still in her pockets. She cleared her throat, and then said aloud: Your friends were just telling me how great this person Caroline is. The girl you're seeing. They all seem very fond of her, she's obviously made a big impression.

Simon was looking at Eileen as she spoke, but she was staring fixedly at the pavement ahead. Right, he said.

I didn't realise you'd introduced her to

280

everyone.

Not everyone, he said. She's come out for drinks with us a couple of times, that's all.

Almost inaudibly Eileen murmured: Jesus.

For a time neither of them spoke again. Finally he said: I did tell you I'd been seeing someone.

Am I the only one of your friends who hasn't met her? she asked.

I know how this sounds, but I really have been trying to do everything right. It's just — You know, it's not the most straightforward situation.

Eileen let out a harsh laugh. Yeah, it must be tough, she said. You can't fuck everyone, right? Or you can, but things eventually get awkward.

Simon seemed to consider this. After a moment he said: Look, I understand you're feeling upset, but I'm not sure if you're being completely fair.

I'm not upset, she answered.

His eyes moved over the street ahead of them. Seconds went by in silence while they walked, cars passing beside them on the road. Finally he said: You know, when I asked you out in February, you told me you just wanted to be friends. You never — and I'm not trying to be accusatory, I'm just giving you my perspective — you never showed any interest in me at all until I told you I was seeing someone else. Feel free to correct me if I'm wrong on that.

Eileen's head was bent forward, showing the long line of her neck over the collar of her jacket, her eyes on the pavement. She said nothing.

He went on: And when you did find out I was seeing someone, you decided you wanted to flirt with me and call me on the phone at night, okay, and then you want to come over when I'm in bed and we mess around or whatever, that's fine, I don't mind. As far as I can see, I've been very clear with you, there is someone else, but it's not exclusive, so if you want to sleep over in my apartment there's no problem. I'm not pressuring you to make any decisions about where we stand with each other, I'm happy to just spend time together and see how things go. From everything you said, I assumed that's what you wanted. And it's been really nice, for me at least. I completely understand why it's awkward for you to hear our friends talking about someone else I'm seeing, but it's not like you didn't know she existed.

While he spoke Eileen lifted her hand to her face, pushing her hair back roughly off her forehead, tension visible in her shoulders, in her neck, in the sharp almost jerking movements of her fingers. Jesus, she repeated. How Christian of you.

What does that mean? he asked.

With a laugh that sounded almost frightened she said: I can't believe I've been such a fool.

They had stopped walking, outside the entrance to a block of flats, beneath a streetlight. He was looking at her with concern. No, he said. You haven't been a fool. And I'm sorry I've upset you. It's the last thing I wanted to do, believe me. I haven't even seen Caroline this week. If I gave you the impression that I'd broken things off with her after last weekend, I'm really sorry.

She was covering her face, her hands scrubbing at her eyes, and her voice when she spoke was muffled and indistinct. Oh God, she was murmuring. I just thought — No, I don't even know what I thought.

Eileen, what do you want? Because if you seriously want us to be together, I can end things with Caroline any time. I'd be happy to, more than happy. But if you don't want that, and we're just playing around and having fun, then, you know. I can't be single for the rest of my life because it suits you better. I have to, at some point, I have to get over that. Do you see what I'm saying?

283

I'm just trying to figure out what you want.

Closing her eyes, she said nothing for several seconds. Then she said in a low even voice: I want to go home.

Right, he said. You mean now?

She was nodding her head, her eyes shut.

The fastest thing is probably just to keep walking, he said. Is that okay? I'll see you to your door.

She answered yes. In silence they made their way to Thomas Street and turned left, walking over toward St Catherine's. At the traffic lights a few cars were idling, and a taxi with its light turned on. Without speaking they walked down Bridgefoot Street and crossed the bridge at Usher's Island. Streetlights fragmented and dissolved on the black surface of the river. Finally they reached the entrance of Eileen's apartment building and stood together under the projecting arch of the external doorway. He looked at her, and with her head held straight she looked back at him. After taking a deep breath in, she said effortfully: Let's just forget about it, can we? He waited a moment as if to let her continue, but she didn't. I'm sorry to sound stupid, he answered, but about what, do you mean? She went on looking at him, her face thin and pale. I suppose about the whole thing, she said. And we can just be friends again. He started to nod his head while she watched him. Sure, he said. That's alright. I'm glad we've talked about it. He paused briefly and then added: I'm sorry if you thought I was ignoring you at Paula's house. I had been looking forward to seeing you, very much. I didn't mean to make you feel ignored. But that's all. I'm going to head home now, okay? I may not see you during the week, but in any case we'll see each other at the wedding. She seemed to swallow, and then asked haltingly: Is Caroline going to be there? I know you said you were thinking about bringing her. He looked up at Eileen then, and started to smile. Ah no, he said. I never invited her in the end. But if that was all you wanted, you could have just told me. No need for such advanced tactics. She turned her face away, shaking her head. No, it wasn't that, she said. He went on observing her a moment longer, and then said in a friendly voice: Not to worry. See you soon. He walked away, the wheels of his bicycle padded and quiet on the paved street surface.

Eileen took her keys from her pocket and let herself into the building, making her way directly up the stairs and through the front door of her apartment. Pushing her bedroom door open blindly and banging it shut, she lay down on the bed and started crying. Her face was red, a vein in her temple was visible. She hugged her knees to her chest and sobbed with a painful catching sound in her throat. Taking off one of her flat leather shoes, she threw it hard at the opposite wall and it fell limply on the carpet. She let out a noise almost like a scream then and put her face in her hands, shaking her head. A minute went by. Two minutes. She sat up and wiped her face, leaving black make-up smudged under her eyes and on her hand. Three, four minutes. She got to her feet, went to the window and looked out between the curtains. The headlights of a car swept past. Her eyes were pink and swollen. She scrubbed them once more with her hand and then took her phone from her pocket. The time was 00:41. She opened a messaging app and tapped Simon's name. An exchange from earlier that day appeared on-screen. Into the reply field Eileen slowly typed the words: Jesus Christ Simon I fucking hate you. Calmly she surveyed this message, and then, with apparent deliberation, added the lines: Like in your mind we were really just "having fun" all week and you were seeing someone else the whole time? When you were crying all over me the other night telling me how lonely you are, was that your idea of a joke? What the fuck is wrong with you? Her eyes moved once again over the text, slowly, thoughtfully. Then, holding her thumb to the backspace key, she deleted the draft. Taking deep hard breaths now, she began to type again. Simon I'm sorry. I feel awful. I don't know what I'm doing. Sometimes I hate myself so much I wish something heavy would fall on my head and kill me. You are the only person who is ever nice to me and now you probably don't even want to speak to me anymore. I don't know why I ruin everything good in my life. I'm sorry. By the time she had finished typing, the clock on-screen read 00:54. She scrolled back to reach the top of the message, and down again to read over the final line. Then she held the pad of her thumb down once more on the backspace key. Again the reply field was blank, the cursor blinking rhythmically over greyed-out text that read: Type a message. She locked her phone and lay back down on the bed.

20.

Alice, I am feeling a bit mystified that you're on another work trip already. When we talked back in February, I got the impression you were leaving Dublin because you didn't want to see people, and you needed time to rest and recover. When I expressed my concerns about you being on your own all the time, you actually told me that was what you needed. I find it a little bit strange that you're now sending me these chatty emails about the award ceremonies you're attending in Paris. If you're feeling better and you're happy to be back at work, that's great, obviously. But presumably you're flying from Dublin airport for all these trips? Could you not have let any of your friends know you were going to be in town? You obviously didn't tell Simon or myself, and Roisin has just told me she texted you two weeks ago and got no reply. I completely understand if you're not feeling up to being sociable, but then maybe you're pushing yourself to get back to work too quickly. Do you see what I mean?

I've been thinking about the later parts of your message for a few days now — about whether, as you say, 'the failure is general'. I know we agree that civilisation is presently in its decadent declining phase, and that lurid ugliness is the predominant visual feature of modern life. Cars are ugly, buildings are ugly, mass-produced disposable consumer goods are unspeakably ugly. The air we breathe is toxic, the water we drink is full of microplastics, and our food is contaminated by cancerous Teflon chemicals. Our quality of life is in decline, and along with it, the quality of aesthetic experience available to us. The contemporary novel is (with very few exceptions) irrelevant; mainstream cinema is family-friendly nightmare porn funded by car companies and the US Department of Defense; and visual art is primarily a commodity market for oligarchs. It is hard in these circumstances not to feel that modern living compares poorly with the old ways of life, which have come to represent something more substantial, more connected to the essence of the human condition. This nostalgic impulse is of course extremely powerful, and has recently been harnessed to great effect by reactionary and fascist political movements, but I'm not convinced that this means the impulse itself is intrinsically fascistic. I think it makes sense that people are looking back wistfully to a time before the natural world started dying, before our shared cultural forms degraded into mass marketing and before our cities and towns became anonymous employment hubs.

I know that you personally feel the world ceased to be beautiful after the fall of the Soviet Union. (As an aside, isn't it curious that this event coincided almost exactly with the date of your birth? It might help explain why you feel so much in common with Jesus, who I think also believed himself to be a harbinger of the apocalypse.) But do you ever experience a sort of diluted, personalised version of that feeling, as if your own life, your own world, has slowly but perceptibly become an uglier place? Or even a sense that while you used to be in step with the cultural discourse, you're not anymore, and you feel yourself adrift from the world of ideas, alienated, with no intellectual home? Maybe it is about our specific historical moment, or maybe it's just about getting older and disillusioned, and it happens to everyone. When I look back on what we were like when we first met, I don't think we were really wrong about anything, except about ourselves. The ideas were right, but the mistake was that we thought we mattered. Well, we've both had that particular error ground out of us in different ways — me by achieving precisely nothing in over a decade of adult life, and you (if you'll forgive me) by achieving as much as you possibly could and still not making one grain of difference to the smooth functioning of the capitalist system. When we were young, we thought our responsibilities stretched out to encompass the earth and everything that lived on it. And now we have to content ourselves with trying not to let down our loved ones, trying not to use too much plastic, and in your case trying to write an interesting book once every few years. So far so good on that front. Are you working on a new one yet, by the way?

I still think of myself as someone who is interested in the experience of beauty, but I would never describe myself (except to you, in this email) as 'interested in beauty', because people would assume that I meant I was interested in cosmetics. This I guess is the dominant meaning of the word 'beauty' in our culture now. And it seems telling that this meaning of the word 'beauty' signifies something so profoundly ugly — plastic counters in expensive department stores, discount pharmacies, artificial perfumes, eyelash extensions, jars of 'product'. Having thought about it just now, I think the beauty industry is responsible for some of the worst ugliness we see around us in our visual environment, and the worst, most false aesthetic ideal, which is the ideal of consumerism. All its various trends and looks ultimately signify the same principle — the principle of spending. To be open to aesthetic experience in a serious way probably requires as a first step the complete rejection of this ideal, and even a wholesale reaction against it, which if it seems to require at first a kind of superficial ugliness is still better by far and more substantively 'beautiful' than purchasing increased personal attractiveness at a price. Of course I wish that I personally were better-looking, and of course I enjoy the validation of feeling that I do look good, but to confuse these basically auto-erotic or status-driven impulses with real aesthetic experience seems to me an extremely serious mistake for anyone who cares about culture. Have the two things ever been more widely or deeply confused at any period in history before?

Do you remember when I had that essay

about Natalia Ginzburg published a couple of years ago? I never told you at the time but I actually heard from an agent in London about it, asking if I was working on a book. I didn't tell you because you were busy and because, I suppose, it seemed like something small compared with everything that was going on in your life. I'm embarrassed now to admit that I would even make that comparison. But anyway, I was happy about this email at first, and I showed it to Aidan, although he didn't really know anything about publishing or care very much, and I even told my mother. Then after a day or two I started to feel kind of anxious and stressed about it, because I actually wasn't working on a book, and I didn't have any idea what I could possibly write a book about, and I didn't think I had the stamina to finish a big project like that anyway. And the more I thought about it, the more I felt like it would be really painful and desperate of me to even try to write a book, because I have no intellectual depth or original ideas, and what would I be doing it for anyway, just to say that I had done it? Or just to feel like I was equal to you? I'm sorry if this is all making it sound like you loom large over my inner life. You don't usually, or if you do it's in a good way.

Anyway, in the end I never replied to the email. It just sat there in my inbox making me feel worse and worse and worse until I deleted it. I could have at least thanked the woman and said no, but I didn't, or couldn't, I don't know why. I suppose it doesn't matter now. The stupid thing is that I really liked writing that essay, and I did want to write another one, and after I got that email I never did. I know that if I really had any talent I would have done something with my life by now — I don't delude myself about that. If I tried I'm sure I would fail and that's why I've never tried.

In one of your emails a couple of months ago you wrote that Aidan and I had never been very happy together. That's not exactly true — we were in the beginning, for a while — but I know what you meant. And I do wonder why I've spent all this time feeling depressed about the end of something that wasn't working anyway. I suppose on one level it's just worse to get to the age of thirty without even one really happy relationship behind me. I think I would feel superficially sadder, but less fundamentally broken as a person, if I could just be sad about one break-up, rather than sad about my lifelong inability to sustain a meaningful relation-ship. But on the other hand, maybe it's something else. All those times I thought about breaking up with Aidan, and even talked about doing it, why didn't I? I don't think it was just because I loved him, although I did, and I don't think it was the idea that I would miss him, because it never really occurred to me that I would, and to be honest with myself I haven't. Sometimes I think I was afraid that without him my life would be just the same, or even worse, and I would have to accept that it was my fault. And it was easier and safer to stay in a bad situation than to take responsibility for getting out. Maybe, maybe. I don't know. I tell myself that I want to live a happy life, and that the circumstances for happiness just haven't arisen. But what if that's not true? What if I'm the one who can't let myself be happy? Because I'm scared, or I prefer to wallow in self-pity, or I don't believe I deserve good things, or some other reason. Whenever something good happens to me I always find myself thinking: I wonder how long it will be until this turns out badly. And I almost want the worst to happen sooner, sooner rather than later, and if possible straight away, so at least I don't have to feel anxious about it anymore.

If, as I think is quite possible now, I never have any children and never write any books, I suppose I will leave nothing on this earth to be remembered by. And maybe that's better. It makes me feel that rather than worrying and theorising about the state of the world, which helps no one, I should put my energy into living and being happy. When I try to picture for myself what a happy life might look like, the picture hasn't changed very much since I was a child — a house with flowers and trees around it, and a river nearby, and a room full of books, and someone there to love me, that's all. Just to make a home there, and to care for my parents when they grow older. Never to move, never to board a plane again, just to live quietly and then be buried in the earth. What else is life for? But even that seems so beyond me that it's like a dream, completely unrelated to anything in reality. And yes, when it comes to myself and Simon, two bedrooms please. All my love always. E.

21

The following night, a Wednesday, Alice went out to meet Felix and some of his friends at a bar called The Sailor's Friend, on a street corner near the pier. She arrived at the bar around nine o'clock, flushed from the walk, wearing a grey turtleneck and tapered trousers. Inside, it was warm and noisy. A long dark counter ran the length of the left wall, and behind it, above the spirit bottles, was a collection of colourful postcards. In front of an open hearth, a lurcher lay sleeping, its long delicate face resting on its paws. Felix and his friends were seated near a window at the back, in the midst of a good-natured argument about the marketing of online gambling. When Felix saw Alice approaching, he stood up, greeted her, touched her waist, and asked what she would like to drink. Gesturing back at his friends, he added: You know them crowd, you've met them before. Sit down, I'll go and get you something. She sat with his friends while he went to the bar. A woman named Siobhán was telling a story about a man she knew who had taken out a sixty-thousand-euro loan to cover his gambling debts. Alice appeared to find the story very interesting, and asked several specific questions. When Felix came back with the vodka tonic, he sat down beside her and put his hand on her lower back, smoothing the wool of her sweater under his fingers.

At midnight they walked back together from the bar to his house. Upstairs in bed Alice lay flat on her back, and Felix was on top of her. Her eyelids were fluttering and she was breathing rapidly, noisily. He rested his weight on one elbow, pressing her right leg back against her chest. Did you think about me while you were away, he asked. In a tight voice she replied: I think about you every night. He shut his eyes then. Her breath seemed to come over her in waves, forcing itself into her lungs and out again through her open mouth. Still his eyes were closed. Alice, he said, can I come, is it okay? She put her arms around him.

In the morning, he dropped her home on his way to work. Before she got out of the car, she asked him if she would see him for dinner that night and he said yes. Do your friends think I'm your girlfriend? she asked. He smiled at that. Well, we have been going around together a fair bit, he replied. I doubt they're kept awake at night thinking about it, but yeah, they might assume. He paused and added: And people in town are saying it. I don't care, I'm just telling you so you know. Alice asked what, exactly, people in town were saying, and Felix frowned. Ah, you know, he said. Nothing really. That author lady who lives above in the parochial house is hanging around with the Brady lad. That kind of thing. Alice said that they were, after all, 'hanging around', and Felix agreed that they were. There might be a few eyebrows raised, he added, but I wouldn't mind that. She asked why anyone should raise an eyebrow at the idea of two young single people hanging around together, and he handled the gearstick thoughtfully under his hand. I wouldn't be known as a great catch, he said, I'll put it that way. Not the most reliable character going. And speaking honestly, I owe a bit of money around town as well. He cleared his throat. But sure look, if you like me, that's your own business, he said. And I won't go borrowing money from you, don't worry. Hop out now or I'll be late, good woman. She unbuckled her seatbelt. I do like you, she said. I know, he answered. Go on, get out.

That morning, while Felix was at work, Alice had a phone call with her agent, discussing invitations she had received to literary festivals and universities. While this phone call took place, Felix was using a handheld scanner to identify and sort various packages into labelled stillage carts, which were then collected and wheeled away by other workers. Some of these workers greeted Felix when they came to collect the boxes, and others didn't. He was wearing a black zip-up, with the zip pulled right up, and occasionally he tucked his chin under the raised collar, evidently cold. While speaking to her agent, Alice made notes on her laptop in a draft email with the subject heading 'summer book dates'. After the phone call, she closed that email and opened a text file containing notes for a book review she was writing for a literary magazine in London. In the warehouse, Felix was pushing one of the tall steel stillage carts along an aisle of shelves illuminated by white fluorescent bulbs. Occasionally he stopped, squinted at a label, checked his scanner, and then scanned the item and placed it into the cart. Alice ate two pieces of buttered bread from a small plate, cut up an

apple, made herself a cup of coffee and
opened a draft email to Eileen.

Felix finished his shift at seven in the
evening, while Alice was cooking. On his
way out of the warehouse, he texted her.

Felix: Hey sorry but im actually not
gonna be there for dinner
Felix: Heading out w people from work
Felix: I wouldnt be any fun anyways bc
im in foul humor
Felix: Might see u tomorrow depending
on how wrecked I get
Alice: oh
Alice: I'll be sorry to miss you
Felix: Not in the form im in right now
believe me
Alice: I like you no matter what form
you're in
Felix: Well you can send me a love letter
on here while im out getting locked
Felix: And ill read it when I get home

Alice put her phone away and for a few
seconds stared blankly down into the empty
kitchen sink. Felix told his friend Brian he
could give him a lift as far as Mulroy's and
then he was going to drop the car home and
walk in. Alice passed the following few

hours preparing a pasta sauce, boiling water, laying the table, and eating. Felix drove home, fed his dog, showered quickly, changed his clothes, looked at Tinder, and then walked into the village to meet his work friends. Between the hours of eight p.m. and midnight he drank six pints of Danish lager. Alice washed up after dinner and read an article on the internet about Annie Ernaux. Around twelve, Felix and his friends got in a minivan taxi to a nightclub outside town and sang several verses of 'Come Out Ye Black and Tans' on the way there. Alice sat on the living room couch writing an email to a female friend of hers who now lived in Stockholm, asking about her job and her new relationship. At the club, Felix took two pills, drank a shot of vodka, and then went to the bathroom. He opened Tinder again, swiped left on several profiles, checked his messages, looked at the BBC Sports home page, and then went back out to the club. By one in the morning Alice was drinking peppermint tea and working on her book review, while Felix was on the dance floor with two of his friends and two people he had never met before. He had an easy and natural way of dancing, as if it cost him no effort, moving his body lightly into and against the beat of the music. After another drink he went outside and threw up behind a wheelie bin. Alice was lying in bed by then, reading over the messages Felix had sent earlier, the screen of her phone casting a greyish-blue light over her face. Felix took out his phone at the same moment and opened the messages app.

Felix: Hey
Felix: You up?
Alice: in bed but awake
Alice: having fun?
Felix: Ill be honest alice
Felix: I m yipped out of my tree
Felix: And I did haveto throw up
Felix: But yea good night so far
Alice: well, I'm glad
Felix: What are u doign in bed
Felix: Weairng anything or?
Felix: Describe
Alice: I'm wearing a white nightdress
Alice: I hope we can see each other tomorrow
Felix: Yeahhhh or
Felix: I cojld get a taxi back to yours
Felix: Now I mnea
Felix: Mean
Alice: if you want, of course
Felix: Yea are you sure?

Alice: I'm awake anyway, I don't mind
Felix: Cool
Felix: See u soon

She got out of bed and put on her dressing gown, turned on a bedside lamp and looked at herself in the mirror. Felix called the taxi company, went back inside, got his jacket, ordered another shot of vodka, swilled it around in his mouth, swallowed, found Brian and told him to tell the others he was heading off, and then went to get in the taxi. Alice opened his profile on the dating app where they'd first met, and read his bio note again. On the way out to her house, Felix was having an involved conversation with the taxi driver about the relative strengths and weaknesses of the current Mayo GAA side. When Felix pointed out the house, the driver asked if his parents lived there.

Nah, it's my bird's place, said Felix.

In an amused tone of voice, the driver replied: Must be a rich lady.

Yeah, and she's famous. You can Google her. She writes books.

Oh yeah? You'd better keep a hold of her.

Don't worry, she's fairly keen on me, Felix said.

They pulled into the driveway then. Turning around, the driver said: She'd want to be, letting you knock on her door at two in the morning. State you're in. I wouldn't be surprised if you're calling me again in a few minutes when she's had a look at you. Ten euro eighty, please.

Felix handed over the money.

Do you want me to wait? asked the driver.

Don't be jealous now, good lad. You go away and enjoy your Lyric FM.

He got out of the car and knocked on the door. Alice came downstairs to answer it as the taxi was pulling out of the gate. Felix came inside, kicked the door shut, and put his arms around Alice, lifting her up a little and pressing her back against the wall. They kissed for a while and then he untied the sash of her dressing gown. She held it shut with one hand.

Oh, you are drunk, she said.

I know, yeah. I said that in the messages.

He tried to open her dressing gown again and she folded her arms tightly to prevent him.

Here, what's the problem? he said. Are you on your period or something? I don't care if you are, I'm a grown-up.

Alice retied her dressing gown grimly and said: You're trying to embarrass me.

No, no. I'm just wondering what's the

matter. I'm not trying anything, I'm happy to be here. The taxi driver was very impressed I had a girlfriend who lived in such a big house.

Alice looked up at him and finally said: Are you on drugs?

God yeah, he said. Wouldn't be much of a night out if I wasn't.

She stood there with her arms folded. I don't know, she said. Would other people let you behave like this? Other girlfriends or boyfriends you've had. Is this normal? You go out with your friends and get hammered and then show up in the middle of the night looking for sex?

He seemed to consider this, leaning his arm against the wall beside her head. I would often give it a go, yeah, he said. Not everyone would be up for it, obviously.

Right. You must think I'm a complete fucking idiot.

No, I think you're highly intelligent. It's not lucky for you, in a lot of ways. If you were a little bit stupider you might have an easier life.

He stood up straight and put his hands on her hips, in a way that seemed to convey fondness and even contrition.

The taxi driver told me you were going to fuck me out of it, Felix said. He told me, no

306

way is she going to let you call around at this hour of the night looking like that. What I look like, I don't actually know, I haven't seen myself. But I can imagine not good.

You just look drunk.

Ah, do I? I don't know, I suppose I shouldn't have texted you. The stupid thing is, I was actually having a good night. I mean, okay, I went a bit overboard getting sick, but I was having a good time other than that. And you were probably having a fine time as well, lying in bed or whatever. So I shouldn't have texted you really.

Right, but you felt like having sex, she said.

Well, I'm only human. Nah, but if that's all I was after I could have gone elsewhere, couldn't I? No need to bother you just for that.

She shut her eyes and said in a quiet, inexpressive voice: I'm sure that's true.

Alice, don't be looking so serious, he said. I haven't been off with anyone else. Obviously I could if I wanted to, but so could you. Look, I'm sorry if I've annoyed you, alright?

For a moment she said nothing.

And you probably don't like being around drunk people anyway, he said.

No, I don't.

No, why would you? I'd say you had

enough of that growing up.

She stared up at him and he kept his hands on her hips, holding her against the wall.

Yes, I did, she said.

If you want me to go home, just say.

She shook her head. He kissed her again. They went upstairs together, Alice holding Felix's hand and following behind him. In her room he took off her dressing gown and lifted her nightdress off over her head. She lay back on the bed and he went down on her. Her body looked compact, androgynous. She pressed her hand flat over her mouth. He broke off then to undress himself and take his watch off. Looking down at her where she lay stretched out naked on the mattress, he said with a smile: Do you know what you look like? One of those girl statues we saw in Rome.

She laughed and covered her face.

Is that not nice? he said. It was meant nicely.

She said it was. He lay down beside her, his head propped up on the pillows, his hand toying idly with her small soft breast.

I was thinking about you at work today, he said. I find it makes me feel a bit better for a while but then I actually feel worse, because you're lying around here all day and I'm stuck in a warehouse packing boxes. Not that I'm put out with you about it. I'm not going to be able to explain this the right way, but the difference between what we're doing right now and what I do all day, I actually can't describe. It's hard to believe I have to use the same body for both things, I'll say it like that. And it doesn't feel like the same. These hands touching you now, I use them to pack boxes? I don't know. At work my hands are fucking freezing all the time. And like, basically numb. Even if you wear gloves they go numb eventually, everyone says that. Sometimes I'll get a little cut or a scrape or something and I won't even notice until I see it's bleeding. And these are the same hands touching you? I don't know, you probably think I'm off my head talking like that. But you're very, very soft and nice to touch, that's all. And warm. When you let me come inside you, I feel so good, I can't even describe. I was thinking about that at work today and I wanted it so much I started getting annoyed. Like, annoyed, yeah, pissed off. That's the other thing I will say about work, your feelings get really messed up in there. You start feeling things that make no sense. I should have been looking forward to seeing you, but I actually felt pissed off. And then I didn't even want to see you anymore. There's no point trying to explain it because it doesn't make any sense, I'm just saying what I felt. I'm sorry.

She told him it was okay. For a little while he kissed her and said nothing. Then he asked if she would go on top because he was tired, and she said yes. Once he was inside her she was still for a few seconds, breathing hard. Okay? he said. She nodded. He looked content to wait. You have such a perfect cunt, he said. A shudder dropped over her, from her head down to her pelvic bone. She put a hand on his shoulder. They fucked slowly for a couple of minutes while he touched her. In a high uneven voice she said: Oh God, I'm in love with you, I really am. He looked up at her then. Are you, yeah? he said. That's good. Say it again. Trembling, out of breath, she bent her head low, and said: I love you, I love you. He put his hands around her waist, his fingers pressing into the flesh of her back, and pulled her down hard onto him, again and again quickly, and she was wincing almost as if in pain.

Afterwards they were still for a while, resting against one another. Then she climbed off him, sat on the side of the mattress and took a drink from the water bottle on her bedside table. He lay down with his head nestled among the pillows, watching her. Pass me that when you're finished, he said. She gave him the bottle and he drank without lifting his head.

Handing the bottle back, he said: Here, I want to know something. You know you're always saying that you're rich. What do you mean, are you a millionaire or what?

She screwed the cap back onto the bottle. About that, she said.

He watched her in silence. A million, really, he said. That's a lot of money.

Yes it is.

All that just from books?

She nodded.

And just sitting in your bank account, or it's all tied into things? he said.

Rubbing her eyes, she said it was mostly just sitting in her bank account. He was still watching her, his eyes moving quickly and discreetly over her face, her arms, her shoulders. After a time, he said: Come here and tell me you love me again. I could get to like it. With heavy, tired movements she lay back down beside him.

I love you, she said.

And when did you realise this? Love at first sight kind of thing, was it?

No, I don't think so.

A bit later on, then, he said. In Rome?

She turned to him and he draped his arm over her body. Her eyes were half-closed. His face was thoughtful, alert.

I suppose so, she said.

That's pretty quick to be falling in love with someone. What was it, maybe three weeks?

Letting her eyes close, she said: About that.

Would that be usual for you?

I don't know. I don't fall in love very often.

He lay watching her for a second or two. And vice versa, I assume, he said.

She smiled faintly and said: People don't fall in love with me very often, you mean? No, indeed they don't.

And you don't seem to have many friends either, he said.

She stopped smiling then. She turned to look at Felix in silence for several seconds while all expression emptied from her features. Then she said simply: No, I suppose not.

No, yeah. Because since you moved in here, I don't think anyone's been to see you, have they? Your family haven't. And your friend Eileen, you talk about her a lot, but she hasn't bothered. I think I'm the only person who's been in the house since you

312

arrived, would that be right? And you're here at least a few months.

Alice stared at him and said nothing. He seemed to take this as permission to continue, and tucked his arm up under his pillow thoughtfully.

I was thinking about it over in Italy, he said. Watching you do your reading and your autographs and all that. I wouldn't go so far as to say you work hard, because your job's a laugh compared to mine. But you have a lot of people wanting things off you. And I just think, for all the fuss they make over you, none of them actually care about you one bit. I don't know if anyone does.

They looked at one another for several long seconds. As Felix watched her, his initial self-assurance, even sadistic triumph, changed gradually into something else, as if recognising too late his own misapprehension.

You must really hate me, she said coolly.

No, I don't, he replied. But I don't love you either.

Of course not. Why should you? I wasn't deluded about that.

She turned over then, quite calmly, and switched off the lamp on the bedside locker. The darkness dissolved their faces and only the outlines of their bodies were visible under the sheets. Neither of them moved at all and every line, every shadow in the room was still.

You can leave if you'd like, she said. But you're welcome to stay. You might flatter yourself you've hurt me very badly, but I can promise you I've been through worse.

He lay there in silence, not responding.

And when I said I loved you I was telling the truth, she added.

He made a noise that sounded like a strangled laugh, and then said: Ah, I like your style. I'll give you that. You're not easy to get the upper hand on, are you? Obviously I'm not going to manage it. It's funny, because you carry on like you'd let me walk all over you, answering my texts at two in the morning, and then telling me you're in love with me, blah blah blah. But that's all your way of saying, just try and catch me, because you won't. And I can see I won't. You're not going to let me have it for a minute. Nine times out of ten you'd have someone fooled with the way you go on. They'd be delighted with themselves, thinking they were really the boss of you. Yeah, yeah, but I'm not an idiot. You're only letting me act badly because it puts you above me, and that's where you like to be. Above, above. And I don't take it personally, by the way, I don't think you'd let anyone near you. Actually, I respect it. You're looking out for yourself, and I'm sure you have your reasons. I'm sorry I was so harsh on you with what I said, because you were right, I was just trying to hurt you. And I probably did hurt you, big deal. Anyone can hurt anyone if they go out of their way. But then instead of getting mad with me, you go saying I'm welcome to stay over and you still love me and all this. Because you have to be perfect, don't you? No, you really have a way about you, I must say. And I'm sorry, alright? I won't be trying to take a jab at you again. Lesson learned. But from now on you don't need to act like you're under my thumb, when we both know I'm no-where near you. Alright?

Another long silence fell. Their faces were invisible in darkness. Eventually, in a high and strained voice, straining perhaps for an evenness or lightness it did not attain, she replied: Alright.

If I ever do get a hold of you, you won't need to tell me, he said. I'll know. But I'm not going to chase too much. I'll just stay where I am and see if you come to me.

Yes, that's what hunters do with deer, she said. Before they kill them.

22.

Eileen, I'm sorry if my last email alarmed you. I did cancel all my public engagements for several months, as you know, but I was always planning to go back to work eventually. Surely you understand that this is my job? No one finds that fact more tiresome and degrading than I do, but I never meant you to think that I had actually retired from public life altogether. You have never been off work sick for more than four days at a time, so I should think my taking four months off would strike you as a pretty protracted break. And yes, I did fly out of Dublin, and back into Dublin again, at seven in the morning and one in the morning respectively. Since you also have a job, at which I understand you keep regular hours, I didn't think waking you up in the middle of the night for a quick cup of tea and a chat would have been particularly polite. You can't possibly think I don't want

316

to see you, since I have been asking you repeatedly for months on end to come and visit me, and I only live three hours away. As for the unanswered text message from Roisin, I'm confused — are you writing to me personally, or in your capacity as friendship ambassador for the greater Dublin region? You're right, I didn't reply to her text, because I've been busy. With all due love and affection, I don't intend to file a report with you every time I fall behind on my correspondence.

As for the rest of your message: what exactly do you mean when you say 'beauty'? You wrote that to confuse personal vanity with aesthetic experience is a grave mistake. But is it another mistake, and maybe a related one, to take aesthetic experience seriously in the first place? No doubt it is possible to be moved in a personally disinterested way by artistic beauty or by the beauty of the natural world. I even think it's possible to enjoy the good looks of other people, their faces and bodies, in a way that's 'purely' aesthetic, i.e. without the element of desire. Personally I often find people beautiful to look at without feeling any inclination to draw them into a particular relationship with myself — in fact I don't find beauty much of an inducement to desire anyway. In other words I exercise no volition in perceiving beauty and I experience no conscious will as a result. This I suppose is what the Enlightenment philosophers meant by aesthetic judgement, and it corresponds rightly enough to the kind of experience I've had with certain works of visual art, passages of music, scenic vistas, and so on. I find them beautiful, and their beauty moves me and gives me a pleasurable feeling. I agree that the spectacle of mass consumerism marketed to us as 'beauty' is in reality hideous and gives me none of the aesthetic pleasure I get from, e.g., sunlight falling through leaves, or the 'Demoiselles d'Avignon', or 'Kind of Blue'. But I'm inclined to ask: so what? Even if we suppose that the beauty of 'Kind of Blue' is in some sense objectively superior to the beauty of a Chanel handbag, which philosophically speaking is a lot of ground to give, why does it matter? You seem to think that aesthetic experience is, rather than merely pleasurable, somehow important. And what I want to know is: important in what way?

I'm not a painter or a musician, for good reason, but I am a novelist, and I do try to take the novel seriously — partly because I'm conscious of the extraordinary privilege of being allowed to make a living from something as definitionally useless as art. But if I tried to describe my experience of reading the great novels, it would not be remotely like the aesthetic experience I've described above, in which no volition is involved and no personal desires are stirred. Personally I have to exercise a lot of agency in reading, and understanding what I read, and bearing it all in mind for long enough to make sense of the book as I go along. In no sense does it feel like a passive process by which beauty is transmitted to me without my involvement; it feels like an active effort, of which an experience of beauty is the constructed result. But, I think more importantly, great novels engage my sympathies and make me desire things. When I look at the 'Demoiselles d'Avignon', I don't 'want' anything from it. The pleasure is in seeing it as it is. But when I read books, I do experience desire: I want Isabel Archer to be happy, I want things to work out for Anna and Vronsky, I even want Jesus to be pardoned instead of Barabbas. Again it might be that I am a narrow-minded and rather vapid reader, sentimentally wishing the best for everyone (except Barabbas); but if I wished the opposite, that Isabel should make a bad marriage, that Anna should throw herself under the train, it would just be a variation on the same experience. The point is that my sympathies are engaged, I'm no longer disinterested.

Have you talked to Simon about any of this? I think you could rely on him to present a more coherent view of the thing than I can, because his worldview has a consistency mine lacks. In Catholic doctrine, as far as my understanding goes, beauty, truth and goodness are properties of being which are one with God. God kind of literally 'is' beauty (and also truth, which maybe is what Keats meant, I'm not sure). Humankind strives to possess and understand these properties as a way of turning toward God and understanding his nature; therefore whatever is beautiful leads us toward contemplation of the divine. As critics we may quibble about what is and isn't beautiful, because we are only human and God's will isn't perfectly accessible to us, but we can all agree on the surpassing importance of beauty itself. It's all very nice and self-contained, isn't it? I could riff on it a little to explain my sympathetic engagement with the great novels. For example, God made us the way we are, as complex human beings with desires and impulses, and compassionate attachment to purely fictional people

— from whom we obviously can't expect to derive any material satisfaction or advantage — is a way of understanding the deep complexities of the human condition, and thus the complexities of God's love for us. I can even go further: in his life and death, Jesus emphasised the necessity of loving others without regard to our own self-interest. In a way, when we love fictional characters, knowing that they can never love us in return, is that not a method of practising in miniature the kind of personally disinterested love to which Jesus calls us? I mean that sympathetic engagement is a form of desire with an object but without a subject, a way of wanting without wanting; desiring for others not what I want for myself but the way I want for myself.

I suppose the point I'm making is that there's no end of fun to be had once you get into the Christian mindset. For you and me it's harder, because we can't seem to shake the conviction that nothing matters, life is random, our sincerest feelings are reducible to chemical reactions, and no objective moral law structures the universe. It's possible to live with those convictions, of course, but not really possible, I don't think, to believe the things that you and I say we believe. That some experiences of beauty are serious and others trivial. Or that some things are right and others wrong. To what standard are we appealing? Before what judge do we argue our case? I'm not trying to tear you down, by the way — I occupy what I suspect is exactly your position. I can't believe that the difference between right and wrong is simply a matter of taste or preference; but I also can't bring myself to believe in absolute morality, which is to say, in God. This leaves me in a philosophical nowhere place, lacking the courage of my convictions on both sides. I can't have the satisfaction of feeling that I serve God by doing right, and yet the idea of doing wrong disgusts me. Even more to the point, I find my own work morally and politically worthless, and yet it's what I do with my life, the only thing I want to do.

When I was younger, I think what I wanted was to travel the world, to lead a glamorous life, to be celebrated for my work, to marry a great intellectual, to reject everything I had been raised with, to cut myself off from the narrow world. I feel very embarrassed by all that now, but I was lonely and unhappy, and I didn't understand that these feelings were ordinary, that there was nothing singular about my loneliness, my unhappiness. Maybe if I had understood that, as I think I do now, at least a little bit, I would never have written those books, I would never have become this person. I don't know. I know that I couldn't write them again, or feel the way I felt about myself at that time. It was important to me then to prove that I was a special person. And in my attempt to prove it, I made it true. Only afterwards, when I had received the money and acclaim which I believed I deserved, did I understand that it was not possible for anyone to deserve these things, and by then it was too late. I had already become the person I had once longed to be, and now energetically despised. I don't say this to slight my work. But why should anyone be rich and famous while other people live in desperate poverty?

The last time I fell in love, it ended badly, as you know, and then in the aftermath I wrote two novels. While I was in love, I tried to write a little here and there, but my thoughts always returned to the object of my affection, and my feelings ran back inexorably toward her, so my work could never develop any substance of its own, and I had no meaningful place for it in my life. We were happy, and then we were unhappy, and after some misery and recrimination, we broke up — and only then could I start giving myself to my work in a serious way. It was like I had cleared a space inside myself, and I had to fill it up somehow, and that's how I came to sit down and write. I had to empty my life out first and begin from there. Looking back now on the period when I wrote the books, I feel like it was a good time in my life, because I had work I needed to do, and I did it. I was perennially broke, and lonely, and anxious about money, but I also had this other thing, this part of my life which was secret and protected, and my thoughts returned to it all the time, and my feelings orbited around it, and it belonged to me completely. In a way it was like a love affair, or an infatuation, except that it only involved myself and it was all within my own control. (The opposite of a love affair, then.) For all the frustration and difficulty of writing a novel, I knew from the beginning of the process that I had been given something very important, a special gift, a blessing. It was like God had put his hand on my head and filled me with the most intense desire I had ever felt, not desire for another person, but desire to bring something into being that had never existed before. When I look back at those years, I feel touched and almost pained by the simplicity of the life I was living, because I knew what I had to do, and I did it, that was all.

Other than a little criticism and some very long emails, I haven't written anything now for almost two years. And I think the space in my life has been cleared out at this stage, and it's empty, and maybe for that reason it's time for me to fall in love again. I need to feel that my life has some kind of centre, somewhere for my thoughts to return and rest. I know, by the way, that most people don't need any such thing, and I would be much healthier if I didn't. Felix doesn't feel the need to arrange his life around a central principle, and I don't think you do either. Simon does, but he has God. When it comes to putting something at the centre of life, God strikes me as a good option — better at least than making up stories about people who don't exist, or falling in love with people who hate me. But here we are. It's still better to love something than nothing, better to love someone than no one, and I'm here, living in the world, not wishing for a moment that I wasn't. Isn't that in its own way a special gift, a blessing, something very important? Eileen, I am sorry, and I do miss you. When we see each other after all these emails I'm going to get very shy and hide my head under my wing like a little bird. Give your sister and her groom my best wishes this weekend — and then, if it's not too much trouble, come and see me, please.

23.

On the morning of the wedding, Eileen sat on the bed in the bridal suite while Lola was at the dressing table. Touching a finger to her face, Lola said: I think she did the eyes too heavy. She was wearing a white wedding gown, strapless, simple in its shape. You look beautiful, said Eileen. Their eyes met in the mirror and Lola grimaced, rose, went to the window. Outside, the early afternoon was white, casting a thin watery light, but Lola stood with her back to the glass, facing Eileen, studying her where she sat on the ample mattress. For a time they looked at one another, aggrieved, guilty, mistrustful, contrite. Finally Lola said: Well? Eileen glanced down at a thin gold watch she wore on her left wrist. It's only ten to, she said. She was wearing a pale-green dress, celadon, her hair pinned back, she was thinking of something else then, they both were. Lola remembered paddling in the sea at Strandhill, or was it Rosses Point that day, or Enniscrone. The gritty texture of sand under her fingernails and in her scalp, also the taste of salt. Then she had fallen and found herself swallowing seawater, painful in her nose and throat, a confusion of light and sensation, she remembered crying, and being carried up the beach in her father's arms. A red-and-orange towel. Later, driving back to Sligo town, strapped into the back seat, with the radio crackling, pinpoints of light visible in the distance. In the darkness by the side of the road, a van that sold sausages and chips, the hatch open, the sting of vinegar. Sleeping in a cousin's bedroom that night, with different books on the shelf, the furniture casting different shadows in the light from an unfamiliar window. At midnight the cathedral bells. Downstairs the adults were talking, downstairs the lights were on and there were glasses of beer. Eileen was thinking also of childhood, one of Lola's make-believe games, a hidden kingdom, palaces, dukes and peasants, enchanted rivers, forests, lights in the sky. All the twists and turns were lost now, the invented names in magic languages, the loyalties and betrayals. What remained were the real-life places over which the fictive world had been imposed:

the cowshed behind their house, the over-grown reaches of the garden, gaps behind hedges, the damp shale running down to the river. And in the house: the attic, the staircase, the coat closet. Still these places gave Eileen a special feeling, or at least she could, if she willed, tune into a special feeling that was in them, an aesthetic frequency. They filled her with pleasure, with a thrill of something like excitement. Like good stationery, heavy pens, unlined paper, they represented to her the possibility of imagination, a possibility so much finer in itself and more delicate than anything she had ever managed to imagine. No, her imagination let her down. It was something other people either had or didn't want anyway. Eileen wanted and didn't have it. Like Alice in her moral philosophy, she was caught between two positions. Maybe everyone was, in everything that mattered. At a knock on the door they looked up and their mother Mary entered, wearing her blue dress, her patent shoes, a feather dangling upright in her hair. Then they all began talking, quickly, remonstrating, laughing, complaining, adjusting each other's clothing, and the activity in the room was rapid and noisy, like the activity of birds. Lola wanted to repin Eileen's hair, to make it looser at the back, and Mary wanted to try on at the last minute an alternative pair of shoes, and Eileen, with her slim white arms like reeds, like branches, began to unpin her hair, held a shawl up to Mary's shoulders, removed a stray eyelash from Lola's powdered cheekbone, laughing, speaking in a quick light voice and breaking into laughter once again. Mary too was thinking of her childhood, their little terraced house with the shop next door, slivers of ice cream between wafers, chequered oilcloth on the kitchen table, patterned crockery behind glass. Cold bright summer days, air clear as cold water, and the gorse a blaze of yellow. To think of childhood gave her a funny queasy feeling, because it had been real life once and now it was something else. The old people had died, the babies had grown old. It would happen also to Eileen, also to Lola, who were young and beautiful now, loving and hating one another, laughing with white teeth, smelling of perfume. Another knock sounded on the door, and they fell silent and looked around. Their father Pat entered. How are the women, he said. It was time to go to the church then, the car was waiting, Pat was wearing his suit. He was thinking about his wife, about Mary, how like a stranger she had seemed to him the first time she was pregnant, how something had come over her, some seriousness, some strange purpose in her words, in her movements, and he found it uncomfortable, it made him want to laugh, he didn't know why. She was changing, turning her face away from him, toward some other experience. In time it passed, Lola was born, healthy thank God, and he told himself they'd never do it again. Too much strangeness for one life. As usual, as usual, he had been wrong. Outside, the air stirred the trees, sifted its cool breath over their faces. They climbed into the car together. Lola pressed her nose to the window and left a tiny circle of powder on the glass. The church was squat and grey with long thin stained-glass windows, rose-coloured and blue and amber. As they entered, the electric organ played, the scent of incense touched them, damp and fragrant, and the rustle of cloth, the creaking of pews, as everyone stood and watched them processing together up the polished floor of the aisle, Lola stately and magnificent in white, radiant with the realisation of cherished plans, accepting with composure the gazes offered to her, not bowed but upright, Pat in his suit, dignified, tender in his awkwardness, Mary smiling nervously, clutching Eileen's hand with a damp grip, and Eileen herself slim and pale in green, dark hair pinned loosely behind her, arms bare, head held aloft on her long neck like a flower, and turning her eyes quietly she looked for him but did not see him. Matthew was waiting at the altar, frightened, joyful, and the priest spoke, the vows were exchanged. O my dove, in the clefts of the rock, in the covert of the cliff, let me see your face, let me hear your voice, for your voice is sweet, and your face is lovely. Afterwards on the gravel outside the church, the white daylight, the chill of wind, spindly fingers of foliage, everyone laughing, shaking hands, embracing. The bridal party stood together under a tree to have their photograph taken, inching closer and further apart, murmuring to one another with fixed smiles. Only then Eileen saw him, Simon, standing at the church door watching her. They looked at one another for a long moment without moving, without speaking, and in the soil of that look many years were buried. He remembered when she was born, the Lydons' new baby, and the first time he was allowed to see her, the red wrinkled face more like an old creature than something new, baby Eileen, and his parents said he was always asking for a sister after that, not just any sibling, a sister, like what Lola had. She remembered him too, the older boy who went to a different school, lively, intelligent, with those strange seizures he suffered from, an object of sympathy among the adults, which made him, though he was a beautiful child, somehow freakish. Her mother always saying how lovely his manners were, a little gentleman. And she was the adolescent girl he remembered, thin and freckled, standing at the kitchen counter with her legs twisted one around the other, fifteen, always frowning. Speaking not at all or suddenly and too much, her bad tempers, her friendlessness. And those frank looks she turned on him, pink in the face and almost cross. He was that too, for her, the boy, the young man of twenty, who helped out on the farm for the summer, she had seen him, with incomparable tenderness, bottle-feeding a baby lamb, she would spend a week in agony over a glance from him, the breath knocked out of her when she entered a room to find him there. The day all three of them cycled to the woods and left their bikes in a clearing together. Dark clouds surreal-looking behind bright sunlit treetops. Lola telling a long, embellished story about someone who had been murdered in the forest, Simon murmuring things like, Hm, I'm not sure about that, and, Oh dear, that's a bit grisly, isn't it? Eileen absorbed in kicking a pebble along the path before her, occasionally glancing up at Simon to observe his face. Stabbed so many times she was almost decapitated, Lola was saying. Gosh, said Simon, I'd rather not think about it. Lola laughed and told him he was a mouse. Well, if it comes to that, I am a bit, he said. It was starting to rain then and Lola untied her jacket from around her waist. You're like Eileen, she said. He looked over at Eileen and said: I'd like to be more like her. Lola said that Eileen was only a baby. In a quick, heated, strangely loud voice, Eileen said: Imagine someone saying that to you when you were my age. Lola looked around at her sympathetically. But to be fair, she answered, when I was your age I was a lot more mature. Simon said he thought Eileen was very mature. Lola frowned and said: Don't be creepy. Simon's ears were red then and his voice came out sounding different. I meant intellectually, he said. He didn't say anything else and neither did Lola, but neither of them were happy. Lola put her hood up against the rain and walked ahead. With fast long strides she marched on around a bend in the path, out of sight. Eileen looked down at the path, which had been dry dirt and was now turning to mud, little streams running between the stones. The rain was growing harder, making a pattern of dark dots on the front of her jeans, wetting her hair. When they came around the next bend, Lola still wasn't visible. She might have been further ahead, or she might have gone down some other path. Do you know where we are? Eileen asked. Simon smiled and said he thought so. We won't get lost, he said, don't worry. We might get drowned, though. Eileen wiped her forehead with her sleeve. Hopefully no one will come along and stab us thirty-eight times, she remarked. Simon laughed. The victims always seem to be on their own in those stories, he said. So I think we'll be fine. Eileen said that was all very well unless he was the murderer. He laughed again. No, no, he said. You're safe with me. She glanced up at him again, shyly. I feel that way, she said. He looked around at her and said: Hm? She shook her head, wiped her face with her sleeve again, swallowed. I feel that I'm safe, she said, when I'm with you. For a few seconds Simon was silent. Presently he said: That's nice. I'm glad to hear it. She watched him. Then with no warning she stopped walking and stood under a tree. Her face and hair were very wet. When

Simon noticed she was no longer beside him, he turned around. Hello, he said. What are you doing? She gazed at him with intense concentration in her eyes. Can you come here for a second? she said. He walked toward her a few steps. Very quietly but with some agitation she said: No, I mean here. Where I'm standing. He paused. Well, why? he said. Instead of answering she merely went on looking at him with a kind of pleading, distressed expression. He came toward her, and she put her hand on his forearm and held it. The cloth of his shirt was damp. She pulled him a little closer, so their bodies were almost touching, and her lips wet, rain streaming down her cheeks and nose. He didn't pull away from her, in fact he stood very close, and his mouth was almost at her ear. She said nothing and her breath came fast and high. Softly he said: Eileen, I know. I understand. But it can't be like that, okay? She was trembling and her lips looked pale. I'm sorry, she said. He didn't pull away, he stood there letting her hold on to his arm. There's nothing to be sorry for, he said. You haven't done anything wrong. I understand, okay? There's nothing to say sorry for. Can we walk on now, do you think? They walked on, Eileen staring down at her feet. In the clearing behind the gate Lola was waiting, holding her bicycle upright. At the sight of them, she kicked one pedal impatiently with her foot and sent it spinning. Where have you been? she called out as they approached. You ran ahead, said Eileen. Simon retrieved Eileen's bike from the grass and handed it over to her before lifting out his own. I hardly ran, said Lola. With a strange look on her face, she reached out and tousled Eileen's wet hair. You look like a drowned rat, she said. Let's go. He let them walk on together. Silently with his eyes on the wheel of his bicycle he prayed: Dear God, let her live a happy life. I'll do anything, anything, please, please. When she was twenty-one, she went to see him in Paris, where he was spending the summer living in an old apartment building with a mechanical lift shaft. They were friends then, writing each other amusing postcards with famous nude paintings on the front. When they walked together along the Champs-Élysées, women turned their heads to watch him, he was so tall and beautiful, so austere, and he never looked back at them. The night she arrived in his apartment she told him the story of how she had lost her virginity, only a few weeks before, and while she was talking her face was so hot it felt painful, and the story was so terribly bad and awkward, but somehow perversely she liked telling it to him, she liked the funny unshockable tone he took with her. He even made her laugh. They were lying close together, their shoulders almost touching. That was the first time. To be held in his arms and to feel him move inside her, this man who kept himself apart from everyone, to feel him giving in, taking comfort in her, that was her whole idea of sexuality, it had never surpassed that, still. And for him, to have her in that way, when she was so innocent and nervous, trembling all over, so unconscious it seemed of what she was giving him, he almost felt guilty. But it could never be wrong with her, no matter what they did together, because she had nothing evil in her, and he would give his life away to make her happy. His life, whatever that was. And the years afterwards, with Natalie in Paris, his youth, gone now, never to be had back again. Living with you is like living with depression, Natalie told him. He wanted, he tried to make her happy, and he couldn't. Alone afterwards, washing his dishes after dinner, the single plate and fork on the draining board. And not even young anymore, not really. For Eileen those years had passed also somehow, sitting on floorboards unboxing flat-pack furniture, bickering, drinking warm white wine from plastic cups. Watching all her friends move away, move on, to New York, to Paris, while she stayed behind, working in the same little office, having the same four arguments over and over again with the same man. Unable to remember anymore what she had thought her life would be. Hadn't there been a time when it had meant something to her, to be alive, to be living? But what? One weekend last year, they were both at home, and Simon borrowed his parents' car to drive her into Galway. She wore a red tweed jacket with a brooch on the lapel, her hair loose around her shoulders, dark, soft, her hands lying in her lap, white like doves. They talked about their families, about her mother, his mother. She was still living with her boyfriend then. Driving back that night, the crescent moon lopsided and golden like a lifted saucer of champagne, the top buttons of her blouse were undone, she put her hand inside, touching her breastbone, they were talking about children, she had never wanted any before, but lately she wondered, and it was impossible for him not to think about it, he felt a hard low ache inside himself, let me do it to you, he wanted to say, I have money, I'll take care of everything. Jesus Christ. What about you, she asked, do you want kids? Very much, he said. Yeah. That dead noise when she closed the car door behind her. Thinking of it again that night, imagining that she would let him, that she would want him to, and afterwards feeling empty, and ashamed of himself. He saw her on O'Connell Street a few weeks later, it was August, she was walking with a friend he didn't know, all the way across the road, heading toward the river, and she was wearing a white dress, it was a hot day. How graceful she looked in the crowd, his eyes followed her, her long beautiful neck, her shoulders gleaming in the sunlight. Like watching his life walk away from him. One evening in Dublin around Christmas, she saw him from the window of a bus, he was crossing the street, on his way home from work probably, wearing his long winter overcoat, tall and golden-headed under the streetlights, God it was an awful time, Alice in hospital, and Aidan saying he needed to think about things, and there, out the window of the bus, there was Simon, crossing the street. It was so peaceful just to watch him, his fine handsome figure, making his way through the deep blue liquid darkness of December, his quiet solitude, his self-containment, and she felt so happy, so grateful that they lived in the same city, where she could see him even without meaning to, where he could appear like this in front of her just when she needed most to see him, someone who had loved her for her entire life. All of that. And their phone calls, the messages they wrote to one another, their jealousies, the years of looks, suppressed smiles, their dictionary of little touches. All the stories they had told about each other, about themselves. This much was in their eyes and passed between them. Facing this way, please, the photographer said. Simon inclined his head and let her turn away. When the photographs were finished, the party dispersed across the gravel, talking, waving, and she went to him where he was standing on the step. You look very beautiful, he said. Her face was flushed, she was holding a bouquet of flowers in her arms. Already someone else was calling her, wanting something. Simon, she said. Tenderly, it seemed almost painfully, they smiled at one another, saying nothing, and their questions were the same, am I the one you think about, when we made love were you happy, have I hurt you, do you love me, will you always. From the church gate now, her mother was calling her name. Reaching to touch Simon's hand Eileen said: I'll be back. He nodded, he was smiling at her. Don't worry, he said. I'll be here.

24.

Dearest Alice — just a quick note to say the wedding was very beautiful, and we're on the train heading for Ballina as we speak. I always forget Simon is in essence (though he denies this) a politician, and therefore knows literally everyone in the country. He is currently in a long conversation with some random man I have never seen in my life while I sit here typing this message. It's making me think about what you wrote in your email about beauty, and how difficult it is to believe that beauty could be important or meaningful when it's just random. But it brings some pleasure into life, doesn't it? You don't need to be religious to appreciate that, I believe. It's funny that I have only two best friends in the world and neither of them remind me of myself at all. In fact the person who reminds me most of myself is my sister — because she is completely insane, which I also am, and because she makes me so angry, which I also do. She looked very beautiful yesterday, by the way, although her dress was strapless, and I know you disapprove of those. The random man who's talking to Simon is now sitting down at our table and showing him something on his phone. I think it might be a picture of a bird? Maybe the man is some kind of bird enthusiast? I don't know, I haven't been listening. Anyway, I'm looking forward to seeing you. I think I had an idea in my mind about beauty, or about the wedding, or about you and Simon and how you don't remind me of myself, but I can't remember what the idea was. You know the first time I went to bed with Simon was almost ten years ago? I sometimes think it would have been a nice life for me if he had done the Christian thing and asked me to marry him then. We could have had several children by now and they would probably be sitting on the train with us at this very moment, overhearing their father's conversation with a bird enthusiast. I just have this sense that if Simon had taken me under his wing earlier in life, I might have turned out a lot better. And even he might have, if he'd had someone to care for and confide in all that time. But I'm sorry to say that I think it is too late to change the way we have turned out. The turning-out process has come to an end, and we are to a very great extent what we are. Our parents are getting older, and Lola is married, and I will probably continue to make poor life decisions and suffer recurrent depressive episodes, and Simon will probably continue to be a highly competent and good-natured but emotionally inaccessible person. But maybe it was always going to be that way, and there was never anything we could have done. It makes me think about the first day I ever saw you, and I remember the knitted green cardigan I was wearing, and the hairband you had in your hair. I mean the life we've had since then, together and not together — whether it was already there with us that day. The truth is that I really love Lola, and my mother, and I think that they love me, although we can't seem to get along with one another, and maybe we never will. In a funny way maybe it's not important to get along, and more important just to love each other anyway. I know, I know — she goes to Mass a couple of times and suddenly she wants to love everyone. Anyway, we're already at Athlone so I should probably stop writing this email. Just remind me that I have an idea for an essay about 'The Golden Bowl' that I want to run by you. Have you ever read such a juicy novel?? I threw it across the room when it was finished. Can't wait to see you. Love love love. Eileen.

25.

On the platform of a train station, late morning, early June: two women embracing after a separation of several months. Behind them, a tall fair-haired man alighting from the train carrying two suitcases. The women unspeaking, their eyes closed tight, their arms wrapped around one another, for a second, two seconds, three. Were they aware, in the intensity of their embrace, of something slightly ridiculous about this tableau, something almost comical, as someone nearby sneezed violently into a crumpled tissue; as a dirty discarded plastic bottle scuttled along the platform under a breath of wind; as a mechanised billboard on the station wall rotated from an advertisement for hair products to an advertisement for car insurance; as life in its ordinariness and even ugly vulgarity imposed itself everywhere all around them? Or were they in this moment unaware, or something more than unaware — were they somehow invulnerable to, untouched by, vulgarity and ugliness, glancing for a moment into something deeper, something concealed beneath the surface of life, not unreality but a hidden reality: the presence at all times, in all places, of a beautiful world?

When Felix pulled up outside Alice's house after work that night, the lights were on in the windows. It was after seven o'clock, still bright out, but colder now, and beyond the trees the sea showed green and silver. With a backpack over his shoulder he walked with a jogging step up to the front door, rapping the knocker twice in quick succession against the brass plate. Chill salt air stirred over him, and his hands were cold. When the door came open, it was not Alice standing inside, but another woman, the same age, taller, with darker hair, dark eyes. Hello, she said. You must be Felix, I'm Eileen. Come on in. He entered and allowed her to close the door behind him. He was smiling distractedly. Yeah, he said. Eileen, I've heard about you. Glancing at him she said: Good things, I hope. She told him Alice was cooking dinner, and he followed her down the hallway, watching the back of her head and her neat narrow shoulders proceeding ahead of him to the kitchen door. Inside, a man was seated at the table and Alice was at the stove, wearing a dirty white apron tied around her waist. Hello, she said. I was just draining the pasta. You've met Eileen, this is Simon. Felix nodded, fingering the strap of his backpack as Simon greeted him. The kitchen was a little dim, with just the worktop lights switched on, and candles on the table. The back window was fogged with steam, the glass velvety and blue. Can I give you a hand with anything? Felix asked. Alice was patting her forehead with the back of her wrist, as if to cool herself. I think it's all under control, she said. But thank you. Eileen was just telling us about her sister's wedding. Felix hesitated for a moment, and then sat down at the table. At the weekend, was it? he asked. Turning her attention on him with a delighted expression, Eileen began talking again about the wedding. She was funny and moved her hands a lot. Occasionally she invited input from Simon, who spoke in a relaxed voice and seemed to find everything amusing. He too paid a good deal of attention to Felix, catching his eye now and then and smiling in a vague conspiratorial way, as if pleased by the presence of another man, or pleased by the presence of the women but wanting to share or acknowledge this pleasure with Felix. He was handsome, wearing a linen shirt, thanking Alice in a low easy way when she refilled his glass of wine. The table was set with small patterned side plates, silver cutlery, white cloth napkins. A large yellow salad bowl, the leaves inside oiled and glistening. Alice brought a plate of pasta to the table and laid it down in front of Eileen. Felix, I'm serving you last, she said, because the other two are my guests of honour. Their eyes met. He smiled at her, a little nervously, and said aloud: That's alright, I know my place. She made a sarcastic face and went back to the cooker. He watched.

When they had finished eating, Alice got up to clear the plates from the table. The rattling and scraping of cutlery, the noise of the tap. Simon was asking Felix about work. Tired now and contented, Eileen sat quietly with her eyes half-closed. A fruit crumble warming in the oven. On the table the detritus of the meal, a soiled napkin, sodden leaves in the salad bowl, soft drops of blue-white candle wax on the tablecloth. Alice asked whether anyone wanted coffee. For me, please, said Simon. A carton of ice cream melting slowly on the countertop, wet rivulets running down the sides. Alice unscrewed the base of a silver coffee pot. And what do you do for a job? Felix was saying. Alice told me you work in politics or something. In the sink a dirty saucepan, a wooden chopping board. Then the hiss and spark of the gas burner, and Alice saying: Do you still take it black? Eileen opening her eyes simply to see Simon half-turn toward Alice where she stood at the burner and say over his shoulder: Yes, thank you. No need for sugar, thanks. His attention returning to Felix then, resettling, and Eileen's eyes fluttering almost closed once more. The white of his throat. When he trembled over her, blushing, murmuring, is that okay, I'm sorry. The clanking noise of the oven door, the fragrance of butter and apples. Alice's white apron discarded over the back of a chair, strings trailing. Right, we worked with him on something last year, Simon was saying. I don't know him well, but his staff speak very highly of him. And the house around them quiet and solid with its nailed-down floorboards, with its bright burnished tiles in the candlelight. And the gardens dim and silent. The sea breathing peacefully outside, breathing its salt air through the windows. To think of Alice living here. Alone, or not alone. She was standing at the countertop then, serving the crumble out into bowls with a spoon. Everything in one place. All of life knotted into this house for the night, like a necklace knotted at the bottom of a drawer.

After dinner Felix went outside to smoke, and Eileen went upstairs to make a phone call. In the kitchen Simon and Alice washed the dishes together. Through the window over the sink Felix's slim small figure was now and then visible as he wandered around the darkening garden. The lit tip of his cigarette. Alice watched for the sight of him while she dried the dishes with a chequered tea towel and stacked them away in the cupboards. When Simon asked her how her work was going, she shook her head. Oh, I can't talk about that, she said. It's secret. No, I'm retired. I don't write books anymore. He handed her the damp dripping salad bowl and she patted at it with her tea towel. I find that hard to believe, he said. Felix was no longer visible out the window then, he had gone around the other side of the house, or further back among the trees. You'll have to believe it, she said. I'm burned out. I only had two good ideas. No, it was too painful anyway. And I'm rich now, you know. I think I'm richer than you are.

Leaving the salad tongs down on the wire rack beside the sink, Simon said: I'll bet. Alice put the bowl away and closed the cupboard door again. I paid off my mother's mortgage last year, she said. Did I tell you that? I have so much money I just do things kind of randomly. I will do other things, I have plans, but I'm very disorganised. Simon looked at her but she looked away, taking the salad tongs off the rack, wrapping them up in the tea towel to dry them. That was generous of you, he said. She was embarrassed. Yes, well, I'm only telling you so you'll think I'm a good person, she said. You know I long for your approval. She dropped the tongs into the cutlery drawer. I approve of you completely, he said. Her shoulders jolted up, and she replied, half-joking: Oh no, I'm not to be completely approved of. But you can approve of me a little bit. He was silent for a moment, wiping down a roasting dish with the sponge. Restless now, she glanced out the window again and saw nothing. The light fading. Silhouettes of trees. Anyway, she isn't speaking to me anymore, she said. Neither of them are. Simon paused, and then put the dish down on the rack. Your mother and your brother, he said. She took the dish up and started dabbing at it with the towel, quick hard little dabs, saying: Or I'm not speaking to them, I can't remember which. We had a falling-out when I was in hospital. You know they're living together again now. He had let the sponge float down through the dishwater to the base of the sink. I'm sorry, he said. That sounds miserable. She gave a raw laugh, scalding her throat, and went on dabbing at the roasting dish. The sad thing is, I feel better when I don't have to see them, she said. It's not very Christian, I know. I hope they're happy. But I prefer to be with people who like me. She could feel him watching her as she bent down and thrust the roasting dish noisily into the back of a cupboard. I don't think that's un-Christian, he said. She gave another trembling laugh. Oh, what a nice thing to say, she replied. Thank you. I feel much better. He retrieved the sponge from the bottom of the sink. And how are you? she asked. He smiled down at the dishwater, a resigned smile. I'm alright, he said. She went on watching him. Glancing at her he said humorously: What? She raised her eyebrows, innocuous. I'm not sure what the story is, she said. I mean, with you and Eileen. At that he returned his attention to the sink. Join the club, he answered. She was twisting the tea towel thoughtfully between her hands. But you're just friends now, she said. He was nodding his head, dropping a spatula on the drying rack, answering yes. And you're happy, she went on. Finally he gave a laugh. I wouldn't go that far, he said. No, it's the old life of quiet desperation for me, I'm afraid. The back door opened and Felix came inside, stamping his shoes on the mat, closing the door behind him. Beautiful evening out there, he said. And overhead the creak of footsteps, Eileen's soft tread down the stairs. Alice folded the damp wilted tea towel in her hands. They had all come to see her. For this reason they were all in her house, for no other reason, and now that they were here it did not matter much what they did or said. Felix asking Simon if he had ever been a smoker. No, I didn't think so. Too healthy-looking. And I'd say you drink a lot of water as well, do you? Conversation and laughter, these were just pleasant arrangements of sounds in the air. Eileen in the doorway and Alice getting up to pour her another glass of wine, to ask her about work. She had come to see her, they were together again, it did not matter much now what they said or did.

A little after one in the morning they went upstairs to bed. Lights switched on and off

355

again, the noises of taps running, cisterns refilling, doors opened and closed. Alice let the blind down in her room while Felix sat on the side of the bed. She came to him and he started to unbutton her dress. I'm sorry, he said. She put her hand on his head, smoothing his hair back. Why are you saying that? she asked. Because we had a fight? He exhaled slowly and for a moment said nothing. It wasn't really a fight, though, was it? he said. I don't mind. You can call it that if you want. It won't happen again, whatever it was. Sadly she went on looking down at him a little longer, and then she turned away and finished unbuttoning her dress. Are you giving up on me? she asked. He watched her slip the dress from her shoulders and drop it into the laundry basket. Ah no, he said. I'm just going to try being nice to you for a while. Unhooking her bra, she let out a high laugh. I might not like that, she answered. He got onto the bed then, smiling to himself. No, I thought not, he said. But you can't always get what you want. She lay down on the bed beside him. Stroking her breast with his hand, he said: You're happy she's here, aren't you? Your friend. After a moment, Alice said yes. Yeah, it's cute the way you love each other so much, he said. Girls are like that. You should get time on your own with her while she's around, don't let the lads crowd in on you. Alice smiled. We've been apart for too long, she said. We're shy with each other now. He turned over on his back and looked up at the ceiling. That won't last, he said. And I like her, by the way. Alice smoothed her hand slowly down his shoulder, down his arm. Will you spend some time with us tomorrow? she said. He made a kind of shrugging gesture. Yeah, why not, he said. Closing his eyes, he thought again, and then added: I'd like to.

Slowly the breath of the sea drew the tide out away from the shore, leaving the sand flat and glimmering under the stars. The seaweed wet, bedraggled, crawling with insects. The dunes massed and quiet, dune grass smoothed by the cool wind. The paved walkway up from the beach in silence now under a film of white sand, the curved roofs of the caravans glowing dimly, parked cars huddled dark on the grass. Then the amusements, the ice cream kiosk with its shutter pulled down, and up the street and into town, the post office, the hotel, the restaurant. The Sailor's Friend with its doors closed, stickers on the windows illegible. The sweeping headlights of a single car passing. Rear lights red like coals. Further up the street, a row of houses, windows reflecting the streetlights blankly, bins lined up outside, and then the coast road out of town, silent, empty, trees rising through the darkness. The sea to the west, a length of dark cloth. And to the east, up through the gates, the old rectory, blue as milk. Inside, four bodies sleeping, waking, sleeping again. On their sides, or lying on their backs, with the quilts kicked down, through dreams they passed in silence. And already now behind the house the sun was rising. On the back walls of the house and through the branches of the trees, through the coloured leaves of the trees and through the damp green grasses, the light of dawn was sifting. Summer morning. Cold clear water cupped in the palm of a hand.

26.

At nine o'clock they were eating breakfast together in the kitchen, with clouds of steam from the kettle, clattering of plates and cups, sunlight billowing through the back window. Footsteps up and down the staircase after that, and voices calling. Alice threw a straw basket full of beach towels into the boot of the car while Felix stood leaning against the bonnet. Her sunglasses on her head, pushing her damp hair back off her face. He came and put his arms around her from behind, kissed the back of her neck, said something in her ear, and she laughed. The four of them in the car then with the windows rolled down, the smell of hot plastic and stale cigarette smoke, Thin Lizzy on the radio, a crackle of static. Simon in the back seat, saying to Alice: God no, I haven't heard from her in ages. Eileen's face at the open window, the wind whipping hard through her hair. When they parked up, the beach ahead was white and glittering, dotted with bathers, people in wetsuits, families with sun umbrellas and coloured plastic buckets. Eleven o'clock on a Tuesday. Down by the dunes Alice and Eileen spread their towels out on the sand, one orange, the other with a pink-and-yellow pattern of seashells. Taking his shoes off, Simon said he would go and see what the water was like. Felix, toying with the drawstring on his swimming shorts, smiled to himself. I knew you'd say that, he said. Go on, I'll go with you, why not. The tide was out and as they walked the sand was darker, firmer underfoot, crusted with coloured stones and fragments of shell, dried seaweed, the whitened remains of crabs. Ahead of them the sea. The sun beat down hot on their necks and shoulders. Beside Simon, Felix looked small and compact, dark-haired, nimble. Simon's shadow longer over the flat wet sand. Felix started asking about his job again, asking what he actually did all day. He said he mostly attended meetings, sometimes with politicians, and sometimes with activists and community groups. Saltwater mild over their feet, and then cold on their ankles, colder still up at their knees. In the last few months Simon said they had been working a lot with an organisation for refugees.

Helping them, said Felix. Trying to, said Simon. Is the water always this cold, by the way? Felix laughed, his teeth were chattering. Yeah, it's always horrible, he answered. Don't know why I came in, I usually never do. And you're renting in Dublin, or you own a place? He was hugging his arms against his chest as he spoke, shivering his shoulders. Right, I have an apartment, Simon said. I mean, I have a mortgage. Felix splashed his hand idly through the surface of the water, kicking up a little white spray in Simon's direction. Without raising his eyes, he said: Yeah, my mam died there last year and she left us the house. But that's still got ten years on the mortgage as well. He rubbed the back of his neck with his wet fingertips. I don't live there or anything, he added. My brother is actually in the middle of selling it now. Simon listened in silence, wading along to keep pace, the water waist-high now. He said gently that he was very sorry to hear that Felix had lost his mother. Felix looked at him, screwed one eye shut, and then looked back down at the water. Yep, he said. Simon asked how he felt about selling the house and he gave a strange, hard laugh. It's funny, he replied. I'm avoiding my brother for the last six weeks trying to get out of signing it over.

Isn't that mad? I don't know why I'm doing it. It's not like I want to live there. And I really need the money. But that's me, can't do things the easy way. He splashed his hand through the water again aimlessly. It's good you're doing that stuff you were saying, about the asylum seekers, he said. God love them. Simon seemed to consider this a moment, and then said that he felt increasingly frustrated with his work, because all he really did was go to meetings and write reports that no one ever read. But at least you care, said Felix. A lot of people don't. Simon said that while of course he did care, in theory, it didn't seem to make much difference whether he did or not. Most of the time I'm going about my life like it's not even happening, he added. I mean, I meet with these people who've gone through things I can't even begin to understand. And as much as I'm on their side in principle, and I go to work every day and do my job, in reality I spend most of my time thinking about — I don't know. Felix gestured back toward the shore, at the reclining forms of Alice and Eileen. The likes of them, he said. Smiling now, Simon turned his eyes away and said yes, the likes of them. Felix was observing him carefully. You're religious, are you? he asked. Simon paused a moment before looking back up at him. Did Alice tell you that, he said, or did you just guess? Felix gave another cheerful laugh. The Catholic guilt was a giveaway, he answered. Nah, she told me. For a few seconds they were silent, walking on. Quietly, Simon said that at one time in his life he had thought about joining the priesthood. Felix was observing him, mild, interested. And why didn't you, he said, if you don't mind me asking? Simon was looking down into the cold cloudy water, the surface broken up here and there by fragments of reflected light. Then he answered: I was going to say that I thought politics would be more practical. But the truth is, I didn't want to be alone. Felix was grinning to himself. That's your problem, he said, you're hard on yourself for not being more like Jesus. You should do what I do, just be a dickhead and enjoy your life. Simon looked up then, smiling. You don't seem like a dickhead, he said. But I'm glad to know you enjoy your life. Felix waded a little further ahead into the water. Without turning back he said aloud: I've definitely done a lot of stuff I shouldn't have done. But there's no point crying over it, is there? I mean, maybe I do cry over it sometimes, but I try not to. Simon watched him for another second or two, the water lapping up around his small white body. Well, we're all sinners, Simon said. Felix turned around and looked at him then. Oh yeah, he said. He started laughing again. I forgot you lot believed that, he added. Absolute freaks, no offence. Come on, we're not going to get a swim in at all if you stay standing there. He walked in a few steps further and then dipped his whole body under the surface of the water, disappearing completely.

On the shore Eileen was sitting up, cross-legged, leafing through a collection of short stories. Alice was lying on a towel beside her, sunlight glistening on her damp eyelids. A breath of wind caught at a page of Eileen's book and she smoothed it back down impatiently with her hand. Without opening her eyes Alice said: So what's the situation? Eileen made no reply at first, did not even lift her head. Then she said: With Simon, you mean. I don't know what the situation is. You know, I think we're very different people. Alice's eyes were open now, shielded by the flat of a hand, looking up at her. What does that mean? she asked. Eileen frowned down at a page of dense black type and then closed the book. He's seeing someone else, she said. But I don't know if it would have worked out between us anyway. You know, we're just very different. Alice still had her hand up, shading her eyes. You said that before, but what does it mean? she asked. Eileen put the book down then and took a drink of water from her bottle. After swallowing she said: You're being intrusive. Alice dropped her hand away and closed her eyes again. Sorry, she said. Eileen put the cap back on the bottle, saying: It's a touchy subject. A small insect landed on Alice's towel and zipped away again through the air. Understandably, said Alice. Eileen was looking out at the horizon, two figures dropping down now below the surface of the water, and now emerging again, changing places with one another. If it didn't work out, it would be too depressing, she remarked. Alice sat up on her elbows, digging two little hollows in the soft sand. But if it did work out, said Alice. That's gambling mentality, Eileen replied. Alice was nodding her head, her eyes travelling up and down the seated figure of her friend beside her. The slender black shoulder strap of her swimsuit. That's risk aversion, said Alice. Eileen was half-smiling. Self-sabotage, then, Eileen answered. Alice was smiling too, cocking her head to one side. That's arguable either way, she said. He does love you, though. Eileen glanced around at her then, saying: What, he said that to you? Alice shook her head. No, I just mean it's obvious, she replied. Eileen bent forward over her crossed legs, planting her hands down on the rough pink-patterned towel in front of her, the little ridges of her spine showing through the thin synthetic cloth of her swimsuit. Right, in a way he loves me, she said. Because I'm a little idiot who can't do anything for myself, that's his big thing. She straightened up again and rubbed her eyes with her hands. Earlier in the year, around January or February, I started getting really bad headaches, she said. And one night I went down this rabbit hole online looking up my symptoms, and I convinced myself I had a brain tumour. This is a completely stupid story, by the way. Anyway, I called Simon at like one in the morning to tell him I was scared I had brain cancer and he got a taxi over to my apartment and let me cry on him for like an hour. He didn't even seem annoyed, he was just very chilled out. Not that I wanted him to be annoyed. But would I ever do that for him? If he called me in the middle of the night saying, oh hey Eileen, what's up, I've irrationally convinced myself I have a rare form of cancer, do you want to come over and let me cry on you until I tire myself out and fall asleep? There's no point even imagining how I would react, because it's just something he would never do. In fact if he did that, I would assume there genuinely was something wrong with his brain. Alice was laughing. You have all these stories where you're a hypochondriac, she said. But you never come across that way to me. Eileen had taken her sunglasses from her bag and was cleaning them on a corner of the sweater she had taken off. No, that's what I'm saying, she said. Simon gets the absolute dregs of my personality. I don't know why I'm criticising him, I should be criticising myself. What adult woman would behave like that? It's awful. Alice was digging her elbows down into the towel contemplatively. After a moment she said aloud: You mean you don't like who you are, when you're with him. Eileen frowned to herself then, inspecting the sunglasses under the light. No, not that, she said. I just feel like our relationship is very one-way. Like he's always fixing things for me and I never fix anything for him. I mean, it's great that he's so helpful. And I need that, in a way. But he doesn't need anything back from me. After a pause she added: Anyway, it doesn't matter. He has this twenty-three-year-old girlfriend who everyone says is great. Alice lay back down on the beach towel. The figures of Simon and Felix were no longer visible from where Eileen was sitting, just the vast haze of light and water, thin waves breaking like thread. Behind them the village glittered white along the coast, as far as the lighthouse, and to the left were the empty sand dunes. Alice put the back of her hand to her forehead as if to cool it. Could you really live here, do you think? Eileen asked. Alice looked over at her with no surprise. I do live here, she said. A frown flickered over Eileen's features and instantly receded. No, I know that, she said. But I mean in the long term. Mildly Alice replied: I don't know. I'd like to. Behind them a young family made their way down from the caravan park, two children toddling ahead in matching dungarees. Why? asked Eileen. Alice gave a smile. Why not? she said. It's beautiful, isn't it? In a low tone Eileen answered: Sure, obviously. She was looking down at the towel then, smoothing out creases with her long fingers, while Alice watched her. You could always come and live with me, Alice replied. Eileen shut her eyes and opened them again. Unfortunately I have to work for a living, she said. Alice hesitated for a moment, and then answered lightly: Don't we all. The men were coming out of the water then, glistening wet, reflecting the light of the sun, and they were speaking to one another, at first inaudibly, their shadows cast behind them on the sand, dappled blue, and the women fell silent and watched them.

At two o'clock, Felix went out to work and the other three walked around the village. It was a hot afternoon, black patches of tar softening on the roads, school exam students dawdling in their uniforms. In the charity shop beside the church Eileen bought a green silk blouse for six euro fifty. Felix meanwhile was wheeling a tall stillage trolley through the aisles of the warehouse, angling his body against the mechanism of the trolley in a certain precise manner in order to guide it around corners, placing his left foot just behind the back wheels while his hands loosed and then regripped the handles. He carried out this action identically again and again, never seeming to think about it except when he miscalculated and the weight of the trolley slipped briefly out of his control. In Alice's kitchen, Simon was making dinner, and Alice was encouraging Eileen to write a book. For some reason Eileen was holding in her lap the silk blouse she had purchased earlier in the day. Occasionally while Alice spoke she petted the blouse absent-mindedly as if it were an animal. She seemed in one sense to be giving her conversation with Alice a very deep and sustained attention, but in another sense she hardly seemed to be listening at all. She looked down at the tiles, apparently thinking, her lips sometimes moving silently as if to form words, but saying nothing.

After dinner, they walked down to meet Felix for a drink. A cool light was fading over the sea, blue and faintly yellow. Felix was standing outside The Sailor's Friend when they arrived, talking on the phone. He waved to them with his free hand, saying into his phone: We'll see, I'll ask. Listen, I'll let you go, alright? They went inside together then. If it isn't the bold Felix Brady, said the barman. My best customer. To the others, Felix said: That's his idea of a joke. The four of them sat down together in a booth near the empty fireplace, drinking, and talking about different cities they had lived in. Felix asked Alice about New York, and she said she had found it stressful and confusing. She said everybody there lived in very strange buildings, with hallways and staircases that led nowhere, and none of the doors ever closed properly, even bathroom doors, even in expensive places. Felix said he had moved to London after he finished school and spent some time there working as a barman, including a short stint at a strip club, which he told them was the most depressing job he'd ever had. Addressing Simon, he asked: Have you ever been to a strip club? Politely, Simon said no. Awful places, said Felix. You should have a look sometime, if you ever feel like things are going okay in the world. Simon said he had never lived in London but had spent a bit of time there when he was at university, and after that he had lived in Paris for several years. Felix asked whether he spoke any French, and Simon said yes, adding that his partner at the time had been Parisian and they had spoken French at home. You lived together? said Felix. Simon was taking a drink from his glass. He nodded. How long for? said Felix. Sorry, I'm like interviewing you now. I'm just curious. Simon said about four or five years. Raising his eyebrows, Felix said: Oh right. And you're single now, are you? Simon gave a wry smile at that, and Felix laughed. Eileen was plaiting a lock of her hair idly with her fingers, watching them. Yes, I'm single, Simon said. Dropping the half-finished braid, Eileen interjected: Well, you're seeing someone. This remark seemed to interest Felix, and he glanced back at Simon quickly. No, not at the moment, Simon replied. You mean Caroline, we're not seeing each other anymore. Eileen affected a surprised face, opening her mouth up in the shape of an 'o', and then, perhaps to mask some real surprise, returned to plaiting her hair. So secretive, she said. You weren't going to tell me? To Felix, she added: He never tells me anything. Simon sat watching her, amused. I was going to tell you, he said. I was just waiting for the opportune moment. She let out a little laugh, her face turning pink. Opportune in what sense? she asked. Cheerfully Felix put his glass down on the table. Now we're having fun, he said.

After another drink, another, and one more, they left the bar and went to get ice cream. Eileen and Alice were laughing, talking about someone they had hated in college, who had recently married someone else they had also hated in college. Have they always been so mean? Felix said to Simon. In a humorous tone, Simon answered that Eileen had actually been a nice girl before she met Alice, and Alice called back: I knew you were going to say that. The shop on the corner with its sliding automatic doors, buzzing white light fixtures, glossy floor tiles. By the fruit and vegetable crates, a display of fresh flowers.

Gravy granules, rolls of baking paper, identical bottles of vegetable oil. Alice slid open the freezer door and they each selected a pre-packaged ice cream. Then she remembered they would need milk and soda bread for breakfast, and kitchen roll, and Eileen wanted toothpaste. As they approached the till with these items, Alice took her purse from her bag, and Simon said: No, no, let me. Eileen watched him fish his wallet from his pocket, a slim leather wallet, which he unfolded with one hand to take out his card. Glancing up, he caught her looking, and sheepishly she smiled, touching her ear, and he smiled back at her. Quietly Felix looked on, while Alice packed the items into a cloth bag. Walking back up the coast road, they ate their ice creams and talked about whether they had gotten any sunburn at the beach earlier. Alice and Eileen falling behind together, arm in arm, smelling of perfume and sun lotion, talking about Henry James. I never know what to think until I talk to you, Alice said. Simon and Felix striding up the hill ahead, Felix asking about Simon's family, about where he grew up, about his previous relationships. Politely and pleasantly Simon answered his questions, or else smiled and said only: No comment. Felix nodding his head, amused, hands in his pockets. Just girls, is it, he said. Simon looked around at him then. Sorry? he asked. With a serene expression Felix looked back at him. Is it just girls you like, he said. For a moment Simon said nothing, and then in a low easy tone of voice answered: So far. Felix's high laughter then echoing off the facades of houses. Past the street entrance to the caravan park, the golf links silent and blue, the hotel with its bright glass lobby, they walked.

At the house they wished one another goodnight and went upstairs. In the en suite Alice brushed her teeth while Felix sat up in bed scrolling through the notifications on his phone. You know my friend Dani, he said, she's having people over for her birthday tomorrow. Nothing wild, her nieces and nephews will be there and all that. I might just show the face, is that alright? Alice appeared in the doorway of the bathroom, drying her hands on a towel. Of course, she said. He was nodding his head, looking her up and down. You can come if you want, he added. And the other two. She hung the towel up then and came to sit down on the bed, taking her necklace off. That might be fun, she said. Would Dani mind? He sat up and reached to help her with the clasp. No, not at all, he said. She told me to say it to you. Alice let the necklace spool out into her hand and then dropped it on the bedside cabinet. Attractive, isn't he? Felix added. Your friend. Simon. Alice gave a feline little smile then and got onto the bed. I told you he was, she said. Felix put his hand behind his head, looking up at her. He reminds me of you, he replied. Keeps his cards close. She picked up her pillow and batted him with it. Sadly, I suspect he might be heterosexual, she said. Tucking the pillow behind his head, Felix answered mildly: Yeah? We'll see. She laughed, climbing on top of him. You're not going to leave me for him, are you? she asked. Smoothing his hands down from her hips, down her thighs, he said: Leave you? No, not at all. You don't think the three of us could have a bit of fun together, no? She was shaking her head. And where would Eileen be in this scenario? she asked. Downstairs knitting? Felix pouted his bottom lip thoughtfully, and then remarked: I wouldn't rule her out. Alice ran a finger over one of his dark eyebrows. This is what I get for having such good-looking friends, she said. He was smiling. You're not so bad yourself, you know, he said. Come here.

Eileen meanwhile was sitting on her bed scrolling on her phone through a series of wedding photographs her mother had sent her. On the floor, a discarded cardigan, her swimsuit with its straps tangled, sandals with the buckles hanging open. On the bedside table a lamp with a pleated pink shade. When a knock sounded softly on her door she looked up and said aloud: Hello? Simon opened the door a crack. His face in the shadow, his hand on the handle. I'll just leave your toothpaste in the bathroom, he said. Sleep well. With her arm she gestured for him to come inside. I'm looking at wedding photos, she said. He closed the door behind him and sat down on the side of the bed. The photograph on her screen showed Lola and Matthew standing together outside the church, Lola holding a bouquet of pink and white flowers. That's nice, said Simon. She scrolled on to the next image then, the bridal party standing together, Eileen in her pale-green dress, half-smiling. Ah, you look beautiful, Simon said. She moved over on the bed and patted the mattress to invite him. He sat beside her, their backs against the headboard, and she scrolled on. Photographs from the drinks reception. Lola laughing with her mouth open, a flute of champagne in her hand. Yawning now, Eileen nestled her head against Simon's shoulder, and he settled his arm around her, warm and heavy. After a minute or two she put the phone down on her lap and let her eyes drift closed. Today was fun, she said. His fingers moved idly over the back of her neck, up into her hair, and she gave a soft pleasurable sigh. Mm, he said. She rested her hand on his chest, her eyes half-open. So what happened with Caroline? she asked. Looking down at her hand, he answered: I told her there was someone else. Eileen paused, as if waiting for him to continue. Then she said: Anyone I know? His fingers behind her ear, through her hair. Oh, just the same girl I've been in love with all along, he said. Now and then she likes to toy with my feelings to make sure I'm still interested. She sucked on her lower lip and released it. Heartless woman, she said. He was smiling to himself. Well, it's my fault for spoiling her, he said. I'm a terrible fool about her, really. She moved her hand down over his shirt buttons, down to the buckle of his belt. Simon, she said. You know the night I came over to your apartment, when you were sleeping. He said yes. When we got into bed that night, she went on, you just turned over on your side, away from me. Do you remember that? With a self-conscious smile he said he remembered. She was tracing the buckle of his belt with her fingers. You didn't want to touch me? she asked. He let out a kind of laugh, looking down at her small white hand. Yes, of course I did, he replied. But when you came upstairs I thought you seemed upset about something. She was thoughtful for a moment. I was, kind of, she said. I suppose I thought it would make me feel better if we slept together. I'm sorry if you think that's bad. But when you turned away from me, I felt like, maybe you didn't really want me after all. He was smoothing his hand down over the back of her neck. Oh, he said. That didn't occur to me. I mean, I had no idea you wanted to sleep with me to cheer yourself up. I was doing it purely because I wanted to, and you let me. I wasn't even really sure why you were letting me, to be honest. I suppose I thought, maybe it was good for your self-esteem to get in bed with someone who wanted you so badly. I've had that feeling before, like it's flattering to be the object of desire, and maybe it's so flattering that it's even kind of sexy in a way. But it never went through my mind that you would think I didn't want you. I suppose the way I think about these things — I mean, even when we do make love, I some-times feel like it's something that I'm doing to you, for my own reasons. And maybe you get some kind of innocent physical pleasure out of it, I hope you do, but for me it's different. I know you're going to say that's sexist. She was laughing, her mouth was open. It is sexist, she said. Not that I mind. It's flattering, like you were saying. You have this primal desire to subjugate and possess me. It's very masculine, I think it's sexy. Lifting his hand, he touched his thumb to her lower lip. I do feel that, he said. But at the same time, you have to want it. She looked up at him, her eyes were wide and dark. I do, she said. He turned over then and kissed her mouth. For a time they lay like that with their arms around one another, his hand caressing the small hard bone of her hip, her breath hot and damp on his neck. When he put his hand under her dress, she shut her eyes and let out a low breath. Ah, you're being very good, he murmured. She gave a kind of animal cry, she was shaking her head. Oh God, she said. Please. Laughing again now, he asked: What does that mean, 'please'? She went on shaking her head against the pillow. You know what it means, she replied. He smoothed a strand of her hair behind her ear. I don't have a condom, he said. She told him it was okay. Then she added: As long as you're not having unprotected sex with anyone else.

379

His ears were red, he was smiling. No, no, he said. Just you. Can I take this off? She sat up and he lifted her dress off over her head. Underneath she was wearing a soft white bra and he reached behind her to unhook it. Watching him while he slipped the straps off her shoulders, she gave a little shiver. She lay down on her back then and took off her underwear. Simon, she said. He was unbuttoning his shirt, looking over at her attentively. Do you do this with all your girlfriends? she asked. I mean, the way you talk to me, telling me that I'm being good. Do you do it a lot? Not that it's my business, I'm just curious. He gave a kind of shy smile. No, never, really, he said. I'm improvising. Is it okay? She laughed then and so did he, embarrassed. Oh, I love it, she said. I was just wondering, after the last time. You know, maybe this is his thing, maybe he's like this with all the other women. He was leaving his clothes down on the floorboards. There haven't really been that many women anyway, he said. Not that I want to spoil the fantasy for you. She shaded her eyes, and she was smiling. How many, she said. He lay down on top of her then. Let's not, he answered. With her arms around his neck she asked: Less than twenty? He gave a funny frown. Fewer, he said. Yes. Is that what you think, twenty? She was grinning, she licked her teeth. Fewer than ten? she asked. He took in a patient breath and then answered: I thought you were going to be good. She bit her lip. I am, she said. When he moved inside her she made a hard little gasping sound and said nothing. He closed his eyes. Oh, I love you, he murmured. In a small childish voice she said: And am I the only one you love? He kissed the side of her face then, saying: Jesus, God, yes.

Afterwards, she turned over on her belly, her arms folded on the pillow, her head turned to look at him. He pulled a corner of the quilt up over himself and lay down on his back with his hand behind his head. His eyes were closed, he was sweating. Sometimes I wish I was your wife, she said. Catching his breath still, he smiled to himself. Go on, he answered. She settled her chin down on her arms. But when I think about being married to you, she went on, I picture it too much like this. Like we get to spend the whole day with our friends, and then at night we lie in bed together making love. In real life you'd probably be away all the time at conferences. Having affairs with people's secretaries. Without opening his eyes he replied that he had never had an affair in his life. But you've never been married, she pointed out. See, your girlfriends are always the same age. A wife gets older. He laughed then. Such a brat, he said. If you were my wife I'd put manners on you. She watched him for a moment in silence. Then she remarked: But if I was your wife we wouldn't be friends. Languidly he opened an eye to look at her. What do you mean? he asked. She gazed down at her arms, thin, and freckled from the sun. I've just been thinking about these situations, she said, where people who are friends get into relationships. And usually it ends badly. I mean, of course that's true in any case when people get together. But in most cases you can just block the person's number and move on. Whereas I don't really want to block your number, personally speaking. She propped herself upright on her elbows, looking down at him. Do you remember when I was like, fourteen or fifteen, you told me we were going to be friends for the rest of our lives? she asked. I know you probably don't remember, but I do. He was lying very still and listening to her. Sure, he said. Of course I remember. She nodded her head several times in quick succession, sitting up now on the mattress, gathering the quilt around her body. And what about that? she asked. If we get together and then break up — Even saying that is so painful, I just, I don't even want to think about it. With everything the way it is — I mean, Alice living out here in the middle of nowhere, and all our friends like, emigrating constantly, and I have to buy illegal antibiotics on the internet when I get a urinary tract infection because I'm too poor to go to the doctor, and every election everywhere on earth makes me feel like I'm physically getting kicked in the face. And then not to have you in my life? Jesus, I don't know. It's hard for me to imagine going on in those circumstances. Whereas, if we just stay friends, okay we can't sleep together, but what's the likelihood we'll ever fall out of each other's lives? I can't imagine it, can you? Quietly he answered: No. I see what you mean. She rubbed her hands down her face, shaking her head. In some ways, maybe our friendship is actually more important, she said. I don't know. When I was living with Aidan, I sometimes thought, it's a little bit sad that I'll never find out what might have happened with Simon. But maybe, in a way, it's better not to know. We'll always be in each other's lives and we'll always have this feeling between us, and it's better. Sometimes when I get really sad and depressed, you know, I lie in bed and think about you. I don't mean in a sexual way. I just think about the goodness of you as a person. And since you like me, or you love me, I must be okay. I can feel that feeling inside myself even now while I'm describing it to you. It's like, when everything is really bad, it's this one small feeling the size of an acorn, and it's inside me, here. She gestured to the base of her breastbone, between her ribs. It's like the way, when I'm upset, I know I can call you, and you'll say soothing things to me, she said. And when I think about that, most of the time I don't even need to call you, because I can feel it, the way I'm describing. I can feel that you're with me. I know that probably sounds stupid. But if we got together and then broke up, would I not be able to feel that anymore? And what would I have inside here instead? She tapped the base of her breastbone again with anxious fingers. Nothing? she asked. He lay there on the bed watching her, and for a few moments was silent. Then he said: I don't know. It's very difficult. I understand what you're saying. With a desperate, almost disbelieving look, she stared at him. But you're not saying anything back to me, she said. He gave a kind of self-deprecating smile, looking up at the ceiling. Well, it's complicated, he replied. Maybe you're right, it's better to draw a line under it, and not put ourselves through all this anymore. I do find it very difficult, hearing you say these things. You know, I felt terrible about the situation with Caroline, and I really wanted to fix it. But from what you're saying now, I suppose it wasn't really about that, it was something else. I do understand your reasons, but from what you're saying, it sounds like you don't actually want to be with me. She stayed there staring at him, her hand still pressed to her chest. He rubbed his jaw and sat up from the bed with his feet on the floorboards. His back was turned to her. I'll let you get some sleep, he said. He picked his clothes up off the floor and put them back on again. She sat on the mattress, the quilt wound around her body, saying nothing. Finally he finished buttoning his shirt and turned to look at her. When you came over that night, he said, after I got back from London, I felt very excited to see you. I don't know if I said that, or maybe I did. To be honest, I was nervous, because I was so happy. She was silent, wiping her nose with her fingers, and he nodded to himself, acknowledging her silence. I hope you don't regret it, he said. Softly she answered: No. He smiled then. That's something, he said.

I'm glad. After a pause he added: I'm sorry that I couldn't be what you wanted. She sat staring a few seconds longer. Then she said: But you are. He laughed at that, his eyes on the floor. The feeling is mutual, he replied. But no, I understand. I do, really. I won't keep you up any later. Sleep well, alright? He left the room then. Eileen sat still on the bed, her shoulders drawn up, her arms folded. She picked up her phone and dropped it again without looking, pushed her hair off her forehead, closed her eyes. Remembering absently a line of poetry: Well now that's done: and I'm glad it's over. Her underarms prickling wet, her back aching, shoulders hot and sore from the sun. Across the landing Simon enters his own room and closes the door behind him. And if in the silence and solitude of his room he kneels down on the floorboards, is he praying? And for what? To be free of selfish desires — maybe. Or maybe with his elbows on the mattress, his hands clasped before him, he is only thinking: What do you want from me? Please God show me what you want.

27.

At six forty-five in the morning, Felix's alarm rang out, a flat repetitive beeping noise. The room was dim, the west-facing windows letting in only a little cool white light through the blinds. What time is it, Alice murmured. He turned the alarm off and got out of bed. Time for work, he said. Go back to sleep. He showered in the en suite bathroom and came out again with a towel around his shoulders, pulling on his underwear. When he was dressed he went to the bedside and bent to kiss Alice's forehead, warm and damp. I'll see you later on, he said. With her eyes closed she answered: I love you. He touched her forehead with the back of his hand as if taking her temperature. You do, yeah, he said. He went downstairs then and into the kitchen. Eileen was leaning against the countertop, unscrewing the base of the coffee pot. Her eyes were swollen and red. Good morning, she said.

From the doorway Felix looked at her. What are you doing up? he asked. She gave a tired smile and said she couldn't sleep. Studying her face, Felix replied: You look a bit wrecked alright. He opened the fridge and took out a pot of yoghurt, while she dumped yesterday's coffee grounds into the sink. Sitting down at the table, he asked: So what do you do for a job? Alice told me you're a journalist or something. Eileen shook her head, filling the pot with water from the tap. No, no, she said. I just work for a magazine. I'm an editor, kind of. Felix was stirring the yoghurt with his spoon. What kind of magazine? he asked. She said it was a literary journal. Ah right, he said. I don't really know what that is. She was lighting the burner then. Yeah, we don't have a wide readership, she said. We publish poetry and essays and things like that. He asked how the magazine made money in that case. Oh, it doesn't, she said. It's just funded with grants. Felix looked interested then. You mean like from the taxpayer? he asked. She sat down at the other end of the table, smiling faintly. Yes, she said. Do you object? After swallowing he answered: Not at all. And you get paid from the taxpayer as well, do you? She said yes. Although not a lot, she added. He was licking the back of the spoon. What's not a lot to you? he asked. She took a tangerine from the fruit bowl and started to unpeel it. About twenty thousand a year, she said. His eyebrows shot up, and he put the yoghurt down. You're not serious, he said. After tax? She said no, before. He was shaking his head. I make more than that, he said. She left a long spiralling piece of orange peel down on the table. And why shouldn't you? she asked. He was staring at her. How do you even live? he said. She broke the tangerine in half with her fingers. I often wonder, she replied. He went back to his yoghurt, murmuring in a friendly tone of voice: Fuck's sake. After swallowing another mouthful, he added: And you went to college for that? She was chewing. No, I went to college to learn, she said. He laughed. Fair enough, he answered. Anyway, you probably like your job, do you? She moved her head from side to side uncertainly, and then said: I don't hate it. He was nodding, looking down into the yoghurt pot. That's where we're different, so, he said. She asked him how long he had been at the warehouse and he told her eight or ten months. The coffee pot started sputtering and she got up to look inside. Pulling her sleeve down over her hand, she poured two cups and carried them to the table. He watched her, and then said: Here, can I ask you something? Sitting back down at the table, she replied: Sure. He was frowning to himself. How come you're only visiting her now? he said. I mean, you live in Dublin, it's not that far away. And she's been here for ages. Eileen's posture stiffened while he spoke, but she said nothing, made no particular expression with her face. She added a spoonful of sugar to her coffee without speaking. The way she talks about you, he added, she makes it sound like you're best friends. Quickly and coolly Eileen answered: We are best friends. Behind her a little rain speckled the kitchen window. Right, so how come it took you all this time to come and see her? he asked. I'm just curious. If she's your best friend I would have thought you'd want to visit her before. Eileen's face was white, her nostrils were white when she took in a deep breath and released it. You know I have a job, she said. He was screwing one eye closed then, frowning. Yeah, so do I, he said. But you hardly work weekends, do you? Eileen's arms were folded now, her hands gripping her upper arms through the sleeves of her dressing gown. And why didn't she come and visit me? she asked. If she's so keen on seeing me. She doesn't work weekends, does she? Felix seemed to find this remark peculiar, and he turned it over a moment before answering. I didn't say she was so keen on seeing you, he asked. Maybe neither of you were that keen on seeing each other, I don't know. That's why I'm asking. Gripping her arms very tightly now Eileen said: Well, maybe we weren't. He was nodding his head then. Did you have a falling-out or something? he asked. Irritably she moved a strand of hair out of her face. You don't actually know anything about me, she said. He took this in, and after a moment answered: You don't know anything about me either. She folded her arms again. That's why I'm not interrogating you, she said. He smiled at that. Fair enough, he replied. He swallowed the last of his coffee and got to his feet, taking his jacket from the back of a chair where he'd left it the night before. My theory would be, people like them two are different from you and me, he said. You'll only drive yourself crazy trying to make them act the way you want. Eileen watched him for a few seconds and then replied: I'm not trying to make either of them do anything. Felix had unzipped his backpack and was stuffing his jacket down inside. You have to ask yourself, he said, if they wreck your head so much, why bother? He put his bag over his shoulder then. There must be some reason on your side, he went on. Why you care. Staring down into her coffee cup then, she said very quietly: Fuck off. He gave a surprised little laugh. Eileen, he said, I'm not attacking you. I like you, alright? She was silent. Maybe you should go back to bed, he added. You look tired. I'm off anyway, see you later on. Outside the front door, a mist of morning rain. He got into the car, turned the CD player on and pulled out of the driveway. Watching the road, he whistled along with the music, adding little riffs and variations to the melody now and then, as he drove past the turn-off for the village, along the coast road to the industrial estate.

When Felix got home after work that evening, his dog came bounding up from the kitchen, letting out several high yelps in quick succession, claws clicking on the laminate. Reaching him, she leapt up with her front paws on his legs, her tongue lolling out, panting. He put his hands on her head, tousling her ears, and she let out another yelp. Shh, he said. I've missed you too. Is anyone home? Gently he pushed her back down onto the floor, where she ran around in a circle and sneezed. Felix made his way down the hall then and she trotted behind him. The kitchen was empty, the lights turned off, a few breakfast dishes soaking in the sink. He sat idly on a kitchen chair and took his phone out, while the dog sat at his feet and settled her head in his lap. Scrolling through his notifications with one hand, he rubbed at the scruff of her neck with the other. Alice had sent him a text reading: Still on for Danielle's party this evening? I baked a cake just in case. Hope work was ok. He opened the message then and typed a quick reply: Yeah still on. Said we would be there around 7 is that ok? Dont get your hopes up too much haha it will prob just be a lot of old people and kids. But dani will be glad to see you. The dog emitted a low whining noise and he returned his hand to her head, saying: I've only been gone two days, you know. Are they feeding you alright? She reared her head back to lick his hand. Thanks, he said. That's disgusting. His phone vibrated and he checked it again. Alice was asking if he wanted to eat dinner with them and he said he had eaten already. Will swing by and pick you up in a bit, he typed. She replied: Great. Eileen is in a weird mood, just to let you know . . . . Raising his eyebrows, he typed back: Ahaha. I know anyway, saw her this morning. Your friends are as bad as you are. He got up then, pocketing his phone, and went to the sink to turn on the hot tap. On the left side of his left hand, below the joint of his smallest finger, was a blue sticking plaster. While the hot tap ran, he peeled it off gingerly and looked underneath. A deep pink cut ran just under his knuckle, around to the palm of his hand on the other side. The white cotton pad of the sticking plaster was stained with blood, but the wound was no longer bleeding. He rolled the plaster up and dropped it in the bin under the sink, then washed his hands with soap and water, wincing as he rinsed the cut under the tap. Still sitting at the foot of the kitchen chair, the dog thumped her tail against the floor. Turning around to look down at her, drying his hands carefully on a clean dishcloth, he asked: Do you remember Alice? She's been here a few times, you've met her. The dog got up from the floor and padded over to him. I don't know if she's allowed dogs at her house, he remarked. I'll find out for you. He refilled the dog's bowl with water then. While she was drinking, he went upstairs and changed his clothes, taking off the black running shoes he had worn to work and leaving them under his bed. A clean pair of black sweatpants, a white T-shirt, grey cotton pullover. Against the back of his bedroom door was a full-length mirror, in which he checked his reflection. His eyes travelling over the slim figure in the mirror, he shook his head, as if amused by some remembered idea. Down in the hall then, he sat on the staircase to lace up a pair of white sneakers. The dog came up from the kitchen and sat in front of him, prodding his knee with her long delicate jaw. You haven't been cooped up in here the whole time, have you? he said. Gavin said he was going to take you out yesterday. She tried to lick his hand again and gently he pushed her muzzle away. Now you're making me feel bad, he said. She let out a low whining noise and put her head down on the bottom step, looking up. Getting to his feet, he said: You have a lot in common with her, you know. You're both in love with me. The dog followed him to the door, whimpering, and he patted her head once more before he left. God love you, he muttered. Then he shut the front door behind him and got in the car.

A warm still evening, blue showing softly through white cloud. Felix knocked on Alice's front door once before opening it, calling out: Hey, it's me. Inside, the lights were on. From upstairs, her voice answered:

We're up here. He shut the door behind him and jogged up the staircase. At the back of the landing, Simon was standing in the open doorway of Eileen's room. He turned to greet Felix and they looked at one another a moment, Simon with a resigned expression, tired. Hello, handsome, Felix said. Simon smiled then, and gestured for Felix to enter the room ahead of him, saying: Nice to see you too. Inside, Eileen was sitting at the dressing table and Alice was leaning against it, unscrewing a tube of lipstick. Felix sat down on the end of the bed, watching Eileen put on make-up. His eyes moved over her shoulders, the back of her head, over her reflection in the mirror, the slightly rigid expression on her face, while Alice and Simon were talking about something that had been in the news that day. Brandishing a small plastic wand, Eileen met Felix's eyes in the mirror and said: Would you like some? He got up and examined the object. What is it, mascara? he said. Go on, why not. She moved over on the little bench to let him sit beside her. He sat down with his back to the mirror, and Eileen said: Look up for a second. He obliged. She ran the brush over his left lower lid with a delicate gesture of her wrist.

Simon, how about you? said Alice.

396

From the doorway Simon replied peaceably: No, thanks.

He's pretty enough already, Felix said.

Alice clicked her tongue, putting the cap back on the lipstick. Don't make personal remarks, she said.

With his hand in his pocket Simon said: Don't listen to her, Felix.

Eileen withdrew the mascara brush and Felix opened his eyes again. Turning around, he glanced at his own reflection in the mirror impassively and then rose from the seat. Can any of you sing, by the way? he asked. They all looked at him. Just sometimes these things involve a bit of singing, he said. You don't have to if you really can't, obviously. Alice said that Simon had been in a choir at Oxford, and Simon said he didn't think anyone at the party would be in the mood to hear the bass part of the *Miserere* for fourteen minutes. What about you, Eileen? Felix said. Can you sing? She was screwing the cap back on the mascara. He looked at her but she avoided his eyes. No, I can't, she answered. She rose to her feet then, smoothing her hands over her hips. I'm ready to go when everyone else is, she said.

In the car Alice sat in the front seat, carrying a sponge cake wrapped in clingfilm on a plate. Eileen and Simon sat in the back, the middle seat between them. Felix glanced at them in the rear-view mirror and then drummed his fingers cheerfully on the steering wheel. So what do you do in the gym? he asked. Like, rowing machine, or what. Simon met his eyes in the mirror, and Alice turned her face away, smiling, or trying not to laugh. I do a little bit on the rowing machine, yeah, Simon answered. Felix asked if he lifted weights at all and Simon said not a lot. Alice started laughing then and pretending to cough. What? said Eileen. Nothing, she answered. Felix hit the indicator as they approached the turn off the coast road into town. And what height are you? he asked. Out of curiosity. With a lazy smile Simon looked out the window. Shameless, Alice said. I don't get it, said Eileen. Clearing his throat, Simon answered in a low voice: Six foot three. Felix was grinning then. See, it's just a question, he said. Six foot three. And now I know. Tapping his fingers on the steering wheel again he added: I'm like five foot eight, by the way. Not that you care, just telling you. From the back seat Eileen said she was also five foot eight. Felix glanced at her over his shoulder and then back at the road again. Are you, he said. Interesting. For a girl it's a good tall height. Still looking out the window at the passing facades of summer homes, Simon remarked: I think it's a fine height for anyone. Felix laughed. Thanks, big guy, he said. They were driving down the main street then, past the turn-off for the amusements. We don't have to stay that long or anything, he remarked. At this thing. I just said I'd swing by for a bit. Hitting the indicator once more, he added: And if you get talking to anyone who says anything bad about me, they're lying. Simon started to laugh. Do people say bad things about you? Eileen asked. Felix glanced at her in the mirror again, waiting to turn right. Well, there's nasty people out there in the world, Eileen, he answered. And I'm not for everyone, let's be honest. He took the right turn then, off the main road behind the church, and after a few minutes pulled in outside a bungalow, where several cars were parked already in the driveway. When he turned the engine off he said: Now just be normal, alright? Don't go in there talking about like, world politics and shit like that. People will think you're freaks. Alice turned around in her seat and said: His friends are very nice, don't worry. Eileen said she didn't know anything about world politics anyway.

Felix rang the doorbell and Danielle came

to answer it. She was wearing a short blue summer dress and her hair was loose around her shoulders. Behind her, the house was bright and noisy. She welcomed them inside and Felix kissed her cheek, saying: Hey, happy birthday. You look great. She waved him away with her hand, pleased. Since when do you give compliments? she said. Alice introduced Eileen and Simon, and Danielle said: You're all so glam, I'm jealous. Come on in. The kitchen was a tiled room behind the hallway, with a ceiling light over the table and a back door leading out onto the garden. Inside, seven or eight people were drinking from plastic cups and talking, and from the living room beside them came the sound of music and laughter. On the table were various cans and bottles, empty and unopened, a bowl of crisps, a corkscrew. A tall man standing by the fridge said: Felix Brady, where have you been this week? Another man who was standing at the back door smoking called out: He's been off riding his new girlfriend. When the first man pointed his thumb at Alice, the second man made an apologetic face and stepped inside to say: I am so sorry, I didn't see you there. Alice smiled and said not to worry. Eating a handful of crisps, Felix nodded over his shoulder and said: These are friends of hers. Be nice to them, they're a bitteen odd. Looking at Eileen, Danielle shook her head. How do you put up with him? she said. Let me get you a drink. Alice had put the cake down on a kitchen counter and was peeling off the clingfilm. A woman came out from the living room holding a small child in her arms. Danielle, the woman said, we're going to head off before this man falls asleep. Danielle put her hand on the child's light curls and kissed his forehead. Eileen, she said, this is my precious nephew Ethan. What do you think, isn't he an angel? The woman holding the child reached to untangle one of her earrings from the child's fingers. Eileen asked what age he was and the woman answered: Two years two months. Felix's housemate Gavin was standing with Alice at the countertop asking her if she had baked the cake herself. Felix took a rolled cigarette from his wallet and said casually to Simon: Come outside for one?

The back garden was cooler and quieter. A little way down the grass, a woman, a man and a little girl were playing an improvised game of football, using sweatshirts as goalposts. Felix leaned back against the garden wall, facing the grass, lighting a cigarette, and Simon stood beside him, watching the game in progress. Behind them the back of the house was hidden by the dark bulk of the garage. Energetically the little girl ran back and forth between the two adults, dribbling the ball awkwardly at her feet. Exhaling a mouthful of smoke, Felix said: Do you think Alice would be allowed to have a dog in her house? Simon looked around attentively. Well, if she buys it, she can do what she likes, he said. Why, do you have a dog? Felix was frowning. Is she thinking of buying it? he asked. Simon paused. Oh, he said. I don't know. I thought she told me that on the phone one night, but I might be wrong. With a curious expression, Felix glanced down at the lit tip of his cigarette before taking another drag. Then he answered: Yeah, I have a dog. I mean, she's not really mine. The last people who were renting our place just left her behind when they moved, so we kind of ended up with her by accident. Simon watched him while he spoke. She was really skinny then, Felix added. Like, not healthy at all. And she had anxieties. Didn't like anyone touching her or anything. She'd hide off somewhere while you were putting out food, and then when you were gone away she'd come out and eat it. And actually she had some aggression problems as well. You know, if you went too close to her and she didn't like it, she might snap at you, that kind of thing. Simon was nodding his head slowly. He asked Felix if he thought something traumatic had happened to the dog in the past. Hard to know, Felix said. Maybe the last crowd kind of neglected her. She definitely had problems anyway, wherever she got them from. He tapped some ash off his cigarette and let it float down slowly toward the grass. But she relaxed a bit in the end, he said. Just got used to being fed, and nothing bad happening, and eventually she didn't mind us going near her. She still doesn't like strangers touching her too much, but with me she likes it. Simon was smiling. That's nice, he said. I'm glad. Felix exhaled again, with a grimace. But it did take a good while, he replied. The other lads actually wanted to get rid of her at one stage, because the behaviour was so bad and she didn't really seem to be calming down at all. And not to make myself out to be the hero, but I was the one who said we should keep her. With a laugh Simon said: You can be the hero, I don't mind. Thoughtfully Felix went on smoking. I was just wondering would I be allowed bring her up to Alice's house, he added. Some landlords, they won't let you. But if she's going to buy the place it's different. I didn't know she was thinking about that. Down the garden, the little girl had managed to kick the ball between the goalposts, and the man had lifted her up on his shoulders, cheering. Simon watched them, saying nothing. Felix scraped the last of his cigarette along the wall beside him until it went out. Then he dropped the end down in the grass. So what happened last night? he asked. Simon looked around at him. What do you mean? he said. Felix gave a short cough from his chest. I mean between you and Eileen, he said. You don't have to tell me, but you might as well. The little girl was coming back down the garden toward the house, the man and woman walking behind her, talking. As they passed, the man nodded and said: How's life, Brady? Felix answered: Yeah, not bad, thanks. They went inside, pulling the door behind them. The garden was empty then except for Simon and Felix, standing on the grass together behind the garage. After a long silence, Simon dropped his gaze down to his feet and said: I don't really know what happened. Felix gave a laugh at that. Okay, he said. I'll fill you in. You went into her room after we got home, right? And then a bit later, you went back to your room, and today you're both depressed. I don't know anything more than that, so you tell me.

You had sex with her, or what? Simon passed his hand down over his face, looking tired. Right, he said. No further remark followed, and Felix prompted: Not for the first time, I would guess. Simon gave a wan smile. No, he agreed. Not quite. Felix put his hands in his pockets, watching Simon's face. And then what? he said. You had a fight. Not that I could hear you, by the way. It must have been a quiet kind of fight if it was one. Simon was rubbing the back of his neck with his hand. It wasn't, he said. We just talked. She said she'd prefer to stay friends. That's all. We didn't fight about it. With his eyebrows raised, Felix was staring. Fuck's sake, he said. She said that to you after you just had sex with her? What kind of behaviour is that? Simon gave an awkward laugh, dropped his hand, looked away. Well, we all do things we shouldn't do, he said. I think she's just unhappy. Felix frowned at him for a second or two. There you go, he said. Trying to be like Jesus again. Simon gave another strained laugh. No, he answered, Jesus actually resisted temptation, as I recall. Smiling now, Felix reached to touch Simon's hand, and Simon let him. Down the inside of his wrist, down toward his palm, Felix brushed the back of his fingers slowly. A few seconds passed in silence. Quietly Simon said: She's a very dear friend of mine. Alice. Felix started laughing then, and let go of his hand. That's cute of you to say, he said. What do you mean? Simon stood there looking calm, tired. I just mean, I'm extremely fond of her, he answered. I admire her. Felix gave another cough, shaking his head. You mean like, if I do anything bad to her you'll kick my head in, he said. Simon was touching his own wrist then where Felix had touched it before, circling it in his hand as if it hurt. No, he said, I actually didn't mean that at all. Felix gave a yawn, stretching his arms. You could, though, he said. Kick my head in. Easily. He straightened up and turned to look out at the garden. If she's such a good friend of yours, he asked, how come you've never been to see her all this time she's been living here? Surprised, Simon said he had been trying to arrange to come and see Alice since February, and that she had always told him she was away or that it didn't suit. I also invited her to come and stay with me, he added. But she said she was busy. The impression I got was that she didn't want to see me. I'm not saying that in an accusatory way, I thought maybe she just wanted a break. We had been seeing quite a lot of each other, you know, before she left Dublin. Felix was nodding to himself. When she was in hospital, was it? he asked. Simon looked at him for a time, and answered: Yes. Felix put his hands in his pockets and walked away for a moment, aimlessly, before returning to the wall, facing Simon. So all this time you've been on at her, saying you want to see her, and she's been saying, no, I'm busy? he asked. Simon replied: Sure, but as I say, there's nothing wrong with that. Felix grinned. It didn't hurt your feelings? he said. Simon smiled back at him. No, no, he replied. I'm very grown-up about these things. Kicking the toe of his shoe against the wall, Felix asked: What was she like in hospital? In a bad way, was she? Simon seemed to think about the question, and then answered: She seems much better now. Felix wandered away again, far enough beyond the garage to look back at the house. Well, he said, if you see her in there, tell her I want to talk to her. Simon nodded his head and for a few seconds said nothing, did nothing. Then he stood up straight and went back inside.

In the kitchen, Alice was standing with Danielle, eating a slice of cake from a paper plate. Raking over the sponge with her fork, she said: It didn't really rise, but it tastes alright. Closing the door behind him, Simon said it looked delicious. Felix is outside, he added. I think he wants to talk to you. Danielle laughed. Oh my God, she said. Is he drunk already? He's always being deep and meaningful when he's drunk. Helping himself to a slice of cake, Simon said: No, I don't think he's drinking. But he was getting a little deep and meaningful with me just now. Alice put her plate on the countertop. That sounds ominous, she said. I'll be back in a bit. When she was gone, Danielle asked Simon what he did for a living, and he started telling her about Leinster House, making her laugh. However bad you think it is, he said, it's worse. Eileen was in the living room looking through the Spotify account connected to the speakers, a man over her shoulder saying: Real tunes, please. Outside, Alice closed the back door behind her and said into the empty garden: Felix? He looked out from behind the garage. Hey, he said. I'm down here. With her arms folded she came down onto the grass. On the wall he had spread out a cigarette paper and was taking a pinch of tobacco from a small plastic pouch. You know why they're in a weird mood? he said. The other pair. They hooked up last night, and then she turned around and said she just wanted to be friends. The drama in your house, it's unreal. Alice was leaning against the wall, watching him roll the cigarette. Did Simon tell you that? she asked. He sealed the paper with the wet of his tongue and tapped it shut. Yeah, he said. Why, what did she tell you? Watching him light his cigarette, Alice answered: She just said it was a mistake. But she didn't really go into details. I could see she was upset, I didn't want to press her. Glancing down at her fingernails, she added: She says he's impossible to talk to. She thinks he grew up in an emotionally repressive family, and he's fucked up. He can't say what he needs. Felix started laughing, coughing. Jesus, he said. That's harsh. I wouldn't have said he was fucked up. I like him. I actually tried it on with him a little bit while he was out here, and he started talking about how you're his great friend and he looks up to you so much. He was tempted, though, I could tell. I was on the point of being like, relax, she's cool with it. Alice was laughing then too. God, he's such a lamb, she said. Do you think he has low self-esteem? Felix frowned and answered: No. He might be losing the will to live a bit. But low self-esteem, I don't think so. And he's not that much of a lamb either. He's like yourself. His self-esteem is alright, he just fucking hates his life. Alice was smiling, brushing crumbs off the skirt of her dress. I don't hate my life, she replied. Felix breathed out a cloud of smoke and dispersed it idly with his hand. You told me you did, he said. Last time we went outside for a cigarette together. Do you remember? Before we went to Rome. You were smoking yourself that time. She tucked her hair behind her ears, embarrassed. Oh yes, she said. Did I say I hated my life? Felix said he was pretty sure. Well, maybe I did then, she replied. But I don't now. He said nothing, looking down at his hand as he smoked. Then he said: Here, look what happened me at work today. He held out the hand and showed her the deep horizontal wound running under the knuckle of his smallest finger. The cut itself was darker now, healing over, while the surrounding skin was red and inflamed. Wincing, Alice clutched her face. Felix moved his hand around, as if to examine the wound from different angles. I didn't even notice it until it started bleeding everywhere, he said. He looked up at her, saw her face and added: Shit like that happens all the time in there, it didn't hurt that much or anything. She took his hand without speaking and lifted it against her cheek. He gave an uncertain kind of laugh. Ah, you're very soft, he said. It's just a scrape, I shouldn't have even showed it to you.

Does it hurt now? she asked.

No, not really. Washing my hands it stings a bit.

It's not fair, Alice said.

You think everything is unfair.

The back door behind them opened then, and Alice let Felix's hand fall away from her cheek, though she still held it in hers. After a moment, another man came down onto the grass nearby. He was tall, with reddish fair hair, wearing a close-fitting patterned shirt. Seeing them, he started to laugh, and Felix said nothing.

Am I interrupting something? said the man.

Not to worry, Felix said. Didn't know you were here.

The man removed a packet of cigarettes from his pocket and began lighting one. This must be the new girlfriend, he said. Alice, isn't it? They were just talking about you in there. Someone got up an article about you online.

She looked at Felix, but he did not return her eye contact. Oh dear, she said.

You have some big fans out there on the internet, the man added.

Yes, I believe so, she replied. Also a lot of

people who hate me and wish me ill.

The man seemed to accept this neutrally. Didn't see any of those, he said, but I suppose everyone has them. How's things with you, Felix?

Can't complain.

How'd you land yourself a famous girl-friend?

Tinder, he said.

The man exhaled a stream of smoke. Yeah? I'm on there all the time, never see anyone famous. Are you going to introduce us or what?

Alice glanced uncertainly at Felix, who looked perfectly relaxed.

Alice, that's my brother there, he said. Damian. You don't have to shake his hand or anything, you can just nod at him from a distance.

She looked back over at the man with some surprise. Oh, it's good to meet you, she said. You don't look anything alike.

He smiled back at her. I'll take that as a compliment, he said. I heard you were in Rome together there a few weeks ago, is that right? You must have swept him off his feet, Alice. He wouldn't usually be the type for romantic mini-breaks.

Really he was just keeping me company on a work trip, she said.

Damian seemed to find the whole exchange increasingly amusing. He went along to your book events and that, did he? he asked.

Some of them, said Alice.

Well, well. On top of everything else he must have learned to read since I last saw him.

Ah no, Felix said. But why would I bother, she can tell me the good bits in person.

Ignoring his brother, Damian looked Alice up and down with some curiosity. After another drag on his cigarette, he said: Mad few years you've had, isn't it?

I suppose so, she said.

Yeah, I've a friend who's a big fan of yours, actually. She was saying your film must be coming out soon, is that right?

Politely, Alice replied: It's not really my film, it's just based on one of my books.

Putting his hand on Alice's back, Felix said: Here, you're annoying her talking about that stuff. She doesn't like it.

Damian nodded, unfazed, smiling to himself. Does she not, he said. Addressing Alice then, he went on: He's not being nice, you know. He seriously doesn't have a fucking clue who you are. He's never read a book in his life.

She's hardly stuck for meeting people who

like reading, said Felix. Sure they never leave her alone.

Damian took another drag on his cigarette. After a moment he said to Alice: Do you know he's been avoiding me?

Alice looked at Felix, who was gazing down at his feet, shaking his head.

See, when our mam died, Damian went on, she left us both the house, yeah? Together. And we agreed we were going to sell it. Are you following me? You're a smart lady, I'm sure you are. Anyway, I can't sell it without his signature on all these documents. And in the last few weeks, he's just disappeared. Won't answer my calls, texts, nothing. What do you think that's about?

Alice said quietly that it was none of her business.

You'd think he'd be happy to have a bit of money coming his way, Damian added. God knows he's been short of it often enough.

Anything else you want to rat on me about while you're here? Felix asked.

Ignoring him, Damian went on thoughtfully: Tom Heffernan gave him an awful lot of money there at one stage. Auld lad who lives in town with his wife. Wonder why that was. What's the connection, do you know?

Felix was shaking his head again, flicking the end of his cigarette away into the grass, and in the dimming light of the eastern sky his face was flushed.

Look, you seem like a nice girl, Damian remarked. Maybe a bit too nice, yeah? Don't let him make a fool of you, that's my advice.

Coolly Alice answered: I wonder what makes you believe I could possibly want life advice from you.

Felix started laughing at that, high wild laughter. Damian said nothing for a moment, smoking slowly. Then he said: You've got it all figured out, have you?

Oh, I'd say I'm doing alright, she answered.

In a conciliatory tone now, still grinning, Felix said: Here, Damian. I'll come over tomorrow morning before work and do that for you. Okay? And you can leave off harassing me. Is that fair enough?

Still looking at Alice, Damian answered: Fine. He dropped his cigarette in the grass. God help you both, he added. Turning around then, he went back inside. The door clicked shut behind him. Felix stepped out from behind the garage as if to check he was really gone, and then laced his fingers together and placed his hands on the back of his head. She watched him.

Yeah, he said. Damian. We hate each other, by the way, I don't know if I said that to you before.

You didn't.

Ah, right. Sorry.

Felix dropped his hands from his head and held them loosely at his side, still looking at the door through which his brother had exited. It was a wooden door with yellow glass panes inset.

We were never great buddies, he added. But the whole thing with Mam getting sick, yeah. I really won't get into it because I'll be here all night giving you the details. But anyway, me and him have not been getting on the best in the last few years. If I knew we were going to run into him I would have given you more background.

Still she said nothing. He turned around to look at her, his expression agitated now or unhappy.

I can read, by the way, he said. I don't know why he went down that line of saying I'm illiterate and all that. I'm not great at reading, but I can read. And I don't think you really care anyway.

Of course I don't.

Yeah, he was always better than me in school so I suppose he likes to bring it up in front of people. He's one of these lads who has to put other people down so he can feel like the big man. Mam used to criticise him on that and he didn't like it. Anyway, it doesn't matter. Stupid thing is, he actually annoys me. I mean I'm annoyed now.

I'm sorry.

He looked back at her again. Not your fault, he said. You were good. I could have watched you and him have it out for a while, that side was funny to me. That's the thing about you being so intimidating, it's enjoyable when you do it to other people.

She dropped her gaze to the ground and said softly: I don't enjoy it.

Do you not? A small bit, you must.

No, I don't.

Why do you do it, then? he asked.

Intimidate people? she said. I don't intend to.

He frowned. But you know the way you act, he said. Putting the fear of God into people. You know what I'm talking about. I'm not having a go at you.

You may find it hard to believe this, she said, but when I meet people, I actually try to be nice.

He let out a yelp of laughter and in response Alice gave a sigh, leaning against the wall, covering her eyes.

Is the idea so amusing? she said.

If you're trying to be nice, why do you

417

make cutting remarks all the time?

I don't all the time.

No, but you come out with them when it suits you, he said. I'm not saying you're a nasty person or anything. Just that people wouldn't want to get on the wrong side of you.

Sharply she replied: Yes, you've made that point.

He raised his eyebrows, and for a few seconds was silent. Finally he said mildly: Jesus, I'm getting attacked on all sides this evening. She bowed her head, as if despondent or tired, but made no reply. You're not the easiest person to get along with, he added, but you know that yourself.

Felix, is it too much to ask that you might stop criticising my personality? she asked. I don't want you to flatter me. You really don't have to say anything about me at all. I just don't find the negative feedback useful.

He watched her uncertainly for a few seconds. Alright, he said. I'm not trying to upset you.

She said nothing. Her silence seemed to bother him, and he put his hands in his pockets before taking them out again.

Yeah, it's like Damian was saying, he said. You think I don't appreciate you. Fair enough, maybe I don't.

Still she said nothing, and stared down at her feet. He looked restless, irritable, anxious.

See, you're used to getting treated differently, he went on. From people who know about you and think you're really important and everything. And then when I treat you in a normal way it's not good enough. I think if I'm honest, you'll find someone who appreciates you better, and you'll be happier.

After a long pause, she said: I think I'd like to go inside now if that's alright.

He looked down at the ground, frowning. I can't stop you, he said.

She walked back up the grass toward the house. Before she reached the door, he cleared his throat and said aloud: You know, when I fucked my hand up earlier, the first thing I thought was, I bet Alice won't be happy about this.

She turned back to him before replying: And I wasn't.

Yeah, he said. And it's nice to have someone who would care about something like that. I get sliced to bits every other week out in that place, and it's not like I have a lot of people saying, oh, that must have hurt, what happened? And look, maybe there is certain things about you I can't appreciate, and sometimes I don't like the tone you put on with me, I've admitted that. But say you were above in your house on your own and you weren't feeling well, or you hurt yourself or something, I would want to know about it. And if you wanted me to come up and look after you, I would. And I'm sure you'd do the same. Is that not enough to be going on with? Maybe for you it's not, but it is for me.

They looked at one another. Let me think about it, Alice said.

Inside the house, a bumblebee had flown into the living room and two of Danielle's friends were shrieking and laughing, trying to guide it back out the window. Simon was sitting at the kitchen table with Danielle's cousin Gemma, who was holding in her lap the little girl who had been playing football earlier. And do you prefer school, Simon was saying, or do you prefer being on your holidays? Eileen was at the countertop splashing some vodka into a plastic cup, while the same man she had been talking with earlier said: It's not that great, but it's something to watch anyway. Felix and Alice came back in the patio door, Felix cutting himself a slice of the birthday cake, Alice putting on her cardigan, saying cheerfully: That's a lovely big garden out there. She laid a hand absently, fondly, on Simon's shoulder, and he looked up at her, curious, half-smiling, and neither of them spoke.

At ten o'clock, Danielle tapped a spoon on a glass and said they would have a few songs. Gradually the room fell quiet, conversations tailing off, people entering from the living room to listen. A cousin of Danielle's began by singing 'She Moved Through the Fair'. Some who knew the lyrics sang along, while others hummed the melody. From the doorway Eileen was watching Simon where he leaned against the fridge next to Alice, holding a glass of wine. Danielle asked Felix to sing something next. Give us 'Carrickfergus', said Gavin. Felix gave a nonchalant yawn. I'll do 'The Lass of Aughrim', he said. He put down the paper plate he had been holding, cleared his throat and began to sing. His voice was clear and tuneful, with a kind of tonal purity, rising to fill the quiet and then falling very low, so low it almost had the quality of silence. From across the room Alice watched him. He was standing against the counter, under the ceiling lamp, so that his hair and face and the slim slanting figure of his body were bathed in light, and his eyes were dark, and his mouth also. For some reason, because of the low rich quality of his voice, or because of the

421

melancholy lyrics of the song, or perhaps because of some prior association the melody brought to her mind, Alice's eyes filled with tears as she watched him. He caught sight of her for a moment and then looked away. His voice sounded strangely similar to his ordinary speaking voice, the pronunciations were the same, but with sudden resounding depths. Tears began to run from Alice's eyes, and her nose was running also. She smiled as if at her own absurdity, but the tears went on streaming regardless, and she wiped her nose with her fingers. Her face was pink and gleaming wet. The song finished and into a single moment of silence spilled the sound of cheering and applause. Gavin put his fingers in his mouth to whistle approvingly. Felix leaned against the sink, looking at Alice, and she looked back at him, almost shrugging, embarrassed. She wiped her cheeks with her hands. He was smiling. You made her cry, said Gavin. People looked around at Alice then, and she laughed, awkwardly, and the laugh seemed to catch in her throat. She was wiping her face again. She's alright, Felix said. Danielle asked for another song, but no one volunteered. A hard act to follow, someone said. Danielle's cousin Gemma suggested 'The Fields of Athenry', and people began to talk amongst themselves. Felix had made his way around behind the table and was pouring wine into a plastic cup. Handing it to Alice he said: You're okay, aren't you? She nodded, and he rubbed her back consolingly. Don't worry, he said. It's usually the old ladies who cry at that one, but we'll allow it. You didn't know I could sing, did you? Well, I used to be a lot better before I wrecked myself with smoking. He was talking lightly, almost inattentively, and stroking her back with his hand, as if he was not listening to himself. Look, Simon's not crying, Felix said. He must not be impressed with me. Smiling, Simon answered in a low voice: Multi-talented. Alice gave another little laugh, sipping from her cup. Cheeky, said Felix. From the living room doorway Eileen watched them, Felix with his hand on Alice's back, Simon standing beside her, the three of them talking together. And out the windows the sky was still dimming, darkening, the vast earth turning slowly on its axis.

28.

When they left Danielle's house, it was pitch-dark, without streetlights, and Eileen lit the torch on her phone so they could find their way down the driveway. In the car, with the doors shut behind them, it was quiet and warm. Felix, you have a beautiful singing voice, Eileen said. He switched the headlights on and started to pull back out onto the road. Yeah, that was for you, he said. Well, for the pair of you, since you're both from around there. Aughrim. Aren't you? Not that I really know what the song is about, to be honest. I thought it was a man singing to a woman, but then in the chorus I think it's a woman singing. Saying her babe lies cold in her arms. It's probably one of those old songs that's got a few different lyrics mixed up together. It's a sad one anyway, whatever it's about. Simon asked if he played music as well as singing, and Felix answered: A bit. Fiddle mainly.

And I'd get by alright on guitar if I had to. Few friends of mine play together, like at weddings and that. I have done weddings before, but from the music side it's not really my thing. You're just doing Celine Dion all night or whatever. Alice said she'd had no idea he was so musical. Yeah, he said. Everyone around here would be like that, though. It's only in Dublin you meet tone-deaf people. No offence. Glancing at Alice before returning his attention to the road, he went on: So you're thinking of buying the house, are you? I didn't know that. From the back seat Eileen looked up. Sorry, what? she asked. Alice was putting on lip balm, pleased, a little drunk. Thinking about it, she said. Haven't decided yet. Eileen burst out laughing then, and Alice turned around in her seat to face her. No, great, said Eileen. I'm happy for you. You're moving to the countryside. Alice was looking at her with a puzzled frown. Eileen, I already live in the countryside, Alice said. We're talking about the house where I currently live. Eileen was smiling, shaking her head. No, totally, she replied. You came here on holiday and now you're going to like, stay on holiday forever. Why not? Simon was watching Eileen, but Eileen was still smiling at Alice. Seriously, Eileen added. It's great.

The house is amazing. Such high ceilings, wow. Slowly, Alice was nodding her head. Right, she replied. Well, I haven't made any decisions yet. She put the lip balm back in her bag. I don't know why you're saying I'm on holiday, she added. Whenever I do go to work, you send me a disapproving email telling me I should be at home. Eileen was laughing again, her face emptied of colour. I'm sorry, she said. I misunderstood the situation, I can see that now. Simon was still watching her, and she turned to him with a bright insincere smile, as if to say: what? Felix remarked that, before buying the house, Alice should get someone in to look at it properly, and Alice said it would need a lot of work anyway, no doubt. They were driving past the hotel then, the lit windows of the lobby, and along the coast road.

Back at the house, Eileen went straight upstairs to her room while the others were still in the hallway. Her lips were pale, her breath shallow and uneven as she turned on the bedside lamp. The darkened bedroom window reflected the faint grey ellipse of her face, and she jerked the curtain closed, the hooks rasping on the rail. From downstairs, the sound of voices, Alice saying: No, no, not me. Simon made some low indistinct reply, and then the others were laughing, high laughter carrying up the stairs. Eileen rubbed her fingers into her closed eyelids. The sound of the fridge door unsealing softly, and a clinking noise like glass. She started to unknot the waist tie of her dress, the linen creased and softened now after a day's wear, smelling of sun cream and deodorant. Downstairs, the noise of a door opening. She pulled the dress down off her shoulders, taking deep hard breaths in through her nose and releasing them between her lips, and then put on a striped blue nightdress. The noises from downstairs were quieter now, the voices intermingled. Sitting on the side of the mattress, she began to unpin her hair. Downstairs, one of the others was walking along the hallway, whistling. She removed one long black hairpin and dropped it with a faint click on the bedside locker. Her jaw was held tight, her back teeth grinding together. From outside the house, the noise of the sea, low, repetitive, and the air moving soft through the full heavy leaves of the trees. When her hair was loose she combed it out roughly with her fingers and then lay down on the bed and shut her eyes. A crisp snapping sound came from downstairs like a cork popping. She filled her lungs with breath. Her hands clenched into fists and then opened out again, stretching her fingers wide on the duvet, twice, three times. Alice's voice again. And the other two laughing, the men laughing, at whatever Alice had said. With a quick jerking movement Eileen got to her feet. She tugged a quilted yellow dressing gown from the back of a chair and pulled her arms into the sleeves. Making her way downstairs, she tied the sash of the gown loosely at her waist. At the end of the hallway the kitchen door was pulled shut, the light turned on, a sweet heavy fragrance of smoke in the air. She put her hand to the door handle. From inside, Alice's voice saying: Oh, I don't know, not for months. Eileen opened the door. Inside, the room was warm and dimly lit, Alice sitting at one end of the table, Felix and Simon seated together against the wall, sharing a joint. They all looked up at Eileen with surprise, with something like wariness, where she stood in the doorway in her dressing gown. Bravely she smiled at them. Can I join? she asked.

Please do, Alice replied.

Pulling a chair back and sitting down, Eileen asked: What are we talking about?

Felix passed her the joint over the tabletop. Alice was just telling us about her parents, he said.

Eileen took a quick drag and exhaled, nodding her head, everything in her face and bearing showing an effort to be cheerful.

Well, you already know, Alice said to Eileen. You've met them.

Mm, Eileen said. Long time ago. But go on.

Turning back to the others, Alice went on: With my mother it's actually less complicated, because she and my brother are like, suffocatingly close. And then my mother never liked me much anyway.

Yeah? Felix said. That's funny. My mother loved me. I was her golden boy. Sad, really, because I turned out to be such a fuck-up. But she doted on me, God knows why.

You're not a fuck-up, said Alice.

To Simon, Felix said: What about you? Were you your mother's pet?

Well, I was an only child, Simon answered. Certainly my mother was very fond of me, yes. Is very fond of me, I mean. He was turning the base of his wine glass around on the tabletop. It's not the easiest relationship in my life, he added. I think she sometimes feels kind of confused and frustrated with me. Like in terms of my career, the decisions I've made. I suppose she has friends whose children are the same age I am, and they're all doctors or lawyers now and they have children of their own. And I'm basically still a parliamentary assistant with no girlfriend. I mean, I don't blame my mother for being confused. I don't know what happened to my life either.

Felix gave a short cough, and asked: But you have a fairly important job, do you not?

Simon looked around at him, as if the question was surprising, and answered: Oh God, no. Not at all. Not that I think my mother is obsessed with status, by the way. I'm sure she would have liked to have had a son who was a doctor, but I don't think she's disappointed in me for not wanting that. Felix passed him the joint and he accepted it. We don't really have serious conversations, he added. You know, she doesn't like things to get serious, she just wants everyone to get along. I think in a way she finds me intimidating. Which makes me feel awful. He took a short drag and, after exhaling, added: Whenever I think about my parents I feel guilty. I was just the wrong son for them, it wasn't their fault.

But it wasn't your fault either, said Alice.

Intently Eileen was watching this exchange, her jaw held tight, still half-smiling.

What about you, Eileen? said Felix. You get along okay with your parents?

The question seemed to surprise her. Oh, she said. Then, after a pause: They're not bad. I have an insane sister who they're both afraid of. And she made my life hell when we were kids. But otherwise they're okay.

The sister who got married, said Felix.

Yeah, that's the one, she said. Lola. She's not really evil, she's just chaotic. And maybe a bit evil, sometimes. She was really popular in school and I was a loser. I mean, I literally had not one friend. Looking back, I think it's lucky I didn't kill myself, because I used to think about it constantly. Around the age of fourteen, fifteen. I tried talking to my mother, but she said there was nothing wrong with me and I was just being dramatic. Here she hesitated, looking down at the bare surface of the table. Then she went on: Really I think I would have done it, but when I was fifteen, I met someone who wanted to be friends with me. And he saved my life.

Quietly Simon said: If that's true, I'm glad.

Felix sat up then, surprised. What? he said. Was it you?

Eileen was smiling more naturally now, still a little pale and drawn, but enjoying the rehearsal of a familiar story. You know we were neighbours growing up, she said. And when Simon was home from college one summer, he came to help my dad out on the farm. I don't know why. I suppose your parents told you to.

In a low humorous voice, Simon said: No, I think at the time I'd just finished reading *Anna Karenina*. And I wanted to go and work on a farm so I could be like Levin. You know he has these profound experiences while he's cutting grass with a sickle or something, and it makes him believe in God. I don't really remember the details now, but that was my general idea.

Eileen was laughing, moving her hair around with her hands. Did you really come to work for Pat because you thought it would be like Anna Karenina? she said. I never knew that. I suppose if you were Levin, we were the muzhiks. Addressing the others again, she went on: Anyway, that's how Simon and I became friends. I was one of the little peasant girls who lived near his family's estate. Indulgently Simon murmured: I wouldn't put it quite like that. Eileen dismissed this intervention with a flapping gesture of her hand. And our parents know each other, obviously, she said. My mother actually has an inferiority complex about Simon's mother. Every year on Christmas Eve, Simon and his parents come over for a drink and we have to scrub the entire house from top to bottom before they arrive. And we put special towels in the bathroom. You know that kind of way.

Smoking again now, leaning back against the wall, Felix said: And what do they think of Alice?

Eileen looked at him. Who, my parents? she asked. He nodded. Yeah, she said. They've met a couple of times. They don't know each other really well or anything.

With a smile Alice said: They disapprove of me.

Felix laughed. Do they really? he asked.

Eileen was shaking her head. No, she said. They don't disapprove. They just don't know you very well.

They never liked us living together in college, Alice went on. They wanted Eileen to make friends with nice middle-class girls.

Eileen let out a breath with a raw kind of laughing sound. To Felix, she said: I think they found Alice's personality a bit challenging.

And now that I'm successful, they resent me, Alice added.

I don't know where you get that from, said Eileen.

Well, they didn't like you visiting me in hospital. Did they?

Eileen was shaking her head again, pulling at her earlobe distractedly. That had nothing to do with you being successful, she said.

What did it have to do with? Alice asked.

Felix seemed to have forgotten he was smoking, and let the joint go out between his fingers. Looking up at him, Eileen said: You see, when Alice moved back from New York, she didn't tell me she was coming home. I was sending her all these emails and messages, hearing nothing back for weeks, and getting really worried and panicky that something had happened to her. And the whole time she was living five minutes away from my apartment. Pointing at Simon, she went on: He knew. I was the only one who didn't know. And she told him not to tell me, so he had to put up with me complaining to him that I hadn't heard from her, and all the time he knew she was living on fucking Clanbrassil Street.

In a restrained voice Alice said: Obviously it wasn't a great time for me.

Eileen was nodding her head, with the same bright effortful smile. Yeah, she said. Not a great time for me either, because my partner of like three years was breaking up with me, and I had nowhere to live. And my best friend wasn't speaking to me, and my other best friend was acting really weird because he wasn't allowed to tell me anything.

Eileen, said Alice calmly, with all due respect, I was having a psychiatric breakdown.

Yes, I know. I remember, because when you were admitted to hospital, I was there pretty much every day.

Alice said nothing.

The reason my parents didn't like me visiting you so much had nothing to do with you being successful, Eileen went on. They just don't think you're a very good friend. Remember when you got out of hospital, you told me you were leaving Dublin for a few weeks to get some rest? And now it turns out you weren't leaving for a few weeks, you were leaving forever. Which everyone seemed to realise except me. But no need to keep me in the loop, obviously. I'm just the idiot who put my bank account into overdraft getting buses to see you in hospital every day. See, I suppose my parents would say you just don't really care about me.

Simon had bowed his head while Eileen was speaking, but Felix went on watching them both. Alice stared across the table, patches of colour flaring on her cheeks.

You have no idea what I've been through,

435

Alice said.

Eileen laughed, a high brittle laugh. Couldn't I say exactly the same thing to you? she asked.

Alice closed her eyes and opened them again. Right, she said. You mean some guy you didn't even really like broke up with you. Must have been rough.

From the other end of the table, Simon said: Alice.

No, Alice went on. None of you have any idea. Don't lecture me. Not one of you understands anything about my life.

Eileen got to her feet and let her chair fall backward onto the floor, slamming the kitchen door shut behind her. Simon sat up, watching her go, and Alice glanced over at him impassively. Go on, she said. She needs you, I don't.

Looking back at her, Simon answered in a gentle tone of voice: But that hasn't always been true, has it?

Fuck you, said Alice.

He went on looking at her. I know you're angry, he said. But I think you also know that what you're saying isn't right.

You know nothing about me, she answered.

Gazing down at the surface of the table then, he seemed to smile. Okay, he said. He rose to his feet and left the room, closing the door quietly after him. Alice put her fingertips on her temples briefly, as if her head ached, and then she got to her feet and went to the sink, rinsing out her glass. You can't trust people, she said. Any time you think you can, they just throw it back at you. Simon is the worst of all. You know what's wrong with him? I'm serious, it's called a martyr complex. He never needs anything from anyone, and he thinks that makes him a superior being. Whereas in reality he just leads a sad sterile life, sitting alone in his apartment telling himself what a good person he is. When I was really sick, I called him on the phone one night and he brought me to the hospital. That's all. And now I have to hear about it whenever I see him. What has he done with his life? Nothing. At least I can say I've contributed something to the world. And he thinks he's superior to me because he picked up the phone once. He goes around making friends with unstable people just so he can feel good about himself. Especially women, especially younger women. And if they have no money, that's even better. You know he's six years older than me. What has he done with his life?

Felix, who had not spoken in a long time

now, was still sitting on the bench seat with his back against the wall, nursing his bottle of beer. Nothing, he replied. You said that already. I've done nothing either so I don't know why you think I care. Alice stood at the kitchen counter with her back to him, watching him in the reflective surface of the kitchen window. Gradually he noticed her looking, their eyes met. What? he said. I'm not scared of you. She lowered her gaze then. Maybe that's because you don't know me very well, she said. He gave an offhanded laugh. She said nothing. He went on watching her back for a few seconds longer. Her face very white, she took an empty wine glass from the draining board and held it in her hand for a moment before dropping it hard down onto the tiles. The bowl part of the glass hit the floor with a crashing noise and shattered into fragments, while the stem remained largely intact, rolling away toward the fridge. In silence he observed her, not moving. If you're thinking of doing something to hurt yourself, he said, don't bother. You'll only make a scene and you won't feel better afterwards anyway. Her hands were braced against the kitchen counter, her eyes closed. Very quietly she answered: No, don't worry. I won't do anything while you're all here. He raised his eyebrows and looked

438

down at his drink. I'd better stick around so, he said. Her knuckles stood out white where she gripped the counter. I don't honestly think you care whether I live or die, she said. Felix took a sip of his drink and swallowed. I should be pissed off with you talking to me like that, he remarked. But what's the point? You're not even really talking to me anyway. In your head you're still talking to her. Alice bent down over the sink, her face buried in her hands, and he got up from his seat to go to her. Without turning around she said: Come near me and I'll fucking hit you, Felix. I will. He stopped there at the table while she stood with her head in her arms. Time passed this way in silence. At length he came out from behind the table and pulled out one of the kitchen chairs, dislodging some of the larger shards of glass on the tiles. For a few seconds she just continued standing against the sink, as if she had not even heard him approaching, and then without looking at him, she sat down. She was shivering, her teeth were chattering. In a low kind of groan she said: Oh God. I feel like I'm going to kill myself. He was leaning against the kitchen table, watching her. Yeah, I've felt that way before, he answered. But I haven't done it. And neither will you. She looked up at him, the expression on her face frightened, penitent, ashamed. No, she said. I suppose you're right. I'm sorry. Faintly he smiled and lowered his eyes. You're alright, he answered. And I do care whether you live or die, by the way. You know well I do. She went on looking at him for a few long seconds, her eyes moving absently over his figure, his hands, his face. I'm sorry, she said. I'm ashamed of myself. I thought — I don't know, I thought I was starting to get better. I'm sorry. He sat up on the surface of the kitchen table then. Yeah, you are getting better, he said. This is just a small little — whatever they call it, a little episode. Are you taking something? Antidepressants or something. She nodded her head. Yeah, she said. Prozac. He looked down at her sympathetically where she sat on the chair. Oh yeah? he said. You're doing pretty well on it, then. When I was on that stuff I had no sex drive at all. She laughed, and her hands were trembling, as if in relief after some averted disaster. Felix, she said, I can't believe I told you I was going to hit you. I feel like a monster. I don't know what to say. I'm so sorry. Calmly he met her eye. You didn't want me coming near you, that's all, he said. You didn't really know what you were saying. And you're a psychiatric case, remember. Confused, she looked down at her shaking hands. But I thought I wasn't anymore, she said. He shrugged his shoulders, taking his lighter from his pocket. Well, you still are, he said. It's okay, it takes time. She touched her lips, watching him. When were you on Prozac? she asked. Without looking up he answered: Last year, I went on it for a month or two and then came off again. And I was doing a lot worse stuff than dropping a few wine glasses, believe me. Getting into fights all the time. Stupid things. He rasped his thumb over the spark-wheel of the lighter. You and your friend will be alright, he said. Alice stared down at her lap and said: I don't know. I think it's one of those friendships where one person cares a lot more than the other. He clicked the button down to light the flame and then released it again. You think she doesn't care about you? he said. Alice was still looking down into her lap, smoothing her hands over her skirt. She does, she said. But it's not the same. He got down from the table and crossed over to the back door, avoiding the larger fragments of glass. Opening the door out wide, he leaned on the frame and looked out at the damp garden, breathing in the cool night air. For a while neither of them said anything. Alice got up and took a dustpan and brush from under the sink to sweep up the glass. The very smallest shards had scattered the furthest, under the radiator, between the fridge and the countertop, glittering silver with reflected light. When she was finished sweeping up, she dumped the contents of the pan onto a sheet of newspaper and then wrapped that up and put it into the dustbin. Felix was leaning on the door-jamb, looking outside. It's the same thing you think about me, he remarked. Just interesting, that it's the same. Inside, she straightened up and looked at him. What? she asked. He took a deep breath and exhaled before answering. You think Eileen doesn't care as much as you do, he said. And you think the same about me, that you care more. Maybe that's why you got to like me in the first place, I don't know. Part of me thinks you just hate yourself. Everything you're doing, moving out here on your own with no car or anything, getting your feelings involved with some randomer you met online, it's like you're trying to make yourself miserable. And maybe you want someone to fuck you over and hurt you. At least that would make sense why you would pick me out, because you think I'm the type of person who could do that. Or would want to. She was standing at the sink, saying nothing. Slowly he nodded his head. Well, I'm not going to, he said. If that's what you want, I'm sorry. He cleared his throat and added: And I don't think you like me more. I think we like each other the same. I know I don't show it in my actions all the time, but I can try to be better on that. And I will try. I love you, alright? She had a strange, dazed look on her face as she listened, holding her hand to her cheek. Even though I'm a psychiatric case, she said. He laughed, standing upright and closing the door behind him. Yeah, he answered. Even though we both are.

After leaving the room, Simon had gone upstairs to the landing and stood for a moment at the door of Eileen's room. From inside came a high ragged sobbing sound, punctuated by gasps of breath. Gently he knocked on the door with the back of his hand and a sudden silence fell. Hey, he said aloud, it's just me. Can I come in? The noise of crying started again. He opened the door and went inside. Eileen was lying on her side with her knees pulled up to her chest, one hand in her hair, the other hiding her eyes. Simon closed the door behind him and went to sit down on the side of the bed, near the pillows. I can't believe this is my life, she said. He sat looking down at her with a friendly expression. Come here, he said. She sobbed again and clutched hard at her hair. In a thick voice she answered: You don't love me. She doesn't love me. I have no one in my life. No one. I can't believe I have to live like this. I don't understand. He laid a broad square hand on her head. What are you talking about? he said. Of course I love you. Come here. For a moment she scrubbed at her face crossly with her hands, not speaking, and then, with the same tense irritated manner, she moved over and rested her head in his lap, her cheek against his knee. That's better, he said. She was frowning, rubbing at her eyes with her fingers. I ruin everything good in my life, she said. Everything. He went on moving his hand over her hair, smoothing the stray damp strands back off her face. With Alice I've ruined everything, she went on. And with you. At that she let out another sob, covering her eyes. He moved his hand slowly back over her forehead, over her hair. You haven't ruined anything, he said. Ignoring this remark, she paused for breath, and went on: When we were having drinks last night in town — She broke off again to take another heaving breath, and with some effort continued: I actually felt happy for once in my life. I even thought that to myself at the time, for once in my life I feel happy. Sometimes I think I'm being punished, like God is punishing me. Or I'm doing it to myself, I don't know. Because any time I feel good for even five minutes something bad has to happen. Like in your apartment the other week when we were watching TV together. I should have known it would all get ruined after that, because I was sitting there on your couch thinking to myself, I can't remember the last time I felt this happy. Any time something really good happens, my life has to fall apart. Maybe it's me, maybe I'm the one doing it. I don't know. Aidan couldn't put up with me. And now Alice can't either, and neither can you. In a low voice Simon murmured peaceably: Yes I can. Impatiently Eileen wiped away the tears that were still streaming from her eyes. I don't know, maybe I'm not that great of a person, she said. Maybe I don't really think about other people, the way I think about myself. Like with you. For all I know you're more miserable than I am, but you just never say it. And you're always nice to me. Always. Even right now I'm crying on your lap. When have you ever cried on my lap? Never, you never have. Tenderly he looked down at her, the freckles along her cheekbone, her hot pink ear. No, he agreed.

But we're different people. And I'm not miserable, don't worry. Sometimes I'm sad, but that's okay. She gave her head a little shake without lifting it from his lap. But I don't take care of you the way you take care of me, she said. He was smoothing his thumb slowly over her cheekbone. Well, maybe I'm not very good at being taken care of, he answered. Her tears had subsided, and she lay there on his lap for a moment without speaking. Then she asked: Why not? He gave an awkward smile. I don't know, he said. Anyway, we were talking about you, I think. She turned her head to look up at him. I wish we could talk about you for once, she said. Looking back down at her, he was quiet a moment. I'm sorry that you feel like God is punishing you, he said. It's not something I believe he would do. She looked at him a few seconds longer, and then said: When we were on the train the other day I wrote Alice a message saying, I wish Simon had asked me to marry him ten years ago. For a moment he said nothing, apparently in thought. When you were nineteen, he remarked. Would you have accepted such a proposal? She gave a feeble laugh and shrugged her shoulders. Her eyes were hot and swollen. If I had any sense I would have, she answered. But I can't remember now if I had any sense at that age or not. I think I would have found it extremely romantic, so maybe yes. It would have been a better life, you know. Than whatever I've had instead. He was nodding his head, smiling wryly, a little sadly. For me too, he said. I'm sorry. She took hold of his hand then, and they were quiet for a time. I know Alice upset you, he said. She was tracing her thumb over his knuckles. In the kitchen this morning, Felix asked me why I didn't come to see her sooner, she said. And I started saying, well, what was stopping Alice from coming to see me? Where has she been? It's not like she has a lot on. Any time she felt like it, she could have hopped on a train and come to visit me. If she loves me so much, why did she move here in the first place? No one made her do it. It's like she went out of her way to make it difficult for us to see each other, and now she's nursing her hurt feelings, telling herself I don't care about her. When actually, she was the one who left. I didn't want her to go. With this last remark, Eileen started crying again, her face in her hands. I didn't want her to go, she repeated. Simon was touching her hair, saying nothing. Without looking up she said in a painful voice: Please don't leave me. Smoothing a lock of her hair back behind her ear, he murmured: No, never. Of course not. For a minute longer, two minutes, she went on crying, and he sat quietly cradling her head in his lap. Finally she sat upright beside him on the mattress, drying her face with her sleeve. I never have been very good at it, he remarked. Being looked after. With a frail little laugh she said: Watch and learn. I'm an expert. Absently he smiled, looking down at his lap. I suppose I'm afraid of imposing myself, he went on. I mean, I don't like to feel someone is doing something just because they think I want them to, or they feel obliged. Maybe I'm not explaining that properly. It's not that I never want anything for myself. There are obviously some things I do want, very much. He broke off, shaking his head. Ah, I'm not expressing myself well, he said. Her eyes moved over his face. But Simon, she said, you don't really let me get near you. Do you know what I mean? And whenever I do get near, you just push me away. He cleared his throat, looking down at his hands. We can talk about it another time, he said. I know you're upset about Alice, we don't need to discuss all this now. With a faint crease between her brows she was frowning. But that's just pushing me away again, she said. He gave a kind of pained smile. I don't want you to be in my life just because you think I'll be miserable without you, he said. I like to feel that you like being around me, for your own sake. He was massaging the palm of his hand, under his thumb joint. I never want you to feel obliged to me, he went on. If I've ever done anything for you, it was really for myself, because I've wanted to be close to you. And, if I'm honest, I've wanted to feel that you needed me, that you couldn't do without me. Do you understand what I'm saying? I don't think I'm being very clear at all. I mean that you've done much more for me, really, than I've ever done for you. And I've needed you more. I do need you more, a lot more, than you need me. He let out a breath. She was watching him in silence. He went on distractedly, almost as if talking to himself: But maybe I'm saying all the wrong things. I find it very hard to talk like this. Again he exhaled, almost like a sigh, and touched his hand to his brow. She went on watching him, only listening, not speaking. Finally he looked up at her and said: I know you're scared. And maybe you really meant all those things you said about our friendship, just wanting to be friends, and if you did, I'll accept that. But I feel maybe it's possible you said those

449

things, at least in some way, because you wanted me to make the other case. As if I would come out and say, no, Eileen, it's you or no one, I can't be happy without you. Or whatever, whatever you wanted me to say. And maybe even when you're getting angry at Alice, saying that she doesn't care about you — I don't know, maybe it's the same idea. At some level you want her to say, oh but Eileen, I love you very much, you're my best friend. But the problem is that you seem to be drawn to people who aren't very good at giving you those responses. I mean, anyone could have told you — certainly Felix and myself both knew — that Alice was never going to react that way just now. And maybe it's the same with me, in a way. If you tell me you don't want to be with me, I might feel very hurt and humiliated, but I'm not going to start begging and pleading with you. At some level, I actually think you know I won't. But then you get left with the impression that I don't love you, or I don't want you, because you're not getting this response from me — this response that you basically know you won't get, because I'm not the type of person who can give it to you. I don't know. I'm not excusing myself, and I'm not excusing Alice. I know you think I'm always defending her, and I suppose when I do that I'm really defending myself, to be honest. Because I see myself in her, and I feel sorry for her. I can see her pushing you away, even though she doesn't want to, and it hurts her. And I know how that feels. Look, if you meant what you said about just wanting to be friends, I understand, really. I'm not an easy person to be with, I know that. But if you think there's any chance that I could make you happy, I wish you would let me try. Because it's the only thing I really want to do with my life. She put her arms around his neck then, turning toward him where they sat on the side of the bed, pressing her face to his throat, and she whispered something only he could hear.

When Alice reached the bottom of the staircase a few minutes later, Eileen was coming out onto the landing. By the low light of a lamp in the hallway they saw one another and paused, Eileen at the top of the stairs looking down, Alice looking up, their faces anxious, wary, aggrieved, each like a dim mirror of the other, hanging there pale and suspended as the seconds passed. Then they went to each other, meeting halfway down the stairs, and they embraced, holding one another tightly, their arms clasped hard around each other's bodies, and then

Alice was saying: I'm sorry, I'm sorry, and Eileen was saying: Don't apologise, I'm sorry, I don't know why we're fighting. Both of them laughing then, with strange hiccupping laughter, and wiping their faces with their hands, saying: I don't even know what we're fighting about. I'm sorry. They sat down then on the staircase, exhausted, Alice one step below Eileen, their backs against the wall. Do you remember in college we had a fight and you wrote me a mean letter, said Eileen. On refill paper. I don't remember what it said, but I know it wasn't nice. Alice gave the hiccupping laugh again weakly. You were my only friend, she said. You had other friends, but I only had you. Eileen took her hand, lacing their fingers together. For a time they sat there on the stairs, not speaking, or speaking absently about things that had happened a long time ago, silly arguments they'd had, people they used to know, things they had laughed about together. Old conversations, repeated many times before. Then quiet again for a little while. I just want everything to be like it was, Eileen said. And for us to be young again and live near each other, and nothing to be different. Alice was smiling sadly. But if things are different, can we still be friends? she asked. Eileen put her arm around Alice's shoulders. If you weren't my friend I wouldn't know who I was, she said. Alice rested her face in Eileen's arm, closing her eyes. No, she agreed. I wouldn't know who I was either. And actually for a while I didn't. Eileen looked down at Alice's small blonde head, nestled on the sleeve of her sweatshirt. Neither did I, she said. Half past two in the morning. Outside, astronomical twilight. Crescent moon hanging low over the dark water. Tide returning now with a faint repeating rush over the sand. Another place, another time.

29.

Hello — I have attached a draft of the essay with notes below. It's reading really nicely the way it is, but I wonder what you think about the idea of switching the two middle sections? So the biographical part would come later on. Have a look and see how you feel. Did JP ever get back to you with his notes? I suspect he would be much more useful than I am!

I have so completely lost any sense of linear time that I was lying in bed last night thinking: it must be nearly a year now since the first time Eileen and Simon were here. And only very gradually — as I became conscious that I was lying under our big warm duvet rather than the light summer blanket — did I remember that it is now almost December, eighteen months since that first visit last summer. Eighteen months!! Is this how it's going to be for the rest of our lives? Time dissolving into thick dark fog, things that happened last week seeming years ago, and things that happened last year feeling like yesterday. I hope this is a side effect of lockdown and not simply a consequence of growing older. Speaking of which: happy belated. I did put a gift in the post on time, but have no idea when or whether it will arrive . . .

No news on our end. Felix is as well as can be expected. He continues to experience periodic episodes of despair about the pandemic, and to hint darkly that if the situation continues much longer he won't be responsible for his actions. But he usually cheers up again afterwards. In the meantime he has been doing the grocery shopping for several elderly people in the village, which gives him lots of opportunities to complain about elderly people, and he also spends quite a bit of time down at the community garden, making compost, complaining about making compost, and so on. For my part, the difference between lockdown and normal life is (depressingly?) minimal. Eighty to ninety per cent of my days are the same as they would be anyway — working from home, reading, avoiding social gatherings. But then it turns out that even a tiny amount of socialising is very different from none — I mean, one dinner party every two weeks is categorically different from no parties at all. And of course I continue to miss you passionately, and your boyfriend too. Seeing him on the news the other night was the thrill of our lives, by the way. Felix is convinced the dog recognised him, because she barked at the screen, but between you and me she barks at the television all the time.

I don't know if you've been following any of this, but about a month ago I was doing an interview over email and the journalist asked me what my partner thought of my books. Unthinkingly, I wrote back that he had never read them. So of course this became the headline of the interview — 'Alice Kelleher: my boyfriend has never read my books' — and afterwards Felix saw a popular tweet saying something like, 'this is tragic . . . she deserves better'. He showed me the tweet on the screen of his phone one evening without saying anything, and when I asked him what he thought about it, he just shrugged. At first I thought: a perfect example of our shallow self-congratulatory 'book culture', in which non-readers are shunned as morally and intellectually inferior, and the more books you read, the smarter and better you are than everyone else. But then I thought: no, what we really have here is an example of a presumably normal and sane person whose thinking has been deranged by the concept of celebrity. An example of someone who genuinely believes that because she has seen my photograph and read my novels, she knows me personally — and in fact knows better than I do what is best for my life. And it's normal! It's normal for her not only to think these bizarre thoughts privately, but to express them in public, and receive positive feedback and attention as a result. She has no idea that she is, in this small limited respect, quite literally insane, because everyone around her is also insane in exactly the same way. They really cannot tell the difference between someone they have heard of, and someone they personally know. And they believe that the feelings they have about this person they imagine me to be — intimacy, resentment, hatred, pity — are as real as the feelings they have about their own friends. It makes me wonder whether celebrity culture has sort of metastasised to fill the emptiness left by religion. A sort of malignant growth where the sacred used to be.

In other news that isn't news, the saga of my poor health continues as before. With one thing and another I am in pain almost every day now. In my better moods, I tell myself this is just a consequence of all the accumulated stress and exhaustion of the last few years, and it will resolve itself with time and patience. And in my worse moods I think: this is it, this is my life. I have been reading a lot about 'stress' in the medical literature. Everyone seems to agree it is about as bad for your health as smoking, and beyond a certain point practically guarantees a major adverse health outcome. And yet the only recommended treatment for stress is not to experience it in the first place. It's not like anxiety or depression, where you can go to your doctor and get treated and hopefully experience some degree of symptomatic improvement. It's like taking illegal drugs — you're just not supposed to do it, and if you do, you should try to do it less. There is no available medication to treat the problem, and no therapeutic regime backed by any real evidence. Just don't get stressed! It's very important, or you could make yourself really sick!! Anyway, from an aetiological stand-point I feel like I've been locked in a smoke-filled room with thousands of people shouting at me incomprehensibly day and night for the last several years. And I don't know when it will end, or how long it will take me to feel better afterwards, or if I ever will. On one hand, I know the human body can be incredibly resilient. On the other, my sturdy peasant ancestors did little to prepare me for a career as a widely despised celebrity novelist. What do you think? Gradual return to a state of fair-to-moderate physical health? Or gradual acceptance of chronic poor health, perhaps presenting new opportunities for spiritual growth?

Speaking of which: when Felix saw I was writing you an email, he said, 'You should tell her you're Catholic now.' This is because he recently asked me if I believed in God, and I said I didn't know. He went around shaking his head all day after that, and then told me that if I go off and join a convent, I shouldn't expect any visits from him. Needless to say, I am not going to join a convent, nor am I even Catholic, as far as I know I only feel, rightly or wrongly, that there is something underneath everything. When one person kills or harms another person, then there is 'something' — isn't there? Not simply atoms flying around in various configurations through empty space. I don't know how to explain myself, really. But I feel that it does matter — not to hurt other people, even in one's own self-interest. Felix of course agrees with this sentiment as far as it goes, and he points out (quite reasonably) that nobody goes around committing mass murders just because they don't believe in God. But increasingly I think it's because, in one way or another, they do believe in God — they believe in the God that is the deep buried principle of goodness and love underneath everything. Goodness regardless of reward, regardless of our own desires, regardless of whether anyone is watching or anyone will know. If that's God, then Felix says fine, it's just a word, it means nothing. And of course it doesn't mean heaven and angels and the resurrection of Christ — but maybe those things can help in some way to put us in touch with what it does mean. That most of our attempts throughout human history to describe the difference between right and wrong have been feeble and cruel and unjust, but that the difference still remains — beyond ourselves, beyond each specific culture, beyond every individual person who has ever lived or died. And we spend our lives trying to know that difference and to live by it, trying to love other people instead of hating them, and there is nothing else that matters on the earth.

The book was proceeding by leaps before, but has now slowed to a kind of intermittent trickle. Naturally my sanguine temperament has prevented me from reading anything ominous into this turn of events. Haha! But really, I am trying not to go down that rabbit hole again this time — worrying that my brain has stopped working and that I'll never write another novel. One day I'll be right, and then I can't imagine I'll be glad that I spent so much time feeling anxious in advance. I know I am lucky in so many ways. And when I forget that, I just remind myself of the fact that Felix is alive, and you are, and Simon is, and then I feel wonderfully and almost frighteningly lucky, and I pray that nothing bad will ever happen to any of you. Now write back and tell me how you are.

30.

Alice — thank you so much for your notes — and the birthday gift, which arrived in a timely fashion and was characteristically generous! — and sorry for the short delay. I know you'll forgive me, because I am writing with important and confidential news. Confidential for the moment, though, as you'll soon figure out, not for long. The news is this: I'm pregnant. I found out for certain a few days ago by cutting a test out of its plastic packaging using a kitchen scissors and then urinating on it in the bathroom before Simon got home from a committee hearing he had to attend in person. When the test was positive I sat down at the kitchen table and started crying. I'm not really sure why. I can't say I was shocked, because my doctor had taken me off the pill months ago, and my period was three weeks late. I won't bore or embarrass you with any more specific details about how I came to be pregnant — I'm sure you cannot at this stage in our friendship be surprised by any irresponsible behaviours on my part, but suffice it to say that even Simon is only human. Anyway, I had no idea when he was going to get home from this hearing — in an hour, two hours, or maybe he would be really late and I'd be sitting there alone all evening in the apartment — and then just as I was thinking that, I heard his keys in the door. He came inside and saw me sitting at the table, doing nothing, and I asked him to sit with me. He stood there looking at me for what seemed like a long time, and then without speaking he came over and sat down. Even before I said anything, I knew that he knew. I told him I was pregnant, and he asked me what I wanted to do. As strange as this might sound, I hadn't thought about that at all until he asked me. But only a few minutes had passed, really, and all I had thought about in that time was where he was — whether he was still at work or on his way back, whether he had stopped in a pharmacy or a supermarket — and how long it would take him to get home. When he asked me, I found it was easy to answer, I didn't have to think about it. I told him I wanted to have the baby. He cried then and said he was very happy. And

I believed him, because I was very happy too.

Alice, is this the worst idea I've ever had? In one sense, maybe yes. If everything goes right with the pregnancy, the baby will probably be due around the start of July next year, at which point we may still be in lockdown, and I would have to give birth alone in a hospital ward during a global pandemic. Even shelving that more immediate concern, neither you nor I have any confidence that human civilisation as we know it is going to persist beyond our lifetimes. But then again, no matter what I do, hundreds of thousands of babies will be born on the same day as this hypothetical baby of mine. Their futures are surely just as important as the future of my hypothetical baby, who is distinguished only by its relationship to me and also to the man I love. I suppose I mean that children are coming anyway, and in the grand scheme of things it won't matter much whether any of them are mine or his. We have to try either way to build a world they can live in. And I feel in a strange sense that I want to be on the children's side, and on the side of their mothers; to be with them, not just an observer, admiring them from a distance, speculating about their best interests, but one of them. I'm not saying, by the way, that I think that's important for everyone. I only think, and I can't explain why, that it's important for me. Also, I could not stomach the idea of having an abortion just because I'm afraid of climate change. For me (and maybe only for me) it would be a sort of sick, insane thing to do, a way of mutilating my real life as a gesture of submission to an imagined future. I don't want to belong to a political movement that makes me view my own body with suspicion and terror. No matter what we think or fear about the future of civilisation, women all over the world will go on having babies, and I belong with them, and any child I might have belongs with their children. I know in a thin rationalist way that what I'm saying doesn't make any sense. But I feel it, I feel it, and I know it to be true.

The other question, which may seem to you even more pressing — I wish I knew what you thought! please write back quickly and tell me! — is whether I am fit to parent a child in the first place. On the one hand, I'm in good health, I have a supportive partner who loves me, we're financially secure, I have great friends and family, I'm in my thirties. The circumstances are probably as good as they're going to get. On the other hand, Simon and I have only been together for eighteen months (!), we live in a one-bed apartment, we don't have a car, and I'm a huge idiot who recently broke down in tears because I couldn't answer any of the starter questions on 'University Challenge'. Is that appropriate behavioural modelling for a child? When I spend the day moving commas around and then cook dinner and then wash the dishes, and after this simple set of tasks I feel so tired I could physically sink through the floor and become one with the earth — is that the mentality of someone who's ready to have a baby? I have talked with Simon about this, and he says feeling tired after dinner is probably normal in your thirties and nothing to worry about, and that 'all women' have crying spells, and although I know that's not true, I do find his paternalistic beliefs about women charming. Sometimes I think he's so perfectly suited to being a parent, so relaxed and dependable and good-humoured, that no matter how awful I am, the child will turn out fine anyway. And he loves so much the idea of us having a baby together — already I can tell how happy and proud he is, and how excited — and it's so intoxicating to make him happy in that way. I find it hard to believe anything really bad about myself when I consider how much he loves me. I do try to remind myself that men can be foolish about women. But maybe he's right — maybe I'm not so bad, maybe even a good person, and we'll have a happy family together. Some people do, don't they? Have happy families, I mean. I know you didn't, and I didn't. But Alice, I'm still so glad we were born. As for the apartment, Simon says not to worry about that, because we can just buy a house in a less expensive area. And of course, he has suggested again that we might think about getting married, if I want to . . .

Can you imagine me, a mother, a married woman, owning a little terraced house somewhere in the Liberties? With crayon on the wallpaper and Lego bricks all over the floor. I'm laughing even typing that — you have to admit it doesn't sound like me at all. But then, last year, I couldn't really imagine myself as Simon's girlfriend. I don't just mean that it was hard to imagine what our families would say, or what our friends would think. I mean, I couldn't imagine we were going to be happy together. I thought it would be the same as everything else in my life — difficult and sad — because I was a difficult and sad person. But that's not what I am anymore, if I ever was. And life is more changeable than I thought. I mean a life can be miserable for a long time and then later happy. It's not just one thing or another — it doesn't get fixed into a groove called 'personality' and then run along that way until the end. But I really used to believe that it did. Every evening now when we've finished our work, Simon turns on the news while I cook dinner, or I turn on the news while he cooks dinner, and we talk about the latest public health guidance, and what's been reported about what everyone is saying in cabinet and what Simon has privately heard everyone is actually saying in cabinet, and then we eat and wash up, and afterwards I read him a chapter of 'David Copperfield' while we lie on the couch, and then we look through the trailers on various streaming services for an hour until one or both of us falls asleep and then we go to bed. And in the morning I wake up feeling almost painfully happy. To live with someone I really love and respect, who really loves and respects me — what a difference it has made to my life. Of course everything is terrible at the moment, and I miss you ardently, and I miss my family, and I miss parties and book launches and going to the cinema, but all that really means is that I love my life, and I'm excited to have it back again, excited to feel that it's going to continue, that new things will keep happening, that nothing is over yet.

I wish I knew what you thought of all this. I still have no idea what it will be like — what it will feel like, or how the days will pass, whether I'll still want to write or be able to, what will become of my life. I suppose I think that having a child is simply the most ordinary thing I can imagine doing. And I want that — to prove that the most ordinary thing about human beings is not violence or greed but love and care. To prove it to whom, I wonder. Myself, maybe. Anyway: no one else knows, and we're not going to tell anyone for a few more weeks, except for you and Felix. You can tell him if you want, of course, or Simon can tell him on the phone. I know that it's not the life you imagined for me, Alice — buying a house and having children with a boy I grew up with. It's not the life I used to imagine for myself either. But it's the life I have, the only one. And as I write you this message I'm very happy. All my love.

ACKNOWLEDGEMENTS

The title of this book is a literal translation of a phrase from Friedrich Schiller's poem 'Die Götter Griechenlandes' ('The Gods of Greece'), first published in 1788. In the original German, the phrase reads: 'Schöne Welt, wo bist du?' Franz Schubert set a fragment of the poem to music in 1819. Beautiful World, Where Are You? was also the title of the 2018 Liverpool Biennial, which I visited during the Liverpool Literary Festival in October of that year.

I would like to acknowledge here some of the support I received while I worked on this book. Above all, I want to thank my husband, who makes it possible for me to live and work the way I do. John, I can only try to express in my writing some small measure of the love and happiness you have brought into my life. And to my friends Aoife Comey and Kate Oliver: I am grateful every day for your friendship, and I can never thank you enough.

I owe a great debt of gratitude to John Patrick McHugh, whose excellent early feedback led me to find a much-needed new direction for this book. And I am likewise indebted to my editor Mitzi Angel, who from the beginning helped me to see what was good in the novel, and how it could be better. I also want to thank Alex Bowler for his thorough and very insightful notes. Further thanks, personal and professional, to Thomas Morris, and to my agent and dear friend Tracy Bohan. For conversations that helped me to tease out the problems of the book, and in some cases for help with factual and practical queries, I would like to thank — as well as those previously mentioned — Sheila, Emily, Zadie, Sunniva, William, Katie and Marie.

I spent a blissful period working on this novel at Santa Maddalena in Tuscany. I would like to thank Beatrice Monti della Corte von Rezzori and the Santa Maddalena Foundation for their generosity in inviting me to take part in a residency there. And to Rasika, Sean, Nico, Kate, Fredrik — how can I ever thank you for those heavenly weeks?

I would also like to acknowledge the support of the Cullman Center at the New York

Public Library, where I was a fellow from 2019 to 2020. My thanks are due not only to the wonderful staff there but also to my 'fellow fellows', in particular Ken Chen, Justin E. H. Smith, and Josephine Quinn. Josephine's 2016 piece on the Bronze Age collapse ('Your own ships did this!', *London Review of Books*) has clearly informed Eileen's thinking in chapter 16 of this novel (though of course any errors are Eileen's and mine).

Finally, to everyone who has worked on the publication, distribution or sale of this book, my warmest thanks.

ABOUT THE AUTHOR

Sally Rooney is an Irish novelist. She is the author of *Conversations with Friends* and *Normal People.* She also contributed to the writing and production of the Hulu/BBC television adaptation of *Normal People.*